RAVE REVIEWS FOR
THE AUTHORS OF *WISH LIST*!

LISA KLEYPAS

RITA Award-winner for "I Will"

"Kleypas knows what secrets lie in a woman's heart and is able to play upon them like a virtuoso."

—*Romantic Times*

LISA CACH

"Ms. Cach's writing is open, bawdy, and laugh-out-loud funny."

—*Romantic Times*

"Cach's descriptive writing is brilliant."

—*All About Romance*

CLAUDIA DAIN

"Claudia Dain writes with intelligence, sensuality, and heart and the results are extraordinary!"

—Connie Brockaway, bestselling author

"One of the genre's fastest rising stars."

—*Publishers Weekly*

LYNSAY SANDS

"Lynsay Sands has just the right touch of humor to hold you in her grasp."

—*Romantic Times*

Sands is a skilled writer [who] takes more than a few chances."

—*All About Romance*

LISA KLEYPAS
LISA CACH * CLAUDIA DAIN
LYNSAY SANDS

Wish List

LEISURE BOOKS **NEW YORK CITY**

LEISURE BOOKS ®

October 2003

Published by

Dorchester Publishing Co., Inc.
200 Madison Avenue
New York, NY 10016

ISBN 0-8439-5102-8

Visit us on the web at www.dorchesterpub.com.

MAR – – 2006

Table of Contents

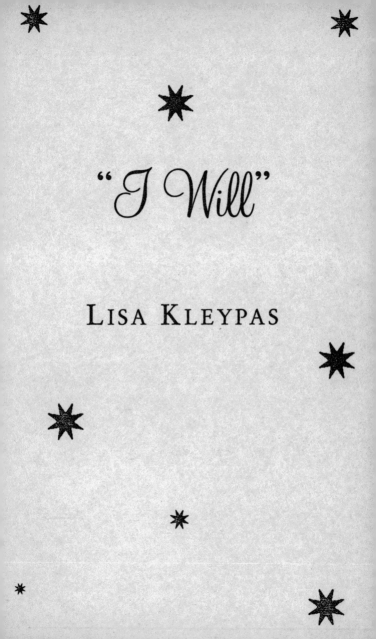

"I Will"

LISA KLEYPAS

* Chapter One *

London, 1833

*I*t was not easy to ask a favor of a woman who despised him. But Andrew, Lord Drake, had always been beyond shame, and today was no exception. He needed a favor from a morally upright woman, and Miss Caroline Hargreaves was the only decent female he knew. She was proper and straitlaced to a fault . . . and he wasn't the only man to think so, judging by the fact that she was still unmarried at the age of twenty-six.

"Why are you here?" Caroline asked, her voice threaded with quiet hostility. She kept her gaze fastened on the large square frame propped by the settee, a wooden lace stretcher used to reshape curtains and tablecloths after they were washed. The task was a meticulous one, involving sticking a pin through each tiny loop of lace and affixing it to the edge of the frame until the cloth was drawn tight. Although Caroline's

3

face was expressionless, her inner tension was betrayed by the stiffness of her fingers as she fumbled with a paper of pins.

"I need something from you," Andrew said, staring at her intently. It was probably the first time he had ever been completely sober around her, and now that he was free of his habitual alcoholic haze, he had noticed a few things about Miss Caroline Hargreaves that intrigued him.

She was far prettier than he had thought. Despite the little spectacles perched on her nose, and her frumpy manner of dressing, she possessed a subtle beauty that had escaped him before. Her figure was not at all spectacular—Caroline was small and slight, with practically no hips or breasts to speak of. Andrew preferred big, voluptuous women who were willing to engage in the vigorous bedroom romps he enjoyed. But Caroline had a lovely face, with velvety brown eyes and thick black lashes, surmounted by dark brows that arched with the precision of a hawk's wing. Her hair was a neatly pinned mass of sable silk, and her complexion was as fine and clear as a child's. And that mouth . . . why in God's name had he never noticed her mouth before? Delicate, expressive, the upper lip small and bow shaped, the lower curved with generous fullness.

Right now those tempting lips were pulled tight with displeasure, and her brow was furrowed in a perplexed expression. "I can't conceive of what you could possibly want from me, Lord Drake," Caroline said crisply. "However, I can assure you that you won't get it."

Andrew laughed suddenly. He threw a glance at his friend Cade—Caroline's younger brother—who had brought him to the parlor of the Hargreaves family home. Having predicted that Caroline would not be willing to help him in any way, Cade now looked both annoyed and resigned at his sister's stubbornness. "I told you," Cade murmured.

Not willing to give up so easily, Andrew returned his attention to the woman seated before him. He considered her thoughtfully, trying to decide what approach to use. No doubt she was going to make him crawl . . . not that he blamed her for that in the least.

Caroline had never made a secret of her dislike for him, and Andrew knew exactly why. For one thing, he was a bad influence on her younger brother Cade, a pleasant-natured fellow who was far too easily swayed by the opinions of his friends. Andrew had invited Cade along on far too many wild evenings of gambling, drinking, and debauchery, and returned him home in a sorry condition.

As Cade's father was dead, and his mother was a hopeless feather-wit, Caroline was the closest thing to a parent that Cade had. She tried her best to keep her twenty-four-year-old brother on the straight-and-narrow path, wanting him to assume his responsibilities as the man of the family. However, Cade naturally found it more tempting to emulate Andrew's profligate lifestyle, and the two of them had indulged in more than a few dissolute evenings.

The other reason that Caroline despised Andrew was the simple fact that they were complete opposites. She was pure. He was tarnished. She was honest. He tailored the truth to fit his own purposes. She was self-disciplined. He had never restrained himself in any regard. She was calm and serene. He had never known a moment's peace in his life. Andrew envied her, and so he had mocked her mercilessly on the few previous occasions when they had met.

Now Caroline hated him, and he had come to ask for a favor—a favor he desperately needed. Andrew found the situation so amusing that a wry smile cut through tension on his face.

Abruptly he decided to be blunt. Miss Caroline Hargreaves did not seem to be the kind of woman who would tolerate game playing and prevarication. "I'm here because my father is dying," he said.

The words caused her to accidentally prick her finger, and she jumped slightly. Her gaze lifted from the lace stretcher. "I am sorry," she murmured.

"I'm not."

Andrew saw from the widening of her eyes that she was shocked by his coldness. He did not care. Nothing could make him feign sorrow at the passing of a man who had always been a poor excuse for a father. The earl had never given a damn about him, and Andrew had long ago given up trying to earn the love of a manipulative son of a bitch whose heart was as soft and warm as a block of granite. "The only thing I'm sorry about," Andrew continued calmly, "is that the earl has decided to disinherit me. You and he seem to share similar feelings about my sinful way of living. My father has accused me of being the most self-indulgent and debased creature he has ever encountered." A slight smile crossed his lips. "I can only hope that he is right."

Caroline seemed more than a little perturbed by his statement. "You sound proud of being such a disappointment to him," she said.

"Oh, I am," he assured her easily. "My goal was to become as great a disappointment to him as he has been to me. Not an easy task, you understand, but I proved myself equal to it. It has been the greatest success of my life."

He saw Caroline throw a troubled glance at Cade, who merely shrugged sheepishly and wandered to the window to contemplate the serene spring day outside.

The Hargreaves house was located on the west side of London. It was a pleasant Georgian-style manor house, pink-washed and framed by large beech trees, the kind of home that a solid English family should possess.

"And so," Andrew continued, "in an eleventh-hour effort to inspire me to reform, the earl has cut me out of his will."

"But surely he cannot do so entirely," Caroline said. "The titles, the property in town, and your family's country estate . . . I would have thought they were entailed."

"Yes, they are entailed." Andrew smiled bitterly. "I'll get the titles and the property no matter what the earl does. He can't break the entailment any more than I can. But the money—the entire family fortune—that is *not* entailed. He can leave it to anyone he wishes. And so I'll likely find myself turning into one of those damned fortune-hunting aristocrats who has to marry some horse-faced heiress with a nice fat dowry."

"How terrible." Suddenly Caroline's eyes were lit with a challenging gleam. "For the heiress, I mean."

"Caro," came Cade's protesting voice.

"That's all right," Andrew said. "Any bride of mine would deserve a great deal of sympathy. I don't treat women well. I've never pretended to."

"What do you mean, you don't treat women well?" Caroline fumbled with a pin and stuck her finger again. "Are you abusive?"

"No." He scowled suddenly. "I would never physically harm a woman."

"You are merely disrespectful to them, then. And no doubt neglectful, and unreliable, and offensive and ungentlemanly." She paused and looked at him expectantly. When Andrew made no comment, she prompted with an edge to her tone, "Well?"

"Well, what?" he countered with a mocking smile. "Were you asking a question? I thought you were making a speech."

They regarded each other with narrowed eyes, and Caroline's pale complexion took on the rosy hue of anger. The atmosphere in the room changed, becoming strangely charged and hot, snapping with tension. Andrew wondered how in the hell a skinny little spinster could affect him like this. He, who had made it a lifetime's habit never to care about anything or anyone, including himself, was suddenly more troubled and aroused than he could ever recall being before. *My God*, he thought, *I must be one perverted bastard to desire Cade Hargreaves's sister*. But he did. His blood was pumping with heat and energy, and his nerves simmered relentlessly as he thought of the various ways he would like to put that delicate, innocent mouth to use.

It was a good thing that Cade was there. Otherwise Andrew was not certain he could have stopped himself from showing Miss Caroline Hargreaves exactly how depraved he was. In fact, standing up as he was, that fact was soon going to become all too obvious through the thin covering of his fashionably snug fawn-colored trousers. "May I have a seat?" he asked abruptly, gesturing to the chair near the settee she occupied.

Unworldly as she was, Caroline did not seem to notice his burgeoning arousal. "Please do. I can hardly wait to hear the details of this favor you intend to ask, especially in light of the charm and good manners you have displayed so far."

God, she made him want to laugh, even as he wanted to strangle her. "Thank you." He sat and leaned forward casually, bracing his forearms on his knees. "If I want to be reinstated in the earl's will, I have no choice but to indulge him," he said.

"You intend to change your ways?" Caroline asked skeptically. "To reform yourself?"

"Of course not. My cesspool of a life suits me quite well.

8

I'm only going to *pretend* to reform until the old man meets his maker. Then I'll be on my way, with my rightful fortune intact."

"How nice for you." Distaste flickered in her dark eyes.

For some reason Andrew was stung by her reaction—he, who had never given a damn what anyone thought of him. He felt the need to justify himself to her, to explain somehow that he wasn't nearly as contemptible as he seemed. But he kept silent. He would be damned if he would try to explain anything about himself to her.

Her gaze continued to hold his. "What role am I supposed to play in your plans?"

"I need you to pretend an interest in me," he said flatly. "A romantic interest. I'm going to convince my father that I've given up drinking, gambling, and skirt chasing . . . and that I am courting a decent woman with the intention of marrying her."

Caroline shook her head, clearly startled. "You want a sham engagement?"

"It doesn't have to go that far," he replied. "All I am asking is that you allow me to escort you to a few social functions . . . share a few dances, a carriage ride or two . . . enough to start a few tongues wagging until the rumors reach my father."

She regarded him as if he belonged in Bedlam. "Why in heaven's name do you think anyone would believe such a ruse? You and I are worlds apart. I cannot conceive of a more ill-suited pair."

"It's not all that unbelievable. A woman your age . . ." Andrew hesitated, considering the most tactful way to express himself.

"You are trying to say that since I am twenty-six years old, it naturally follows that I must be desperate to marry. So desperate, in fact, that I would accept your advances no matter how repulsive I find you. That is what people will think."

"You have a sharp tongue, Miss Hargreaves," he commented softly.

She frowned at him from behind her glinting spectacles. "That is correct, Lord Drake. I am sharp-tongued, I am a bluestocking, and I have resigned myself to being an old maid. Why would anyone of good sense believe that you have a romantic interest in me?"

Well, that was a good question. Just a few minutes ago Andrew himself would have laughed at the very idea. But as he sat close to her, his knees not far from hers, the stirring of attraction ignited in a sudden burst of heat. He could smell her fragrance—warm female skin and some fresh out-of-doors scent, as if she had just walked in from the garden. Cade had confided that his sister spent a great deal of time in the garden and the hothouse, cultivating roses and experimenting with plants. Caroline seemed like a rose herself—exquisite, sweetly fragrant, more than a little prickly. Andrew could scarcely believe that he had never noticed her before.

He flashed a glance at Cade, who was shrugging to indicate that arguing with Caroline was a hopeless endeavor. "Hargreaves, leave us alone for a few minutes," he said curtly.

"Why?" Caroline asked suspiciously.

"I want to talk privately with you. Unless . . ." He gave her a taunting smile that was guaranteed to annoy. "Are you afraid to be alone with me, Miss Hargreaves?"

"Certainly not!" She threw her brother a commanding glance. "Leave, Cade, while I deal with your so-called friend."

"All right." Cade paused at the threshold of the doorway,

his boyishly handsome face stamped with concern as he added, "Just give a shout if you need help."

"I will not need help," Caroline assured him firmly. "I am capable of handling Lord Drake by myself."

"I wasn't speaking to you," Cade replied ruefully. "I was speaking to Drake."

Andrew struggled to suppress a grin as he watched his friend leave the room. Returning his attention to Caroline, he moved beside her on the settee, placing their bodies into closer proximity.

"Don't sit there," she said sharply.

"Why?" He gave her a seductive look, the kind that had melted many a reluctant woman's resistance in the past. "Do I make you nervous?"

"No, I left a paper of pins there, and your backside is about to resemble a hedgehog's."

Andrew laughed suddenly, fishing for the packet until he located it beneath his left buttock. "Thanks for the warning," he said dryly. "You could have let me find out for myself."

"I was tempted," Caroline admitted.

Andrew was amazed by how pretty she was, with amusement glimmering in her brown eyes, and her cheeks still flushed pink. Her earlier question—why anyone would believe he would be interested in her—abruptly seemed ludicrous. Why would he *not* be interested in her? Vague fantasies drifted through his mind . . . he would like to lift that dainty body in his arms right now, settle her on his lap, and kiss her senseless. He wanted to reach under the skirts of her plain brown cambric gown and slide his hands over her legs. Most of all he wanted to pull down the top of her bodice and uncover her pert little breasts. He had never been so intrigued by a pair of breasts, which was odd when one considered that he had always been interested in well-endowed women.

He watched as she turned her attentions back to the wooden frame. Clearly she was distracted, for she fumbled with the pins and managed to prick her fingers yet again as she tried to fasten the lace properly. Suddenly exasperated, Andrew took the pins from her. "Allow me," he said. Expertly he stretched the lace with just the right amount of tension and secured it with a row of pins, each miniature loop fastened exactly on the edge of the frame.

Caroline did not bother to hide her amazement as she watched him. "How did you learn to do that?"

Andrew regarded the lace panel with a critical eye before setting it aside. "I grew up as the only child on a large estate, with few playmates. On rainy days I would help the housekeeper with her tasks." He gave her a self-mocking grin. "If you are impressed by my lace stretching, you should see me polish silver."

She did not return his smile, but stared at him with new curiosity. When she spoke, her tone had softened a few degrees. "No one would believe the charade you propose. I know what kind of women you pursue. I have talked with Cade, you see. And your reputation is well established. You would never take an interest in a woman like me."

"I could play the part convincingly," he said. "I've got a huge fortune at stake. For that I would court the devil himself. The question is, can you?"

"I suppose I could," she returned evenly. "You are not a bad-looking man. I suppose some might even regard you as handsome in a debauched, slovenly sort of way."

Andrew scowled at her. He was not vain, and rarely considered his own appearance other than to make certain he was clean and his clothes were decently tailored. But without conceit, he knew that he was tall and well proportioned, and that women often praised his long black hair and blue eyes. The problem was his way of life. He spent too much time indoors, too little time sleeping, and he drank too often and too long. More often that not, he woke up at midday with bloodshot, dark-circled eyes, his complexion pasty from a night of hard drinking. And he had never cared . . . until now. In comparison to the dainty creature before him, he felt like a huge, untidy mess.

"What incentive were you planning to offer me?" Caroline asked. It was clear that she would not consider his plan; she was merely interested to discover how he would have tried to entice her.

Unfortunately that was the weak aspect of his scheme. He had little to entice her with. No money, no social advantage, no possessions that would allure her. There was only one thing he had been able to come up with that might be sufficiently tempting.

"If you agree to help me," he said slowly, "I will leave your brother alone. You know what kind of influence I am on him. He is in debt up to his ears, and he is doing his best to keep pace with the pack of miscreants and degenerates I like to call friends. Before long Cade is going to end up exactly like me—rotten, cynical, and beyond all hope of redemption."

Caroline's expressive face revealed that this was exactly what she feared.

"How far in debt is he?" she asked stiffly.

He named a sum that astonished and sickened her. Reading the horror in her eyes, Andrew experienced a surge of predatory satisfaction. *Yes* . . . he had guessed correctly. She loved her younger brother enough to do anything to save him. Even pretend to fall in love with a man she despised.

"That is only the beginning," Andrew told her. "Before long Cade will be in a pit so deep that he'll never be able to climb out."

"And you would be willing to let that happen? You would simply stand by and let him ruin his life? And impoverish my mother and myself?"

Andrew responded with a casual shrug. "It is his life," he pointed out matter-of-factly. "I'm not his keeper."

"My God," she said unsteadily. "You don't care about anyone but yourself, do you?"

He kept his expression blank, and studied the scuffed, unpolished surface of his very expensive boot. "No, I don't give a damn who gets dragged down with me. But if you decide to help me, I'll take care of Cade. I'll make certain the others in our set don't invite him to their clubs or their favorite bawdy houses. I will ensure that all the listmakers I know—and believe me, that is a considerable number— will not extend him credit. He won't be allowed into any high-stakes games in London. Moreover, if I am reinstated in my father's will, I will assume all of Cade's financial obligations."

"Does Cade know about your plan?" Caroline was pale and intent as she stared at him.

"No. But it would prove his salvation."

"And if I refuse to accept your offer?"

A hard, somewhat cruel smile curved his lips. His father's smile, Andrew thought, with bitter self-awareness. "Then your brother is on the path to hell . . . right alongside me. And you will be left to pick up the pieces. I would hate to see your family's estate sold to pay off Cade's debts. Not a pleasant prospect for your mother, being forced to live off the charity of relatives in her old age. Or you, for that matter." He gave her an insultingly thorough glance, his gaze lingering on her bosom. "What skills do you have that would earn enough to support a family?"

"You fiend," Caroline whispered, visibly trembling, though it was impossible to discern whether her emotion was fear or anger, or perhaps a mixture of both.

In the silence, Andrew was aware of a twisting sensation somewhere in his chest, and suddenly he wanted to take it all back . . . reassure and soothe her . . . promise her that he would never allow a bit of harm to come to her family. He had a terrible feeling of tenderness that he struggled to thrust away, but it remained stubbornly lodged within him.

"What choice do I have?" Caroline asked angrily, forestalling any repentant words from him.

"Then you agree to my plan? You'll pretend to engage in a courtship with me?"

"Yes . . . I will." She sent him a simmering glare. "How long must this last? Weeks? Months?"

"Until the earl reinstates me in his will. If you and I are sufficiently convincing, it shouldn't take long."

"I don't know if I can bear it," she said, regarding him with patent loathing. "Exactly how far will this charade have to go? Words? Embraces? Kisses?" The prospect of kissing him seemed as enthralling as if she had been required to kiss a goat. "I warn you, I will not allow my reputation to be compromised, not even for Cade!"

"I haven't thought out the details yet." He kept his face unreadable, although relief shot through him in a piercing note. "I won't compromise you. All I want is the appearance of pleasant companionship."

Caroline sprang from the settee as if she had suddenly been released from the law of gravity. Agitation was evident in every line of her body. "This is intolerable," she muttered. "I cannot believe that through no fault of my own . . ." She whirled around to glare at Andrew. "When do we start? Let it be soon. I want this outrageous charade to be done with as quickly as possible."

"Your enthusiasm is gratifying," Andrew remarked, with a sudden flare of laughter in his eyes. "Let's begin in a fortnight. My half brother and his wife are giving a weekend party at their country estate. I will prevail on them to invite your family. With any luck, my father will attend as well."

"And then to all appearances, you and I will develop a sudden overwhelming attraction to each other," she said, rolling her eyes heavenward.

"Why not? Many a romantic liaison has begun that way. In the past, I've had more than a few—"

"*Please*," she interrupted fervently. "Please do not regale me with stories of your sordid affairs. I find you repulsive enough as it is."

"All right," he said agreeably. "From now on I'll leave the subjects of conversation to you. Your brother tells me that you enjoy gardening. No doubt we'll have enthralling discourses on the wonders of manure." He was satisfied to see her porcelain complexion turn mottled with fury.

"If I can manage to convince a single person that I am attracted to you," Caroline said through gritted teeth, "I vow to begin a career on the stage."

"That could be arranged," Andrew replied dryly. His half brother, Logan Scott, was the most celebrated actor of the day, as well as being the owner and manager of the Capital Theater. Although Andrew and Logan had been friends since childhood, they had only recently discovered that they were related. Logan was the by-blow of an affair the earl had conducted with a young actress long ago. Whereas Andrew had been raised in an atmosphere of luxury and privilege, Logan had grown up in a hovel, frequently starving and abused by the family that had taken him in. Andrew doubted that he would ever rid himself of the guilt of that, even though it hadn't been his fault.

Noticing that Caroline's spectacles were smudged, he approached her with a quiet murmur. "Hold still."

She froze as he reached out and plucked the steel-framed spectacles from her nose. "Wh-what are you doing? I . . . *stop*; give those back. . . ."

"In a minute," he said, using a fold of his soft linen shirt to polish the lenses until they gleamed brightly. He paused to examine them, and glanced at Caroline's face. Bereft of the spectacles, her eyes looked large and fathomless, her gaze slightly unfocused. How vulnerable she seemed. Again he experienced an odd surge of protectiveness. "How well can you see without them?" he asked, carefully replacing them on her small face.

"Not well at all," she admitted in a low voice, her composure seeming fractured. As soon as the spectacles were safely on her nose, she backed away from Andrew and sought to collect herself. "Now I suppose you are going to make some jest at my expense."

"Not at all. I like your spectacles."

"You do?" she asked with clear disbelief. "Why?"

"They make you look like a wise little owl."

Clearly she did not consider that a compliment, although Andrew meant it as one. He couldn't help imagining what she would look like wearing nothing *but* the spectacles, so prim and modest until he coaxed her into passionate abandonment, her small body writhing uncontrollably against his—

Abruptly aware that his erection was swelling again, Andrew shoved the images out of his mind. Damn, but he had never expected to be so fascinated by Hargreaves's spinster sister! He would have to make certain that she never realized it, or she would have even more contempt for him. The only way to keep her from guessing at his attraction to her was to keep her thoroughly annoyed and hostile. No problem there, he thought sardonically.

"You may leave now," Caroline said sharply. "I assume our business is concluded for the time being."

"It is," he agreed. "However, there is one last thing. Could you manage to dress with a bit more style during the weekend party? The guests—not to mention my father—would find it easier to accept my interest in you if you didn't wear something quite so . . ."

Now even the lobes of her ears were purple. "Quite so *what*?" she said in a hiss.

"Matronly."

Caroline was silent for a moment, obviously suppressing an urge to commit murder. "I will try," she finally said in a strangled voice. "And you, perhaps, might engage the services of a decent valet. Or if you already have one, replace him with someone else."

Now it was Andrew's turn to be offended. He felt a scowl twitching at the muscles of his face. "Why is that?"

"Because your hair is too long, and your boots need polish, and the way *you* dress reminds me of an unmade bed!"

"Does that mean you'd like to lie on top of me?" he asked.

He slipped around the door of the parlor and closed it just before she threw a vase.

The sound of shattering porcelain echoed through the house.

"Drake!" Cade strode toward him from the entrance hall, looking at him expectantly. "How did it go? Did you get her to agree?"

"She agreed," Andrew said.

The words caused a flashing grin to cross Cade's boyishly handsome face. "Well done! Now you'll get back in your father's good graces, and everything will go swimmingly for us, eh, old fellow? Gaming, drinking, carousing . . . oh, the times we're going to have!"

"Hargreaves, I have something to tell you," Andrew said carefully. "I don't think you're going to like it."

✳
Chapter Two
✳

Caroline sat alone for a long time after Lord Drake left. She wondered uneasily what would become of her. Gossip would certainly abound once the news got out that she and Drake were courting. The unlikeliness of such a match would cause no end of jokes and snickers. Especially in light of the fact that she was notoriously particular in her choice of companionship.

Caroline had never been able to explain even to herself why she had never fallen in love. Certainly she was not a cold person—she had always had warm relationships with friends and relatives, and she knew herself to be a woman of very deep feeling. And she enjoyed dancing and talking and even flirting on occasion. But when she had tried to make herself feel something beyond casual liking for any one gentleman, her heart had remained stubbornly uninvolved.

"For heaven's sake, love is not a prerequisite for marriage," her mother had often exclaimed in exasperation.

"You cannot *afford* to wait for love, Caro. You have neither the fortune nor the social position to be so fastidious!"

True, her father had been a viscount, but like the majority of viscounts, he did not possess a significant amount of land. A title and a small London estate were all the Hargreaves could boast of. It would have benefitted the family tremendously if Caroline, the only daughter, could have married an earl or perhaps even a marquess. Unfortunately most of the available peers were either decrepit old men, or spoiled, selfish rakes such as Andrew, Lord Drake. Given such a choice, it was no wonder that Caroline had chosen to remain unwed.

Dwelling on the subject of Andrew, Caroline frowned pensively. Her reaction to him was troubling. Not only did he seem to have a remarkable ability to provoke her, but he seemed to do it intentionally, as if he delighted in stoking her temper. But somewhere in the midst of her annoyance, she had felt a strange sort of fascination for him.

It couldn't possibly be his looks. After all, she was not so shallow as to be undone by mere handsomeness. But she had found herself staring compulsively at the dark, ruined beauty of his face . . . the deep blue eyes shadowed from too little sleep, the cynical mouth . . . the slightly bloated look of a heavy drinker. Andrew possessed the face of a man who was determined to destroy himself. Oh, what terrible company he was for her brother Cade! Not to mention herself.

Her thoughts were interrupted by the arrival of her mother, Fanny, who had returned from a pleasant afternoon of visiting with friends. Strangers were often surprised to learn that the two were mother and daughter, for they did not resemble each other in any way except for their brown eyes. Caroline and Cade had inherited their late father's looks and temperament. Fanny, by contrast, was blond and plump, with the mercurial disposition of a child. It was always disconcerting to try to converse with Fanny, for she disliked serious subjects and did not choose to face unpleasant realities.

"Caro," Fanny exclaimed, coming into the parlor after giving her frilly plumed hat and light summer wrap to the housekeeper. "You look rather displeased, dear. What has caused such a sour expression? Has our darling Cade been up to his usual pranks?"

"Our darling Cade is doing his best to ensure that you will spend your final years in a workhouse," Caroline replied dryly.

Her mother's face wrinkled in confusion. "I'm afraid I don't understand, dear. What do you mean?"

"Cade has been gambling," Caroline said. "He is going through all our money. Soon there will be nothing left. If he doesn't stop soon, we'll have to sell everything we own . . . and even *that* won't fully satisfy his debts."

"Oh, but you're teasing!" Fanny said with an anxious laugh. "Cade promised me that he would try to restrain himself at the hazard tables."

"Well, he hasn't," Caroline replied flatly. "And now we're all going to suffer for it."

Reading the truth in her daughter's eyes, Fanny sat down heavily on the pink brocade settee. In the grim silence that followed, she folded her hands in her lap like a punished child, her rosebud mouth forming an *O* of dismay. "It's all your fault!" she burst out suddenly.

"My fault?" Caroline gave her an incredulous stare. "Why on earth would you say that, Mother?"

"We wouldn't be in this predicament if you had married! A rich husband would have provided enough funds for Cade to indulge his little habits with his friends, and taken care of us as well. Now you've waited too long . . . your bloom has faded, and you're almost *twenty-seven*. . . ." Pausing, Fanny became a bit tearful at the thought of having an unmarried daughter of such an advanced age. Pulling a lace handkerchief from her sleeve, she dabbed delicately at her eyes. "Yes, your best years are behind you, and now the family will come to ruin. All because you refused to set your cap for a wealthy man."

Caroline opened her mouth to argue, then closed it with an exasperated sound. It was impossible to debate with someone so inured to the concept of logic. She had tried to argue with Fanny in the past, but it had served only to frustrate them both. "Mother," she said deliberately. "Mother, stop crying. I have some news that might cheer you. This afternoon I received a visit from one of Cade's friends—Lord Drake . . . do you remember him?"

"No, dear. Cade has so many acquaintances, I can never keep them all straight."

"Drake is the Earl of Rochester's only legitimate heir."

"Oh, that one." Fanny's expression brightened with interest, her tears vanishing instantly. "Yes, what a fortune he will come into! I do indeed remember him. A handsome man, I recollect, with long, dark hair and blue eyes—"

"And the manners of a swine," Caroline added.

"With an inheritance like that, Caro, one can overlook a few tiny breaches in etiquette. Do tell, what did Lord Drake say during his visit?"

"He . . ." Caroline hesitated, galled by the words she was about to say. She did not dare tell Fanny that the courtship between her and Drake would be only a charade. Her mother was a notorious gossip, and it would be only a matter of days—no, hours—before she let the truth slip to someone. "He expressed an interest in courting me," Caroline said, stone-faced. "Toward that end, you and I will allow him to escort us to a weekend party given by Mr. and Mrs. Logan Scott, to be held within a fortnight."

The news was almost too much for Fanny to digest at once. "Oh, Caro," she exclaimed. "An earl's son, interested in *you* . . . I can scarcely believe . . . Well, it's nothing less than a miracle! And if you can bring him to scratch . . . what a fortune you will have! What land, what jewels! You would certainly have your own carriage, and accounts at the finest shops. . . . Oh, this is the answer to all our problems!"

"So it would seem," Caroline said dryly. "But do not get your hopes too high, Mother. The courtship hasn't yet begun, and there is no guarantee that it will lead to marriage."

"Oh, but it will, it will!" Fanny practically danced around the room. Her blond curls fluttered and her well-rounded form jiggled with excitement. "I have a feeling in my bones. Now, Caro, you must heed my advice—I will tell you exactly how to set the hook and reel him in. You must be agreeable, and flatter his vanity, and give him admiring gazes . . . and you must never, never argue with him. And we must do something about your bosom."

"My bosom," Caroline repeated blankly.

"You will let me sew some quilted lining into the bodice of your chemise. You are a lovely girl, Caro, but you are in definite need of enhancement."

Assailed by a mixture of outrage and rueful laughter, Caro shook her head and smiled. "Quilted lining is not going to fool anyone. Especially not Lord Drake. But even if I did manage to deceive him, don't you think it would be a great disappointment on our wedding night to discover that my bosom was false?"

"By then it would be too late for him to do anything about it," her mother pointed out pragmatically. "And I would not call it a deception, Caro dear. After all, everyone must try to present herself or himself in the best light possible . . . that is what courtship is all about. The trick is to disguise all the unpleasant little faults that may put a man off, and maintain an air of mystery until you have finally landed him."

"No wonder I have never caught a husband," Caroline said with a faint smile. "I've always tried to be open and honest with men."

Her mother regarded her sadly. "I do not know where you have gotten these ideas, dear. Honesty has never fanned the flames of a man's ardor."

"I will try to remember that," Caroline replied gravely, fighting the temptation to laugh.

"The carriage is here," Fanny said with a squeal, staring out the parlor window at the vehicle moving along the front drive. "Oh, it is so fine! All that red lacquer and a Salisbury boot and crane neck, and what a fine large wrought-iron baggage rack. And no less than *four* outriders. Hurry, Caroline, do come and have a look."

"I had no idea you were so versed in the features of carriage construction, Mother," Caroline said dryly. She joined her mother at the window, and her stomach clenched with anxiety as she saw the Rochester coat of arms on the side of the carriage. It was time for the charade to begin. "Where is Cade?" she asked.

"In the library, I believe." Fanny continued to stare out the window, enthralled. "That dear, dear Lord Drake. Of all Cade's acquaintances, he has always been my favorite."

Amused despite her nervousness, Caroline laughed. "You didn't even remember who he was until I told you!"

"But then I recalled how much I liked him," Fanny countered.

Smiling wryly, Caroline wandered from the parlor to the small library, where her treasured collection of books was neatly stacked in the mahogany cases. Cade was at the sideboard, pouring a snifter of brandy from a crystal decanter.

"Are you ready to depart?" Caroline asked. "Lord Drake's carriage is here."

Cade turned with a glass in hand. His features, so like her own, were stamped with a scowl. "No, I am not ready," he said sourly. "Perhaps after I drink the rest of this bottle, I will be."

"Come, Cade," she chided. "One would think you were being sent to Newgate instead of attending a weekend party with friends."

"Drake is no friend of mine," Cade muttered. "He has seen to it that I am deprived of everything I enjoy. I'm not welcome at any hazard table in town, and I have not been invited to a single damned club for the past two weeks. I've been reduced to playing vingt-et-un for shillings. How will I ever earn enough to repay my debts?"

"Perhaps working?"

Cade snorted at what he perceived was a great insult. "No Hargreaves has occupied himself with trade or commerce for at least four generations."

"You should have thought of that before you gambled away everything Father left us. Then we wouldn't have to attend this dratted weekend party, and I would not have to pretend interest in a man I detest."

Suddenly shamefaced, Cade turned away from her. "I am sorry, Caro. But my luck was about to turn. I would have won back all the money, and more."

"Oh, Cade." She approached him and slid her arms around him, pressing her cheek against his stiff back. "Let us make the best of things," she said. "We'll go to the Scotts' estate, and I'll make calf eyes at Lord Drake, and you'll make yourself agreeable to everyone. And someday Lord Drake will be back in his father's will, and he will take care of your debts. And life will return to normal."

Suddenly they were interrupted by the housekeeper's voice. "Miss Hargreaves, Lord Drake has arrived. Shall I show him to the parlor?"

"Is my mother still in there?" Caroline asked.

"No, miss, she has gone upstairs to put on her traveling cloak and bonnet."

Wishing to avoid being alone with Drake, Caroline prodded her brother. "Cade, why don't you go welcome your friend?"

Evidently he was no more eager to see Drake than she. "No, I am going to show the footmen how I want our trunks and bags loaded on the carriage. You be the one to make small talk with him." Cade turned to glance at her, and a rueful grin spread across his face. "It is what you will be doing all weekend, sweet sister. You may as well practice now."

Giving him a damning look, Caroline left with an exasperated sigh and went to the parlor. She saw Andrew's tall form in the center of the room, his face partially concealed as he stared at a landscape that hung on the wall. "Good day, my lord," she said evenly. "I trust that you are . . ."

Her voice died away as he turned to face her. For a fraction of a second, she thought that the visitor was not Andrew, Lord Drake, but some other man. Stunned, she struggled silently to comprehend the changes that had taken place in him. The long, trailing locks of his dark hair had been cut in a new short style, cropped closely at the nape of his neck and the sides of his head. The alcoholic bloat of his face was gone, leaving behind a marvelously clean-lined jaw and hard-edged cheekbones. It seemed that he must have spent some time out-of-doors, for the paleness of his skin had been replaced by a light tan and the touch of windburn on the crests of his high cheekbones. And the eyes ... oh, the eyes. No longer dark-circled and bloodshot, they were the clear, bright blue of sapphires. And they contained a flash of something—perhaps uncertainty?—that unraveled Caroline's composure. Andrew seemed so young, so vital, remarkably different from the man who had stood with her in this very parlor just a fortnight ago.

Then he spoke, and it became evident that although his outward appearance had changed, he was still the same insufferable rake. "Miss Hargreaves," he said evenly. "No doubt Cade has seen fit to tell you that I have upheld my part of the bargain. Now it is your turn. I hope you've been practicing your love-struck glances and flirtatious repartee."

Somehow Caroline recovered herself enough to reply. "I thought all you wanted was 'the appearance of pleasant companionship' ... those were your exact words, were they not? I think 'love-struck' is a bit much to ask, don't you?"

"This past week I've gotten a complete accounting of Cade's debts," he returned grimly. "For what I'm going to have to pay, you owe me 'love-struck' and a damn sight more."

"You have yourself to blame for that. If you hadn't taken Cade along with you so many evenings—"

"It's not entirely my fault. But at this point I'm not inclined to quarrel. Gather your things, and let's be off."

Caroline nodded. However, she couldn't seem to make herself move. Her knees had locked, and she strongly suspected that if she took one step forward, she would fall flat on her face. She stared at him helplessly, while her heart thumped in a hard, uncontrollable rhythm, and her body flooded with heat. She had never experienced such a response to anyone in her life. Awareness of him pounded through her, and she realized how badly she wanted to touch him, draw her fingertips down the side of his lean cheek, kiss his firm, cynical mouth until it softened against hers in passion.

It can't be, she thought with a burst of panic. She could not feel such things for a man as immoral and depraved as Andrew, Lord Drake.

Something in her round-eyed gaze made him uncomfortable, for he shifted his weight from one leg to another, and shot her a baleful glance. "What are you staring at?"

"You," she said pertly. "I believe all your buttons have been fastened in the correct holes. Your hair appears to have been brushed. And for once you don't reek of spirits. I was merely reflecting on the surprising discovery that you can be made to look like a gentleman. Although it seems that your temper is as foul as ever."

"There is good reason for that," he informed her tersely. "It's been two weeks since I've had a drink or a wh— a female companion, and I've spent nearly every day at the family estate in the proximity of my father. I've visited with tenants and managers, and I've read account books until I've nearly gone blind. If I'm not fortunate enough to die of boredom soon, I'm going to shoot myself. And to top it all off, I have this damned weekend to look forward to."

"You poor man," she said pityingly. "It's terrible to be an aristocrat, isn't it?" He scowled at her, and she smiled. "You do look well, however," she said. "It appears that abstinence becomes you."

"I don't like it," he grumbled.

"That is hardly a surprise."

He stared down into her smiling face, and his expression

softened. Before Caroline could react, he reached out and plucked her spectacles from her nose.

"My lord," she said, unsettled, "I wish you would stop doing that! Hand those back at once. I can't see."

Andrew extracted a folded handkerchief from his pocket and polished the lenses. "It's no wonder your eyes are weak, the way you go about with your spectacles smudged." Ignoring her protests, he polished them meticulously and held them up to the light from the window. Only when he was satisfied that they were perfectly clean did he replace them on her nose.

"I could see perfectly well," she said.

"There was a thumbprint in the middle of the right lens."

"From now on, I would appreciate it if you simply *told* me about a smudge, rather than ripping my spectacles off my face!" Caroline knew she was being ungrateful and thorny-tempered. Some part of her mind was appalled by her own bad manners. However, she had the suspicion that if she did not maintain a strategic animosity toward him, she might do something horribly embarrassing—such as throw herself against his tall, hard body and kiss him. He was so large and irascible and tempting, and the mere sight of him sent an inexplicable heat ripping through her.

She did not understand herself—she had always thought that one had to *like* a man before experiencing this dizzying swirl of attraction. But evidently her body was not reconciled with her emotions, for whether she liked him or not, she wanted him. To feel his big, warm hands on her skin. To feel his lips on her throat and breast.

A flaming blush swept all the way from her bodice to her hairline, and she knew his perceptive gaze did not miss the tide of betraying color.

Mercifully, he did not comment on it, but answered her

earlier remark. "Very well," he said. "What do I care if you walk into walls or trip over paving stones when you can't see through your damn spectacles?"

It was the most peculiar carriage-ride Andrew had ever experienced. For three hours he suffered under Cade's disapproving glare—the lad regarded him as an utter Judas, and this in spite of the fact that Andrew was willing to pay all his debts in the not-too-distant future. Then there was the mother, Fanny, surely one of the most empty-headed matrons he had ever met in his life. She chattered in unending monologues and seemed never to require a reply other than the occasional grunt or nod. Every time he made the mistake of replying to one of her comments, it fueled a new round of inane babble. And then there was Caroline sitting opposite him, silent and outwardly serene as she focused on the ever-changing array of scenery outside the window.

Andrew stared at her openly, while she seemed completely oblivious to his perusal. She was wearing a blue dress with a white pelisse fastened over the top. The scooped neck of her bodice was modest, not revealing even a hint of cleavage— not that she had much cleavage to display. And yet he was unbearably stimulated by the little expanse of skin that she displayed, that exquisite hollow at the base of her throat, and the porcelain smoothness of her upper chest. She was tiny, almost doll-like, and yet he was spellbound by her, to the extent of being half-aroused despite the presence of her brother *and* mother.

"What are you looking at?" he asked after a while, irritated by her steadfast refusal to glance his way. "Find the sight of cows and hedges enthralling, do you?"

"I have to stare at the scenery," Caroline replied without

moving her gaze. "The moment I try to focus on something inside the carriage, I start to feel ill, especially when the road is uneven. I've been this way since childhood."

Fanny interceded anxiously. "Caroline, you must try to cure yourself of that. How vexing it must be for a fine gentleman such as Lord Drake to have you staring constantly out the window rather than participating in our conversation."

Andrew grinned at hearing himself described as a "fine gentleman."

Cade spoke then. "She's not going to change, Mother. And I daresay that Drake would prefer Caro to stare at the scenery rather than cast her accounts all over his shoes."

"Cade, how vulgar!" Fanny exclaimed, frowning at him. "Apologize to Lord Drake at once."

"No need," Andrew said hastily.

Fanny beamed at him. "How magnanimous of you, my lord, to overlook my son's bad manners. As for my daughter's unfortunate condition, I am quite certain that it is not a defect that might be passed on to any sons or daughters."

"That is good news," Andrew said blandly. "But I rather enjoy Miss Hargreaves's charming habit. It affords me the privilege of viewing her lovely profile."

Caroline glanced at him then, quickly, rolling her eyes at the compliment before turning her attention back to the window. He saw her lips curve slightly, however, betraying her amusement at the flattery.

Eventually they arrived at the Scotts' estate, which featured a house that was reputed to be one of the most attractive residences in England. The great stone mansion was surrounded with magnificent expanses of green lawn and gardens, and an oak-filled park in the back. The row of eight stone pillars in front was topped by huge sparkling windows, making the facade of the building more glass than wall. It seemed that only royalty should live in such a place, which made it rather appropriate for the family of Logan Scott. He was royalty of a sort, albeit of the London stage.

Caroline had been fortunate enough to see Scott perform in a production at the Capital Theater, and like every other member of the audience, she had found Scott to be breathtaking in his ability and presence. It was said that his Hamlet surpassed even the legendary David Garrick's, and that people would someday read of him in history books.

"How interesting that a man like Mr. Scott is your half brother," Caroline murmured, staring at the great estate as Andrew assisted her from the carriage. "Is there much likeness between you?"

"Not a farthing's worth," Andrew said, his face expressionless. "Logan was given a damned poor start in life, and he climbed to the top of his profession armed with nothing but talent and determination. Whereas I was given every advantage, and I've accomplished nothing."

They spoke in quiet murmurs, too low to be heard by Cade and Fanny.

"Are you jealous of him?" Caroline could not help asking.

Surprise flickered across Andrew's face, and it was clear that few people ever spoke so openly to him. "No, how could I be? Logan has earned everything he's gotten. And he's tolerated a great deal from me. He's even forgiven me for the time I tried to kill him."

"What?" Caroline stumbled slightly, and stopped to look up at him in astonishment. "You didn't really, did you?"

A grin crossed his dark face. "I wouldn't have gone through with it. But I was drunk as a wheelbarrow at the time, and I had just discovered that he had known we were brothers and hadn't told me. So I cornered him in his theater, brandishing a pistol."

"My God." Caroline stared up at him uneasily. "That is the behavior of a madman."

"No, I wasn't mad. Just foxed." Amusement danced in his blue eyes. "Don't worry, sweetheart. I plan to stay sober for a while . . . and even if I weren't, I would be no danger to you."

The word *sweetheart*, spoken in that low, intimate voice, did something strange to her insides. Caroline began to reprove him for his familiarity, then realized that was their entire purpose for being here—to create the impression that they were indeed sweethearts.

They entered the two-story great hall, which was lined with dark wood paneling and rich tapestries, and were welcomed by Mr. Scott's wife, Madeline. The girl was absolutely lovely, her golden brown hair coiled atop her head, her hazel eyes sparkling as she greeted Andrew with youthful exuberance. It was clear that the two liked each other immensely.

"Lord Drake," Madeline exclaimed, clasping his hands in her own small ones, her cheek turned upward to receive his brotherly kiss. "How well you look! It has been at least a month since we've seen you. I am terribly vexed with you for remaining away so long."

Andrew smiled at his sister-in-law with a warmth that transformed his dark face, making Caroline's breath catch. "How is my niece?" he asked.

"You won't recognize her, I vow. She has grown at least two inches, and she has a tooth now!" Releasing his hands, Madeline turned toward Cade, Fanny, and Caroline, and curtsied gracefully. "Good morning, my lord, and Lady Hargreaves, and Miss Hargreaves." Her vivacious gaze locked with Caroline's. "My husband and I are delighted that you will be joining us this weekend. Any friends of Lord Drake's are always welcome at our home."

"You always despise my friends," Andrew remarked dryly, and Madeline gave him a quick frown.

"Your usual ones, yes. But friends like *these* are definitely welcome."

Caroline interceded then, smiling at Madeline. "Mrs. Scott, I promise we will do our best to distinguish ourselves from Lord Drake's usual sort of companions."

"Thank you," came the girl's fervent reply, and they shared a sudden laugh.

"Wait a minute," Andrew said, only half in jest. "I didn't plan for the two of you to become friendly with each other. You had better stay away from my sister-in-law, Miss Hargreaves—she's an incurable gossip."

"Yes," Madeline confirmed, sending Caroline a conspiratorial smile. "And some of my best gossip is about Lord Drake. You'll find it vastly entertaining."

Fanny, who had been so in awe of their grandiose surroundings as to be rendered speechless, suddenly recovered her voice. "Mrs. Scott, we are so looking forward to meeting your esteemed husband. Such a celebrated man, so talented, so remarkable—"

A new voice entered the conversation, a voice so deep and distinctive that it could only belong to one man. "Madam, you do me too much honor, I assure you."

Logan Scott had approached them from behind, as large and handsome as he appeared on the stage, his tall form impeccably dressed in gray trousers, a formfitting black coat, and a crisp white cravat tied in an elaborate knot.

Looking from Andrew to his half brother, Caroline could see a vague likeness between them. They were both tall, physically imposing men, with strong, even features. Their coloring was not the same, however. Andrew's hair was as black as jet, whereas Logan Scott's was fiery mahogany. And Andrew's skin had a golden cast, as opposed to Scott's ruddier hue.

Watching them stand together, Caroline reflected that the main difference between the two men was in their bearing. It was clear that Logan Scott was accustomed to the attention that his celebrity had earned—he was self-confident, a bit larger than life, his gestures relaxed and yet expansive. Andrew, however, was quieter, far more closed and private, his emotions ruthlessly buried deep below the surface.

"Brother," Logan Scott murmured, as they exchanged a hearty handshake. It was clear that there was deep affection between the two.

Andrew introduced Scott to the Hargreaves family, and Caroline was amused to see that the presence of this living legend had reduced her mother to speechlessness once more. Scott's penetrating gaze moved from one face to another, until he finally focused on Andrew. "Father is here," he said.

The brothers exchanged a look that was difficult to interpret, and it was obvious that the two shared an understanding of the man that no one else in the world did.

"How is he?" Andrew asked.

"Better today. He didn't need quite so much of his medicine during the night. At the moment he is conserving his strength for the ball tonight." Scott paused before adding. "He wanted to see you as soon as you arrived. Shall I take you to his room?"

Andrew nodded. "No doubt I have committed a hundred offenses he'll wish to upbraid me for. I should hate to deprive him of such entertainment."

"Good," Scott said sardonically. "Since I've already had to

run through that particular gauntlet today, there is no reason that you should be spared."

Turning to Caroline, Andrew murmured, "Will you excuse me, Miss Hargreaves?"

"Of course." She found herself giving him a brief reassuring smile. "I hope it goes well, my lord."

As their gazes met, she saw his eyes change, the hard opaqueness softening to warm blue. "Later, then," he murmured, and bowed before leaving.

The intimacy of their shared gaze had caused warm flutters in the pit of her stomach, and a sensation of giddy lightness that floated all through her. Slightly bemused, Caroline reflected that Logan Scott was not the only man in the family with acting ability. Andrew was playing his part so convincingly that anyone would believe he had a real interest in her. She could almost believe it herself. Sternly she concentrated on the thought that it was all a pretense. Money, not courtship, was Andrew's ultimate goal.

Andrew and Logan entered the house and crossed through the marble hall, its plasterwork ceiling embellished with mythological scenes and a mask-and-ribbon motif. Approaching the grand staircase, which curved in a huge gentle spiral, the brothers made their way upward at a leisurely pace.

"Your Miss Hargreaves seems a charming girl," Logan remarked.

Andrew smiled sardonically. "She is not *my* Miss Hargreaves."

"She's a pretty sort," Logan said. "Delicate in appearance, but she seems to possess a certain liveliness of spirit."

"Spirit," Andrew repeated wryly. "Yes . . . she has plenty of that."

"Interesting."

"What is interesting?" Andrew asked warily, disliking his half brother's speculative tone.

"To my knowledge, you've never courted a lady before."

"It's not a real courtship," Andrew informed him. "It's merely a ruse to fool Father."

"What?" Logan stopped on the stairs and stared at him in surprise. "Would you care to explain, Andrew?"

"As you know, I've been cut out of the will. To be reinstated I've got to convince Father that I've changed my wicked ways, or he'll die without leaving me a damned shilling." Andrew proceeded to explain his bargain with Caroline, and the terms they had struck.

Logan listened intently, finally giving a gruff laugh. "Well, if you wish to change Father's mind about his will, I suppose your involvement with a woman like Miss Hargreaves is a good idea."

"It's not an 'involvement,'" Andrew said, feeling unaccountably defensive. "As I told you, it's merely a charade."

Logan slid a speculative glance his way. "I have a suspicion, Andrew, that your relationship with Miss Hargreaves is something more than a charade, whether you are willing to admit it or not."

"It's all for Father's benefit," Andrew said swiftly. "I am telling you, Scott, I have no designs on her. And even if I did, believe me, I would be the last man on earth whom she would take an interest in."

Chapter Three

"Not if he were the last man on earth," Caroline said, glaring at her brother. "I am telling you, Cade, I feel no sort of attraction whatsoever to that . . . that *libertine*. Don't be obtuse. You know quite well that it is all a pretense."

"I thought it was," Cade said reflectively, "until I watched the two of you during that deuced long carriage ride today. Now I'm not so certain. Drake stared at you like at cat after a mouse. He didn't take his eyes off you once."

Caroline sternly suppressed an unwanted twinge of pleasure at her brother's words. She turned toward the long looking glass, needlessly fluffing the short sleeves of her pale blue evening gown. "The only reason he may have glanced my way was to distract himself from Mother's babbling," she said crisply.

"And the way you smiled at him this afternoon, before he left to see his father," Cade continued. "You looked positively besotted."

"Besotted?" She let out a burst of disbelieving laughter. "Cade, that is the most ridiculous thing I've ever heard you say. Not only am I *not* besotted with Lord Drake, I can barely stand to be in the same room with him!"

"Then why the new gown and hairstyle?" he asked. "Are you certain you're not trying to attract him?"

Caroline surveyed her reflection critically. Her gown was simple but stylish, a thin white muslin underskirt overlaid with transparent blue silk. The bodice was low-cut and square, edged with a row of glinting silver beadwork. Her dark, glossy brown hair had been pulled to the crown of her head with blue ribbons, and left to hang down the back in a mass of ringlets. She knew that she had never looked better in her life. "I am wearing a new gown because I am tired of looking so matronly," she said. "Just because I am a spinster doesn't mean I have to appear a complete dowd."

"Caro," her brother said affectionately, coming up behind her and putting his hands on her upper arms, "you're a spinster only by choice. You've always been a lovely girl. The only reason you haven't landed a husband is because you haven't yet seen fit to set your cap for someone."

She turned to hug him, heedless of mussing her gown, and smiled at him warmly. "Thank you, Cade. And just to be quite clear, I have *not* set my cap for Lord Drake. As I have told you a dozen times, we are simply acting. As in a stage performance."

"All right," he said, drawing back to look at her skeptically. "But in my opinion, you are both throwing yourself into your roles with a bit more zeal than necessary."

The sounds of the ball drifted to Caroline's ears as they went down the grand staircase. The luminous, agile melody of a waltz swirled through the air, undercut by the flow of laughter and chatter as the guests moved through the circuit of rooms that branched off from the central hall. The atmosphere was heavily perfumed from huge arrangements of lilies and roses, while a garden breeze wafted gently through the rows of open windows.

Caroline's gloved fingertips slid easily over the carved marble balustrade as they descended. She gripped Cade's arm with her other hand. She was strangely nervous, wondering if her evening spent in Andrew's company would prove to be a delight or torture. Fanny chattered excitedly as she accompanied them, mentioning the names of several guests she had already seen at the estate, including peers of the realm, politicians, a celebrated artist, and a noted playwright.

As they reached the lower landing, Caroline saw Andrew waiting for them at the nadir of the staircase, his dark hair gleaming in the brilliant light shed by legions of candles. As if he sensed her approach, he turned and glanced upward. His white teeth flashed in a smile as he saw her, and Caroline's heartbeat hastened to a hard, driving rhythm.

Dressed in a formal, fashionable scheme of black and white, with a starched cravat and a formfitting gray waistcoat, Andrew was so handsome that it was almost unseemly. He was as polished and immaculate as any gentleman present, but his striking blue eyes gleamed with the devil's charm. When he looked at her like that, his gaze hot and interested, she did not feel as if this entire situation were an obligation. She did not feel as if it were a charade. The lamentable fact was, she felt excited, and glad, and thoroughly beguiled.

"Miss Hargreaves, you look ravishing," he murmured, after greeting Fanny and Cade. He offered her his arm and guided her toward the ballroom.

"Not matronly?" Caroline asked tartly.

"Not in the least." He smiled faintly. "You never did, actually. When I made that comment, I was just trying to annoy you."

"You succeeded," she said, and paused with a perplexed frown. "Why did you want to annoy me?"

"Because annoying you is safer than—" For some reason he broke off abruptly and clamped his mouth shut.

"Safer than what?" Caroline asked, intensely curious as he led her into the ballroom. "What? What?"

Ignoring her questions, Andrew swept her into a waltz so intoxicating and potent that its melody seemed to throb inside her veins. She was at best a competent dancer, but Andrew was exceptional, and there were few pleasures to equal dancing with a man who was truly accomplished at it. His arm was supportive, his hands gentle but authoritative as he guided her in smooth, sweeping circles.

Caroline was vaguely aware that people were staring at them. No doubt the crowd was amazed by the fact that the dissolute Lord Drake was waltzing with the proper Miss Hargreaves. They were an obvious mismatch . . . and yet, Caroline wondered, was it really so inconceivable that a rake and a spinster could find something alluring in each other?

"You are a wonderful dancer," she could not help exclaiming.

"Of course I am," he said. "I'm proficient at all the trivial activities in life. It's only the meaningful pursuits that present a problem."

"It doesn't have to be that way."

"Oh, it does," he assured her with a self-mocking smile.

An uncomfortable silence ensued until Caroline sought a way to break it. "Has your father come downstairs yet?" she asked. "Surely you will want him to see us dance together."

"I don't know where he is," Andrew returned. "And right now I don't give a damn if he sees us or not."

In the upper galleries that overlooked the ballroom, Logan Scott directed a pair of footmen to settle his father's fragile, tumor-ridden form onto a soft upholstered chaise longue. A maidservant settled into a nearby chair, ready to fetch anything that the earl might require. A light blanket was draped over Rochester's bony knees, and a goblet of rare Rhenish wine was placed in his claw-like fingers.

Logan watched the man for a moment, inwardly amazed that Rochester, a figure who had loomed over his entire life with such power and malevolence, should have come to this. The once-handsome face, with its hawklike perfection, had shrunk to a mask of skeletal paleness and delicacy. The vigorous, muscular body had deteriorated until he could barely walk without assistance. One might have thought that the imminent approach of death would have softened the cruel earl, and perhaps taught him some regret over the past. But Rochester, true to form, admitted to no shred of remorse.

Not for the first time, Logan felt an acute stab of sympathy for his half brother. Though Logan had been raised by a tenant farmer who had abused him physically, he had fared better than Andrew, whose father had abused his very soul. Surely no man in existence was colder and more unloving than the Earl of Rochester. It was a wonder that Andrew had survived such a childhood.

Tearing his thoughts away from the past, Logan glanced at the assemblage below. His gaze located the tall form of his brother, who was dancing with Miss Caroline Hargreaves.

The petite woman seemed to have bewitched Andrew, who for once did not seem bored, bitter, or sullen. In fact, for the first time in his life, it appeared that Andrew was exactly where he wanted to be.

"There," Logan said, easily adjusting the heavy weight of the chaise longue so that his father could see better. "That is the woman Andrew brought here."

Rochester's mouth compressed into a parchment-thin line of disdain. "A girl of no consequence," he pronounced. "Her looks are adequate, I suppose. However, they say she is a bluestocking. Do not presume to tell me that your brother would have designs on such a creature."

Logan smiled slightly, long accustomed to the elderly man's caustic tongue. "Watch them together," he murmured. "See how he is with her."

"It's a ruse," Rochester said flatly. "I know all about my worthless son and his scheming ways. I could have predicted this from the moment I removed his name from the will. He seeks to deceive me into believing that he can change his ways." He let out a sour cackle. "Andrew can court a multitude of respectable spinsters if he wishes. But I will go to hell before I reinstate him."

Logan forbore to reply that such a scenario was quite likely, and bent to wedge a velvet-covered pillow behind the old man's frail back. Satisfied that his father had a comfortable place from which to view the activities down below, he stood and rested a hand on the carved mahogany railing. "Even if it were a ruse," he mused aloud, "wouldn't it be interesting if Andrew were caught in a snare of his own making?"

"What did you say?" The old man stared at him with rheumy, slitted eyes, and raised a goblet of wine to his lips. "What manner of snare is that, pray tell?"

"I mean it is possible that Andrew could fall in love with Miss Hargreaves."

The earl sneered into his cup. "It's not in him to love anyone other than himself."

"You're wrong, Father," Logan said quietly. "It's only that Andrew has had little acquaintance with that emotion—particularly to be on the receiving end of it."

Understanding the subtle criticism of the cold manner in which he had always treated his sons, the legitimate one and the bastard, Rochester gave him a disdainful smile. "You lay the blame for his selfishness at *my* door, of course. You've always made excuses for him. Take care, my superior fellow, or I will cut *you* out of my will as well."

To Rochester's obvious annoyance, Logan burst out laughing. "I don't give a damn," he said. "I don't need a shilling from you. But have a care when you speak about Andrew. He is the only reason you're here. For some reason that I'll never be able to comprehend, Andrew loves you. A miracle, that you could have produced a son who managed to survive your tender mercies and still have the capability to love. I freely admit that I would not."

"You are fond of making me out to be a monster," the earl remarked frostily. "When the truth is, I only give people what they deserve. If Andrew had ever done anything to merit my love, I would have accorded it to him. But he will have to earn it first."

"Good God, man, you're nearly on your deathbed," Logan muttered. "Don't you think you've waited long enough? Do you have any damned idea of what Andrew would do for one word of praise or affection from you?"

Rochester did not reply, his face stubbornly set as he drank from his goblet and watched the glittering, whirling mass of couples below.

*   *   *

The rule was that a gentleman should never dance more than three times with any one girl at a ball. Caroline did not know why such a rule had been invented, and she had never resented it as she did now. To her astonishment, she discovered that she liked dancing with Andrew, Lord Drake, and she was more than a little sorry when the waltz was over. She was further surprised to learn that Andrew could be an agreeable companion when he chose.

"I wouldn't have suspected you to be so well-informed on so many subjects," she told him, while servants filled their plates at the refreshment tables. "I assumed you had spent most of your time drinking, and yet you are remarkably well-read."

"I can drink and hold a book at the same time," he said.

She frowned at him. "Don't make light of it, when I am trying to express that . . . you are not . . ."

"I am not what?" he prompted softly.

"You are not exactly what you seem."

He gave her a slightly crooked grin. "Is that a compliment, Miss Hargreaves?"

She was slightly dazed as she stared into the warm blue intensity of his eyes. "I suppose it must be."

A woman's voice intruded on the moment, cutting through the spell of intimacy with the exquisite precision of a surgeon's blade. "Why, Cousin Caroline," the woman exclaimed, "I am *astonished* to see how stylish you look. It is a great pity that you cannot rid yourself of the spectacles, dear, and then you would be the toast of the ball."

The speaker was Julianne, Lady Brenton, the most beautiful and treacherous woman that Caroline had ever known. Even the people who despised her—and there were no end of those—had to concede that she was physically flawless. Julianne was slender, of medium height, with perfectly curved hips and a lavishly endowed bosom. Her features were positively angelic, her nose small and narrow, her lips naturally hued a deep pink, her eyes blue and heavily lashed. Crowning all of this perfection was a heavy swirl of blond hair in a silvery shade that seemed to have been distilled from moonlight. It was difficult, if not impossible, to believe that Caroline and this radiant creature could be related in any way, and yet they were first cousins on her father's side.

Caroline had grown up in awe of Julianne, who was only a year older than herself. In adulthood, however, admiration had gradually turned to disenchantment as she realized that her cousin's outward beauty concealed a heart that was monstrously selfish and calculating. When she was seventeen, Julianne had married a man forty years older than herself, a wealthy earl with a penchant for collecting fine objects. There had been frequent rumors that Julianne was unfaithful to her elderly spouse, but she was far too clever to have been caught. Three years ago her husband died in his bed, ostensibly of a weak heart. There were whispered suspicions that his death was not of natural causes, but no proof was ever discovered.

Julianne's blue eyes sparkled wickedly as she stood before Caroline. Her immaculate blondness was complemented by a shimmering white gown that draped so low in front that the upper halves of her breasts were exposed.

Sliding a flirtatious glance at Andrew, Julianne remarked, "My poor little cousin is quite blind without her spectacles . . . a pity, is it not?"

"She is lovely with or without them," Andrew replied coldly. "And Miss Hargreaves's considerable beauty is matched by her interior qualities. It is unfortunate that one cannot say the same of other women."

Julianne's entrancing smile dimmed, and she and Andrew regarded each other with cool challenge. Unspoken messages were exchanged between them. Caroline's pleasure in the evening evaporated as a few things became instantly clear. It was obvious that Julianne and Andrew were well acquainted. There seemed to be some remnant of intimacy, of sexual knowledge between them, that could have resulted only from a past affair.

Of course they had once been lovers, Caroline thought resentfully. Andrew would surely have been intrigued by a woman of such sensuous beauty . . . and there was no doubt that Julianne would have been more than willing to grant her favors to a man who was the heir to a great fortune.

"Lord Drake," Julianne said lightly, "you are more handsome than ever . . . why, you seem quite reinvigorated. To whom do we owe our gratitude for such a pleasing transformation?"

"My father," Andrew replied bluntly, with a smile that didn't reach his eyes. "He cut me out of his will—indeed a transforming experience."

"Yes, I had heard about that." Julianne's bow-shaped lips pursed in a little moue of disappointment. "Your inheritance was one of your most agreeable attributes, dear. A pity that you've lost it." She shot Caroline a snide smile before adding, "Clearly your prospects have dwindled considerably."

"Don't let us keep you, Julianne," Caroline said. "No doubt you have much to accomplish tonight, with so many wealthy men present."

Julianne's blue eyes narrowed at the veiled insult. "Very well. Good evening, Cousin Caroline. And pray do show Lord Drake more of your 'interior beauty'—it may be your only chance of retaining his attention." A catlike smile spread across her face as she murmured, "If you can manage to lure Drake to your bed, cousin, you will find him a most exciting and talented partner. I can give you my personal assurance on that point." Julianne departed with a luscious swaying of her hips that caused her skirts to swish silkily.

Scores of male gazes followed her movement across the room, but Andrew's was not one of them. Instead he focused on Caroline, who met his scowling gaze with an accusing glare. "Despite my cousin's subtlety and discretion," Caroline said coolly, "I managed to receive the impression that you and she were once lovers. Is that true?"

Until Lady Brenton's interruption, Andrew had actually been enjoying himself. He had always disliked attending balls and soirees, at which one was expected to make dull conversation with matrimonially minded girls and their even duller chaperones. But Caroline Hargreaves, with her quick wit and spirit, was surprisingly entertaining. For the last half hour he had felt a peculiar sense of well-being, a glow that had nothing to do with alcohol.

Then Julianne had appeared, reminding him of all his past debauchery, and the fragile sensation of happiness had abruptly vanished. Andrew had always tried to emulate his father in having no regrets over the past . . . but there it was, the unmistakable stab of rue, of embarrassment, over the affair with Julianne. And the hell of it was, the liaison hadn't even been worth the trouble. Julianne was like those elaborate French desserts that never tasted as good as they looked, and certainly never satisfied the palate.

Andrew forced himself to return Caroline's gaze as he answered her question. "It is true," he said gruffly. "We had an affair two years ago . . . brief and not worth remembering."

He resented the way Caroline stared at him, as if she were so flawless that she had never done anything worthy of regret. Damn her, he had never lied to her, or pretended to be anything other than what he was. She knew he was a scoundrel, a villain . . . for God's sake, he'd nearly resorted to blackmail to get her to attend the weekend party in the first place.

Grimly he wondered why the hell Logan and Madeline had invited Julianne here in the first place. Well, he couldn't object to her presence here merely because he'd once had an affair with her. If he tried to get her booted off the estate for that reason, there were at least half a dozen other women present who would have to be thrown out on the same grounds.

As if she had followed the turn of his thoughts, Caroline scowled at him. "I am not surprised that you've slept with my cousin," she said. "No doubt you've slept with at least half the women here."

"What if I have? What difference does it make to you?"

"No difference at all. It only serves to confirm my low opinion of you. How inconvenient it must be to have all the self-control of a March hare."

"It's better than being an ice maiden," he said with a sneer.

Her brown eyes widened behind the spectacles, and a flush spread over her face. "What? What did you call me?"

The edge in her tone alerted a couple nearby to the fact that a quarrel was brewing, and Andrew became aware that they were the focus of a few speculative stares. "Outside," he ground out. "We'll continue this in the rose garden."

"By all means," Caroline agreed in a vengeful tone, struggling to keep her face impassive.

Ten minutes later they had each managed to slip outside.

The rose garden, referred to by Madeline Scott as her "rose room," was a southwest section of the garden delineated by posts and rope swags covered with climbing roses. White gravel covered the ground, and fragrant lavender hedges led to the arch at the entrance. There was a massive stone urn on a pedestal in the center of the rose room, surrounded by a velvety blue bed of catmint.

The exotic perfumed air did nothing to soothe Andrew's frustration. As he saw Caroline's slight figure enter the rustling garden, he could barely restrain himself from pouncing on her. He kept still and silent instead, his jaw set as he watched her approach.

She stopped within arm's length of him, her head tilted back so that she could meet his gaze directly. "I have only one thing to say, my lord." Agitation pulled her voice taut and high. "Unlike you, I have a high regard for the truth. And while I would never take exception to an honest remark, no matter how unflattering, I *do* resent what you said back there. Because it is not true! You are categorically wrong, and I will not go back inside that house until you admit it!"

"Wrong about what?" he asked. "That you're an ice maiden?"

For some reason the term had incensed her. He saw her chin quiver with indignation. "Yes, that," she said in a hiss.

He gave her a smile designed to heighten her fury. "I can prove it," he said in a matter-of-fact tone. "What is your age . . . twenty-six?"

"Yes."

"And despite the fact that you're far prettier than average, and you possess good blood and a respected family name, you've never accepted a proposal of marriage from any man."

"Correct," she said, looking briefly bemused at the compliment.

He paced around her, giving her an insultingly thorough inspection. "And you're a virgin . . . aren't you?"

It was obvious that the question affronted her. He could easily read the outrage in her expression, and her blush was evident even in the starlit darkness. No proper young woman should even think of answering such an inquiry. After a long, silent struggle, she gave a brief nod.

That small confirmation did something to his insides, made them tighten and throb with savage frustration. *Damn* her, he had never found a virgin desirable before. And yet he wanted her with volcanic intensity . . . he wanted to possess and kiss every inch of her innocent body . . . he wanted to make her cry and moan for him. He wanted the lazy minutes afterward when they would lie together, sweaty and peaceful in the aftermath of passion. The right to touch her intimately, however and whenever he wanted, seemed worth any price. And yet he would never have her. He had relinquished any chance of that long ago, before they had ever met. Perhaps if he had led his life in a completely different manner . . . But he could not escape the consequences of his past.

Covering his yearning with a mocking smile, Andrew gestured with his hands to indicate that the facts spoke for themselves. "Pretty, unmarried, twenty-six, and a virgin. That leads to only one conclusion . . . ice maiden."

"I am *not!* I have far more passion, more honest feeling, than you'll ever possess!" Her eyes narrowed as she saw his amusement. "Don't you dare laugh at me!" She launched herself at him, her hands raised as if to attack.

With a smothered laugh, Andrew grabbed her upper arms and held her at bay . . . until he realized that she was not trying to claw his face, but rather to put her hands around his neck. Startled, he loosened his hold, and she immediately seized his nape. She exerted as much pressure as she was able, using her full weight to try to pull his head down. He resisted her easily, staring into her small face with a baffled smile. He was so much larger than she that any attempt on her part to physically coerce him was laughable. "Caroline," he said, his voice unsteady with equal parts of amusement and desire, "are you by chance trying to *kiss* me?"

She continued to tug at him furiously, wrathful and determined. She was saying something beneath her breath, spitting like an irate kitten. "... show you ... make you sorry ... I am *not* made of ice, you arrogant, presumptuous *libertine* ..."

Andrew could not stand it any longer. As he viewed the tiny, indignant female in his arms, he lost the capability of rational thought. All he could think of was how much he desired her, and how a few stolen moments in the rose garden would not matter in the great scheme of things. He was nearly mad with the need to taste her, to touch her, to drag her body full-length against his, and the rest of the world could go to hell. And so he let it happen. He relaxed his neck and lowered his head, and let her tug his mouth down to hers.

Something unexpected happened with that first sweet pressure of her lips—innocently closed lips because she did not know how to kiss properly. He felt a terrible aching pressure around his heart, squeezing and clenching until he felt the hard wall around it crack, and heat came rushing inside. She was so light and soft in his arms, the smell of her skin a hundred times more alluring than roses, the fragile line of her spine arching as she tried to press closer to him. The sensation came too hard, too fast, and he froze in sudden paralysis, not knowing where to put his hands, afraid that if he moved at all, he would crush her.

He fumbled with his gloves, ripped them off, and dropped them to the ground. Carefully he touched Caroline's back and slid his palm to her waist. His other hand shook as he gently grasped the nape of her neck. Oh, God, she was exquisite, a bundle of muslin and silk in his hands, too luscious to be real. His breath rushed from his lungs in hard bursts, and he fought to keep his movements gentle as he urged her closer against his fiercely aroused body. Increasing the pressure of the kiss, he coaxed her lips to part, touched his tongue to hers, found the intoxicating taste of her. She started slightly at the unfamiliar intimacy. He knew it was wrong to kiss a virgin that way, but he couldn't help himself. A soothing sound came from deep in his throat, and he licked deeper, searching the sweet, dark heat of her mouth. To his astonishment, Caroline moaned and relaxed in his arms, her lips parting, her tongue sliding hotly against his.

Andrew had not expected her to be so ardent, so receptive. She should have been repelled by him. But she yielded herself with a terrible trust that devastated him. He couldn't stop his hands from wandering over her hungrily, reaching over the curves of her buttocks to hitch her higher against his body. He pulled her upward, nestling her closer into the huge ridge of his sex until she fit exactly the way he wanted. The thin layers of her clothes—and his—did nothing to muffle the sensation. She gasped and wriggled deliciously, and tightened her arms around his neck until her toes nearly left the ground.

"Caroline," he said hoarsely, his mouth stealing down the tender line of her throat, "you're making me insane. We have to stop now. I shouldn't be doing this—"

"Yes. Yes." Her breath puffed in rapid, hot expulsions, and she twined herself around him, rubbing herself against the rock-hard protrusion of his loins. They kissed again, her mouth clinging to his with frantic sweetness, and Andrew made a quiet, despairing sound.

"Stop me," he muttered, clamping his hand over her writhing bottom. "Tell me to let go of you. . . . Slap me. . . ."

She tilted her head back, purring like a kitten as he nuzzled the soft space beneath her ear. "Where should I slap you?" she asked throatily.

She was too innocent to fully comprehend the sexual connotations of her question. Even so, Andrew felt himself turn impossibly hard, and he suppressed a low groan of desire. "Caroline," he whispered harshly, "you win. I was wrong when I called you a . . . No, don't do that anymore; I can't bear it. You win." He eased her away from his aching body. "Now stay back," he added curtly, "or you're going to lose your virginity in this damned garden."

Recognizing the vehemence in his tone, Caroline prudently kept a few feet of distance between them. She wrapped her slender arms around herself, trembling. For a while there was no sound other than their labored breathing.

"We should go back," she finally said. "People will notice that we're both absent. I . . . I have no wish to be compromised . . . that is, my reputation . . ." Her voice trailed into an awkward silence, and she risked a glance at him. "Andrew," she confessed shakily, "I've never felt this way bef—"

"Don't say it," he interrupted. "For your sake, and mine, we are not going to let this happen again. We are going to keep to our bargain—I don't want complications."

"But don't you want to—"

"No," he said tersely. "I want only the pretense of a relationship with you, nothing more. If I truly became involved with you, I would have to transform my life completely.

And it's too bloody late for that. I am beyond redemption, and no one, not even you, is worth changing my ways for."

She was quiet for a long moment, her dazed eyes focused on his set face. "I know someone who *is* worth it," she finally said.

"Who?"

"You." Her stare was direct and guileless. "You are worth saving, Andrew."

With just a few words, she demolished him. Andrew shook his head, unable to speak. He wanted to seize her in his arms again . . . worship her . . . ravish her. No woman had ever expressed the slightest hint of faith in him, in his worthless soul, and though he wanted to respond with utter scorn, he could not. One impossible wish consumed him in a great purifying blaze—that somehow he could become worthy of her. He yearned to tell her how he felt. Instead he averted his face and managed a few rasping words. "You go inside first."

For the rest of the weekend party, and for the next three months, Andrew was a perfect gentleman. He was attentive, thoughtful, and good-humored, prompting jokes from all who knew him that somehow the wicked Lord Drake had been abducted and replaced by an identical stranger. Those who were aware of the Earl of Rochester's poor health surmised that Andrew was making an effort to court his father's favor before the old man died and left him bereft of the family fortune. It was a transparent effort, the gossips snickered, and very much in character for the devious Lord Drake.

The strange thing was, the longer that Andrew's pretend reformation lasted, the more it seemed to Caroline that he was changing in reality. He met with the Rochester estate agents and developed a plan to improve the land in ways that would help the tenants immeasurably. Then to the perplexity of all who knew him, Andrew sold much of his personal property, including a prize string of thoroughbreds, in order to finance the improvements.

It was not in character for Andrew to take such a risk, especially when there was no guarantee that he would inherit the Rochester fortune. But when Caroline asked him why he seemed determined to help the Rochester tenants, he laughed and shrugged as if it were a matter of no consequence. "The changes would have to be made whether or not I get the earl's money," he said. "And I was tired of maintaining all those damned horses—too expensive by half."

"Then what about your properties in town?" Caroline asked. "I've heard that your father planned to evict some poor tenants from a slum in Whitefriars rather than repair it—and you are letting them stay, and are renovating the entire building besides."

Andrew's face was carefully expressionless as he replied. "Unlike my father, I have no desire to be known as a slum lord. But don't mistake my motives as altruistic—it is merely a business decision. Any money I spend on the property will increase its value."

Caroline smiled at him and leaned close as if to confide a secret. "I think, my lord, that you actually care about those people."

"I'm practically a saint," he agreed sardonically, with a derisive arch of his brow.

She continued to smile, however, realizing that Andrew was not nearly as blackhearted as he pretended to be.

Just why Andrew should have begun to care about the people whose existence he had never bothered to notice before was a mystery. Perhaps it had something to do with his father's imminent demise . . . perhaps it had finally dawned on Andrew that the weight of responsibility would soon be transferred to his own shoulders. But he could easily have let things go on just as they were, allowing his father's managers and estate agents to make the decisions. Instead he took the reins in his own hands, tentatively at first, then with increasing confidence.

In accordance with their bargain, Andrew took Caroline riding in the park, and escorted her to musical evenings and soirees and the theater. Since Fanny was required to act as chaperon, there were few occasions for Caroline to talk privately with Andrew. They were forced instead to discuss seemly subjects such as literature or gardening, and their physical contact was limited to the occasional brush of their fingertips, or the pressure of his shoulder against hers as they sat next to each other. And yet these fleeting moments of closeness—a wordless stare, a stolen caress of her arm or hand—were impossibly exciting.

Caroline's awareness of Andrew was so excruciating that she sometimes thought she would burst into flames. She could not stop thinking about their impassioned embrace in the Scotts' rose garden, the pleasure of Andrew's mouth on hers. But he was so unrelentingly courteous now that she began to wonder if the episode had perhaps been some torrid dream conjured by her own fevered imagination.

Andrew, Lord Drake, was a fascinating puzzle. It seemed to Caroline that he was two different men—the arrogant, self-indulgent libertine, and the attractive stranger who was stumbling uncertainly on his way to becoming a gentleman. The first man had not appealed to her in the least. The second one . . . well, he was a far different matter. She saw that he was struggling, torn between the easy pleasures of the past and the duties that loomed before him. He still had not resumed his drinking and skirt chasing—he would have admitted it to her freely if he had. And according to Cade, Andrew seldom visited their club these days. Instead he spent his time fencing, boxing, or riding until he nearly dropped from exhaustion. He lost weight, perhaps a stone, until his trousers hung unfashionably loose and had to be altered. Although Andrew had always been a well-formed man, his body was now lean and impossibly hard, the muscles of his arms and back straining the seams of his coat.

"Why do you keep so active?" Caroline could not resist asking one day, as she pruned a lush bed of purple penstemons in her garden. Andrew lounged nearby on a small bench as he watched her carefully snip the dried heads of each stem. "My brother says that you were at the Pugilistic Club almost every day last week."

When Andrew took too long in answering, Caroline paused in her gardening and glanced over her shoulder. It was a cool November day, and a breeze caught a lock of her sable hair that had escaped her bonnet, and blew it across her cheek. She used her gloved hand to push away the errant lock, inadvertently smudging her face with dirt. Her heart lurched in sudden anticipation as she saw the expression in Andrew's searching blue eyes.

"Keeping active serves to distract me from . . . things." Andrew stood and came to her slowly, pulling a handkerchief from his pocket. "Here, hold still." He gently wiped away the dirt streak, then reached for her spectacles to clean them in a gesture that had become habitual.

Deprived of the corrective lenses, Caroline stared up at his dark, blurred face with myopic attentiveness. "What things?" she asked, breathless at his nearness. "I presume that you must mean your drinking and gaming. . . ."

"No, it's not that." He replaced her spectacles with great care, and used a fingertip to stroke the silky tendril of hair behind her ear. "Can't you guess what is bothering me?" he asked softly. "What keeps me awake unless I exhaust myself before going to bed each night?"

He stood very close, his gaze holding hers intimately. Even though he was not touching her, Caroline felt surrounded by his virile presence. The shears dropped from her suddenly nerveless fingers, falling to the earth with a soft thud. "Oh, I . . ." She paused to moisten her dry lips. "I suppose you miss h-having a woman. But there is no reason that you could not . . . that is, with so many who would be willing . . ." Flushing, she caught her bottom lip with her teeth and floundered into silence.

"I've become too damned particular." He leaned closer, and his breath fell gently against her ear, sending a pleasurable thrill down her spine. "Caroline, look at me. There is something I have no right to ask . . . but . . ."

"Yes?" she whispered.

"I've been considering my situation," he said carefully. "Caroline . . . even if my father doesn't leave me a shilling, I could manage to provide a comfortable existence for someone. I have a few investments, as well as the estate. It wouldn't be a grand mode of living, but . . ."

"Yes?" Caroline managed to say, her heart hammering madly in her chest. "Go on."

"You see—"

"Caroline!" came her mother's shrill voice from the French doors that opened onto the garden from the parlor. "Caroline, I insist that you come inside and act as a proper hostess, rather than make poor Lord Drake stand outside and watch you dig holes in the dirt! I suspect you have offered him no manner of refreshment, and . . . Why, this wind is intolerable, you will cause him to catch his death of cold. Come in at once, I bid you both!"

"Yes, Mother," Caroline said grimly, filled with frustration. She glanced at Andrew, who had lost his serious intensity, and was regarding her with a sudden smile. "Before we go inside," she suggested, "you may finish what you were going to say—"

"Later," he said, bending to retrieve her fallen shears.

Her fists clenched, and she nearly stamped her foot in annoyance. She wanted to strangle her mother for breaking into what was undoubtedly the most supremely interesting moment of her life. What if Andrew had been trying to propose? Her heart turned over at the thought. Would she have decided to accept such a risk . . . would she be able to trust that he would remain the way he was now, instead of changing back into the rake he had always been?

Yes, she thought in a rush of giddy wonder. *Yes, I would take that chance.*

Because she had fallen in love with him, imperfect as he was. She loved every handsome, tarnished inch of him, inside and out. She wanted to help him in his quest to become a better man. And if a little bit of the scoundrel remained . . . An irresistible smile tugged at her lips. Well, she would enjoy that part of him too.

A fortnight later, at the beginning of December, Caroline received word that the Earl of Rochester was on his deathbed. The brief message from Andrew also included a surprising request. The earl wanted to see her, for reasons that he would explain to no one, not even Andrew. *I humbly ask for your indulgence in this matter*, Andrew had written,

*as your presence may bring the earl some peace in his last
hours. My carriage will convey you to the estate if you wish
to come . . . and if you do not, I understand and respect your
decision. Your servant.*

And he had signed his name *Andrew,* with a familiarity that
was improper and yet touching, bespeaking his distracted turn
of mind. Or perhaps it betrayed his feelings for her.

"Miss Hargreaves?" the liveried footman murmured, evidently having been informed of the possibility that she might
return with them. "Shall we convey you to the Rochester
estate?"

"Yes," Caroline said instantly. "I will need but a few minutes to be ready. I will bring a maidservant with me."

"Yes, miss."

Caroline was consumed with thoughts of Andrew as the
carriage traveled to Rochester Hall in Buckinghamshire,
where the earl had chosen to spend his last days. Although
Caroline had never seen the place, Andrew had described it
to her. The Rochesters owned fifteen hundred acres,
including the local village, the woods surrounding it, and
some of the most fertile farmland in England. It had been
granted to the family by Henry II in the twelfth century,
Andrew had said, and he had gone on to make a sarcastic
comment about the fact that the family's proud and ancient
heritage would soon pass to a complete reprobate. Caroline
understood that Andrew did not feel at all worthy of the
title and the responsibilities that he would inherit. She felt
an aching need to comfort him, to somehow find a way to
convince him that he was a much better man than he
believed himself to be.

With her thoughts in turmoil, Caroline kept her gaze
focused on the scenery outside the window, the land covered with woods and vineyards, the villages filled with cot-

tages made of flint garnered from the Chiltern hills. Finally they came to the massive structure of Rochester Hall, constructed of honey yellow ironstone and gray sandstone, hewn with stalwart medieval masonry. A gate centered in the entrance gave the carriage access to an open courtyard.

Caroline was escorted by a footman to the central great hall, which was large, drafty, and ornamented with dull-colored tapestries. Rochester Hall had once been a fortress, its roof studded with parapets and crenellation, the windows long and narrow to allow archers to defend the building. Now it was merely a cold, vast home that seemed badly in need of a woman's hand to soften the place and make it more comfortable.

"Miss Hargreaves." Andrew's deep voice echoed against the polished sandstone walls as he approached her.

She felt a thrill of gladness as he came to her and took her hands. The heat of his fingers penetrated the barrier of her gloves as he held her hands in a secure clasp. "Caro," he said softly, and nodded to the footman to leave them.

She stared up at him with a searching gaze. His emotions were held in tight rein . . . it was impossible to read the thoughts behind the expressionless mask of his face. But somehow she sensed his hidden anguish, and she longed to put her arms around him and comfort him.

"How was the carriage ride?" he asked, still retaining her hands. "I hope it didn't make you too uncomfortable."

Caroline smiled slightly, realizing that he had remembered how the motion of a long carriage ride made her sick. "No, I was perfectly fine. I stared out the window the entire way."

"Thank you for coming," he muttered. "I wouldn't have blamed you if you had refused. God knows why Rochester asked for you—it's because of some whim that he won't explain—"

"I am glad to be here," she interrupted gently. "Not for his sake, but for yours. To be here as your friend, as your . . ." Her voice trailed away as she fumbled for an appropriate word.

Her consternation elicited a brief smile from Andrew, and his blue eyes were suddenly tender. "Darling little friend," he whispered, bringing her gloved hand to his mouth.

Emotion welled up inside her, a singular deep joy that seemed to fill her chest and throat with sweet warmth. The happiness of being needed by him, welcomed by him, was almost too much to be borne.

Caroline glanced at the heavy oak staircase that led to the second floor, its openwork balustrade casting long, jagged shadows across the great hall. What a cavernous, sterile place for a little boy to grow up in, she thought. Andrew had told her that his mother had died a few weeks after giving birth to him. He had spent his childhood here, at the mercy of a father whose heart was as warm and soft as a glacier. "Shall we go up to him?" she asked, referring to the earl.

"In a minute," Andrew replied. "Logan and his wife are with him now. The doctor says it is only a matter of hours before he—" He stopped, his throat seeming to close, and he gave her a look that was filled with baffled fury, most of it directed at himself. "My God, all the times that I've wished him dead. But now I feel . . ."

"Regret?" Caroline suggested softly, removing her glove and laying her fingers against the hard, smooth-shaven line of his cheek. The muscles of his jaw worked tensely against the delicate palm of her hand. "And perhaps sorrow," she said, "for all that could have been, and for all the disappointment you caused each other."

He could not bring himself to reply, only gave a short nod.

"And maybe just a little fear?" she asked, daring to caress

his cheek softly. "Because soon *you* will be Lord Rochester . . . something you've hated and dreaded all your life."

Andrew began to breathe in deep surges, his eyes locked with hers as if his very survival depended on it. "If only I could stop it from happening," he said hoarsely.

"You are a better man than your father," she whispered. "You will take care of the people who depend on you. There is nothing to fear. I know that you will not fall back into your old ways. You are a good man, even if you don't believe it."

He was very still, giving her a look that burned all through her. Although he did not move to embrace her, she had the sense of being possessed, captured by his gaze and his potent will beyond any hope of release. "Caro," he finally said, his voice tightly controlled, "I can't ever be without you."

She smiled faintly. "You won't have to."

They were interrupted by the approach of a housemaid who had been dispatched from upstairs. "M'lord," the tall, rather ungainly girl murmured, bobbing in an awkward curtsy, "Mr. Scott sent me to ask if Miss Hargreaves is here, and if she would please attend the earl—"

"I will bring her to Rochester," Andrew replied grimly.

"Yes, m'lord." The maid hurried upstairs ahead of them, while Andrew carefully placed Caroline's small hand on his arm.

He looked down at her with concern. "You don't have to see him if you don't wish it."

"Of course I will see the earl," Caroline replied. "I am extremely curious about what he will say."

The Earl of Rochester was attended by two physicians, as well as Mr. Scott and his wife Madeline. The atmosphere in the bedroom was oppressively somber and stifling, with all the windows closed and the heavy velvet drapes pulled shut. A dismal end for an unhappy man, Caroline reflected silently. In her opinion the earl was extremely fortunate to have his two sons with him, considering the appalling way he had always treated them.

The earl was propped to a semireclining position with a pile of pillows behind his back. His head turned as Caroline entered the room, and his rheumy gaze fastened on her. "The Hargreaves chit," he said softly. It seemed to take great effort for him to speak. He addressed the other occupants of the room while still staring at Caroline. "Leave, all of you. I wish . . . to speak to Miss Hargreaves . . . in private."

They complied en masse except for Andrew, who lingered to stare into Caroline's face. She gave him a reassuring smile and motioned for him to leave the room. "I'll be waiting just outside," he murmured. "Call for me if you wish."

When the door closed, Caroline went to the chair by the bedside and sat, folding her hands in her lap. Her face was nearly level with the earl's, and she did not bother to conceal her curiosity as she stared at him. He must have been handsome at one time, she thought, although he wore the innate arrogance of a man who had always taken himself far too seriously.

"My lord," she said, "I have come, as you requested. May I ask why you wished to see me?"

Rochester ignored her question for a moment, his slitted gaze moving over her speculatively. "Attractive, but . . . hardly a great beauty," he observed. "What does . . . he see in you, I wonder?"

"Perhaps you should ask Lord Drake," Caroline suggested calmly.

"He will not discuss you," he replied with frowning contemplation. "I sent for you because . . . I want the answer to one question. When my son proposes . . . will you accept?"

Startled, Caroline stared at him without blinking. "He has not proposed marriage to me, my lord, nor has he given any indication that he is considering such a proposition—"

"He will," Rochester assured her, his face twisting with a spasm of pain. Fumbling, he reached for a small glass on the bedside table. Automatically Caroline moved to help him, catching the noxious fragrance of spirits mixed with medicinal tonic as she brought the edge of the glass to his withered lips. Reclining back on the pillows, the earl viewed her speculatively. "You appear to have wrought . . . a miracle, Miss Hargreaves. Somehow you . . . have drawn my son out of his remarkable self-absorption. I know him . . . quite well, you see. I suspect your liaison began as a plan to deceive me, yet . . . he seems to have changed. He seems to love you, although . . . one never would have believed him capable of it."

"Perhaps you do not know Lord Drake as well as you think you do," Caroline said, unable to keep the edge from her tone. "He only needs someone to believe in him, and to encourage him. He is a good man, a caring one—"

"Please," he murmured, lifting a gnarled hand in a gesture of self-defense. "Do not waste. . . . what little time I have left . . . with rapturous descriptions of my . . . good-for-naught progeny."

"Then I will answer your question," Caroline returned evenly. "Yes, my lord, if your son proposes to me, I will accept gladly. And if you do not leave him your fortune, I will not care one whit . . . and neither will he. Some things are more precious than money, although I am certain you will mock me for saying so."

Rochester surprised her by smiling thinly, relaxing more deeply against the pillows. "I will not mock you," he murmured, seeming exhausted but oddly serene. "I believe . . . you might be the saving of him. Go now, Miss Hargreaves. . . . Tell Andrew to come."

"Yes, my lord."

She left the room quickly, her emotions in chaos, feeling chilly and anxious and wanting to feel the comfort of Andrew's arms around her.

Chapter Four

It had been two weeks since the Earl of Rochester had died, leaving Andrew the entirety of his fortune as well as the title and entailed properties. Two interminable weeks during which Caroline had received no word from Andrew. At first she had been patient, understanding that Andrew must be wading through a morass of funeral arrangements and business decisions. She knew that he would come to her as soon as possible. But as day followed day, and he did not send so much as a single written sentence, Caroline realized that something was very wrong. Consumed with worry, she considered writing to him, or even paying an unexpected visit to Rochester Hall, but it was unthinkable for any unmarried woman under the age of thirty to be so forward. She finally decided to send her brother Cade to find Andrew, bidding him to find out if Andrew was well, if he needed anything . . . if he was thinking of her.

While Cade went on his mission to locate the new Lord

Rochester, Caroline sat alone in her chilly winter garden, gazing forlornly at her clipped-back plants and the bare branches of her prized Japanese maples. There were only two weeks until Christmas, she thought dully. For her family's sake, Caroline had decorated the house with boughs of evergreens and holly, and had adorned the doors with wreaths of fruit and ribbons. But she sensed that instead of a joyous holiday, she was about to experience heartbreak for the first time in her life, and the black misery that awaited her was too awful to contemplate.

Something was indeed wrong, or Andrew would have come to her by now. And yet she could not imagine what was keeping him away. She knew that he needed her, just as she needed him, and that nothing stood in the way of their being together, if he so desired. Why, then, had he not come?

Just as Caroline thought she would go insane from the unanswered questions that plagued her, Cade returned home. The expression on his face did not ease her worry.

"Your hands are like ice," he said, chafing her stiff fingers and guiding her into the parlor, where a warm fire blazed in the hearth. "You've been sitting outside too long—wait, I'll send for some tea."

"I don't want tea." Caroline sat rigidly on the settee, while her brother's large form lowered to the space beside her. "Cade, did you find him? How is he? Oh, tell me something or I'll go mad!"

"Yes, I found him." Cade scowled and took her hands again, warming her tense fingers with his. He let out a slow sigh. "Drake . . . that is, Rochester . . . has been drinking again, quite a lot. I'm afraid he is back to his old ways."

She regarded him with numb disbelief. "But that's not possible."

"That's not all of it," Cade said darkly. "To everyone's surprise, Rochester has suddenly gotten himself engaged—to none other than our own dear cousin Julianne. Now that he's got the family fortune in his possession, it seems that Julianne sees his charms in a new light. The banns will be read in church tomorrow. They'll be married when the new year starts."

"Cade, don't tease like this," Caroline said in raw whisper. "It's not true . . . not true—" She stopped, suddenly unable to breathe, while flurries of brilliant sparks danced madly across her vision. She heard her brother's exclamation as if from a great distance, and she felt the hard, urgent grip of his hands.

"My God"—his voice was overlaid with a strange hum that filled her ears—"here, put your head down . . . Caro, what in the hell is wrong?"

She struggled for air, for equilibrium, while her heart clattered in a painful broken measure. "He c-can't marry her," she said through chattering teeth.

"Caroline." Her brother was unexpectedly steady and strong, holding her against him in a tight grip. "Good Lord . . . I had no idea you felt this way. It was supposed to be a charade. Don't tell me you had the bad sense to fall in love with Rochester, who has to be the worst choice a woman like you could make—"

"Yes, I love him," she choked out. Tears slid down her cheeks in scalding trails. "And he loves me, Cade, he *does* . . . Oh, this doesn't make sense!"

"Has he encouraged you to think that he would marry you?" her brother asked softly. "Did he ever say that he loved you?"

"Not in those words," she said in a sob. "But the way he was with me . . . he made me believe . . ." She buried her head in her arms, weeping violently. "Why would he marry

Julianne, of all people? She is *evil* . . . oh, there are things about her that you don't know . . . things that Father told me about her before he died. She will ruin Andrew!"

"She's already made a good start of it, from all appearances," Cade said grimly. He found a handkerchief in his pocket and swabbed her sodden face with it. "Rochester is as miserable as I've ever seen him. He won't explain anything, other than to say that Julianne is a fit mate for him, and everyone is better off this way. And Caro . . ." His voice turned very gentle. "Perhaps he is right. You and Andrew . . . it is not a good match."

"Leave me alone," Caroline whispered. Gently she extricated herself from his arms and made her way out of the parlor. She hobbled like an old woman as she sought the privacy of her bedroom, ignoring Cade's worried questions. She needed to be alone, to crawl into her bed and hide like a wounded animal. Perhaps there she would find some way to heal the terrible wounds inside.

For two days Caroline remained in her room, too devastated to cry or talk. She could not eat or sleep, as her tired mind combed relentlessly over every memory of Andrew. He had made no promises, had offered no pledge of love, had given her no token to indicate his feelings. She could not accuse him of betrayal. Still, her anguish was evolving into wounded rage. She wanted to confront him, to force him to admit his feelings, or at least to tell her what had been a lie and what had been the truth. Surely it was her right to have an explanation. But Andrew had abandoned her without a word, leaving her to wonder desperately what had gone wrong between them.

This had been his plan all along, she thought with increasing despair. He had only wanted her companionship until his father died and left him the Rochester fortune. Now that Andrew had gotten what he wanted, she was of no further consequence to him. But hadn't he come to care for her just a little? She knew she had not imagined the tenderness in his voice when he had said, *I can't ever be without you. . . .*

Why would he have said that, if he had not meant it?

To Caroline's weary amusement, her mother, Fanny, had received the news of Andrew's impending nuptials with a great display of hysterics. She had taken to her bed at once, loudly insisting that the servants wait on her hand and foot until she recovered. The household centered around Fanny and her delicate nerves, mercifully leaving Caroline in peace.

The only person Caroline spoke to was Cade, who had become a surprisingly steady source of support.

"What can I do?" he asked softly, approaching Caroline as she sat before the window and stared blankly out at the garden. "There must be something that would make you feel better."

She turned toward her brother with a dismal smile. "I suspect I will feel better as time goes by, although right now I doubt that I will ever feel happy again."

"That bastard Rochester," Cade muttered, sinking to his haunches beside her. "Shall I go thrash him for you?"

A wan chuckle escaped her. "No, Cade. That would not satisfy me in the least. And I suspect Andrew has quite enough suffering in store, if he truly plans to go through with his plans to marry Julianne."

"True." Cade considered her thoughtfully. "There is something I should tell you, Caro, although you will probably disapprove. Rochester sent me a message yesterday, informing me that he has settled all my debts. I suppose I should return all the money to him—but I don't want to."

"Do as you like." Listlessly she leaned forward until her forehead was pressed against the cold, hard pane of the window.

"Well, now that I'm out of debt, and you are indirectly responsible for my good fortune . . . I want to do something for you. It's almost Christmas, after all. Let me buy you a pretty necklace, or a new gown . . . just tell me what you want."

"Cade," she returned dully, without opening her eyes, "the only thing I would like to have is Rochester trussed up like a yuletide goose, completely at my mercy. Since you cannot make that happen, I wish for nothing."

An extended silence greeted her statement, and then she felt a gentle pat on her shoulder. "All right, sweet sister."

The next day Caroline made a genuine effort to shake herself from her cloud of melancholy. She took a long, steaming bath and washed her hair, and donned a comfortable gown that was sadly out of style but had always been her favorite. The folds of frayed dull-green velvet draped gently over her body as she sat by the fire to dry her hair. It was cold and blustery outside, and she shivered as she caught a glimpse of the icy gray sky through the window of her bedroom.

Just as she contemplated the idea of sending for a tray of toast and tea, the closed door was attacked by an energetic fist. "Caro," came her brother's voice. "Caro, may I come in? I must speak with you." His fist pounded the wood panels again, as if he were about some urgent matter.

A faint quizzical smile came to her face. "Yes, come in," she said, "before you break the door down."

Cade burst into the room, wearing the strangest expression . . . his face tense and triumphant, while an air of wildness clung to him. His dark brown hair was disheveled, and his black silk cravat hung limply on either side of his neck.

"Cade," Caroline said in concern, "what in heaven's name has happened? Have you been fighting? What is the matter?"

A mixture of jubilation and defiance crossed his face, making him appear more boyish than his twenty-four years. When he spoke, he sounded slightly out of breath. "I've been rather busy today."

"Doing what?" she asked warily.

"I've gotten you a Christmas present. It required a bit of effort, let me tell you. I had to get a couple of the fellows to help me, and . . . Well, we shouldn't waste time talking. Get your traveling cloak."

Caroline stared at him in complete bewilderment. "Cade, is my present outside? Must I fetch it myself, and on such a chilly day? I would prefer to wait. You of all people know what I have been through recently, and—"

"This present won't keep for long," he replied, straight-faced. Reaching into his pocket, he extracted a very small key, with a frivolous red bow attached. "Here, take this." He pressed the key into her palm. "And never say that I don't go to trouble for you."

Stupefied, she stared at the key in her hand. "I've never seen a key like this. What does it belong to?"

Her brother responded with a maddening smile. "Get your cloak and go find out."

Caroline rolled her eyes. "I am not in the mood for one of your pranks," she said pertly. "And I don't wish to go outside. But I will oblige you. Only heed my words: if this present is anything less than a queen's ransom in jewels, I shall be very put out with you. Now, may I at least be granted a few minutes to pin up my hair?"

"Very well," he said impatiently. "But hurry."

Caroline could not help being amused by her brother's suppressed exuberance. He fairly danced around her like some puckish sprite as she followed him down the stairs a minute later. No doubt he thought that his mysterious gift would serve to distract her from her broken heart . . . and though his ploy was transparent, she appreciated the caring thoughts behind it.

Opening the door with a flourish, Cade gestured to the family carriage and a team of two chestnuts stamping and blowing impatiently as the wind gusted around them. The family footman and driver also awaited, wearing heavy overcoats and large hats to shield them from the cold. "Oh, Cade," Caroline said in a groan, turning back into the house, "I am not going anywhere in that carriage. I am tired, and hungry, and I want to have a peaceful evening at home."

Cade startled her by taking her small face in his hands, and staring down at her with dark, entreating eyes. "Please, Caro," he muttered. "For once, don't argue or cause problems. Just do as I ask. Get into that carriage, and take the deuced key with you."

She returned his steady gaze with a perplexed one of her own, shaking her head within the frame of his hands. A dark, strange suspicion blossomed inside her. "Cade," she whispered, "what have you done?"

He did not reply, only guided her to the carriage and helped her inside, while the footman gave her a lap blanket and moved the porcelain foot warmer directly beneath her soles.

"Where will the carriage take me?" Caroline asked, and Cade shrugged casually.

"A friend of mine, Sambrooke, has a family cottage right at the outskirts of London that he uses to meet his . . . Well, that doesn't matter. For today, the place is unoccupied, and at your disposal."

"Why couldn't you have brought my gift here?" She pinned him with a doubtful glare.

For some reason the question made him laugh shortly. "Because you need to view it in privacy." Leaning into the carriage, he brushed her cold cheek with a kiss. "Good luck," he murmured, and withdrew.

She stared blankly through the carriage window as the door closed with a firm snap. Panic shuffled her thoughts, turning them into an incoherent jumble. *Good luck?* What in God's name had he meant by that? Did this by chance have anything to do with Andrew? Oh, she would cheerfully murder her brother if it did!

The carriage brought her past Hyde Park to an area west of London where there were still large tracts of sparsely developed land. As the vehicle came to a stop, Caroline fought to contain her agitation. She wondered wildly what her brother had arranged, and why she had been such an idiot as to fall in with his plans. The footman opened the carriage door and placed a step on the ground. Caroline did not move, however. She remained inside the vehicle and stared at the modest white roughcast house, with its steeply pitched slate roof and gravel-covered courtyard in front.

"Peter," she said to the footman, an old and trusted family servant, "do you have any idea what this is about? You must tell me if you do."

He shook his head. "No, miss, I know nothing. Do you wish to return home?"

Caroline considered the idea and abandoned it almost immediately. She had ventured too far to turn back now.

"No, I'll go inside," she said reluctantly. "Shall you wait for me here?"

"If you wish, miss. But Lord Hargreaves's instructions were to leave you here and return in precisely two hours."

"I have a few choice words for my brother." Straightening her shoulders, she gathered her cloak tightly about herself and hopped down from the carriage. Silently she began to plan a list of the ways in which she would punish Cade. "Very well, Peter. You and the driver will leave, as my brother instructed. One would hate to thwart his wishes, as he seems to have decided exactly what must be done."

Peter opened the door for her, and helped her off with her cloak before returning outside to the carriage. The vehicle rolled gently away, its heavy wheels crunching the ice-covered gravel of the front courtyard.

Cautiously Caroline gripped the key and ventured inside the cottage. The place was simply furnished, with some oak paneling, a few family portraits, a set of ladder-back chairs, a library corner filled with old leather-bound books. The air was cold, but a cheerful little fire had been lit in the main room. Had it been lit for her comfort, or for someone else's?

"Hello?" she called out hesitantly. "If anyone is here, I bid you answer. Hello?"

She heard a muffled shout from some distant corner of the house. The sound gave her an unpleasant start, producing a stinging sensation along the nerves of her shoulders and spine. Her breath issued in flat bursts, and she gripped the key until its ridges dug deeply into her sweating palm. She forced herself to move. One step, then another, until she was running through the cottage, searching for whomever had shouted.

"Hello, where are you?" she called repeatedly, making her way toward the back of the house. "Where—"

The flickering of hearth light issued from one of the rooms at the end of the hall. Grabbing up handfuls of her velvet skirts, Caroline rushed toward the room. She crossed the threshold in a flurry and stopped so suddenly that her hastily arranged hair pitched forward. Impatiently she pushed it back and stared in astonishment at the scene before her. It was a bedroom, so small that it allowed for only three pieces of furniture: a washstand, a night table, and a large carved rosewood bed. However, the other guest at this romantic rendezvous had not come as willingly as herself.

. . . the only thing I would like to have is Rochester trussed up like a yuletide goose, completely at my mercy, she had unthinkingly told her witless brother. And Cade, the insane ass, had somehow managed to accomplish it.

Andrew, the seventh Earl of Rochester, was stretched full-length on the bed, his arms tethered above his head with what seemed to be a pair of metal cuffs linked by a chain and lock. The chain had been passed through a pair of carved openings in the solid rosewood headboard, securely holding Andrew prisoner.

His dark head lifted from the pillow, and his eyes gleamed an unholy shade of blue in his flushed face. He yanked at the cuffs with a force that surely bruised his imprisoned wrists. "Get these the hell off of me," he said in a growl, his voice containing a level of ferocity that made her flinch. He was like some magnificent feral animal, the powerful muscles of his arms bulging against his shirtsleeves, his taut body arching from the bed.

"I am so sorry," she said with a gasp, instinctively rushing forward to help him. "My God . . . it was Cade . . . I don't know what got into his head—"

"I'm going to kill him," Andrew muttered, continuing to tug savagely at his tethered wrists.

"Wait, you'll hurt yourself. I have the key. Just be still and let me—"

"Did you ask him to do this?" he asked with a snarl as she climbed onto the bed beside him.

"No," she said at once, then felt scarlet color flooding her cheeks. "Not exactly. I only said I wished—" She broke off and bit her lip. "He told me about your betrothal to Cousin Julianne, you see, and I—" Continuing to blush, she crawled over him to reach the lock of the handcuffs. The delicate shape of her breast brushed over his chest, and Andrew's entire body jerked as if he had been burned. To Caroline's dismay, the key dropped from her fingers and fell between the mattress and the headboard. "Do be still," she said, keeping her gaze from his face as she levered her body farther over his and fumbled for the key. It was not easy avoiding eye contact with him when their faces were so close. The brawny mass of his body was hard and unmoving beneath her. She heard his breathing change, turning deep and quick as she strained to retrieve the key.

Her fingertips curled around the key and pried it free of the mattress. "I've got it," she murmured, risking a glance at him.

Andrew's eyes were closed, his nose and mouth almost touching the curve of her breast. He seemed to be absorbing her scent, savoring it with peculiar intensity, as if he were a condemned man being offered his last meal.

"Andrew?" she whispered in painful confusion.

His expression became closed and hard, his blue eyes opaque. "Unlock these damned things!" He rattled the chain that linked the cuffs. The noise startled her, jangled across her raw nerves. She saw the deep gouges the chain links had left on the solid rosewood, but despite the relentless tugging and sawing, the wood had so far resisted the grating metal.

Her gaze dropped to the key in her hand. Instead of using it to unlock the handcuffs, she closed her fingers around it. Terrible, wicked thoughts formed in her mind. The right thing to do would be to set Andrew free as quickly as possible. But for the first time in her entire sedate, seemly life, she did not want to do what was right.

"Before I let you go," she said in a low voice that did not quite sound like her own, "I would like the answer to one question. Why did you throw me aside in favor of Julianne?"

He continued to look at her with that arctic gaze. "I'll be damned if I'll answer any questions while I'm chained to a bed."

"And if I set you free? Will you answer me then?"

"No."

She searched his eyes for any sign of the man she had come to love, the Andrew who had been amusing, self-mocking, tender. There was nothing but bitterness in the depths of frozen blue, as if he had lost all feeling for her, himself, and everything that mattered. It would take something catastrophic to reach inside this implacable stranger.

"Why Julianne?" she persisted. "You said the affair with her was not worth remembering. Was that a lie? Have you decided that she can offer you something more, something better, than I can?"

"She is a better match for me than you could ever be."

Suddenly it hurt to breathe. "Because she is more beautiful? More passionate?" she forced herself to ask.

Andrew tried to form the word *yes*, but it would not leave his lips. He settled for a single jerking nod.

That motion should have destroyed her, for it confirmed every self-doubt she had ever possessed. But the look on Andrew's face . . . the twitch of his jaw, the odd glaze of his eyes . . . for a split second he seemed to be caught in a moment of pure agony. And there could be only one reason why.

"You're lying," she whispered.

"No, I'm not."

All at once Caroline gave rein to the desperate impulses that swirled in her head. She was a woman with nothing to lose. "Then I will prove you wrong," she said unsteadily. "I will prove that I can give you a hundred times more satisfaction than Julianne."

"How?"

"I am going to make love to you," she said, sitting up beside him. Her trembling fingers went to the neck of her gown, and she began working the knotted silk loops that fastened the front of her bodice. "Right now, on this bed, while you are helpless to prevent it. And I won't stop until you admit that you are lying. I'll have an explanation out of you, my lord, one way or another."

Clearly she had surprised him. She knew that he had never expected such feminine aggression from a respectable spinster. "You wouldn't have the damn nerve," he said softly.

Well, that sealed his fate. She certainly could not back down after such a challenge. Resolutely Caroline continued on the silk fastenings until the front of her velvet gown gaped open to reveal her thin muslin chemise. A feeling of unreality settled over her as she pulled her arms from one sleeve, then the other. In all her adult life, she had never undressed in front of anyone. Goose bumps rose on her skin, and she rubbed her bare upper arms. The chemise provided so little covering that she might as well have been naked.

She would not have been surprised had Andrew decided to mock her, but he did not seem amused or angry at her display. He seemed . . . fascinated. His gaze slid over her body, lingered at the rose-tinted shadows of her nipples, then returned to her face. "That's enough," he muttered. "Much as I enjoy the view, there is no point to this."

"I disagree." She slid off the bed and pushed the heavy gown to the floor, where it lay in a soft heap. Standing in her chemise and drawers, she tried to still the chattering of her teeth. "I am going to make you talk to me, my lord, no matter what it takes. Before I'm through, I'll have you babbling like an idiot."

His breath caught with an incredulous laugh. The sound heartened her, for it seemed to make him more human and less a frozen stranger. "In the first place, I'm not worth the effort. Second, you don't know what the hell you're doing, which throws your plans very much in doubt."

"I know enough," she said with false bravado. "Sexual intercourse is merely a matter of mechanics . . . and even in my inexperience, I believe I can figure out what goes where."

"It is *not* merely a matter of mechanics." He tugged at the handcuffs with a new urgency, his face suddenly contorted with . . . fear? . . . concern? "Damn it, Caroline. I admire your determination, but you have to *stop this now*, do you understand? You're going to cause yourself nothing but pain and frustration. You deserve better than to have your first experience turn out badly. Let me go, you bloody stubborn witch!"

The flare of desperate fury pleased her. It meant that she was breaking through the walls he had tried to construct between them, leaving him vulnerable to further assault.

"You may scream all you like," she said. "There is no one to hear you."

She crawled onto the bed, while his entire body went rigid.

"You're a fool if you think that I'm going to cooperate," he said between clenched teeth.

"I think that before long you will cooperate with great enthusiasm." Caroline took perverse delight in becoming cooler and calmer as he became more irate. "After all, you haven't had a woman in . . . how many months? At least three. Even if I lack the appropriate skills, I will be able to do as I like with you."

"What about Julianne?" His arms bulged with heavy muscle as he pulled at the handcuffs. "I could have had her a hundred times by now, for all you know."

"You haven't," she said. "You aren't attracted to her—that was evident when I saw the two of you together."

She began on the tight binding of his cravat, unwinding the damp, starch-scented cloth that still contained the heat of his skin. When his long golden throat was revealed, she touched the triangular hollow at the base with a gentle fingertip. "That's better," she said softly. "Now you can breathe."

He was indeed breathing, with the force of a man who had just run ten miles without stopping. His gaze fixed on hers, no longer cold, but gleaming with fury. "Stop it. I warn you, Caroline, stop *now*."

"Or what? What could you possibly do to punish me that would be worse than what you've already done?" Her fingers went to the buttons of his waistcoat and shirt, and she released them in rapid succession. She spread the edges of his garments wide, baring a remarkably muscular torso. The sight of his body, all that ferocious power rendered helpless before her, was awe-inspiring.

"I never meant to hurt you," he said. "You knew from the beginning that our relationship was just a pretense."

"Yes. But it became something else, and you and I both know it." Gently she touched the thick curls that covered his chest, her fingertips delving to the burning skin beneath. He

84

jumped at the brush of her cool hand, the breath hissing between his teeth. How often she had dreamed of doing this, exploring his body, caressing him. The surface of his stomach was laced with tight muscles, so different from the smooth softness of her own. She stroked the taut golden skin, so hard and silken beneath her hand. "Tell me why you would marry Julianne when you've fallen in love with me."

"I . . . haven't," he managed to choke out. "Can't you get it th-through your stubborn head—"

His words ended in a harsh groan as she straddled him in a decisive motion, their loins separated only by the layers of his trousers and her gossamer-thin drawers. Flushed and determined, Caroline sat atop him in a completely wanton posture. She felt the protrusion of his sex nestle into the cleft between her thighs. The lascivious pressure of him against that intimate part of her body caused a silken ripple of heat all through her. She shifted her weight until he nudged right against her most sensitive area, a little peak that throbbed frantically at his nearness.

"All right," he said in a gasp, holding completely still. "All right, I admit it . . . I love you, damned tormenting bitch— now get *off* of me!"

"Marry me," she insisted. "Promise that you'll break off the betrothal to my cousin."

"*No.*"

Caroline reached up to her hair, pulling the pins loose, letting the rippling brown locks cascade down to her waist. He had never seen her hair down before, and his imprisoned fingers twitched as if he ached to touch her.

"I love you," she said, stroking the furry expanse of his chest, flattening her palm over the thundering rhythm of his heart. The textures of his body—rough silk, hard muscle, bone, and sinew—fascinated her. She wanted to kiss and stroke him everywhere. "We belong together. There should be no obstacles between us, Andrew."

"Love doesn't make a damn bit of difference," he almost snarled. "Idealistic little fool—"

His breath snagged in his throat as she grasped the hem of her chemise, pulled it over her head, and tossed the whisper-thin garment aside. Her upper body was completely naked, the small, firm globes of her breasts bouncing delicately, pink tips contracting in the cool air. He stared at her breasts without blinking, and his eyes gleamed with wolfish hunger before he turned his face away.

"Would you like to kiss them?" Caroline whispered, hardly daring to believe her own brazenness. "I know that you've imagined this, Andrew, just as I have." She leaned over him, brushing her nipples against his chest, and he quivered at the shock of their flesh meeting. He kept his face turned away, his mouth taut, his breath coming in hard gusts. "Kiss me," she urged. "Kiss me just once, Andrew. Please. I need you . . . need to taste you . . . kiss me the way I've dreamed about for so long."

A deep groan vibrated within his chest. His mouth lifted, searching for hers. She pressed her lips over his, her tongue slipping daintily into his hot, sweet mouth. Ardently she molded her body against his, wrapped her arms around his head, kissed him again and again. She touched his shackled wrists, her fingertips brushing his palms. He muttered frantically against her throat, "Yes . . . yes . . . let me go, Caroline . . . the key . . ."

"No." She moved higher on his chest, dragging her feverish mouth over the salt-flavored skin of his throat. "Not yet."

His mouth searched the tender place where her neck met the curve of her shoulder, and she wriggled against him, wanting more, her body filled with a craving that she could not seem to satisfy. She levered herself higher, higher, until almost by accident her nipple brushed the edge of his jaw. He seized it immediately, his mouth opening over the tender crest and drawing it deep inside. His tongue circled the delicate peak and feathered it with rapid, tiny strokes. For a long time he sucked and licked, until Caroline moaned imploringly. His mouth released the rosy nipple, his tongue caressing it with one last swipe.

"Give me the other one," he said in a rasping whisper. "Put it in my mouth."

Trembling, she obeyed, guiding her breast to his lips. He feasted on her eagerly, and she gasped at the sensation of being captured by his mouth, held by its heat and urgency. Exquisite tension gathered between her wide-open thighs. She writhed, undulated, pressed as close to him as possible, but it was not close enough. She wanted to be filled by him, crushed and ravished and possessed. "Andrew," she said, her voice low and raw. "I want you . . . I want you so badly I could die of it. Let me . . . let me . . ." She took her breast from his mouth and kissed him again, and reached frantically down to the huge, bulging shape beneath the front of his trousers.

"No," she heard him say hoarsely, but she unfastened his trousers with unsteady fingers. Andrew swore and stared at the ceiling, seeming to will his body not to respond . . . but as her cool little hand slid inside his trousers, he groaned and flushed darkly.

Caroline brought out the hard, pulsing length of his sex, and clasped the thick shaft with trembling fingers. She was fascinated by the satiny feel of his skin, the nest of coarse curls at his groin, the heavy, surprisingly cool weight of his testicles down below. The thought of taking the entire potent length of him inside her own body was as shocking as it was exciting. Awkwardly she caressed him, and was startled by his immediate response, the instinctive upward surge of his hips, the stifled grunt of pleasure that came from his throat.

"Is this the right way?" she asked, her fingers sliding up to the large round head.

"Caroline . . ." His tormented gaze was riveted on her face. "Caroline, listen to me. I don't want this. It won't be good for you. There are things I haven't done for you . . . things your body needs . . . for God's sake—"

"I don't care. I want to make love to you."

She peeled off her drawers and garters and stockings, and returned to crouch over his groin, feeling clumsy and yet inflamed. "Tell me what to do," she begged, and pressed the head of his sex directly against the soft cove of her body. She lowered her weight experimentally, and froze at the intense pressure and pain that threatened. It seemed impossible to make their bodies fit together. Baffled and frustrated, she tried again, but she could not manage to push the stiff length of him through the tightly closed opening. She stared at Andrew's taut face, her gaze pleading. "Help me. Tell me what I'm doing wrong."

Even in this moment of crucial intimacy, he would not relent. "It's time to stop, Caroline."

The finality of his refusal was impossible to ignore.

She was swamped with a feeling of utter defeat. She took a long, shivering breath, and another, but nothing would relieve the burning ache in her lungs. "All right," she managed to whisper. "All right. I'm sorry." Tears stung her eyes, and she reached beneath her spectacles to wipe at them furiously. She had lost him again, this time permanently. Any man who could resist a woman at such a moment, while she begged to make love to him, could not truly be in love with her. Groping for the key, she continued to cry silently.

For some reason the sight of her tears drove him into a sort of contained frenzy, his body stiffening with the effort not to flail at his chains. "Caroline," he said in a shaking whisper. "Please open the damned lock. Please. God . . . don't. Just get the key. Yes. Let me go. Let me—"

As soon as she turned the tiny key in the lock, the world seemed to explode with movement. Andrew moved with the speed of a leaping tiger, freeing his wrists and pouncing on her. Too stunned to react, Caroline found herself being flipped over and pressed flat on her back. The half-naked weight of his body crushed her deep into the mattress, the startling thrust of his erection hard against her quivering stomach. He moved against her once, twice, three times, the pouch of his ballocks dragging tightly through her dark curls, and then he went still, holding her until she could hardly breathe. A groan escaped him, and a liquid wash of heat seeped between their bodies, sliding over her stomach.

Dazed, Caroline lay still and silent, her gaze darting over his taut features. Andrew let out a ragged sigh and opened his eyes, which had turned a brilliant shade of molten blue. "Don't move," he said softly. "Just lie still for a moment."

She had no other choice. Her limbs were weak and trembling . . . she burned as if from a fever. Miserably she watched as he left the bed, then glanced down at her stomach. She touched a fingertip to the glossy smear of liquid there, and she was puzzled and curious and woeful all at the same time. Andrew returned with a wet cloth, and joined her on the bed. Closing her eyes, Caroline flinched at the coldness of the cloth as he gently cleansed her body. She could not bear the sight of his impassive face, nor could she stand the thought of what he might say to her. No doubt he would berate her for her part in this humiliating escapade, and she certainly deserved it. She bit her lip and stiffened her limbs against the tremors that shook her ... she was so hot everywhere, her hips lifting uncontrollably, a sob catching in her throat. "Leave me alone," she whispered, feeling as if she were going to fly into pieces.

The cloth was set aside, and Andrew's fingers carefully hooked under the sidepieces of her spectacles to lift them from her damp face. Her lashes lifted. He was leaning over her, so close that his features were only slightly blurred. His gaze traveled slowly down the length of her slender body. "My God, how I love you," he murmured, shocking her, while his hand cupped her breast and squeezed gently. His fingertips trailed downward in a lazy path, until they slipped into the plump cleft between her thighs.

Caroline arched wildly, completely helpless at his touch, while small, pleading cries came from her throat.

"Yes." His voice was like dark velvet, his tongue flicking the lobe of her ear. "I'll take care of you now. Just tell me what you want, sweetheart. Tell me, and I'll do it."

"Andrew ..." She gasped as he separated the tender lips and stroked right between them. "Don't t-torture me, please. ..."

Amusement threaded through his tone. "After what you've done to me, I think you deserve a few minutes of torture ... don't you?" His fingertip glided in a small circle around the aching little tip of flesh where all sensation was gathering. "Would you like me to kiss you here?" he asked softly. "And touch it with my tongue?"

The questions jolted her—she had never imagined such a thing—and yet her entire body quivered in response.

"Tell me," he prompted gently.

Her lips were dry, and she had to wet them with her tongue before she could speak. To her utter shame, once the first words were out, she could not stop herself from begging shamelessly. "Yes, Andrew . . . kiss me there, use your tongue, I need you now, now *please*—"

Her voice dissolved into wild groans as he moved downward, his dark head dropping between her spread legs, his fingers smoothing the little dark curls and opening her pink lips even wider. His breath touched her first, a soft rush of steam, and then his tongue danced over her, gently prodding the burning little nub, flicking it with rapid strokes.

Caroline bit her lower lip sharply, struggling desperately to keep quiet despite the intense pleasure of his mouth on her. Andrew lifted his head as he heard the muffled sounds she made, and his eyes gleamed devilishly. "Scream all you like," he murmured. "There's no one to hear you."

His mouth returned to her, and she cried out, her bottom lifting eagerly from the mattress as she pushed herself toward him. He grunted with satisfaction and cradled her taut buttocks in his large, warm hands, while his mouth continued to feast on her. She felt the broad tip of his finger stroke against the tiny opening of her body, circling, teasing . . . entering with delicate skill.

"Feel how wet you are," he murmured against her slick flesh. "You're ready to be taken now. I could slide every inch of my cock inside you."

Then she understood why she had not been able to accommodate him before. "Please," she whispered, dying of need. "Please, Andrew."

His lips returned to her vulva, nuzzling the moist, sensitive folds. Gasping, Caroline went still as his finger slid deeply inside her, stroking in time to the sweet, rhythmic tug of his mouth. "My God," she said between frantic pants for breath, "I can't . . . oh, I can't bear it, please Andrew, my God—"

The world vanished in an explosion of fiery bliss. She

sobbed and shivered, riding the current of pure ecstasy until she finally drifted in a tide of lethargy unlike anything she had ever experienced. Only then did his mouth and fingers leave her. Andrew tugged at the covers and linens, half lifting Caroline's body against his own, until they were wrapped in a cocoon of warm bedclothes. She lay beside him, her leg draped over his, her head pillowed on his hard shoulder. Shaken, exhausted, she relaxed in his arms, sharing the utter peace of aftermath, like the calm after a violent storm.

Andrew's hand smoothed over the wild ripples of her hair, spreading them over his own chest. After a long moment of bittersweet contentment, he spoke quietly, his lips brushing her temple.

"It was never a charade for me, Caroline. I fell in love with you from the moment we struck our infernal bargain. I loved your spirit, your strength, your beauty. . . . I realized at once how special you were. And I knew that I didn't deserve you. But I had the damned foolish idea that somehow I might be able to become worthy of you. I wanted to make a new beginning, with you by my side. I even stopped caring about my father's bloody fortune. But in my arrogance I didn't consider the fact that no one can escape his past. And I have a thousand things to atone for . . . things that will keep turning up to haunt me for the rest of my life. You don't want to be part of that ugliness, Caroline. No man who loves a woman would ask her to live with him, wondering every day when some wretched part of his past will reappear."

"I don't understand." She lifted herself onto his chest, staring into his grave, tender expression. "Tell me what Julianne has done to change everything."

He sighed and stroked back a lock of her hair. It was clear that he did not want to tell her, but he would no longer withhold the truth. "You know that Julianne and I once had an affair. For a while afterward, we remained friends of a sort. We are remarkably similar, Julianne and I—both of us selfish and manipulative and coldhearted—"

"No," Caroline said swiftly, placing her fingers on his mouth. "You're not like that, Andrew. At least not anymore."

A bleak smile curved his lips, and he kissed her fingers before continuing. "After the affair was over, Julianne and I amused ourselves by playing a game we had invented. We would each name a certain person—always a virtuous and well-respected one—whom the other had to seduce. The more difficult the target, the more irresistible the challenge. I named a high-ranking magistrate, the father of seven children, whom Julianne enticed into an affair."

"And whom did she select for you?" Caroline asked quietly, experiencing a strange mixture of revulsion and pity as she heard his sordid confession.

"One of her 'friends'—the wife of the Italian ambassador. Pretty, shy, and known for her modesty and God-fearing ways."

"You succeeded with her, I suppose."

He nodded without expression. "She was a good woman with a great deal to lose. She had a happy marriage, a loving husband, three healthy children. . . . God knew how I was able to persuade her into a dalliance. But I did. And afterward, the only way she could assuage her guilt was to convince herself that she had fallen in love with me. She wrote me a few love letters, highly incriminating ones that she soon came to regret. I wanted to burn them—I should have—but I returned them to her, thinking that it would ease her worry if she could destroy them herself. Then she would never have to fear that one of them would turn up and ruin her life.

Instead the little fool kept them, and for some reason I'll never understand, she showed them to Julianne, who was posing as a concerned friend."

"And somehow Julianne gained possession of them," Caroline said softly.

"She's had them for almost five years. And the day after my father died, and it became known that he left me the Rochester fortune, Julianne paid me an unexpected visit. She has gone through her late husband's entire fortune. If she wishes to maintain her current lifestyle, she will have to marry a wealthy man. And it seems I have been given the dubious honor of being her chosen groom."

"She is blackmailing you with the letters?"

He nodded. "Unless I agreed to marry her, Julianne said she would make the damned things public, and ruin her so-called friend's life. And two things immediately became clear to me. I could never have you as my wife knowing that our marriage was based on the destruction of someone else's life. And with my past, it is only a matter of time until something else rears its ugly head. You would come to hate me, being constantly faced with new evidence of the sins I've committed." His mouth twisted bitterly. "Damned inconvenient thing, to develop a conscience. It was a hell of a lot easier before I had one."

Caroline was silent, staring down at his chest as her fingers stroked slowly through the dark curls. It was one thing to be told that a man had a wicked past, and certainly Andrew had never pretended otherwise. But the knowledge made far more of an impression on her now that she knew a few specifics about his former debauchery. The notion of his affair with Julianne, and the revolting games they had played with others' lives, sickened her. No one would blame her for rejecting Andrew, for agreeing that he was far too tarnished and corrupt. And yet . . . the fact that he had learned to feel regret, that he wished to protect the ambassador's wife even at the expense of his own happiness . . . that meant he had changed. It meant he was capable of becoming a far better man than he had been.

Besides, love was about caring for the whole man, including his flaws . . . and trusting that he felt the same about her. To her, that was worth any risk.

She smiled into Andrew's brooding face. "It is no surprise to me that you have a few imperfections." She climbed farther onto his chest, her small breasts pressing into the warm mat of hair. "Well, more than a few. You're a wicked scoundrel, and I fully expect that at some point in the future there will be more unpleasant surprises from your past. But you are *my* scoundrel, and I want to face all the unpleasant moments of life, and the wonderful ones, with no one but you."

His fingers slid into her hair, clasping her scalp, and he stared at her with fierce adoration. When he spoke his voice was slightly hoarse. "What if I decide that you deserve someone better?"

"It's too late now," she said reasonably. "You have to marry me after debauching me this afternoon."

Carefully he brought her forward and kissed her cheeks. "Precious love . . . I didn't debauch you. Not completely, at any rate. You're still a virgin."

"Not for long." She wriggled on his body, feeling his erection rising against the inside of her thigh. "Make love to me." She nuzzled against his throat and spread kisses along the firm line of his jaw. "All the way this time."

He lifted her from his chest as easily as if she were an exploring kitten, and stared at her with anguished yearning. "There's still the matter of Julianne and the ambassador's wife."

"Oh, that." She perched on him, with her hair streaming over her chest and back, and touched his small, dark nipples with her thumbs. "I will deal with my cousin Julianne," she informed him. "You'll have those letters back, Andrew. It will be my Christmas gift to you."

His gaze was patently doubtful. "How?"

"I don't wish to explain right now. What I want is—"

"I know what you want," he said dryly, rolling to pin her beneath him. "But you're not going to get it, Caroline. I won't take your virginity until I'm free to offer you marriage. Now explain to me why you're so confident that you can get the letters back."

She ran her hands over his muscular forearms. "Well . . . I've never told this to anyone, not even Cade, and especially not my mother. But soon after Julianne's rich old husband died—I suppose you've heard the rumors that his death was not of natural causes?"

"There was never any proof otherwise."

"Not that anyone knows of. But right after Lord Brenton passed on to his reward, his valet, Mr. Stevens, paid a visit to my father one night. My father was a well-respected and highly trustworthy man, and the valet had met him before. Stevens behaved oddly that night—he seemed terribly frightened, and he begged my father to help him. He suspected Julianne of having poisoned old Lord Brenton—she had recently been to the chemist's shop, and then Stevens had caught her pouring something into Brenton's medicine bottle the day before he died. But Stevens was afraid to confront Julianne with his suspicions. He thought that she might somehow falsely implicate him in the murder, or punish him in some other devious way. To protect himself, he collected evidence of Julianne's guilt, including the tainted medicine bottle. He begged my father to help him find new employment, and my father recommended him to a friend who was living abroad."

"Why did your father tell you about this?"

"He and I were very close—we were confidantes, and there were few secrets between us." She gave him a small, triumphant smile. "I know exactly where Stevens is located. And I also know where the evidence against Julianne is hidden. So unless my cousin wishes to face being accused and tried for her late husband's murder, she will give me those letters."

"Sweetheart . . ." He pressed a gentle kiss to her forehead. "You're not going to confront Julianne with this. She is a dangerous woman."

"She is no match for me," Caroline replied. "Because I am not going to let her or anyone else stand in the way of what I want."

"And what is that?" he asked.

"You." She slid her hands to his shoulders and lifted her knees to either side of his hips. "All of you . . . including every moment of your past, present, and future."

✳ Chapter Five ✳

The most difficult thing that Andrew, Lord Rochester, had ever done was to wait for the next three days. He paced and fretted alone at the family estate, alternately bored and anxious. He nearly went mad from the suspense. But Caroline had asked him to wait for word from her, and if it killed him, he would keep his promise. Try as he might, he could not summon much hope that she would actually retrieve the letters. Julianne was as sly and devious as Caroline was honest . . . and it was not the easiest trick in the world to blackmail a blackmailer. Moreover, the thought that Caroline was lowering herself in this way in an attempt to clean up a nasty mess that he had helped to create . . . it made him squirm. By now he should be accustomed to feeling the heat of shame, but he still suffered mightily at the thought of it. A man should protect the woman he loved—he should keep her safe and happy—and instead Caroline was having to rescue *him*. Groaning, he thought longingly of having a drink—but he would be damned if he would drown himself in the comforting oblivion of alcohol ever again. From now on he would face life without any convenient crutch. He would allow himself no more excuses, no place to hide.

And then, just a few days before Christmas, a footman dispatched from the Hargreaves residence came to the Rochester estate bearing a small wrapped package.

"Milord," the footman said, bowing respectfully. "Miss Hargreaves instructed me to deliver this into your hands, and no one else's."

Almost frantically Andrew tore open the sealed note attached to the package. His gaze skittered across the neatly written lines:

> *My lord,*
> *Please accept this early Christmas gift. Do with it what you will, and know that it comes with no obligations—save that you cancel your betrothal to my cousin. I believe she will soon be directing her romantic attentions toward some other unfortunate gentleman.*
>
> > *Yours,*
> > *Caroline*

"Lord Rochester, shall I convey your reply to Miss Hargreaves?" the footman asked.

Andrew shook his head, while an odd feeling of lightness came over him. It was the first time in his life that he had ever felt so free, so full of anticipation. "No," he said, his voice slightly gravelly. "I will answer Miss Hargreaves in person. Tell her that I will come to call on Christmas Day."

"Yes, milord."

* * *

Caroline sat before the fire, enjoying the warmth of the yule log as it cast a wash of golden light over the family receiving room. The windows were adorned with glossy branches of holly, and festooned with red ribbons and sprays of berries. Wax tapers wreathed with greens burned on the mantel. After a pleasant morning of exchanging gifts with the family and servants, everyone had departed to pursue various amusements, for there were abundant parties and suppers to choose from. Cade was dutifully escorting Fanny to no less than three different events, and they would likely not return until after midnight. Caroline had resisted their entreaties to come along, and refused to answer their questions concerning her plans. "Is it Lord Rochester?" Fanny had demanded in mingled excitement and worry. "Do you expect him to call, dearest? If so, I must advise you on the right tone to take with him—"

"Mother," Cade had interrupted, flashing Caroline a rueful gaze, "if you do not wish to be late for the Danburys' party, we must be off."

"Yes, but I must tell Caroline—"

"Believe me," Cade said firmly, plopping a hat onto his mother's head and tugging her to the entrance hall, "if Rochester should decide to appear, Caroline will know exactly how to deal with him."

Thank you, Caroline had mouthed to him silently, and they exchanged a grin before he removed their inquisitive mother from the premises.

The servants had all been given the day off, and the house was quiet as Caroline waited. Sounds of Christmas drifted in from outside . . . passing troubadours, children caroling, groups of merry revelers traveling between houses.

Finally, as the clock struck one, a knock came at the door. Caroline felt her heart leap. She rushed to the door with unseemly haste and flung it open.

Andrew stood there, tall and handsome, his expression serious and a touch uncertain. They stared at each other, and although Caroline remained motionless, she felt her entire being reaching for him, her soul expanding with yearning. "You're here," she said, almost frightened of what would happen next. She wanted him to seize her in his arms and kiss her, but instead he removed his hat and spoke softly.

"May I come in?"

She welcomed him inside, helped him with his coat, and watched as he hung the hat on the hall stand. He turned to face her, his vivid blue eyes filled with a heat that caused her to tremble. "Merry Christmas," he said.

Caroline wrung her hands together nervously. "Merry Christmas. Shall we go into the parlor?"

He nodded, his gaze still on her. He didn't seem to care where they went as he followed her wordlessly into the parlor. "Are we alone?" he asked, having noticed the stillness of the house.

"Yes." Too agitated to sit, Caroline stood before the fire and stared up at his half-shadowed face. "Andrew," she said impulsively, "before you tell me anything, I want to make it clear . . . my gift to you . . . the letters . . . you are not obligated to give me anything in return. That is, you needn't feel as if you owe me—"

He touched her then, his large, gentle hands lightly framing the sides of her face, thumbs skimming over the blushing surface of her cheeks. The way he looked at her, tender and yet somehow devouring, caused her entire body to tingle in delight. "But I am obligated," he murmured, "by my heart, soul, and too many parts of my anatomy to name." A smile curved his lips. "Unfortunately the only thing I can offer you is a rather questionable gift . . . somewhat tarnished and damaged, and of very doubtful value. Myself." He reached for her small, slender hands and brought them to his mouth, pressing hot kisses to the backs of her fingers. "Will you have me, Caroline?"

Happiness rose inside her, making her throat tight. "I will. You are exactly what I want."

He laughed suddenly, and broke the fervent clasp of their hands to fish for something in his pocket. "God help you, then." He extracted a glittering object and slipped it onto her fourth finger. The fit was just a little loose. Caroline balled her hand into a fist as she stared the ring. It was an ornately carved gold band adorned with a huge rose-cut diamond. The gem sparkled with heavenly brilliance in the light of the yule log, making her breath catch. "It belonged to my mother," Andrew said, watching her face closely. "She willed it to me, and hoped that I would someday give it to my wife."

"It is lovely," Caroline said, her eyes stinging. She lifted her mouth for his kiss, and felt the soft brush of his lips over hers.

"Here," he murmured, a smile coloring his voice, and he removed her spectacles to clean them. "You can't even see the damned thing, the way these are smudged." Replacing the polished spectacles, he took hold of her waist and pulled her body against his. His tone sobered as he spoke again. "Was it difficult to get the letters from Julianne?"

"Not at all." Caroline could not suppress a trace of smugness as she replied. "I enjoyed it, actually. Julianne was furious—I have no doubt she wanted to scratch my eyes out. And naturally she denied having had anything to do with Lord Brenton's death. But she gave me the letters all the same. I can assure you that she will never trouble us again."

Andrew hugged her tightly, his hands sliding repeatedly over her back. Then he spoke quietly in her hair, with a meaningful tone that made the hairs on the back of her neck prickle in excitement. "There is a matter I have yet to take care of. As I recall, I left you a virgin the last time we met."

"You did," Caroline replied with a wobbly smile. "Much to my displeasure."

His mouth covered hers, and he kissed her with a mixture of adoration and avid lust that caused her knees to weaken. She leaned heavily against him, her tongue sliding and curling against his. Excitement thumped inside her, and she arched against him in an effort to make the embrace closer, her body craving the weight and pressure of him.

"Then I'll do my best to oblige you this time," he said when their lips parted. "Take me to your bedroom."

"Now? Here?"

"Why not?" She felt him smile against her cheek. "Are you worried about propriety? You, who had me handcuffed to a bed—"

"That was Cade's doing, not mine," she said, blushing.

"Well, you didn't mind taking advantage of the situation, did you?"

"I was desperate!"

"Yes, I remember." Still smiling, he kissed the side of her neck and slid his hand to her breast, caressing the gentle curve until her nipple contracted into a hard point. "Would you rather wait until we marry?" he murmured.

She took his hand and pulled him out of the parlor, leading him upstairs to her bedroom. The walls were covered with flower-patterned paper that matched the pink-and-white embroidered counterpane on the bed. In such dainty surroundings, Andrew looked larger and more masculine than ever. Caroline watched in fascinated delight as he began to remove his clothes, discarding his coat, waistcoat, cravat, and shirt, draping the fine garments on a shield-backed chair. She unbuttoned her own gown and stepped out of it, leaving it in a crumpled heap on the floor. As she stood in her undergarments and stockings, Andrew came to her and pulled her against his naked body. The hard, thrusting ridge of his erection burned through the frail muslin of her drawers, and she let out a small gasp.

"Are you afraid?" he whispered, lifting her higher against him, until her toes almost left the ground.

She turned her face into his neck, breathing in the scent of his warm skin, lifting her hands to stroke the thick, cool silk of his hair. "Oh, no," she breathed. "Don't stop, Andrew. I want to be yours. I want to feel you inside me."

He set her on the bed and removed her clothes slowly, kissing every inch of her skin as it was uncovered, until she lay naked and open before him. Murmuring his love to her, he touched her breasts with his mouth, licked and teased until her nipples formed rosy, tight buds. Caroline arched up to him in ardent response, urging him to take her, until he pulled away with a breathless laugh. "Not so fast," he said, his hand descending to her stomach, stroking in soothing circles. "You're not ready for me yet."

"I am," she insisted, her body aching and feverish, her heart pounding.

He smiled and rolled her to her stomach, and she groaned as she felt his mouth trail down her spine, kissing and nibbling. His teeth nipped at her buttocks before his lips traveled to the fragile creases at the backs of her knees. "Andrew," she groaned, writhing in torment. "Please don't make me wait."

He turned her over once again, and his wicked mouth wandered up the inside of her thigh, higher and higher, and his strong hands carefully urged her thighs apart. Caroline whimpered as she felt him lick the damp, soft cleft between her legs. Another, deeper stroke of his tongue, and another, and then he found the excruciatingly tender bud and suckled, his tongue flicking her, until she shuddered and screamed, her ecstatic cries muffled in the folds of the embroidered counterpane.

Andrew kissed her lips and settled between her thighs. She moaned in encouragement as she felt the plum-shaped head of his sex wedge against the slick core of her body. He pushed gently, filling her . . . hesitating as she gasped with discomfort. "No," she said, clutching frantically at his hips, "don't stop . . . I need you . . . please, Andrew . . ."

He groaned and thrust forward, burying himself completely, while her flesh throbbed sweetly around him. "Sweetheart," he whispered, breathing hard, while his hips pushed forward in gentle nudges. His face was damp, suffused with perspiration and heat, his long, dark lashes spiky with moisture. Caroline was transfixed by the sight of him—he was such a beautiful man . . . and he was hers. He invaded her in a slow, patient rhythm, his muscles rigid, his forearms braced on either side of her head. Writhing in pleasure, she lifted her hips to take him more deeply. His mouth caught hers hungrily, his tongue searching and sliding.

"I love you," she whispered between kisses, her wet lips moving against his. "I love you, Andrew, love you. . . ."

The words seemed to break his self-control, and his thrusts became stronger, deeper, until he buried himself inside her and shuddered violently, his passion spending, his breath stopping in the midst of an agonizing burst of pleasure.

Long, lazy minutes later, while they were still tangled together, their heartbeats returning to a regular rhythm, Caroline kissed Andrew's shoulder.

"Darling," she said drowsily, "I want to ask something of you."

"Anything." His fingers played in her hair, sifting through the silken locks.

"Whatever comes, we'll face it together. Promise to trust me, and never to keep secrets from me again."

"I will." Andrew raised himself up on one elbow, staring down at her with a crooked smile. "Now I want to ask something of you. Could we forgo the large wedding, and instead have a small ceremony on New Year's Day?"

"Of course," Caroline said promptly. "I wouldn't have wanted a large wedding in any case. But why so soon?"

He lowered his mouth to hers, his lips warm and caressing. "Because I want my new beginning to coincide with the new year. And because I need you too badly to wait for you."

She smiled and shook her head in wonder, her eyes shining as she stared up at him. "Well, I need you even more."

"Show me," he whispered, and she did just that.

Puddings, Pastries, and Thou

✴

To Valerie

Chapter One

Christmas Eve, 1818
Copley Grange
Near Corfe Castle, England

"Oh dear. Is that the best you have to wear, Miss Ambrose?"

"Your pardon, ma'am. I'm afraid it is," Vivian admitted, holding her hands clasped tightly in front of her and refusing to give in to the urge to smooth the skirt of her navy wool gown. It was a gown meant for a governess or a paid companion, or for what she was: a poor relation.

"Dear me, dear me, this won't do. This won't do at all!" Mrs. Twitchen, her distant cousin, fretted. "We are having Mr. John Sudley, baronet, for dinner, and his wife is the granddaughter of an earl. This won't do!"

"Perhaps, ma'am, it would be better if I did not attend?" Her stomach growled and gurgled beneath her clasped hands. She could, though, feed it just as well off a tray in her room as at the table.

"Nonsense," Captain Twitchen spoke up, sitting by the fire where the oak yule log burned. He placidly read his paper, a bull of a man around which maids and footmen flowed as they hung greenery and positioned silver candelabra newly polished. "If your gown is not suitable, wear one of Penelope's. She won't mind. Will you, girl?"

"Papa!" Penelope, aghast, turned from her inspection of a towering centerpiece of sweetmeats with sprigs of poisonous mistletoe tucked here and there in a creation of the girl's own design.

Vivian's eyes lingered longingly on the pyramid of goodies even as she felt the heat of humiliation in her cheeks. It was bad enough to be sent from one branch of the family to another, treated like a hungry beggar. It was worse yet to land upon a new doorstep only a day before Christmas, when a family had its mind on entertainments planned weeks in advance, and on private traditions. But worst of all was to feel that her presence was an annoyance and an intrusion.

"They would not fit," Penelope said. "Miss Ambrose is much larger than I am, and the colors would be all wrong. She cannot wear one of my gowns."

"I don't see why not," Captain Twitchen disagreed, folding his paper in half to better read an article of interest. "You've got more already than you need for the season, and you'll be having a bushel more made when we return to town, I warrant." He glanced up from his reading, examining his daughter and his wife's cousin. "You look near enough in size to me."

"Might there be one you could spare?" Mrs. Twitchen inquired cautiously of her child.

"Let her stay in her room! You do not wish to dine with a baronet, do you, Miss Ambrose?"

Vivian supposed she didn't much care where or with whom she dined, as long as dine she did. It had been ages since she'd last eaten.

"Penelope," her father said warningly, and gave his daughter a long look.

"But, Papa, it isn't fair! I suppose you'll want me to share all my gowns with her for the season as well, won't you?"

"Hush, child," Mrs. Twitchen said, coming and putting her hands on her daughter's shoulders and steering her out of the room, then gesturing to Vivian to follow. "You'll give him ideas."

Vivian cast a look back at Captain Twitchen and found him once more absorbed in his paper, the troubles of the females of his house best left to its females. For a brief moment, she had a feeling that the man was a sleeping dragon best not wakened.

Turning, she gave a last, loving look at the tower of treats, then followed the fiercely whispering, protesting Penelope and the shushing Mrs. Twitchen up the oaken staircase of Copley Grange and down the hall to Penelope's room.

Her prideful heart wished to refuse a gown so grudgingly lent, but her reasonable mind ordered her to follow the dictates of the captain and his wife. Those two were the ones she needed to please, not Penelope, although she suspected the Twitchen girl could make her life a misery easily enough.

It felt as if it had been a month ago, but it was only this morning that she had arrived here at the home of her first cousin, twice removed—Penelope's mother. They had never met before this day, although the arrangements for Vivian's arrival had been made some weeks past, as soon as old Ann Marbury had died.

Miss Marbury had been the spinster great-aunt of a previous set of cousins—cousins who had found Vivian useful as a companion to their wicked, dotty old relative. For nine years she had fetched and carried, read aloud, and played at cards with the beastly old woman, had endured increasing insults and pinches, and had had food thrown at her as the lady's mind deteriorated.

It had been a blessing to them both when the woman died. Vivian did not think herself hard-hearted for believing so, for as often as Miss Marbury had been cruel and suspicious, she had equally as often spent her days in tearful confusion, inconsolable, asking after those who had died long before Vivian had been born.

Farewell, unfortunate Miss Marbury! And may the angels keep you in good company!

And farewell also, horrid cousins, who kept me caged with an old woman for your convenience and never spared a thought for me or my future!

She was twenty-five years of age, and had never once attended a dance or an assembly, although her family were gentry and such should have been her right. The horrid cousins had preferred keeping her as unpaid help to spending the money to garb her and help her catch a husband and thus be free of their charity.

But now that Miss Marbury was dead and Vivian's usefulness gone with her, Vivian had been passed on to the next relatives willing to take her in and provide for her. She could only hope the Twitchens proved kinder and more generous than her other cousins.

"Penelope, do stop pouting and fussing. You will put wrinkles in your face with such expressions," Mrs. Twitchen said, and opened her daughter's clothespress to examine the possibilities therein.

"Not the green silk—that is my favorite," Penelope said, seeing her mother reaching for the garment. "It brings out my eyes, and would not suit another."

"Miss Ambrose has green eyes as well," Mrs. Twitchen mentioned.

"She cannot!" Penelope cried, then turned to examine Vivian and contradict the distressing statement. But she could not.

Vivian was equally surprised. The two girls were opposites: she herself had dark hair where Penelope had fair; she had a strong build that was underfed where Penelope had a fine build that was too plump. She would not have thought they shared any traits at all. Yet as her seventeen-year-old cousin came near, Vivian saw that indeed they had the same sea green eyes with dark gray rims.

Penelope's face grew red with anger, and she turned away with a flounce.

Mrs. Twitchen was still talking. "She is our cousin, after all, and blood will show. Dear me, we must dress her suitably. I will not be embarrassed in front of the baronet!"

"It is only Cousin John, Mama. I do not see why you need make such a fuss."

Mrs. Twitchen chose several gowns and laid them out over the bed and two upholstered chairs, then spoke to Vivian. "My husband's sister made an excellent match in a baronet. The title has since passed down to Sir John, Captain Twitchen's nephew, whom we have had the great good fortune to entertain on many an occasion, as he adores his uncle so. His wife is descended from the Earl of Surrey."

"Indeed, ma'am," Vivian said, for want of any better comment. She was beginning to wish most heartily that she could be left alone in her new bedroom while the family entertained their guests. Meeting the Twitchens and being installed in their home was strain enough for one day without the addition of baronets and granddaughters of earls.

"He is not half so grand as to deserve such care," Penelope put in.

"Hush, child. You say that because you know no better. When you come out this season, you will see what difference it makes to say your cousin is a baronet."

"And my great-grandfather a baron. I *know*, Mama."

"You help Miss Ambrose choose something, and give her ear bobs and a necklace to wear if she has none of her own, and perhaps some silk flowers for her hair. Really, we cannot have her looking so shabby, and she a relative of mine!"

Mrs. Twitchen hustled off, murmuring worries about Cook and the footmen, and Vivian was left alone with her cousin.

"I am sorry about this," Vivian said to the girl, feeling awkward and unwelcome. And hungry, to add to her misery. "If I had new gowns meant for my season, I should not like to have another wear one of them first, and she a stranger to me."

"I have been looking forward to my first season since I can remember," Penelope said, a quaver in her voice. "And here *you* come, right before it is to start! And we will have to have dresses made for you, and take you about, and all our acquaintances will be asking who you are when this was supposed to be *my* time. And you're too old for a season, too old by half! It's not fair!"

Vivian could tell the spoiled creature a thing or two about fair; she could! But she would not. Such a protected creature as Penelope Twitchen could not know what life was like outside the loving care of her mama and papa, and Vivian herself would have rather been a spoiled creature than an impoverished one, had she the choice. So she held her tongue.

"Please choose your least favorite," she said, knowing that such was what Penelope had in mind anyway.

The girl chewed her upper lip, frowning at the dresses. "I'm not overfond of the yellow," she said. "It makes my hair look dull, although it does have that lovely Valenciennes lace."

"I would be glad enough to wear it," Vivian said.

"You won't spill gravy on it?"

As if she were a child who could not use a spoon! Vivian counted to five, unclenched her jaw, and said, "I shall take great care not to."

"Well, all right, then." Penelope picked up the dress and held it against Vivian's shoulders. "I suppose it might fit, and the color is not completely unattractive on you. Do you have hair ribbons, ear bobs, anything?"

"I'm afraid I will have to ask those of you, as well." She would rather stick a sprig of holly in her hair and call herself decorated. Mrs. Twitchen would be displeased, though, and she didn't want to embarrass the woman.

Penelope sighed, leaving the dress in Vivian's arms and going to her dressing table. "This is really most unfair of Mama and Papa. This was to be *my* season."

"I do not like it any better than you," Vivian snapped, her weariness, tension, and hunger getting the better of her tongue. Last night had been spent very uncomfortably, sharing a bed at an inn with the unwashed, phlegmy woman who had been paid a pittance to accompany her. She had not slept well. "But I am glad that Captain and Mrs. Twitchen are willing to sponsor me for a season, for marriage is the only way I can at last be free of the so-called charity of relations!"

Penelope turned to her, jaw agape. "What an ungrateful wretch you are!"

"Not ungrateful. I shall thank your dear parents every day of my life if they can help me find a husband."

"More's the pity we will not find you one before we return to London, for then I could be rid of you the sooner."

"There is no greater gift I could ask from this Christmas season than that! The three kings didn't bear anything half so precious as a husband would be to me." Certainly such a mercenary view wasn't anything out of a fairy tale, princes scaling castle walls to rescue her from the villainous clutches of evil knights, but she had never expected such. A husband was simply someone to whisk her away from her dependence on her family. There needed to be no drama.

Vivian's green eyes met Penelope's. A moment of consideration stretched between them. Vivian's stomach growled.

"It's not truly possible, is it, to find a husband in such a short time?" Vivian asked.

"I . . . I'm not sure."

"When does the family return to town?"

"Soon after Epiphany," Penelope said. "The parliamentary session will begin in January this year, and Papa is an MP, so we must go back."

Epiphany was January sixth, the day after Twelfth Night. "It is not much time, less than two weeks. It's not possible." Vivian sighed, her momentary hopes sinking.

"No, perhaps it is." Penelope had a pink silk rose in her fingers, which she began to tap against her lower lip as she considered. "Are you particular about whom you marry?"

"I would wed a man forty years my senior who smelled like molding potatoes and had the wit of a particularly stupid rabbit—as long as he had a solid income and could provide me with my own home."

"You are desperate, aren't you? You have no dowry, and no income of your own. You are past the better part of your youth. You might have to make do with such a one."

"I expect little better." And truly she did not. The only

things that saved her from joining the ranks of governesses were that her education was insufficient to qualify her, and that most of her relatives would rather have her as a spinster gentlewoman they had to support than as a spinster with an occupation.

They would rather as well keep her a poor relation than to see her marry below her level, ending up with a man in trade whom they would then have to claim as a relation. Gentry was all that was acceptable, as well as all that was beyond her, given her lack of an inheritance. And what chance had she to go against their wishes and find herself a blacksmith or a carpenter with whom she might make a ruder home? None.

A woman of her age and station, of her poverty and genteel connections, was subject to the tyranny of her relations. They held her welfare within their purses, tied tight with a drawstring cord, and her only escape was marriage.

It was only the average prettiness of her face she could sell, and the youth of a body that could still bear children. It was old men who were forever the most eager buyers of those commodities.

Who said she wasn't in trade, like the lowest grocer or fishmonger? She would do what she had to to sell herself before she went rotten.

"There is one possibility of a match," Penelope said, coming forward and tucking the silk rose into Vivian's hair. "And he will be visiting us this very night!"

Chapter Two

Whatever weariness Vivian had felt was burned away by a new tension. If Penelope had her way, she would be meeting her future husband tonight. And the cruel child refused to tell her anything about him!

"He'll be the only single man present. You can find out what you will about him on your own. I shan't spoil the fun of that for you," Penelope said, then took the curling tongs to Vivian's hair.

As she sat and endured Penelope's primping and trimming of her, she wondered what it could be about this man of which her cousin was unwilling to speak. She did not fool herself: there had to be something wrong with him. Very wrong. Why else would Penelope believe he might be interested in Vivian's own impoverished self, and so eager to wed that the engagement could be accomplished in a mere two weeks?

Penelope was treating her as a large doll to be dressed and

rearranged without complaint. No longer did she fret about her Valenciennes lace garbing another, nor about loaning her yellow topaz ear bobs and the necklace that went with them. She dabbed Vivian's face with powder, and tinted her lips and cheeks with a faint trace of carmine.

"Shhh," Penelope said. "Don't tell Mama I have it."

Penelope held a needle over the candle and used the soot to fill in the spots where Vivian's brows were sparse or uneven. She was as determined as a mama preparing her daughter to snag a young peer at a ball. Her concentration was a testament to her desire to have her season all to herself, yet at the same time it showed a certain pride in her handiwork. Vivian recalled the carefully arranged mountain of sweetmeats and mistletoe, and hoped her own appearance fared better under Penelope's artistic guidance.

She also felt a bit of a fool while Penelope fussed over her. She was twenty-five and had never been a beauty even when she had the freshness of youth to her face. She feared that when at last she was allowed to look in the mirror, it would be a caricature of a young woman that looked back at her, and it would be plain to all that she was pretending to be something she was not, and with only one goal in mind.

There was, though, a small part of her that began to come alive under the attention, watching with interest the way in which Penelope wielded the cosmetics and chose ribbons and flowers for her hair. With a start she realized what it was: vanity.

And so what if it was? It was long past time she had the chance to indulge in that vice that women were said to have perfected.

"There. I think that is the best that can be expected of us," Penelope said, standing back and examining her handiwork.

At last Vivian was allowed the mirror. She stood in front of the cheval glass and blinked in surprise. She had not been transformed into a beauty—that much even Penelope's pastes and lotions could not achieve. But what charms she had were brought out while the flaws were concealed.

Her brow that was too high was shortened now by the dark brown curls that covered it, and that brought attention to her eyes, whose color was brighter for the contrast with the red of her lips and cheeks. The powder helped to conceal the one or two faint pink blemishes, while allowing the whiteness of her skin to shine through.

"Astonishing!" Vivian said. She touched lightly at her hair, the back brought up in a braided coil, flowers and ribbons tucked around it. It was so much lovelier than the plain chignon she usually wore. She could not quite believe it was Vivian Ambrose in the mirror, it was such a change from the familiar reflection.

Penelope tucked her chin in, a tight-lipped smile of pride and satisfaction on her face. "Don't spoil it by acting as if you think yourself plain. He'll value you as you value yourself, or so Mama has told me a thousand times."

At that, the tension crept back, for how could she value herself any higher than what she was? She saw now the way her collarbones were sharp under her skin, and the boniness of her wrists. Her shoulders were too square and broad, and her jaw as well.

She had a prodigious appetite that had never been satisfied with the stingy trays of food sent up to her and Miss Marbury. Her cousins' servants had sensed the disregard with which she was treated, and had in turn treated her accordingly, ignoring requests she made for extra food. The effects showed in the angular body beneath the lace and silk of this new dress, the powders and the ribbons.

She looked what she was: a nervous, hungry spinster.

Noises came from below, voices raised in greeting. Guests were beginning to arrive.

Vivian felt, all at once, the true loss of those years at Miss Marbury's bedside. She had had no training in the rules of society, knew little of making pleasant conversation, and even less of how to win the heart of a man. She was going to make faux pas left and right, and the baronet would wonder indeed where this graceless cousin of his aunt's had come from.

This, though, was her chance, and she would not—could not—let her lack of experience stop her. She straightened her spine and raised her chin.

She had spent nine years waiting for her life to begin, waiting to live as other people did. Her patience was worn away, her hunger all-consuming. She wanted a snug house; she wanted children she could spoil as badly as Penelope had been spoiled; she wanted a husband who, however old and smelly, would look upon her as a treasure and call her "my dear." And she, in return, would make certain he was well fed and that his clothes were fresh and mended, and treat him with tender regard and gratitude.

If Penelope thought Vivian had a chance at this unnamed man, then perhaps she did. And she would take it.

"Mr. Brent, it is good to see you again," Captain Twitchen said. "I hear you'll be giving us Tories a hard time of it."

"As hard a time as I can possibly manage," Richard Brent said. "What's the good of buying oneself a seat in Parliament if one cannot obstruct Tories?"

"By Jove, you're as blunt as I remember! You won't go far without a bit of finesse, though, Mr. Brent. Politics, you know. Can't always say what you think. I shouldn't go about advertising my seat was from a rotten borough, if I were you."

"I don't see why not. I am always honest about my corruptions."

"Ha! Ha! And so you are. If nothing else, you'll be an entertainment this session; that you will."

"I'll do my best to distract you and your cohorts from your duties," he said, grinning. He couldn't help but like the bluff old captain.

"That you will!" the man agreed.

"Richard, you naughty man," his sister Elizabeth said, coming up and taking his arm. "Talking politics? I'd say you should know better, only that would encourage you all the more. Come, there is someone you should meet."

"Must I?" he asked, and the question was not in jest.

"You must. Captain Twitchen," she said, nodding her head to her uncle-by-marriage.

"Lady Sudley," the captain acknowledged with a brief bow.

"Who now?" Richard asked as Elizabeth led him away. He was visiting her and her family at Haverton Hall for the Christmas season, a tradition he had been faithful to since she had married some five years previously. In that time he had met a goodly number of the eminent citizens of Dorset County, and of Corfe Castle, the small village named for the ruined keep that loomed above it.

"You shall see."

Worrisome words. Elizabeth was forever trying to reform, if not his behavior, then at least the appearance his actions took, and her chosen method was unfortunately matrimonial. Despite the evidence that no well-bred gentlewoman would have him, Elizabeth persisted in thinking one would.

Her disappointment was greater than his when most declined so much as even a dance with him.

Blind Elizabeth—she could not see that her brother's presence in the same room with gentlewomen was tolerated only because his family had rank and he had money. For that kind, honest toleration of society he was suitably kind in return, and he gave its hypocrisies the respect they deserved.

"You're not going to frighten some tender young creature by introducing me to her, are you?"

"No one who knew you could possibly be frightened of you, for all your growling."

"So you *are* introducing me to one," he said.

"She may be different."

He sighed. "At least she will have a tale to share with her friends of how she was forced to speak to that dastardly Richard Brent. I shall not disappoint her."

"Be kind, Richard."

"I shall be completely myself, for did you not just say that no one could possibly be frightened of me if they knew me?"

Elizabeth made a rumbling noise in the back of her throat, most unladylike. Then her expression lightened, her smile softened, her grip on his arm loosened, and he knew that the victim was at hand.

"Miss Ambrose, there you are," Elizabeth began as they came up to a dark-haired woman dressed in pale yellow. "I would like to introduce to you my brother, Mr. Richard Brent."

The girl stared at him, blinking great sea green eyes, then raised her hand for him to take.

"Miss Ambrose," he said, taking her fingers and bowing over them. They trembled in his grasp, and when he looked up from under his brows he saw the faint sheen of perspiration on her upper lip and the plane of her bosom. Not that he allowed his eyes to linger there. "How do you do?"

"How do you do?" she whispered back, her voice cracking on the words.

"Miss Ambrose is cousin to Mrs. Twitchen, and newly arrived from Shropshire," Elizabeth said, as he released the young woman's hand.

"Do you find Corfe Castle any improvement?" he asked. She looked to be one of those nervous girls who, if she was not careful, would grow into a sinewy, discontented old woman around whom one could never relax. She was probably thinking disdainful thoughts about him at this very moment.

"I like the people better," she said.

"Do you?" he asked.

"I think the food looks to be better here, as well."

He startled himself by laughing. Miss Ambrose gazed at him with widened eyes, as if not understanding why he found her amusing. Elizabeth smiled and excused herself.

"Let's hope Cook has not tried to be fancy and created a gothic mess of a meal, with four sauces for every dish," Richard said. "I can never decide if a free dinner should be counted as a gift or a curse. I think it is only the meager excitement of discovering which it shall be that draws me into accepting what few invitations come my way."

Miss Ambrose's lips parted, and she stared dumbstruck at him for several seconds. "You came only for the food?" she finally managed to ask.

"You look a hungry sort of girl," he said, intentionally being as blunt as his reputation had him. She would scamper off, and he would be free of another young miss who lived her life by the rules, not by the truth of her heart. "Aren't you looking forward to sitting down to dine more than you are to any songs on the pianoforte or games of whist?"

She gaped at him as if he were an exotic animal, then leaned forward confidentially and whispered, "I am perishing of hunger. I could eat an entire goose, were one to wander in and conveniently fall dead at my feet." Then she pulled back and put her fingertips to her lips as if she could push the words back in. "A lady is not supposed to admit to such things, is she?"

"I hardly think the scandal sheets will pillory you for it," he said, utterly surprised by her answer.

She flashed him a grateful smile, and he wondered if she was ignorant of his minor infamy. He had not killed anyone, he had not cheated anyone of their wealth, he had not ruined any virgins, yet for his past and present choices gentlewomen had closed ranks against him and counted him a nefarious fellow, unworthy of their daughters. He knew he had been a frequent topic of the cruelest sort of gossip. But it did not bother him much; he had not found any daughters worthy of him.

The announcement came for dinner, and he gave this new young woman his arm. After the briefest of hesitations she took it, and he saw that it was shyness that had stayed her for a moment, not offended honor. She really might not know anything about him! He was surprised by his pleasure in that thought.

Mrs. Twitchen indicated with a benevolent nod that he should sit beside Miss Ambrose at the table. Miss Twitchen sat on his other side, the young girl exchanging a long, meaningful look with Miss Ambrose before smartly turning all her attention to the gentleman farmer who sat on her other side. The look sent Miss Ambrose into blinking blushes, and she stared at her dish of soup as if she had never seen such a thing before.

And perhaps she hadn't. The pea soup had chunks of blue-veined Stilton cheese, half-melted, floating about in it.

"Oh, dear," he said from the side of his mouth. "Cook has been creative."

Her spoon clattered into her dish, and she gave a snort of nervous laughter. She peeked at him, a wary look in her eyes.

Had Miss Twitchen spoken of him earlier, and Miss Ambrose not connected the topic of that conversation to him until that long look? How disappointing. He had started to think he might get through a meal with an attractive female companion and not feel as if she thought he might give her fleas.

For Miss Ambrose *was* attractive, in those moments she began to relax and the tendons in her neck smoothed out, and the little worried frown between her brows disappeared. He put her age at about twenty, six years younger than he himself, but even for that age there was a remarkable lack of polish and ease about her.

Ah, well. She'd have her London season, and then her unaffectedness would be gone forever in the name of social graces.

"I would have my dinner backward if I could," she suddenly said in a very soft voice.

"How's that?" he asked, glad she was still speaking to him. His meal need not be passed in icy silence, after all. What *had* that long look with Miss Twitchen meant?

"Dessert and sweatmeats first. I do think pea soup with Stilton should be left as a final deterrent to gluttons who are overlong at table."

For the second time he was surprised by his own laughter. Heads turned in their direction. "Are you going to eat it?" he asked.

"Oh, I must," she said, picking up her spoon. "I could not

embarrass Mrs. Twitchen by not doing so. And I am hungry enough that I don't think even clippings from Cook's toenails in the soup could put me off."

He set his own spoon into his bowl, any intention of tasting the vile stuff gone from his mind. "That is a thoroughly repulsive thought."

She glanced at him, a spoonful of green and white at her lips. She raised her brows, then purposefully sucked it in.

For the third time, he laughed.

"Miss Ambrose," Captain Twitchen said, speaking across the intervening diners, interrupting their conversations. "What *is* it that you are saying to amuse our Mr. Brent so?"

"I really don't know, sir," she said, dipping her spoon back into her soup.

"Damn if it isn't the first time I've seen the man in a good humor. Mr. Brent, what is so funny?"

"You will have to amuse yourself with wondering," Richard said.

"Damn!"

"Captain Twitchen!" his wife admonished from her end of the table.

"But damn, Mary. It must be a confoundingly good joke."

"Direct your attention to the fish, please," Mrs. Twitchen said, and the servants on their silent feet came around and carried off the offending soup, replacing it with a platter of fish that the captain would have to serve to his guests. The man looked somewhat peeved.

The fish was served and eaten, and Richard could not fail to note that Miss Ambrose consumed every sliver of flaky white meat upon her plate. "You enjoyed the fish?" he asked as it was removed and the platters of the main course were arrayed around the table.

"It helped to erase the memory of the soup," she said.

"Where *did* you come from, Miss Ambrose?" he asked, as he served her from the platters nearest to them. "And no, don't tell me Shropshire. You know that is not what I mean."

"Then what do you mean?"

"There, now you're sounding more like the usual young lady, delicately fishing for a compliment."

"I certainly am not! I cannot help if you ask questions of uncertain meaning. I come from Shropshire, and there is very little to add to my history than that."

"Your parents?"

"Deceased."

"Ah."

"'Ah' what, sir?"

"More oysters?"

"Yes, thank you. 'Ah' what?"

"'Ah,' you will be hunting for a husband this season."

"And what girl does not?"

"Have you an inheritance?"

"That is an impertinent question," she replied.

"I thought we were done with illusions of proper conversation, after that mention of Cook's toenails," he said, disappointed that she had retreated behind that false shield of propriety.

She speared a fried oyster on her fork, and met his eyes. "No, I have no inheritance. This is not my gown, nor my jewelry, nor my ribbons, nor my flowers."

"Then 'Ah,' you are going to be whipping your hounds into a fine frenzy to run down and trap a husband, for all that you have a pretty face."

Emotions he could not read flowed across her face. She ate her oyster and speared another. "I shall do my best. Do you have any advice to offer, you who are so worldly?"

"Are you mocking me?"

"Would I dare?" she asked, eating the second oyster and going for a third.

He laughed, genuinely delighted. "You would, wouldn't you? I doubt you are quite so daring as you pretend, though."

"How so?"

She was working her way through the chicken, the lamb, and the stewed venison on her plate. The girl had not been jesting about being hungry. "More oysters?" he asked.

"Please."

He served her, taking all but the last oyster from the dish and depositing them on her plate. "I would wager you are one of those girls who will venture to the edge of propriety, but never take a step beyond. In words you may take a risk, but never in deed."

She finished off the last of the venison and applied herself to the new batch of oysters. "I would not know."

"More pretty obfuscation?"

"No," she said, looking at him with an oyster on her fork, her eyes large and guileless. "I have never had the opportunity to find out." Then she downed the oyster.

He swallowed. Just who *was* this Miss Ambrose?

Vivian collapsed onto a love seat and with shaking fingers pushed back the limp curls that had begun to fall out near her damp face. The oysters, venison, fish, soup, chicken, four different wines, anchovy toasts, pigeon, tarts, fritters, and a cup of syllabub churned and roiled in her stomach.

"Tea?" Penelope asked.

"Yes, please." Perhaps it would settle her. The women of the party had at last retreated to the drawing room, the men still at the table with their claret. She had half an hour or so to compose herself and prepare for another round with Mr. Brent.

"Here you are," Penelope said, handing her a cup of tea, then sitting down beside her and leaning forward confidentially. "I didn't know you had it in you—what an artful thing you are!"

"I didn't know I had it in me, either," Vivian agreed, raising her cup in quivering fingers and taking a cautious sip.

"He's fascinated by you! Fascinated!"

"What is it that is wrong with him?"

"To be fascinated by you? Heaven only knows, but I won't argue with it."

"That is not what I meant."

"You are a handsome couple. How suprised Mama will be when you marry so shortly after coming to us!"

"Must I ask your mama what it is?"

"What what is? Really, cousin, you are being far too suspicious. Why not enjoy that a well-bred man has taken an interest in you? Though I must say that eating so greedily cannot have helped your cause any. No one could fail to remark upon it."

"'Twas Mr. Brent who insisted on serving me."

"You are not a child. You need not eat everything put before you."

But she did need to. Her nervousness with Mr. Brent had only increased her appetite, and however it had looked she had been unable to stop eating. She felt like a boiled Scottish haggis, ready to burst, and still she could not help thinking of the sweetmeats on the mistletoe pyramid.

"But tell me, you like him, don't you?" Penelope asked.

"I do not know him."

"But your impression so far?"

"He is . . . unexpected."

There seemed no other way to describe it. Each man who had been introduced to her this evening, she had wondered if he was the one Penelope meant she should snare. There was the gentleman farmer; but no, he had a wife. The vicar, too, and the baronet, of course. There were a few others, local gentry, but as she forced herself to converse with them, all had soon enough revealed themselves as being out of the marriage market, their wives elsewhere in the room.

And then Mr. Brent had been introduced to her, and she had almost lost her voice altogether. He was average in height, with a trim, square build, dark hair, and eyes of a rich coffee brown. His features were unremarkable, his nose perhaps too large, his eyes set too deep, but the animation of those plain features gave him an unquestionable attractiveness. There were those people whose smiles touched only their lips, but with Mr. Brent his whole face creased and crinkled, and his eyes met hers with intensity and intelligence.

She had never had a man look at her with such interest. She had never had anyone give her such flirtatious, individual attention in all the years of her life.

She was shy under his scrutiny and wanted to run. And at the same time she wanted to take no step that might cool that interest in Mr. Brent's eyes.

Luckily her time with Miss Marbury had taught her one thing well, and that was how to humor one bent on being difficult. It was plain that Mr. Brent fancied himself a bit of a rebel, and she had adjusted her behavior accordingly. She had not had time as yet to decide if he was a man worthy of being humored, or one she could, after all, marry. Her words to Penelope had been more bombast than substance, and she was not at all certain that she would have the courage to marry an odious man if given the opportunity.

Being a beggar among relations might not be a pleasant life, but it was the one she knew. Presented with the opportunity of escape, in reality and not just fantasy, she did not know if she was equal to the challenge.

The oysters in her stomach rolled and turned, and she felt a wave of heat wash over her.

"I'm going to be sick," she said, shoving her teacup at Penelope. Then she left her astonished cousin on the love seat, and ran from the room.

Chapter Three

Christmas Day
The Nativity
Haverton Hall

"*I* do hope Miss Ambrose can make it tonight," Elizabeth said. "I was surprised not to see her in church this morning."

Richard said nothing, pretending to be engrossed in his book. They were in the drawing room, supposedly enjoying a few moments of quiet. The children had been taken upstairs for their naps, and this would be the only lull in the day, for this evening the Twitchens would arrive for a small family dinner, as had been their custom for many years.

"You seemed fond of the girl," his sister's husband, Sir John, said.

Richard grunted and turned a page.

"I thought that was the only reason you came to church, on the chance of seeing her. What, no answer? You, of the famous forthrightness?" Sir John turned to his wife and said in a stage whisper, "By Jove, I think he *is* smitten with the girl. Have you ever seen him without a reply?"

"I am *not* smitten with her," Richard snapped, shutting his book and glaring first at his brother-in-law and then at his sister. "A trifle curious, perhaps. But not smitten."

"Mrs. Twitchen told me some of her history," Elizabeth volunteered, then did not continue.

Richard looked at her, grinding his teeth, the two of them in a duel of stubbornness. "Oh, all right!" he said at last. "Tell me what she said."

"Make him admit he's smitten first," Sir John teased.

"I don't think we should push our luck, darling," Elizabeth said. "He looks ready to pop a vessel as it is."

"But he's making a damn fine show. I haven't had this much fun since the vicar got drunk and came here to beg the hand of that upstairs chambermaid."

"Really, dearest," Elizabeth said. "Just because you've been fortunate enough to marry the perfect woman doesn't mean you should make fun of others in their quest for a similar happiness."

Sir John narrowed his eyes and chewed his upper lip, trying and failing to come up with a suitable rejoinder that would not get him into trouble.

"Now, as I was saying," Elizabeth moved on. "Mrs. Twitchen says that Miss Vivian Ambrose is her first cousin twice removed, and comes from one of the weaker branches of the family. She has no fortune or rank, and her parents were killed in a carriage accident when she was a small child. She has spent these last several years as a companion to an elderly aunt, and has not yet been out in society, although she is twenty-five years of age. Mrs. Twitchen is hoping to make the girl a match in London this season. She says she feels rather sorry for the awkward thing."

"She's not awkward," Richard argued, privately surprised at Miss Ambrose's age. She was only a year younger than himself. Her face did not show her years.

"Isn't she? Of course, I had only a few moments to speak with her. She seemed quite shy."

"I wonder if we spoke to the same young lady."

"It may have been weariness I noted," Elizabeth amended. "Mrs. Twitchen said she had been remiss in having the girl attend the dinner party, as she had only arrived that morning. The strain was too much for her, and she was forced to retire after dinner."

"Is that what happened, then?" he asked. He had been disappointed to arrive in the drawing room only to find the young Miss Ambrose missing, and had consequently been unable to think of anything but her the remainder of the evening.

"She was overcome quite suddenly. She seemed fine when she was talking with Miss Twitchen; then all of a sudden she ran from the room, and Miss Twitchen said she had taken ill."

"More likely Miss Twitchen said something to her," Richard said. "She's a little minx, is Penelope Twitchen." He shifted in his chair, reopening his book and pretending once again to read, although his mind was on what the girl likely had said to scare Miss Ambrose off.

He really should stop thinking about the girl. He was only doing himself damage by brooding over her. It used to be that his hopes would rise upon each introduction to a friendly young woman, but as he'd gotten to know them—those who did not spurn his conversation—his expectations had died, hope squeezed from his heart.

Miss Ambrose had, with her oyster gluttony and her taunting, frank remarks, stirred that last drop of hope remaining in him. He was caught between wishing for it to grow and wishing he could drain it onto the muddy ground and stomp it under his boot, so it could no longer cause him pain.

It would be all the better if Miss Ambrose did not come to dinner tonight. He could put an end to this nonsense in both his heart and mind.

The Twitchen carriage bounced and rolled along the lane leading to Haverton Hall, jostling its four occupants, who sat two across, bundled in their coats and hats. Outside the windows, the heavy, overcast sky blotted out the last hints of day, the countryside blanketed in a layer of shadows.

Vivian almost wished she were still ill, so that she did not need to attend this dinner. The nausea from greasy fried oysters was preferable to that induced by nerves. At least one could throw up oysters and be rid of them.

Last night she had not returned to the drawing room after being ill, for how could one come back? What explanation could one give for such an absence?

This morning had seen her confined to her bed while the family went to church. Mrs. Twitchen had fretted, blaming herself for Vivian's illness. "'Twas entirely too much strain for you, poor girl," the lady had apologized. "No, you must stay abed. I won't have you overexciting yourself. You should have rested yesterday, only I gave you no chance."

And so her breakfast and lunch had been sent up to her on a tray, and she had devoured them with good appetite, not having known that this dinner party was waiting for her in the evening. If she had, she'd have rung for a third tray.

The day abed had given her more time than she wanted to brood upon meeting Mr. Brent, however, and to suffer a dozen embarrassments over her own behavior. She ate a butter tart off the plate by her bed each time such a distressing memory came to mind.

Mr. Brent had coaxed her into being naughty, and she had let him do so. However much he might have enjoyed her antics, though, his opinion of her had to be low because of them. She had painted herself as fast and daring, and he had likely believed her, for what evidence had he to the contrary?

Another butter tart helped her worry over the question.

Men did not marry fast women; that was common knowledge. And yet, if that was what intrigued Mr. Brent, what other choice had she than to play that role?

If it *was* a role. It had come much more easily to her than ladylike behavior, with its subtle rules and unspoken commandments. Perhaps she was a coarse, unrefined woman at heart.

The carriage at last drew up under the porte cochere, and they got down and entered the house. Sir John and Lady Sudley greeted them, servants took their coverings, and they were ushered into the drawing room to pass the time before dinner.

And there was Mr. Brent, looking uncertain, and then their eyes met and for a moment his face lit up, then as quickly composed itself into a bland, noncommittal welcome.

"See if you can make him laugh again," Penelope whispered to Vivian, giving her a playful shove toward him.

"Push me again," Vivian whispered through gritted teeth, "and I'll spill red wine on this dress." It was a periwinkle gown she wore this time, with embroidery and beadwork over the bodice. Penelope had once again done her hair and her face, working with the same care and concentration as if Vivian were a spun-sugar castle to be presented to the king.

"I'm just encouraging you. You need a bit of that, I think," Penelope complained. "Dowdy girls usually do."

"Red wine, and grease from my dinner," she threatened.

"You can overcome many problems of face or figure with a bright personality," Penelope advised in a teasing tone. She seemed to be enjoying this marriage hunt far more than the huntress herself.

"Leave me alone," Vivian said, although Penelope's insults did serve to distract her from the matter at hand.

"And remember, it may be a feast day, but you needn't stuff yourself: we will have had a half-dozen of them by the end of the Christmas season. You're in no danger of starving." Penelope gave her another little shove toward Mr. Brent, and left her. Vivian watched her go, almost wishing she'd stayed, but when she turned she was startled to find Mr. Brent standing before her.

"Miss Ambrose, I was sorry to miss you the remainder of last evening," he said. "And now look, you are being shy with me."

She saw the devilish light in his eyes, and out of the swirling mass of confused choices for how she should behave—innocent or knowing, shy or fast, flirtatious or proper—what came forward was the truth. "I am being shy because I *am* shy, Mr. Brent."

"You do not seem so to me."

"Only because you make outrageous comments that encourage a similarly outrageous response. You are enough to put any young woman on edge."

"Not any young woman would answer as you just have."

"I don't know any better," she said.

He laughed. "And I pray you never learn. Last night's

conversation was one of the most enjoyable I've had in recent memory."

"I had been hoping you would forget it."

"Impossible. And I would never want to."

She blushed, fidgeted, yearned for a bit of spice cake, then looked around for something to comment upon. She was aware of him watching her, taking in each uneasy movement. She combed back through her memory of their conversation at dinner the night before, and finally found something to say.

"You never answered my question last night."

"Which was that?"

"I asked if you had advice for me for hunting a husband during the season," she said, hoping it did not sound as if she were asking advice for hunting *him*—although that actually was what she was doing. Not that she could use whatever information he gave her; it would be too transparent. Oh, heavens, why had she said anything at all?

"That all depends upon which sort you wish to catch. You must dangle the proper bait for the beast."

"I have only one very poor bit of bait to dangle, and it rules out fortune hunters and social climbers."

"That is a shame. Many a young lady has made her match with such," he said. "London is full of them."

"I was rather counting on an elderly gentleman with a comfortable income."

"Simply because they are aged does not mean they are any less likely to want an heiress," Mr. Brent said. "Their greed does not slow with their limbs."

"Dear me. How about impetuous youths who have already inherited, and so cannot be disowned for making a bad match?"

"Those are difficult to catch, and make poor husbands,

being prone to drink and gambling. Like as not you will end up living on credit, and soon enough be bankrupt."

"There is no point in returning from whence I started," she said.

Mr. Brent seemed to be enjoying this vein of conversation. She was almost enjoying it herself. He dared her to say the thoughts that she would normally not utter even to herself. She had spent her life speaking only those words that would please her benefactors, pretending to be much nicer than she knew herself to be, hiding her darkest, most selfish and discontented thoughts for fear they would show on her face and betray her as a woman unworthy of even grudging charity.

"An exceedingly ugly man might prove acceptable," she proposed. "I think I could grow to love him, if he had a sweet temper."

"He will either be so vain as to think himself worthy of a better match, or so shy he will never manage to offer."

"A sick man, then, who needs an heir before he dies?"

"The competition will be fierce. What young lady would not like to be a wealthy widow, free to do as she pleased?"

"That is a harsh view to take," Vivian argued. "I do not believe that one in a thousand young ladies would be so calculating."

"You said yourself you would be willing."

"For the sake of having a husband, not for being his widow. Really, Mr. Brent, you have a jaded view of womankind."

"Not as jaded as I could wish," he said. The next moment dinner was announced, interrupting their conversation and leaving her to wonder what he could possibly mean by such a statement.

* * *

The dinner table was too small, the company too cozy and close to engage in suggestive banter. Vivian was seated next to Captain Twitchen, Mr. Brent across from her. The family spoke of relations not present or long dead, dredging up memories in which she could not share.

She kept a vacant smile on her lips and concentrated on dinner.

Mr. Brent caught her eye several times, looking with a questioning brow at her plate, then at the dishes arrayed around the table. She had only to let her gaze linger upon some platter beyond her reach, and he would move it nearer to her. If the captain was engrossed in telling a tale and did not notice she was waiting to be served yet again, Mr. Brent dared her with his eyes to serve herself.

So she did. There were two removes between main courses, and she was almost feeling full by the time dessert was finished and Lady Sudley signaled the ladies' retreat to the drawing room.

The tea had been poured and distributed, and Penelope had gone to the pianoforte to stumble through some of the sheet music there, when two nursemaids appeared in the doorway, white-gowned toddlers and young children around their knees.

"My lady, the children wished to say good night," one of the maids said, as the plump creatures spilled into the room. One went for the spaniel that had been curled harmlessly by the fire; one waddled to Lady Sudley; another sprang to the table where the tea things stood, his small hands reaching up to play with the sugar dish and creamer; and the last wobbled to the pianoforte and added his own notes to Penelope's soon-halted playing.

The spaniel cast a long-suffering look to the adults in the room, then slunk off to hide beneath a divan. Deprived of her target, the little girl of about four years went to join the younger boy at the tea tray.

"She looks more like you every day," Mrs. Twitchen said, nodding toward another girl, who had crawled into Lady Sudley's lap.

"She has her father's sense of mischief, though. Don't you, my naughty pumpkin?"

"Nooo," the girl protested, wrapping her arms around her mother's neck.

Vivian blinked at the four children, trying to match their ages with the length of Lady Sudley's marriage, wondering how she could have produced so many so quickly.

An altercation arose at the tea tray. The boy—not more than two, surely—had a spoon in his fist, and the girl was trying to take it away. The girl wrenched it from his hand, and the boy wailed, then went with flying fists at his sibling.

"William! Sara!" came a harsh male voice from behind Vivian. "Stop it at once!"

"My 'poon! Mine!" William wailed, striking his sister again.

Sara shoved the boy, and he fell onto his round backside. It was not a long distance to fall, but the indignity of it overtook him, and he threw himself face-first to the carpet and howled.

"Sara! What did I tell you?" Mr. Brent said, stepping into the fray. "Give me the spoon."

"But, Papa!"

"At once!"

Sara held tight to it a moment longer, then with a pout handed it over.

"Now apologize to your brother."

Sara knelt down beside the still-howling William and patted his back. "'S'all right, Willie. I'm sorry."

William took a breath and gave a howl of a higher pitch. Sara bent over and looked at her brother face-to-face. He turned to the other side. She followed and put her hands over her eyes.

"Who's that?" she said, taking them away from her face.

William's howls stopped. Sara covered her eyes again.

"Who's that? Is that Willie?" she asked, revealing herself again.

"'S Sara," he said.

Vivian watched wide-eyed as Mr. Brent picked William up from the floor, holding him against his side, over his hip, with the ease of long practice. William flopped against his father with his arms straight at his sides, his still-red face looking down at his sister with an unreadable expression.

"You're overtired, the both of you," Mr. Brent said, then kissed William on the temple and handed him to one of the nursemaids. Sara had her arms raised and waiting, and he picked her up and carried her after the retreating maid. "You cannot simply grab things from people, Sara," he said gently as he went out the door.

Vivian barely noticed as Lady Sudley said good night to the two remaining children, bundling them off with their nursemaid. She was too caught in the utter shock of what she had just learned.

Mr. Brent had children! Was that why Penelope thought him willing to take anyone for a wife, that and his rather questionable social graces? And what of Mrs. Brent; what had happened to her? Was she dead?

Or perhaps—the most shocking possibility of all—the two had divorced. That would explain Penelope's attitude better than anything. She wondered what terrible deeds could have made them choose such a course, if that was in truth what had happened.

The future she had been planning in her mind without knowing, a future where she and Mr. Brent were married and started their own family, fell to pieces. He had already had a family, and would not be looking with any great eagerness to starting yet another. If they had a child, it would be the third for him, and no astounding miracle.

He had a whole history of which she was unaware, a whole life that had been lived before she met him. There had been a woman he had loved and lost, who had borne him children, and who might very well still be heavy in his thoughts.

She was a fool. Of course he had a previous life. Did she think the world had stood still for everyone as she had tended to Miss Marbury all those years?

Mr. Brent was a father. Although she did not guess their difference in ages to be much, the difference in their experiences was. Her naive plans to entice him into marriage now seemed childish and silly. The man had children! He had had a wife once already! And what was Vivian, but awkward and dowdy in her borrowed finery, playing at being fast for his momentary entertainment, making herself an amusement of no value? He must think her a fool.

And even if he did have an interest in her—even if so!—she did not know if she had the strength to be anyone's step-mama.

The captain and Sir John had rejoined them, and by the time Mr. Brent returned from tucking his children into bed she had managed, she hoped, to hide her distress. She volunteered to play when a game of piquet was called for, and smiled blankly at Mr. Brent when he sat across from her.

After the game was finished she found a plate of small lemon tarts on a side table, and ate them, every one.

*　　*　　*

They had returned to Copley Grange, everyone yawning and speaking of bed, but Vivian followed Penelope into her dressing room nonetheless and badgered her young cousin as she began to undress.

"Why did you not tell me he had children?"

"Oh, la!" Penelope said, waving her hand as if it were nothing. "Two tiny children; they were not worth mentioning. You would not be the first woman to become a stepmother."

"You could have prepared me!"

"I thought it would make a pleasant surprise."

"Pleasant? How could you think so?"

"Dear Vivian, you did say that you wanted to have children, a family of your own. Now here is one ready-made! You needn't ruin your figure in the bearing of them, and they are old enough to speak, which you must admit makes them much more interesting. Think what a lot of fuss and bother you have been saved!"

"But they aren't *mine*."

"They might as well be. There is no one else being a mother to them."

"What happened to Mrs. Brent?"

Penelope turned away and put her ear bobs in her jewelry box, remaining with her back to Vivian. "I really couldn't say anything about their mother."

"Can't, or won't?"

"I am not certain of the entire tale."

"Is she dead? You can surely tell me that much."

"Really, Vivian. You must stop pestering me with such questions. What does any of that matter? It is Mr. Brent who interests you, not a woman from his past. Now if you'll excuse me," she said, stifling a false yawn, "I really must get to bed."

It was plain she would get no more information from Penelope. She tried for several more minutes anyway, then gave up and went to her room, undressing by the light of a single candle and slipping into the cool sheets of her bed.

She could not sleep. In addition to the lemon tarts, she had drunk four or five cups of coffee—she'd lost count—and in consequence was left with her mind running like a wind-up toy, clickety-clack, around and around and around again.

Little Sara and William. *Could* she be a mother to two such children? They were as rosy-faced and plump as any others of their ages, as noisy, as troublesome, as sweet, as innocent. There was no reason she should not grow to love them, and young as they were they would call her Mama, having known no other.

It would not be like caring for Miss Marbury had been, that dark and thankless task. Sara and William might love her back, which would be infinite reward for her caretaking.

Still, it was overwhelming to think of becoming a mother of two upon an instant. When she had imagined marriage, she had never imagined that children would already be present, with their demands upon their father's attention. She could never begrudge a child time with its father—not after having been so unhappily without one herself.

Yet she knew it was possible she might be jealous of the time he gave to them. She was ashamed to admit to such a selfish thought, but she would have to overcome it if she were to seriously consider wedding Mr. Brent. Sara and William were not going away, and if she were to be a step-mother she would rather be a loving one than an evil one.

And if she were to bear Mr. Brent children herself, would they be as dear to him as those from his first wife? Or would they be merely number three and number four?

There was so much to consider. Sara and William had shattered her girlish fantasies, and she was faced with the challenges of what a true marriage might entail. Mr. Brent did not smell like moldy potatoes and had more wit than the usual rabbit, but choosing a life with him would not be easy.

There was one bright spot, though.

Whatever dark stains might be attached to Mr. Brent's name—for surely there were stains, if Penelope yet insisted on remaining silent on the question of his past marriage—the stains could not extend to his true character. For all her shock at seeing that he was a father, she had also seen that he loved his children dearly, and they him. He was gentle where another might have been harsh, and his tenderness toward Sara and William touched her heart deeply.

It was that tenderness—toward children she did not know if she had the courage herself to mother—that eased her mind and allowed her to drift into sleep.

Chapter Four

December 26, Boxing Day
The Feast of Saint Stephen the Martyr

"Look, Vivian, it is Lady Sudley and Mr. Brent. What good fortune!" Penelope crowed.

Vivian's fingers tightened on the strings of the boxes she carried. It was Boxing Day, the day after Christmas, and she, Penelope, and Mrs. Twitchen had descended upon the tradespeople in the village of Corfe Castle to dispense small gifts of money and mincemeat pies, which would be eaten over the remaining days of Christmas. It should be no surprise to find Lady Sudley out with boxes of her own.

Vivian felt the sudden urge to tear open one of the boxes she carried and consume its contents.

Their small group approached Lady Sudley and Mr. Brent, meeting up in the narrow cobbled street in front of the draper's shop. Greetings and pleasantries were exchanged,

Mrs. Twitchen and Lady Sudley talking of who they had already been to see.

Vivian met Mr. Brent's eyes. There was a question in his expression, buried but readable to one who was accustomed to observation. She smiled tentatively, and was rewarded by his own smile and a wink, which made her blush and look down.

"Have you been to see the ruins, Mr. Brent?" Penelope asked in a lull between Mrs. Twitchen and Lady Sudley. It was a rather ingenuous question, Vivian thought. The ruins were in plain sight of the village, and no one who had spent time in Corfe Castle could possibly have missed exploring them. "Vivian has not. It would be a pity for her to leave the district without having once set foot in them."

"You should take the young ladies," Lady Sudley said to her brother. "It is a fine day for it. Don't you think it a grand idea, Mrs. Twitchen?"

Penelope's mother made a faint sound of dismay, while smiling in apparently cheerful agreement.

"Then let us take advantage of the weather," Mr. Brent said. "After luncheon?" he proposed to Vivian and Penelope.

"Oh, yes," Penelope answered.

"Miss Ambrose?"

"Certainly," she said, knowing that her face must show her trace of uncertainty at the prospect. Penelope was going to be worthless as a chaperone, that much she knew, and was probably going to try to persuade her to some indiscretion.

They made their good-byes and continued with the distribution of boxes.

"Miss Ambrose—Vivian, dear," Mrs. Twitchen said, as they left the butcher's shop some minutes later. "I do think I ought to warn you—I was remiss in not saying something sooner—only he *is* brother-in-law to a baronet and the grandson of an earl—but Mr. Brent is not entirely a gentleman, and you should not entertain thoughts—"

"Mama, don't you think we should have a box for Mr. Simms, who ordered that sheet music for me last month?" Penelope interrupted.

"We do have a box for him, darling."

"Do we? No, I don't think we do. I've counted, and we haven't enough."

"Nonsense. Let me check the carriage," Mrs. Twitchen said, leading them back to the vehicle.

"I knew there was something more wrong with him," Vivian whispered to her cousin.

"Don't let Mama fill your head with tales. You seem to like him well enough. Why not judge him by that, rather than stories?"

"They must be terrible stories if your mama wants to warn me away from him."

"She'd be happy enough to have another of the baronet's family as a relation."

"It doesn't sound that way," Vivian said.

"Never mind what she may think. The point is to have you married. You might as well marry Mr. Brent as anyone you would meet in London. I doubt you'll find a richer husband, not without fortune or rank of your own, or a prettier face."

"One would think he would have his choice of young ladies, if he is wealthy," Vivian said, trying to ignore the hurtful comment. While no longer hostile, as she had been upon the day of Vivian's arrival, Penelope still punctuated her kindnesses with instants of thoughtless cruelty.

"Ah, but you are the only choice here. Take advantage of that while you may. I would."

"Yet you do not."

"He's too old for me, and I have to have my season. I wouldn't give that up even for the eldest son of a duke."

She probably wouldn't, either. There were moments Vivian thought nothing mattered to her cousin more than appearing at balls and assemblies in solitary, expensively garbed glory— no matter what it cost, in money or hurt feelings.

"King Edward was murdered here by his stepmother Elfrida in 978," Penelope said as they passed through the arch in the crumbling curtain wall and beheld the hill upon which the ruins of the castle stood. "It was probably just a hunting lodge here at the time. But it was a castle when King John starved twenty-two French nobles to death in the dungeons. It's haunted, you know, by a headless woman in white who floats down the hill and then disappears."

"Who is the ghost?" Vivian asked.

Richard grinned at Penelope's dramatics, and at Vivian's eager interest in spirits. He'd spent little time in Penelope's company in the past, and had assumed her to be a spoiled child with thoughts only for herself. It was surprising that she seemed to have become so quickly attached to her new cousin.

"Some say it is Lady Bankes. She valiantly defended the castle during the civil war, but a member of the garrison betrayed her and let in the parliamentarians. It was they who tore the walls of the castle down, out of pure spite."

"That doesn't account for her losing her head," Richard said. "And I don't know what good it would do to float down the hillside every now and then. Seems a waste of effort, for a ghost."

"Maybe it is Elfrida, then, doomed to roam the scene of her greatest sin," Penelope amended.

"Or maybe it is fog of an evening and a drunken fool. That seems the better explanation, albeit less thrilling."

"Ow!" Penelope exclaimed, stumbling.

Vivian caught at her cousin, helping her keep her balance. "What is it? Are you all right?"

"My ankle. I've twisted it. Help me to that stone over there," the girl said, pointing to a convenient resting place not three steps away.

"Does it hurt? Can you stand?" Vivian asked as she lowered Penelope to the stone.

"It's minor. Just a momentary twist. If I rest here for a spell I should be fine."

"We should take you back to the grange."

"No, no. You and Mr. Brent go up to the ruins. When you return, I promise I shall be quite restored."

"Are you sure?"

"Yes! Go!"

Vivian frowned at her cousin, then turned to him. She raised her brows in question, and he smiled and shrugged, offering his arm. Penelope's acting would never win her a place on the stage, and it was not difficult to see through her little ploy.

Vivian took his arm, and they started up the narrow, muddy track through the grass. The sky was heavy with clouds, the sun occasionally breaking through in pale yellow, and there was a damp breeze from off the sea a few miles distant. The few remaining segments of castle wall stood like towers against the turbulent skies, and bore the pockmarks of the parliamentarians' destructive forces.

"It's a pity they destroyed it," Vivian said, after they had left Penelope out of earshot on her rock. "It must have been lovely."

"They probably had fun doing it. Boys and men, they

both are forever looking for something they can blow up."

"You, too?"

"When I was a boy. My friends and I made a cannon out of an old oak water pipe, and set it off in a field, using a sapling to brace and aim it, and hiding behind a small wall of earth. We were lucky we weren't killed."

"What happened?"

"Damn thing exploded," he said, remembering with a laugh. "The whole cannon: shards of wood everywhere. You'd think we'd been in a sea battle and the deck had been hit—three separate villages heard the blast, and thought Boney had landed and was marching into the countryside. We wouldn't have admitted it was us, only one of my friends got a wedge of oak in his thigh. A hairbreadth to one side, and he would have cut the artery and bled to death."

"Good heavens!"

He shrugged. "Typical for boys. Just as my sister and your cousin are being typical for women, with their matchmaking," he said, taking a risk and wanting to see her reaction.

She gaped up at him.

"Come now, Miss Ambrose. You cannot be unaware of their machinations."

"No," she admitted.

"Did you encourage Miss Twitchen, or was it her own idea?" he asked, breaking all the rules of romantic fencing, and knowing it was unfair of him to do so. He should not ask such a thing without stating his own wishes first. She would be within her rights to abandon him here and go back to rejoin her cousin. Still, he was interested to see if she were as daring as he hoped. He waited to see what she would do.

"What a question!" she said, looking away from him, her bonnet blocking her face from his view.

"Even on such brief acquaintance as we have, you must

know that I am not one for veilings of the truth. Will you answer?" he asked, pushing her.

"And leave you with no mystery to solve?" she asked.

"I don't play games," he said, knowing it for a lie, for what was he doing now, if not trying to trick a confession from her?

"I do not think it is a game for a woman to protect the secrets of her heart," she said.

"So you have secrets?" he asked, not believing it, and yet hoping it was true.

"As do you, apparently."

"You think so?" he asked, suddenly feeling exposed. If he said he wanted to know much more about her, if he said he was attracted to her and enjoyed her company, if he was as forthright in matters of the heart as he made such an issue of being in other aspects of his life, would she run or would she stay? "I may have a secret or two," he admitted.

"I have heard hints."

"You have?"

"Of your former wife . . ."

"Wife? I have had no wife," he said, taken aback by the unexpected turn in conversation.

She stopped and looked to him, confusion in her expression and her tone. "But Sara and William? They are yours, are they not?"

"They are, but I have had no wife." He sighed, feeling his hopes once again draining away. It should get easier to accept rejection over time, and yet it never did. He had attempted to court a handful of women over the past few years, and when they heard what he was about to tell Vivian, they had all turned from him and made it clear that pursuance of his suit would not be welcome. "I thought someone would have told you—last night, surely, if not before."

"You are worrying me, Mr. Brent."

"My children's mother and I were not married. She was my mistress."

"Oh," she said softly, and he saw the hurt of disappointment in her eyes.

"The situation was nothing unusual, I am sorry to say. I am hardly the first man to sire children out of wedlock." The words sounded a miserable excuse even as he said them, as if he were trying to weasel out of his own past. "Sara and William are my heirs. They bear my name, and any woman I marry would have to raise them as her own, beside any children we might have together."

It was that last point that was so unpalatable to gently bred women. Bastards beside their own offspring? Bastards, heirs along with their own children? He could hardly berate them for following dictates of society in which they had been schooled since birth. They could not help their inability to accept bastards into their care.

And he, loving Sara and William as he did, could not accept a woman as wife who would not love his children.

"What of their mother?" Vivian asked softly.

"She is somewhere in London, with a new protector. She broke off our affair shortly after William was born, and did not protest when I demanded the children." He shrugged, beginning to feel angry and defensive on behalf of his offspring. "She sends gifts on occasion, and visits them once or twice a year, although less frequently as time goes on."

"Did you love her?"

"I thought so for a time, but it was based on illusion. I saw her beauty and her charm, and nothing of who she truly was. I was young and stupid, but I would not have Sara and William pay any more of the price for my idiocy than they already must."

"It was . . . quite remarkable of you to claim them as you have."

"I am their father," he said, the simplicity of the statement his only way to express the strength of the bond he shared with them. "I could not leave them without my name, without my protection, to be raised by strangers or by a mother who paid them little care. And I will not wed a woman who cannot give them the love they deserve. Better that they remain motherless than be subject to an unloving and jealous one."

He met Vivian's troubled gaze, holding it with his own. "Now you are wondering what you are doing here alone with me. I am no marriage prospect, as you were led to believe."

"You have surprised me, that is all," Vivian said, the weakness of her voice belying the words. She tried to smile. "I had been expecting to hear that you were divorced, or had beaten your wife, or that she had thrown herself from a window in despair of being married to you."

"That would have been better?"

"No, only more expected," she said, and to his astonishment her strained smile stretched to one more natural, as if she could almost see humor in the situation. Where, he did not know.

"I say, I don't look like a wife beater, do I?" he asked.

"I would not know. But perhaps you are someone a woman would throw herself from a window to avoid."

"I think some have tried."

"Perhaps if you made a habit of being more polite in your speech, a little more fawning and gracious, they might ponder longer before the leap."

"I prefer to have the truth laid out plain and unadorned, and let people think what they may." They resumed walking

156

up the hill toward the ruins, skirting at least for the moment the subject of his past mistress. He did not fool himself into thinking it was an issue she could so easily overlook, and wondered what thoughts would eat away at her later, when she had time to think it through.

"Yes, you seem to have made a special effort to make yourself as blunt in your speech as possible."

"You are well matching me in that," he said, enjoying the banter, and willing to endure whatever arrows she chose to shoot at him as long as she kept talking.

"Only because it seems to be what you respond to best."

"Then you admit to humoring me, for your own ends."

"And what if I do? Don't we all do that?" she asked, slightly out of breath from the climb. Even through her breathing he could hear the trace of bitterness in her voice.

They had reached the top of the hill, and the heart of the ruins. He stopped so that she could catch her breath, and so that they could both take in the stone walls that rose and tilted and tumbled around them.

"It should have been time that did this," he said, gesturing to the stones around them, "not men."

"It does take away the romance," she agreed.

He led her in a slow circuit of the ruins, and paused with her at an opening in the stones that looked down over the valley and the village of Corfe Castle, gray against the green of the rolling hills.

"Do you always humor those around you?" he asked, not willing to let that bitterness escape unexplored.

"I haven't had much choice," she said, still looking down upon the view.

"It seems a hard way to live, always pleasing others and never yourself."

"One becomes trained in it," she said, "like a cook or a

seamstress. It becomes one's work, for it is how one earns one's bread."

"That hardly seems to be a wise thing to admit."

"I am being honest about my dishonesty," she said, and looked up at him with confusion. "Only, with you, the more I seek to be as straightforward as you wish, the less I know if I am seeking to please you, or to please myself. I am growing to like saying what I think."

"And did you calculate that that is precisely the right thing to say to me?" he asked lightly, although his heart was thumping in his chest. It was so long since he had been with someone who could speak plainly to him of her thoughts. He had told himself for nearly two years that if he could find a woman who cared more for the honesty of her heart than for appearances, he would find a woman with whom he could share his life.

He wanted a wife. He wanted someone with whom to grow old, and watch their children grow. He wanted someone to pull into his arms at night, and sleep warm against him. He wanted someone who knew him completely, and whom he could know to the depths of her being. Life was not meant to be lived alone.

"Do stop thinking about yourself and what a grand matrimonial catch you are," she said, stepping away and finding a seat on a fallen bit of wall.

His lips parted in surprise, her words like cold rain against the warmth of his desires. They reminded him that he had not won her yet.

"Are you now thinking that you have created a monster?" she asked. "So be it. My nerves are worn from this, this . . ." She paused, waving her hand around. "Whatever you call this interplay between men and women. You don't have anything to eat, do you?"

"No, I'm sorry," he said, smiling to himself. Perhaps he should carry a pocketful of treats and win her that way. Would that do it?

She put her hand over her stomach and frowned. "That's all right. I don't think I'm as hungry as I thought." She cocked her head, staring at him in surprise. "Actually, the more I say what is on my mind, the less hungry I become. It seems quite beneficial."

"It's what I've come to believe."

She narrowed her eyes at him, and he fidgeted under her assessing gaze. He sat down beside her, if only to escape such frank scrutiny. She had managed to turn the tables neatly upon him, taking on the role of frank examiner that he was accustomed to having as his own.

"I think there's a touch of self-righteousness to your honesty," she said.

"Self-righteousness?" he repeated, appalled.

"Dear me, have I gone too far, and shared too much truth?"

"I am not self-righteous," he said in a priggish tone that seemed to prove the opposite.

"Self-righteous and a bit of a coward," she continued, "as much so as I am."

He crossed his arms over his chest, feeling more uncomfortable by the moment. "Explain yourself."

"All this honesty—you think it makes you unassailable because you are virtuous." The accusation came in a straightforward manner, and she caught him with her eyes. "You use your bluntness to guard yourself, and scare people away."

"Nonsense."

"I am not berating you for it."

"I did not say you were. I'm saying it's nonsense. I say what I think because I'm tired of hypocrisy, not because I want to frighten people." As he spoke, he became aware that he was protesting too much, aware that he would not be defensive if she had not come close to a truth he would rather not examine.

"Mmm."

"You don't believe me?"

"You know your reasoning better than I," she said, in a tone that suggested very much the opposite.

"I'm not trying to scare *you*," he said, and laid his hand over hers.

She laughed nervously, moving her hand beneath his as if she might pull it away. "Aren't you?"

Maybe he was. Maybe he was trying to keep her from seeing clearly into him before he was ready to reveal all his faults and weaknesses. He wanted her to see the better side of him, to focus her attention on what he could offer her rather than what he might lack.

The best defense was an offense, was it not?

He picked up her gloved hand, feeling its fine trembling. He watched her expression, her lips parting, her eyes on their two hands. Her nervous expectation was contagious, and he found his own heart beating rapidly; he was frightened that she would pull away, yet he wanted more than anything to continue.

He raised her hand to his lips and kissed the back of her fingers. She jerked her hand, and he tightened his grip, not letting her go.

"Mr. Brent . . ." she said.

"Richard. My name is Richard." Let her say his name; let her accept him. Let this grow to be more than a brief acquaintance.

He opened her hand and laid her palm against his cheek, then turned his face so that he could kiss the inside of her wrist where it was left exposed at the edge of her glove.

She caught her breath.

He drew in the faint scent of her, mingled with the leather and the wool, delicate and feminine and ineffably precious. This was something he wanted in his life for more than an afternoon.

He pushed up her sleeve an inch, and followed it with his lips, then painted a stroke upon her soft skin with the tip of his tongue, losing himself in the velvety smoothness and warmth.

"Mr. Brent!" The words were breathless, and again she tried to pull her hand away, and again he stopped her.

"Richard. Call me by my Christian name."

"You must stop," she said. But the words were half-hearted.

He sucked against her wrist, using his tongue to rub her, willing her to feel the same heat that was growing in him, willing her to feel the beginnings of a bond between them and the promise it might hold for the future.

"You must . . . Richard . . ." she said, and when he looked up at her from under his brows he saw that her eyes were half-closed, and she was leaning toward him.

He began to slowly peel her glove down her hand, exposing its heel and the base of her thumb. He slid his finger under the thin leather, rubbing against the palm of her hand, which was damp and warm in the confines of the glove. Her fingers curled inward, and her breathing quickened.

"This is indecent," she whispered. Her pupils had grown into black pools against the sea green irises. She wet her lips.

He peeled the glove another two inches, to the base of her fingers, and kissed the palm of her hand. He scraped against her skin with his teeth, and then with the tip of his tongue penetrated into the tight vee exposed between each finger, imagining behind his closed eyes his tongue working more intimate places than her hand, imagining his mouth at the warm heart of her, making her moan with pleasure in the dark confines of his bed.

He felt his own body responding to the feel of her skin against his tongue, and to the sound of her quickened breathing. He wanted more than her hand: he wanted much more than any young lady would permit upon such short acquaintance, however bold she tried to be.

If he allowed this to go any further he might truly scare her away, and that was something he was not willing to risk.

He kissed her palm once more, then reluctantly pulled the glove back down her hand. He released her, then gently brushed the back of his fingers against her cheek, as if his hand could kiss her for him.

"Your cousin will be wondering what has become of us," he said softly.

"Will she?" she asked, as if lost in a dream.

"She will, and she's likely half-frozen by now, which serves her right for pretending to be hurt." He stood and helped Vivian to her feet.

"I do not regret that she did. Good gracious," Vivian said, looking down at her gloved hand. "I had never thought of such a thing happening to my hand."

He laughed, and laid his own hand over hers in the crook of his arm. He felt hopeful, and giddy with it. A quiet voice warned that it was wisest to go slowly, that it was too soon to know if they were right for one another, but he ignored it.

For this one moment, he would allow himself to hope.

* Chapter Five *

December 27
The Feast of Saint John the Evangelist

"Vivian, my dear," Mrs. Twitchen said. "I am so glad to
have found you alone."

Vivian was curled into a corner of a window seat, pillows
beneath and around her to ward off the chill through the
glass, a book in her lap to make it seem she was otherwise
occupied than watching the drive in hopes that Lady Sudley
and Mr. Brent might come to call.

Penelope was upstairs, fussing over whether or not to
change the trim on her white presentation gown. She had
forestalled all her mother's attempts at speaking on the topic
of Mr. Brent, but as Mrs. Twitchen sat herself down on the
window seat Vivian felt no quiver of foreboding.

Richard had already explained about Sara and William's
mother, in more detail than Mrs. Twitchen would share. She

could understand why Mrs. Twitchen had been concerned, but she thought that she would, in time, be able to overcome the discomfort the thought of that fallen woman brought her.

Jealousy nibbled at her heart when she thought of the woman he had loved and who had given him children who were the center of his world. By his own admission the woman was beautiful and charming, and though he discounted those traits as valueless, she knew she would be tempted to hold herself against them in weak comparison, and to wonder if Richard had any last ember of feeling for the woman.

She would be strong, though; she would not let such thoughts destroy her confidence. It was as Penelope had said: he would value Vivian as Vivian valued herself. She would not let thoughts of the former mistress destroy her chance at happiness.

To let the past eat at her would be to invite a lifetime of distress, if it should happen that she and Richard were to wed. The woman, having not had the good grace to die or move to South America, would be making regular, if infrequent, appearances in Sara's and William's lives. Which meant—if Vivian became Mrs. Brent—in her own life, as well.

It was not a pleasant thought.

Neither was it an undigestible thought. There was much she could swallow if it meant becoming Mrs. Brent, and she was almost embarrassed to admit that a fair deal of the persuasion had been done by Richard's mouth on her hand.

She had relived a dozen times his seduction of her hand, and with each remembrance her body flushed anew with pleasure, her blood warming and tingling in intimate places. She schemed in her mind for how they might next find a private moment together, when he could again take her hand and ravish it.

Or ravish all of her. Let him have her! Then they would have to marry, and she would rush to the prize without having to play all the steps in the game. Only the prize was no longer marriage for the sake of marriage, but was Richard himself.

She saw his tenderness for his children; she saw his vulnerability that he hid behind his blunt words; she saw that his scandalous decisions regarding his children were the only choices that had true honor to them, not the false honor of society. He was a good man, with a true and gentle heart.

And he made her body feel things she would not speak of to Penelope or Mrs. Twitchen for all the cakes in France.

She was so consumed with thoughts of Richard that she had eaten only half the gingerbread on her plate. It sat now in a pool of lemon sauce on the small table with her cold cup of tea.

"Is something amiss?" she asked Mrs. Twitchen, as the woman sat next to her in the window seat. She pulled up her feet to make more space.

"Nothing so far, I do hope, and it is my duty to prevent what I may. Only this is so very awkward and embarrassing, Mr. Brent being a relative of sorts. And from such a good family! One hesitates to say anything against him, yet I feel I *must*, I simply *must* warn you away from him."

"Is it the mother of his children that distresses you?"

"You know about that, then?" the lady asked, surprised.

"He told me himself."

"Then he told you as well about the other woman, the young lady of good family whom he jilted?"

Vivian sucked in a breath, taken by the same surprise with which one slips and falls on the ice.

"I see he did not," Mrs. Twitchen said. "Dear me, I do hate telling such tales, and about one almost in my own family! It was a horrible scandal. They were engaged, and he broke it off without explanation. The girl's father sued for breach of contract, and besides for paying her a settlement Mr. Brent was forced to put an apology accepting all blame in the *Gazette*. Of course, no one will have anything to do with him now."

"Surely he had some reason?"

"If he did, he never spoke publicly of it. And who would dare to ask?"

"I can hardly warrant that he is guilty of such a thing," Vivian said, willing herself to disbelieve.

"Mr. Brent may have kind places in his heart, but that does not mean you can trust him. Men are not always what they seem when they have their eye on a young woman and are pursuing her. Remember, even a tyrant like Napoleon probably had one or two good traits amidst all the rest, and I imagine he could be as charming as any other when he pleased."

"Mr. Brent does not seem like such a man," Vivian said faintly, her view of him turned upside down, tumbling away from the image she had built, all her growing affections now in peril of destruction.

"Be careful, my dear," Mrs. Twitchen said. "My husband and I are in agreement. We don't want to see you hurt, or what chances you have at making a match ruined."

"Thank you," Vivian said.

She spent the remainder of the afternoon staring out the window at nothing. And eating gingerbread.

Chapter Six

December 28
The Feast of the Holy Innocents

The great hall at Haverton rang with the excited shouts and laughter of children. The puppet show had just finished, and now the thirty or so children were going at the sweets and the games. Adults milled among them, imposing the barest sense of order.

"It's a Sudley tradition on Innocents' Day," Penelope said, standing beside Vivian as they observed the chaos. "I remember coming here as a child, myself. All the children of the parish are invited, no matter who their parents might be. Mama never liked me playing with the common children, but it didn't bother me overmuch that they were present, and really, it was easy enough to stay away from them."

Watching the children, Vivian thought they showed far

less snobbishness than Penelope. The well- and poorly dressed played games and ran around with the same shrieking joy, and those who stuck to their own kind seemed to do so only because they were known friends.

Her eye lit upon Richard keeping an eye on William, who was trying to play with boys larger than himself. Her heart contracted, and she felt suddenly wistful, wondering what it would have been like to grow up protected by such a loving hand. She had never met a man like Richard Brent, who was so closely involved in the rearing of his children.

Mrs. Twitchen had tried to warn her away from him, and the tale of the jilting preyed upon her mind, adding its weight to the mistress and the children as things she would have to accept, but she had to believe that once she heard Richard's side, he would prove to have had good reason for his actions.

Surely there must have been good reason? She could not have been so wrong about him, could she?

The tables of sweets beckoned to her, and she excused herself from Penelope and wound her way toward them.

Three or four women guarded the tables, ensuring that greedy fingers did not wreak havoc. They talked among themselves, and nodded their greetings to Vivian as she looked over the goods on offer.

"They're darlings, but it's a bit of a madhouse, don't you think?" someone said beside her.

She turned to see Lady Sudley. "It's a lovely idea," she said, feeling a little shy.

"And no doubt every child will go home sick from overeating and excitement." And then to Sara Brent, who had appeared at her side, reaching for a jam tart, "Sara! Little elf, what are you up to?"

"Papa said I could have some," Sara said, her hand hovering over the prize.

"Did he? Well, I suppose that's all right then," Lady Sudley consented. "Miss Ambrose, this is Sara Brent."

"Hello, Miss Brent," Vivian said, waggling her fingers at the girl.

Sara said nothing.

"Sara, Miss Ambrose is going to watch after you for a bit. Do be good for her," Lady Sudley said. And then to Vivian: "You don't mind, do you? There is so much for me to oversee. . . ." She trailed off, looking at Vivian expectantly.

"No, not at all," Vivian agreed.

"Splendid," Lady Sudley said, and with that the woman glided off.

Sara looked up at her, then grabbed the jam tart and took a bite.

"Is it good?" Vivian asked. If it had been anyone's child but Richard's, she would have been at ease, for it would not have mattered if they did or did not like each other. But with this child it did matter, and in consequence she was tense.

Sara nodded.

"Then maybe I'll have one." She picked up one of the small plates and put a tart on it. It looked small and alone on the plate. She put another beside it.

Sara watched her with interest.

"What about those things with the sugar on them, do they look good to you?"

Sara chewed her tart and nodded again.

"I think so, too." She added one to her plate. "The bits with the sausage?"

Sara made a face.

"No, no good, I agree. Who wants sausage when they can have . . . lemon!"

"I like marchpane," Sara said.

"So do I! Oh, marchpane is an excellent choice. Will you choose a piece for me?"

Sara complied. "The little cakes are pretty."

"So they are," Vivian said. "Which do you think is prettiest?"

They went down the length of two tables, Vivian grabbing a second plate to hold all the treats that Sara chose. The overseeing women gave her questioning looks that she tried to ignore.

"Are you going to eat all that?" Sara asked her in amazement when both small plates were piled high.

"Yes, I believe I will."

"Papa won't let me eat so many."

"I'm a big girl, and I can eat as many as I wish, but maybe I need some help. Would you like to help me?"

Sara nodded and followed her over to some empty chairs. There the girl soon began directing Vivian in which to eat when, and nibbled two or three treats herself.

The plates were nearly empty, and she and the little girl, she thought, were on fine and comfortable terms when Richard found them.

"Papa! Miss A'brose ate this many!" Sara said, holding her two hands out, the fingers spread. "She ate more than Stinky!"

"Stinky?" Vivian asked.

"Our old greedy dog at my house in Wiltshire," Richard explained.

"Stinky ate my supper, and he ate Willie's pudding, and he runs around the floor going *snort snort snort*," Sara said, imitating the grunting dog. "He'll eat anything, even green meat—"

"I think Miss Ambrose understands," Richard interrupted, biting his lip.

"Cook yells at Stinky. He goes to the kitchen and steals things. He's a very bad dog. He eats horse poo."

"Oh. Ah. I see," Vivian said.

"Then he licks my face," Sara said. "Ewww!"

"But you love Stinky, don't you?" Richard asked his daughter.

"He smells bad. Can we go home now, Papa?"

"Soon, sweeting. In another week."

"I'm going to go play now," Sara said, and slid off her chair.

"Excuse yourself," Richard reminded the girl.

"Your pardon," Sara said to Vivian, then the child gave her a quick curtsy and ran off.

"Horse poo?" Vivian said faintly. She had thought she and Sara were getting along so well, and here the girl had been wondering if she would eat horse manure off the ground, given the chance.

"She's really very fond of Stinky," Richard said. He sat down beside her, and reached for the one remaining tart on her plate. "May I?"

"Please." She doubted she would ever be able to eat in public again. And maybe that was for the best.

She felt the questions she needed to ask in the back of her throat, waiting to come out, but couldn't bring herself to do so just yet. Instead she watched the children as Richard ate the tart. "Sara seems a very bright child," she said into the brief silence.

"She is, and cheerful. She has enough willful mischief in her that I will have a head of white hair before she is grown and wed."

"And William?"

"He is quieter, more subdued. He'll spend his time reading dreary philosophy, I imagine, and have to be pushed to court a girl."

"He's a handsome little boy. I think he will set hearts aflutter, if he is brooding and introspective as a man. The young ladies will be unable to resist."

"Poor little fellow."

"You don't think he would enjoy the attention?" she asked.

"Perhaps. He might surprise me." Richard was quiet for a long moment, his gaze on the playing children. "There are times my heart almost breaks, thinking of them growing up, and suffering the pains the world has to offer. Their hurts now are so small, and so easily soothed compared to what they will endure when they are older."

"They will have you to help them," she said, lightly touching his arm and drawing his attention. "And while their hurts may grow greater, so will their strength."

He laid his hand over hers, on his forearm. "You had to quickly grow strong, didn't you? When your parents were killed."

She dropped her eyes, not eager to share that pain that she thought deeply buried, but which at times like this could emerge as easily as if it were just beneath the surface. "That was more than any child should be asked to bear." She made herself smile, and met his eyes again. "But I survived."

He lifted her hand off his arm, raised it to his lips, and, heedless of the roomful of people, let his lips graze her knuckles before releasing her. "And you are beautiful in your strength," he said. The look he gave her seemed to say a million things, all of them new to her and oh so wonderful.

She clasped her hands together in her lap to keep them from trembling, and felt her cheeks and neck heat with embarrassment.

She was falling in love with this man. The realization hit her fully, and it scared her.

She had no experience with romantic love, but she felt herself teetering on its brink, and with her fall would go any last vestige of sense or practical hesitation. She did not want to ask about the woman he had jilted—she wanted to assume the best of him—but if she was wrong it might be her own heart that would be crushed in reward for her ignorance.

For as she felt her heart opening to love, she felt how very fragile and defenseless it was. She had only herself to guard and protect it.

"I need to ask you a personal question, Richard," she said. Children still shrieked and played a few feet from them, and she welcomed their presence as a damper against whatever reaction he might have.

"Anything."

Mrs. Twitchen appeared, forestalling the question. "Vivian, dear, here you are," she said.

Richard stood, bowing in greeting. "Mrs. Twitchen, a pleasure to see you."

"Good day, Mr. Brent. You will excuse me if I take my cousin away from you? I fear we must be going."

"Might I have a few moments?" Vivian asked.

"I'm afraid not, my dear," Mrs. Twitchen said, and her expression said she would not be dissuaded. "We really must go."

Vivian had been wrong in thinking she had only herself to guard her heart. Mrs. Twitchen stood before them as resolute as an armored knight, waiting to carry her to safety.

And so, unsatisfied by her lack of answers, yet touched by Mrs. Twitchen's concern, Vivian made her good-byes.

Chapter Seven

December 31
New Year's Eve

It had been three days since she had seen Richard, and her body yearned for him as if he were her other half. She had never before understood what people meant when they said such things, but now she did. It was shocking, but she felt ripped in two, and as if she could not rest until he was with her again. His clever words, his gentleness with his children, his honesty—all these things played in her mind and far outstripped all the bad things that had been said about him. She loved him.

Worse, she did not know if he felt the same way. For an hour after leaving Haverton Hall on Innocents' Day she would have said yes, he did. Yes, he was beginning to care for her as she did for him. But then the doubts had crept in, carried by the unasked, and therefore unanswered, question about the jilted fiancée. Perhaps that girl, too, had thought that he was falling in love with her, and had been surprised to find herself discarded.

Oh, dreaded time apart, that let her mind form horrid futures as often as happy ones! She had doubts and fears and hopes, and no one with whom to discuss them except Penelope, who listened avidly but was too inexperienced herself to have worthwhile advice to offer. The girl's unexpected sympathy was welcome, but did little to soothe.

What could she do? Would she dare to try to catch Mr. Brent in a compromising position to force him to marry her? She supposed that it wouldn't force anything. He had reneged on a promise of marriage before. . . . Still, if they just had time together, Vivian was certain the union would work. She was sure that she could love Mr. Brent's children. That would be easy, as easy as loving Richard himself.

The mirror was revealing the effects of her anxiety: one week in the Twitchen household, and already the hollows and bony protuberances of her face and figure were beginning to soften. She was eating herself to calmness.

"What are you doing, hiding away over here?" Penelope asked, pulling back the curtain that half hid her where she sat in the window seat, looking out at the night and eating a dish of cheese and spiced nuts she had put together as a post-dessert dessert.

"Just thinking."

"Come out of there. People are arriving, and Mama will be playing the piano for dancing."

"Has Mr. Brent . . . ?" she asked, perking up.

"Not yet. I assume he will be here soon, though, and you don't want him to find you with your teeth full of cheese."

Vivian self-consciously put a fingernail to the groove between her front teeth.

"Emily is here, too. You remember, the vicar's daughter. She wants to do fortune-telling for our future husbands."

"I thought you did that with her on Christmas Eve."

"It didn't work. Come with us; maybe it will work with you there."

"All right." Vivian gave in, emerging from her hideaway. Penelope and her silly friend were not the company she desired, but they were better than sitting and stewing in her own thoughts. After all, she wouldn't want Richard to arrive and think she had been waiting for him like a girl with nothing else to occupy her mind. It was New Year's Eve!

The church bells rang out midnight, and the countryside echoed with clanging pans, bells, shouts, and the blasts of guns. It was the first day of the new year, the Eighth Day of Christmas, and the Feast of the Circumcision, and the celebration was all around. Richard waited in the darkness down the drive from Copley Grange, watching as the guests went back inside as the sounds faded away.

The door was closed, and then a minute later it opened again and was left ajar, warm yellow candlelight spilling out into the blue-black winter night. He knew that in back a door had been opened and shut, letting the old year out, and now the front door was letting in the new.

And he would be the man who did First Footing at Copley Grange. The first visitor through the door in the new year, if a dark-haired male, would bring good luck to the house, according to the superstition. He double-checked his satchel with its required gifts, and headed up the drive.

A smiling maid closed the door behind him when he entered, and he made his way to the drawing room.

"Hurrah!" the cheer went up when he stepped inside. The

enthusiastic greeting surprised him, and he felt a flush of surprised embarrassment. It had been so long since he had felt truly welcome in any home but his sister's, he had forgotten what it felt like.

He grinned and gave a courtly bow. In stately manner he walked up to Captain Twitchen, standing by the fire, and drew out of his satchel the first of the gifts, a hunk of coal.

"To keep your home warm," he said, handing the captain the black lump.

"Hear, hear!" the gathering cheered.

Richard turned to Mrs. Twitchen and took out the next gift, a round loaf of bread. "To keep you fed."

Mrs. Twitchen curtsied and accepted, amid another cheer.

"And lastly . . ." Richard said, putting his hand into the satchel and holding it there for a moment, building the suspense, although they all knew what was coming. He pulled out the bottle of whiskey and held it high, then bowed again and presented it to Captain Twitchen. "For your happiness and your health throughout the new year!"

The final presentation was met with a final cheer and a round of applause. Captain Twitchen slapped him on the back, then went to work opening the bottle and sharing the blessings with the male guests.

Still feeling self-conscious in a way his usual bluntness never made him feel, Richard cast his eyes over the room, his gaze lighting upon Vivian. She was smiling, her eyes sparkling, her face aglow. He would like to think it was aglow for him. She was the reason he had persuaded himself to this display of good fellowship, in hopes of impressing her with his long-dormant social graces.

Sara had not been able to stop talking about "Miss A'brose," who had impressed her greatly with her sweet tooth. He himself had been content to let Sara prattle, his own thoughts on how close he had felt to Vivian as they sat and talked on Innocents' Day.

He had known Vivian for only a week, and yet his hopes were quickly growing that this Christmas he had been gifted with the wife he wanted. What did the shortness of the time matter, when you had found the one with whom you were meant to be?

He made conversation with those near him, listening with half an ear as Captain Twitchen, the whiskey bottle turned over to another for distribution, jingled a purse of coins that he then gave to his wife. "Money for pins, my dear," the captain said.

Would that next year he himself had a wife to whom to give pin money, a wife who would laugh and thank him as Mrs. Twitchen thanked her husband now. Vivian.

He moved through the guests, shaking hands and exchanging pleasantries until at last he found his way to her. She ducked her head, a blush on her cheeks, then looked quickly up at him, smiling.

"When will you stop being shy with me upon greeting?" he asked, feeling his own heart pick up its pace, his growing attachment to her leaving his heart vulnerable to the slightest sign of rejection. To want was to risk being denied.

"I could not say. You have surprised me tonight. I would never have expected you to be first through the door."

"You cannot have thought I would let the new year begin without seeing you," he said, then waited an eternity in the space of a heartbeat for her response.

"I had hoped you would not," she answered quietly.

He laughed with relief. He put her hand in the crook of his elbow and led her to a quieter end of the room, where they stood near a bust of a long-dead Twitchen ancestor, pretending to examine it.

"There's a cobweb in your hair," he said, spotting the wisp of gray, and brushing it away with his fingertips. "What have you been doing?"

"Fortune-telling in the cellar. Penelope and the vicar's daughter insisted I come with them."

"Why the cellar?"

"My guess is because it is dark and cold and suitably unnerving. They had a silver dish full of water, in which they dropped a ring, and we sat around it in the light of single candle, waiting for . . ."

"Waiting for?" he prompted.

"For the faces of our future husbands to appear," she said, as if embarrassed to admit it. "Someday Sara will do the same thing with her friends, I imagine."

"And did his face appear?" he asked, moving slightly closer.

"I don't know. It was so dark and cold, and we sat for so long, my mind began to wander."

"Where did it wander?"

"Everywhere," she said.

"Did it wander to me?"

She met his eyes: they were as wide and wary as he knew his own to be. "Would you want it to?"

He reached down and took her hand, and after a glance around the drawing room to check that none were watching, led her through a nearby door that went to the library. She came willingly. The chamber was dimly lit by candles in wall sconces, and it was cool after the body-heated warmth of the drawing room. The voices from the party were but a murmur through the heavy door.

He slowly backed Vivian up against a wall of books, standing with his feet to either side of hers, close enough to touch but not doing so.

"I want your mind wandering to me in every free moment

of your day. I want you to think of me upon rising in the morning, and to find me in your dreams at night."

"You're already there," she whispered, and the words sent a joyous thrill through his heart, frightening in its intensity.

He knew it was foolish to rush things, that he risked scaring her away, but he had to know for certain. To know the depth of her feelings. To know if she was the one. He bent down his head and kissed her. No lady concerned with appearances would stand for such in the middle of a party.

At first her lips were motionless under his—she was likely shocked—but as he continued the kiss she responded, tentatively mirroring his own movements. He pressed up close against her, gently pinning her to the bookcase, until he could feel each soft curve of her body against his own. He deepened the kiss, and she made a small noise in the back of her throat.

He lifted his mouth from hers, his hips still pressed against her lower belly. "Are you all right?"

"Oh, yes," she said, and her slender arms wrapped around his neck.

She wanted him. Against all possibility, all doubt, she wanted him.

He had found the place he belonged, and was finally free. The joy of it sent him wild. He let loose the reins on his desire, exploring her mouth, her neck, the exposed swell of her breasts, each touch making him hungrier for the next. He breathed in the warm, faintly musky scent of her, and then trailed his tongue up to the hollow at the base of her throat where he pressed gently until he could feel the beat of her heart with his lips.

She was his heart, his desire.

He worked his way up and let his tongue play at the sensitive place behind her earlobe, while his hand went down to cup her buttock and pull her against him, where he could press the firmness of his arousal against the softness of her body.

Her breathing was a soft panting against his ear, and he could feel her trembling even as she pressed herself to him.

He fastened his mouth over hers once more and thrust with his tongue in frantic substitute for how he longed to thrust inside her.

She made a soft sound of pleasure, and he felt her fingers working their way into his hair, gripping tight. He pulled her away from the bookcase and backed her slowly to the library table until she bumped up against it. He boosted her up the few inches until she was sitting on its surface.

"What are you doing?" she asked in a whisper.

"Exactly what I wish."

"Good."

Had she said that or sighed? He wasn't sure. He chuckled and parted her knees so he could stand between them, then brought her tight against him. Her eyes widened, and then she wrapped her arms back around his neck and pulled him down on top of her.

He had one hand lost in her hair, the other on her bare thigh, his mouth sucking at her breast and her legs wrapped around his still-clothed hips when the library door opened. The sounds of the party flooded in upon them, accompanied by an outraged gasp.

Vivian heard it as well and reacted with the reflexes of a startled cat, thrusting Richard off her and scrambling to disentangle her legs from his person as he helped her to pull down her skirts. A quick glance told him it was Captain Twitchen who had discovered them.

There could have been no worse—or better—person to

walk through that door. Richard felt a perverse, happy satisfaction stirring within him.

"Mr. Brent!" Captain Twitchen sputtered, then shut the door behind him, blocking off the sounds of the party and the possibility of witnessing eyes. "How dare you, sir! How *dare* you!"

"My deepest apologies, sir."

"A guest in my home, and this is how you repay my hospitality!"

Vivian gave a soft whimper. Richard put his arm around her, pulling her to his side, concerned for her embarrassment. He would not let her be shamed. "It was a transgression against the kindness you have always shown me, and unforgivably ill-mannered," he said. "I hope that you will allow me to make the proper amends."

Captain Twitchen seemed not to have heard. "I never listened to the rumors about you, never let them cloud what I thought I saw before me. But damned if I shouldn't have paid attention. Mrs. Twitchen was right, and even if you are my nephew's brother-in-law, you are unfit for decent company. Vivian! Go to your room, girl, and stay there."

Richard felt her start under his arm, but he held her more firmly. "What we have to say concerns her, as well."

He saw he'd made a mistake when the captain's face, already red, took on a deeper, almost purple shade of rage. His feeling of satisfaction and confidence assumed the barest quiver of uncertainty.

"Contradict my orders, will you? In my own house! My own house!"

"I should go," Vivian whispered.

He did not want her to have to stand here and suffer as a target of Captain Twitchen's fury. The man might say something hurtful. "Perhaps for the moment," he whispered back.

She started to slip away from him, and he bent down and pressed a quick kiss to the top of her head. "Not to worry. You'll be called back down within the hour, I promise."

She cast him a quick glance—was it one of hope and uncertainty?—and he smiled in reassurance.

Once she was safely from the room, Captain Twitchen lent full force to his ire. "Now, sir, are we going to settle this like gentlemen?"

"That is indeed my intention."

"Pistols or swords?"

Richard felt a sinking in his gut. Soothing Captain Twitchen was going to be more difficult than he'd thought.

An hour passed, and there was no call for Vivian to come down. She paced her bedchamber, she listened at her door for footsteps or the distant sound of voices, she watched from her window as guests left in pairs and in groups. She built up the fire in the grate, and wished that there was something to eat.

Horrible, to have been seen by Captain Twitchen with her bare legs wrapped around Richard, flat on her back, his mouth at her breast. She knew that she had briefly entertained causing such a scandal, but . . . The sickening embarrassment of it made her stomach churn. Far worse, was not knowing what was presently happening down in the library.

Another quarter of an hour passed. Was Richard still here? He must be. He and Captain Twitchen must still be arguing. She rubbed her forehead; the muscles there were sore from her frown of worry. Richard had given every indication that he would ask permission to wed her. Captain Twitchen couldn't possibly refuse, could he? Surely his pride could not be so severely offended.

And if it were?

She would marry Richard despite the captain's objections. She would abandon all family ties, if that was what it took. It would be cruel repayment for the generosity the Twitchens had shown her, but there was no other choice. She had to have Richard. She *would* have him.

Only, if she could, she would do so without breaking her ties to her cousins. She found herself surprised. In the short time she had been with them, she had grown fond of them all—Mrs. Twitchen with her social ambitions and motherly heart; Captain Twitchen and his blunt good cheer; even Penelope had become something of a friend, despite her selfishness.

But the one thing Vivian knew about this life was that caring ties to others were more precious than gold, more precious than titles or gowns or beauty. She would not easily give up even the meager ones she had with the Twitchens.

And she would never give up the one she had now with Richard. Never.

Another half hour passed. She was torn between the need to find out what was happening and the fear of interrupting and somehow spoiling whatever advantage Richard may have gained.

She went to the window and gazed down at another pair of partygoers as they departed. She could feel the cold of the night seeping through the glass.

A knock on her door turned her around, and Mrs. Twitchen entered. She rushed towards her cousin, then stopped as she read the distress upon the woman's face.

"Is Mr. Brent still here?" she asked.

"He is, but not for much longer if Captain Twitchen has anything to say about it."

"Tell me, what is happening?"

"This is a fine mess you've managed to get yourself into," Mrs. Twitchen said in a stern voice that quavered on the last word. "A fine mess. I can only be thankful that we are yet in the country, and that it was the captain who came in upon you, and not one of our neighbors—else I don't know how we would have been able to save you from a future with that man."

"The captain hasn't refused Mr. Brent, has he? Surely he could not have!"

"Mr. Brent has nearly caused my husband to fight a duel, that's what he has done! The foolish man!" Mrs. Twitchen wrung her hands and then burst into tears, sinking into the chair by the fire.

Vivian didn't know which man Mrs. Twitchen meant was the foolish one, but she felt a wave a guilt wash over her at the sight of the woman's distress. She went and knelt by her side, and laid her hand on the woman's knee.

"Hush, now. Hush," she said. "Mr. Brent would never engage in the nonsense of a duel."

"Nonsense? This from you, sitting there with your honor in shreds!" Mrs. Twitchen dropped her hands from her wet and reddened face. "Captain Twitchen has more honor in him than Mr. Brent could ever dream of, and knows a coward and a sneak when he sees one. We won't be letting you throw your life away on such a man, that we won't!"

Vivian sat back on her heels, taking her hand from Mrs. Twitchen's knee. She steadied herself to disagree. "Mr. Brent is the most honorable man I have ever known. It may be a peculiar sort of honor, but it is true and deep, and I love him for it. I will marry him, with or without the blessing of you and Mr. Twitchen." She bit her lip. "But I would rather have it."

Mrs. Twitchen's expression softened to one of pity. "You

are not thinking clearly, child. Don't think that because I'm old I do not know what you are feeling, the passions that are in your heart. And that is how I know that this is a time when you must rely on those older and wiser than yourself, who can see with clear eyes. Mr. Brent is a scoundrel, and will bring you nothing but unhappiness. It is too late to save you from the pain of an entanglement with him, but we can at least save you from public dishonor."

She had lived long enough by the rules and wishes of others. No more! "I am past my majority. I can make up my own mind in this."

"Have you forgotten the engagement Mr. Brent broke in the past? Do you not think that other young woman felt as passionately as you do now?"

"I am sure there must have been a good reason behind that." And she was.

"How can you know?" Mrs. Twitchen asked. "You have known Mr. Brent little more than a week. I have been with the captain nigh on two decades, and still do not know him entirely. Anyone can be charming for a week, my dear. Let his history speak to you of who he truly is."

Vivian shook her head and stood. "It is his very history that tells me he is a man worthy of love. You cannot dissuade me from what my heart knows is true." She marched to the door and laid her hand upon the knob.

"Vivian, darling." Mrs. Twitchen rose and came toward her, hands fluttering. "Can you at least give us this one night? Can you at least sleep upon it, and let us know that you have considered fully?"

Vivian took in Mrs. Twitchen's frantic concern, her distress, and wavered. She let her hand fall from the knob. If waiting one night was all that the Twitchens required of her, she would be heartless not to give it. Such was not so much to ask. The bond she felt with Richard would not suffer for a handful of hours apart.

"I will sleep upon it."

Mrs. Twitchen nodded and opened the door herself to go. She was through it and pulling it closed when she paused and turned, her face in the narrow space between door and jamb.

"Forgive me, child. I do this for your own good."

Vivian lunged for the knob, but was too late. The door slammed, and the key turned in the lock from the other side.

She was a prisoner once again, to another's idea of how she should live.

Chapter Eight

Twelfth Night

 $\mathcal{T}$ he few bits of Christmas greenery in her room had been taken down and were waiting now in a dried-out pile to be fed into the fire. Her hopes of a marriage to Richard Brent might as well burn along with it.

Vivian had been locked in her room for five days now, allowed to send no letters nor receive them, and even Penelope was forbidden from visiting. Vivian saw Mrs. Twitchen daily, and suffered through her lectures and, more dangerously, the growth of the seeds of doubt that the woman planted and watered so carefully.

Richard wanted her. She knew he did. He had offered for her, she was sure of it. Did he love her enough to continue to fight for her, whatever the obstacles?

He had never said he loved her. But he must, he surely must! He had given her every indication. She could count her own love for him as nothing, if she could not trust that he would hold steady to his purpose and free her.

The isolation was making her mind play tricks, and she had no biscuits or tarts with which to soothe herself. They were cold meals that were brought to her by Mrs. Twitchen, with nothing of pleasure to be found in them.

As the days passed, her mind turned in upon itself, reluctantly treading garden rows of doubt. She pulled each plant that showed signs of green, whacked them with her hoe, scuffed them over with her shoe, but Mrs. Twitchen always came back to nurse them to health.

Richard Brent was an honest man. He was an honorable man. He would not abandon her. She must hold tight to that truth.

From her window she had twice seen him come to the house, and leave shortly thereafter, always pausing to gaze up at her window, where she stood with her fingers against the glass, as if she could reach through and touch him. But then Captain Twitchen would emerge from the manor and shoo Richard away, preventing any exchange of words between them.

She had not seen him for two days now. Was he himself beginning to doubt the wisdom of pursuing this course? Had the captain convinced him that it would be better for her to marry another, that she would be happier with a man with an unsoiled reputation?

She would not be able to bear it if it were so.

She wished she had lain with him as a wife, there upon the library table, for all to see. There would have been no question then of what their future would be. If she ever saw him again, she knew precisely what she'd do.

✳ ✳ ✳

He had tried reason. He had tried patience. He had put to use all his powers of persuasion, and all to no effect. He had run out of gentle options, a realization that had come to him upon receipt early yesterday of Penelope's letter:

> *Dearest Mr. Brent,*
> *Forgive me for writing to you so, but I feel you must be told: my cousin is being fed only crusts of bread. She has no coal to keep her warm, and is threatened with beatings if she does not give up her insistence that she be allowed to wed you. My father has threatened to send her to a Catholic convent in France, where you would never see her again. I fear for her health—nay! I fear for her very life. She will be dead of grief within a fortnight if she is not saved. I have heard many things about you, but I trust they are not true. Here is your chance to prove yourself.*
>
> > *Yours Faithfully,*
> > *P.*

Of course he knew she was exaggerating—he doubted very much that Vivian would be sent to a French convent, no matter the provocation—and he was somewhat annoyed by Penelope's allusion to his past, but Vivian was confined to her room, that he knew. And he very much doubted that pastries and cakes would be part of the meals sent up to one suffering such a punishment.

His Vivian, without a pudding. What misery must she be suffering! He smiled sadly at the odd thought.

And what might she begin to think, as the days passed and he left her languishing, the only words she heard those painting him as the darkest blackguard. His smile vanished. Might she not begin to think that he had abandoned her? Might she not begin to wonder if the Twitchens were right and if their reasons were ones to which she should listen? Especially since they were so intent upon protecting her that they would lock her up?

That sweet passion she had given him in the library might even now be dying.

He could not let that happen. The time for diplomacy had passed, and it was now time for action. That was the reason he was now creeping toward Copley Grange in the dead of night with a satchel slung over one shoulder and a rope around the other. In a vest pocket he carried a special license to marry, which he had ridden all the way to Dorchester to obtain.

The windows were dark at the grange, as he hoped they would be. He took a handful of gravel from the drive; such stones were the time-honored choice of swains for waking maidens in their bowers. He stood beneath Vivian's window and tossed them at the glass, one by one, wincing at each *plink* of sound.

He was only on his third stone when she appeared, a pale wraith behind the glass. She must have been awake. A moment later she opened the window.

"Richard!" she whispered.

"Shhh! Stand back. I'm going to toss up the end of a rope." He wasn't going to give her the chance to tell him to go away. He was going to rush up, sweep her off her feet, and carry her to safety. This was something he'd always wanted, and he'd finally found someone who was worth his affection. He wasn't going to let her escape—no matter what happened.

He coiled several lengths of his line into a loop heavy enough to throw, and when she had moved away he gave it a heave.

And missed. The rope fell down the side of the house and into the shrubberies.

"Damn!"

"Where's the rope?"

"Shh!" He scrounged around in the bushes, untangling the line, hoping no one in the house heard him thrashing through the branches like a deranged animal.

Coils once again in hand, he gave them another heave, and this time they sailed through the window. He heard the *thunk* as they hit the floorboards, and grimaced.

Vivian appeared again in the window. "What now?"

"Tie it off to the leg of your bed."

"Right." She disappeared, and the dangling rope jerked and swayed in the faint moonlight as she set to work. "Done," she said, appearing again.

He pushed through the shrubberies to the wall of the house, and gave the rope an experimental tug. It felt sound. He jumped up and grabbed as high as he could on the rope, and was rewarded with a groaning screech from above and a slow sinking back to the ground.

"The bed! It's moving!" Vivian whispered.

"Damn! Is there anything heavier in the room?"

"No, nothing. But wait, I think I can brace it."

He waited while she did so, flinching with each sound of dragging furniture, expecting at any moment to see the front door open and an outraged Captain Twitchen appear with pistol in hand. The man would certainly shoot him.

"All right! I think I've got it, but I'm going to have to go sit on the chair."

He didn't inquire what she meant, he just climbed. The rope held, sinking only a few inches, the sounds from the room mere creaks of strained wood rather than groans. His head was almost at the sill when he suddenly dropped several inches. That, and the cry from Vivian were his only warning before he began to fall.

He caught himself by one hand on the sill, releasing the rope that snaked past him and tumbled to the ground. With a grunt of effort he pulled himself up to the window, Vivian grabbing his arm and helping him to where he could straddle the sill.

"My knot gave out," she said.

"I gathered." He released a shaky breath, peering back down at the twenty foot drop to the ground, and to the shadows where their escape route lay twisted in the dirt.

He turned to Vivian. Her hair was down, thick and dark against the white of her nightgown. A nightgown under which, he suspected, she wore nothing at all.

"What are you doing here?" she asked. She looked surprised, bewildered, and awfully pleased.

"Penelope wrote and said you were being starved. I've brought you tarts and cakes." He swung his other leg inside, then took the satchel off and opened it, holding it out for her to see.

"You risked your life to bring me pastries?" She looked a bit sheepish, but moved closer, brushing against him, the satchel ignored. He could smell a hint of flowery soap, and under it the scent that was Vivian's alone.

"I came to take you away." He dropped the sack to the floor and wrapped his arm around her waist, drawing her close. Her flesh was soft and warm under his hand. "Only, I seem to be proving an inept rescuer. I don't know how I'm going to get you safely to the ground without the rope."

"Don't you?"

He was about to say "No, I don't," but then she kissed him and was touching him everywhere, and suddenly there were more important things to do than talk. His other arm went around her, and they stumbled backwards, tripping over the chair laid on its back on the floor as a brace, barely making it to the bed before falling together, sinking into its deep mattress.

Vivian was going to be his wife. If he could not take her through the window, he would take her here, on the bed. Then she would be his forever, and no one could put a door between them ever again.

✳ Chapter Nine ✳

The Feast of the Epiphany

"*It's* almost morning."

"It was the nightingale you heard, and not the lark," Vivian said, and giggled at her paraphrase of Juliet's famous words. She stretched as she lay naked against him, loving the feel of her skin touching his, then threw a leg over his thigh.

"Perhaps you're right." He lay his hand on her leg, his palm gliding up to her buttock.

"Don't move," she said, and slipped from beneath his hand. She found the satchel and brought it back to the bed. "I'm hungry."

"After what we just did, I am not surprised."

She dug a tart out of the satchel and handed it to him. He took it, and she found a half-crushed pastry for herself and downed it. "Heavens, that tastes good." She found another and devoured it while he laughed.

"I have a confession to make," he said, as she handed him a small cake.

She stopped chewing, her heart skipping a beat, a sudden fear taking hold of her. "What is it?" She almost didn't want to hear the answer.

"I seduced you for my own selfish reasons."

"Oh?"

"I was afraid I might not manage to get you out of this house, so I made you mine to be certain Captain Twitchen could not separate us again."

She released her breath and smiled, then started to laugh.

"What?"

"You!" she said, her relief making her giddy.

"Why are you laughing?"

His frown made her laugh all the harder. Then she said, "You didn't seduce me, I seduced you!"

"Nonsense."

She leaned close, her breasts brushing against his chest, and kissed him. Five minutes later they emerged from a tangle of limbs, sheet, and satchel, hearts thumping with newly aroused passion.

"*I* seduced *you*," she said again.

He shrugged, and she could see he was trying to subdue a smile. "All right. But why would you try?"

"For the same reason you gave, and—" she started, and then cut herself off, not knowing if she should continue.

"And what? Speak your heart, Vivian. You know you can always do that with me."

"And I wanted to be sure you could not be rid of me."

He pushed himself upright and grasped her by the shoulders. "Rid of you? I would never want to be rid of you. What could have possibly given you such an idea?"

"Mrs. Twitchen told me about your broken engagement to that other girl," she said weakly.

"Oh, Vivian." He pulled her to him and held her cradled against his chest. "I caught my fiancée pinching Sara, and calling her a little bastard. She had pretended to me that she adored the children, and I had not been wise enough to see the lie."

"She hurt Sara?" Vivian asked in horror, trying to look up at him and seeing only the hard line of his jaw. "How could she? How could anyone?"

"She thought she had the right."

"Why then did you take the blame for breaking the engagement?"

"Because I *did* break it. She would have gone through with the marriage."

"But the public apology . . ." she asked, confused.

"I thought it easier to give them what they asked. I did not need vengeance: I just wanted to be free of her."

"I am so sorry."

"It was not one of the happier times of my life, and I'm afraid it has attached itself to my name. People think I have no honor."

She reached up and lay her hand against his cheek, coaxing him to look at her. "You are the most honorable man I have ever known."

He met her gaze, his dark eyes sheened with tears. "I love you," he said, his voice hoarse with emotion. "You do not know how long I have waited to find you, Vivian Ambrose."

"And I you, my love."

And that was when the door opened, and with a gasp and a cry Mrs. Twitchen fainted to the floor.

* * *

"I think it was only that special license in Mr. Brent's jacket that kept Papa from shooting him," Penelope said, putting the finishing touches to Vivian's hair. "I have never seen him so angry! And the words he used! So vulgar! I'll have a hard time of it in London, with the way he'll be watching me after all this, afraid I'll come to the same bad end. I suppose I deserve it."

"Do you think he'll allow you to visit me?"

"He'll soften in time. Mr. Brent is, after all, a good catch once you overlook a few small details." She paused to examine her work. "There. All done. You look like a princess, as every bride should."

Vivian grasped Penelope's hand, and held it. "Thank you. For everything."

"It's only a gown."

Vivian squeezed her hand and released it, both of them knowing that it was more than the gown that she meant.

And yet, the gown was the gift that, from Penelope, was worth more than all the treasures of the Indies. It was her court presentation gown she had given to Vivian, in which to be wed.

Vivian rose, and together they left the room and walked down the hall to the head of the stairs. Penelope stood to the side and nodded for Vivian to go first, sole focus of the eyes of those who waited below.

She felt like an angel, the heavy white silk of the gown flowing round her in crystal-shimmering waves. She knew she had been blessed, for never in her life had there been a Christmas season as this, where the dearest wishes of her heart had come true.

She descended to the earth, and to the arms of the man she loved. And her family was there to see.

Union

CLAUDIA DAIN

*

To Tom,
who is not only an ideal husband,
but an ideal editor.

Chapter One

London, December 1808

Clarissa Walingford came down the stairs with a step that was so firm and so determined that it came perilously close to being a childish stomp. Her brothers understood both the distinctiveness of her step and the restraint that hobbled it from becoming an all-out tantrum. This evening marked her coming-out.

Clarissa had arrived at that precise moment in a woman's life when a husband must be obtained for her. Clarissa did not want a husband at present, but Clarissa had been well brought up and understood her duty to her family and her name. Clarissa would marry.

But she did not want to marry an Englishman.

"It's not so bad, once you wade in and find your footing," Lindley said.

"Prettily put, Lindley. I can hardly wait," she said, adjusting her shawl.

"Lindley, keep your encouragement to yourself if that's the best you can do," Dalton said, smiling at her.

Dalton's smiles were wasted. She did not want to go.

"It won't be so bad," Perry said, coming close. "You look wonderful. I'm certain that your season will be a smash."

"Kindly keep your vulgar euphemisms to yourself, Perry," Albert said, glowering. "Clarissa will have a successful season because she is a Walingford, has a fine, healthy figure, and lovely, clear eyes. All the Walingfords have done well in their seasons."

Albert, the eldest, had used similar language to describe the new hunter he had just purchased, but Clarissa refrained from making that comparison aloud. She felt that the comparison, though unintentional, was too apt for her tranquillity; she was on the block, so to speak, and would be bid upon by gentlemen who would look her over as carefully as a man purchasing a horse. What else was an offer of marriage but a bid to be rejected or accepted or even negotiated until both seller and buyer each felt himself to have made a good bargain? A woman in such an exchange was neither the seller nor the buyer; she was the horse.

"And your gown is lovely," Jane added with a gentle smile and a brief hug. Jane, sister to Albert's wife, was the soul of compassion, a rare commodity in a houseful of older brothers. Clarissa much appreciated her companionship.

"Yes, what color is that?" Russell asked. "Looks like weak tea with too much milk."

"Lovely," Dalton murmured sarcastically in an undertone just loud enough to be heard by Russell.

"It's called Ivory Bisque, if you must know," Clarissa said, crossing her arms over her chest. "And the decoration around the hem is a thistle design in russet thread. Any other questions or comments about my attire?"

"Well, now that you mention it . . . I don't know why you had to chop off all your hair like that. Makes you look like a boy."

"Clarissa looks nothing like a boy!" Jane protested.

"It's the fashion, you dolt," Dalton said. "Leave the club more than once a month and you'll find out what women are wearing."

"Shut up, Russell," Lindley said, scowling. "You look beautiful, Clarissa. You are beautiful."

"Very fashionable," Perry added.

"Very feminine," Jane said, sounding almost warlike for her.

"I'm quite confident that you'll have an offer of marriage before Christmas," Albert said comfortably.

It was not the sort of compliment she wanted.

She did not want to marry an Englishman.

She was solitary in that opinion and desire. Quite solitary. Even Jane did not understand her distaste for the prospect.

Though even if all understood her reasons, she supposed there was no escape. It was her time and her duty to marry. Certainly Lindley had no desire to marry, and yet he was engaged to Miss Emeline Brookdale, who had agreed to his proposal with the appropriate degree of both eagerness and submission.

She was no Miss Brookdale. She was neither eager nor submissive; in point of fact, she was the exact opposite, a situation that Albert found beyond tolerable. Her other brothers were more tolerant, but then they were not the eldest and had not his duties and responsibilities; oh, yes, she understood all dispassionately. Yet the fact remained: she did not want to marry an Englishman. Small chance of finding anything else in London.

"You'll find someone . . . acceptable," Perry offered.

Acceptable? Perhaps some Scotsman down looking for a wife? That would be more acceptable than having to settle into the rest of her life with an English lord as a husband. As helpful as Perry was trying to be, he was off to a fine military career while she had to tramp about London searching for a husband.

"Will I?" she asked, looking at Perry and then at them all.

"Of course you will, Clarissa; don't be absurd," Albert said. "You must stop this nonsense about not wanting to be married to an Englishman. You are as English as anyone. Whom else would you marry?"

"An Irishman," she answered, her ever-ready answer.

"An Irishman? When all the owners of land and title in Ireland are English?" Albert said gruffly. "Think logically, Clarissa, and be reasonable. You are here for your season. You will attract many admirers and from them you must choose your husband. It is all quite simple."

Yes, it was all quite simple. And there was no avoiding it. Albert, as head of the family, would always have his way in all things.

The carriage was waiting and they went in, Lindley, Perry, and Jane accompanying her on her first of many parties in London. It was a mild night and all that was needed was her shawl, which was somewhat unfortunate, as she would have liked to burrow her face into the folds of a cloak and have a private sulk. Unfortunately, all within the carriage could read her mood well enough.

"Albert is quite right, you know. There is no point in pining for Ireland when we hold all the land worth having," Lindley said.

"Explain the justice of that to me, Lindley, for how that should be so escapes me," Clarissa said.

"I can't change what is in order to suit you, Clarissa,"

Lindley said stiffly. "You know the truth of the situation. You also know that there is no one in Ireland of sufficient station to marry."

"You will find someone, Clarissa," Perry said, taking hold of her hand. "You will be the girl of the season and will have your pick."

"Yes, my pick of Englishmen," she grumbled, squeezing his hand in gratitude before she released him.

"Who holds the land in Ireland, girl? How do you think to regain Ireland if you dismiss the means to grab hold?" Lindley said.

She bit back a reply, forcing herself to consider. Lindley was surly and stubborn half the time, but he had made a valid point. It was beyond question, no matter how unpleasant the prospect, that she would marry an Englishman. Perhaps an Englishman could be found who had an Irish estate. He would, of necessity, remain in England most of the year, while she could live out her life in Ireland. He could come to visit. Or he could not. She would not demand his presence if only she could reside in Ireland again.

Ireland was home.

England, with her destructive policies and disregard for Irish ways, with her planting of British troops on Ireland's soil, was the enemy. And all England's men were English: arrogant and cold, proud and cruel. She understood them well by the soldiers sent to subdue the Irish. Albert was correct: she was English by birth, but her blood and her heart belonged to Ireland. What English husband would understand that?

"Stop scowling, Clarissa," Lindley admonished. "We have arrived."

It was true. The carriage slowed to a stop and the door was opened by a footman. Lindley exited first, followed by

Perry, who then turned to offer a hand to Clarissa. She hesitated, against her better judgment. She had few options. In truth, she had none. It was time to marry, and the only dignity left to her was to put a good face upon it and not disgrace herself or her family.

"'Tis not so bad, Clarissa, to come out into society. I would be much surprised if you did not enjoy yourself completely," Jane said by way of encouragement.

"I cannot disagree if it were only balls and parties and concerts to be enjoyed, but the goal of all the entertainment is to acquire a husband for myself."

"You will have your choice, my dear. None shall force a decision upon you," Jane said softly, taking her hand.

"You are correct in that, and I take what comfort I can in it," Clarissa said. She had to marry, but her brothers knew well enough that she would do her own choosing. "Perhaps 'twill not be so vexing if I can but remember that I do have a choice."

"Clarissa," Lindley called, clearly impatient. A choice she surely had, but Lindley was eager for her to make it.

Without another word to either bolster her courage or delay the inevitable, Clarissa stepped down from the carriage and walked up the steps into the brick town house on Grosvenor Street. Host and house had been amply prepared for a small gathering of twenty-five or so, all friends to greater or lesser degree of the host. Jane was an old friend of their hostess, Lady Morland, and it was to her good grace that Clarissa owed her invitation.

Good breeding required that she be polite anyway.

Lindley and Perry disappeared readily enough after being greeted by Lord and Lady Morland, leaving Clarissa and Jane and Lady Morland—or Fanny, as Jane called her—in an intimate conversation of three, two of whom were happily engaged in conversation, one of whom was pretending to be.

"A lovely gathering," Jane said to Fanny. "The candlelight looks so well against these walls. When did you repaint?"

"In the autumn," Fanny replied. "I found myself dismally bored with the green and chose this tawny gold instead, just for the warmth and light it seemed to offer."

"It is wonderful. Very daring," Jane said.

"I suppose I should confess, or perhaps it is obvious, that I chose the color after a month of cold rain and heavy cloud. I was yearning for the gleam of sunlight, I daresay."

"What nature will not provide, man must supply." Jane smiled. "Don't you think it a lovely color, Clarissa?"

"Yes, it is lovely. So . . . warm," Clarissa said. She did not care about the color of the walls.

The room was full of pleasant-looking people, fully half of them men, and perhaps six of them under thirty, excluding Perry and Lindley. Was she to choose from this random collection? And if so, how was she to go about making her choice? Age was one factor to be considered. She did not want a husband more than twice her age; the tendency would be for him to be rather fatherly, and she did not yearn for that characteristic in a husband.

"And how is your mother, Fanny? Has her cough abated? I have been most concerned about her."

"That is very kind of you, Jane. No, she is still weak and abed much of the day. I think a walk in the gardens would do much to clear her lungs, but the weather is so damp yet that it is not to be."

"Perhaps the weather will clear by Christmas," Jane said.

"Perhaps. In the interim, Dr. Spenser has prescribed a soothing tonic that has the added benefit of aiding her sleep. I think all will be well in time."

"Clarissa, what was it you drank when you suffered last winter from that sharp cough?"

"It was chamomile added to my tea that brought me some relief," Clarissa said quietly, forcing her eyes away from the corners of the room and the men who loitered there. It would not do to appear too forward; naturally all knew that she was looking for a husband, but to be blatant in her search would not put her in a good light. It would be a very tedious search if she had to practice such discretion week after week. She did hope to have the whole thing settled by the new year.

Across the room, loitering in a dimly lit corner, Lindley was aiding her in her search, though she could not know it.

"Did I not tell you? Such beauty you will rarely find," Lindley said softly.

"It is rare as well to find such eagerness on the part of a brother to rid himself of a sister," Beau answered.

"I do not rid myself of her, but rather encourage you to become a part of my family. I do not do so lightly," Lindley said stiffly.

Beau, known to most as Henry Wakefield, Lord of Montwyn, laughed and said, "Still more starch than sense, Walingford. I was jesting. She is a fine-looking woman, as you said."

And she was. Hair of bright auburn, skin pale and smooth as milk, eyes the dark brown of rich chocolate; she was a beauty. Shapely and of a good height, not as petite as the current fashion, but then, he had no desire for a small wife, fearing that carrying his babe and delivering herself of it might kill her. Too many women died so. He was a large-knit man and he wanted a wife he wouldn't dwarf.

"She is just come out, so the field may well be yours. If you do not hesitate," Lindley said.

"You *are* eager, aren't you?" Beau chuckled. "Well, the

season is early and I do not fear a more protracted interlude before the rigors of matrimony. Do not mistake me," Beau said into Lindley's frown. "I am interested, particularly if her manner matches her look, for she does please the eye, and, of course, her family is impeccable." He smiled. "I will look and I will woo, if the mood strikes."

"Does one require a certain mood to obtain a wife?"

"No, but the mood for haste is certainly not upon me. I need a wife. Why not the sister of a friend? Yet there is time to enjoy the season and to undertake my introduction to your sister slowly."

"You are not the only man in London this season," Lindley said grimly.

"Nor is she the only woman. Come." Beau laughed lightly. "Let us not come to blows over this. I am taken with her. You spoke truly when you described her to me. Let it proceed as it will. By all that I can see, I will offer for her. But I will not be rushed to the altar, no matter how eager or fetching the maid."

Lindley kept his tongue firmly between his teeth so that Beau would not so soon know that Clarissa was anything but eager.

Jane was battling that knowledge at that precise moment.

"He is a rather handsome gentleman," Jane said softly into her glass, her observation for Clarissa's ears only. "A friend of Lindley's, by the look of it."

Clarissa had taken note of him. How could she not? He was a man of above average height, dark of hair, with a fine brow and a well-shaped mouth. His dress was of the highest quality and cut, his hair well-groomed, and his cravat impeccable. It was equally obvious that he knew he cut a fine figure. His pride affected her mood like cold water on a frigid day; there was no warmth in her toward him, as she could detect no warmth in him. He called from her, for all his masculine appeal, only the chill of winter. Though it was difficult to keep her eyes from him.

"He has a loose button. I cannot abide a slovenly man," Clarissa said, turning her face away from the sight of him.

"A loose button?" Jane was incredulous. "At this distance? And surely, if so, his valet is to be blamed and not the man himself."

"You are of a generous nature, Jane, a trait I find most welcome, most comforting, but in this instance, when I must choose a husband, I must be exacting in my standards. I will not wed a slattern."

"Surely a wife would be of assistance to him. If a slattern he is—and I do not say so, for I think he is a most fine-looking gentleman—then a wife's gentle counsel would cure such an ill. He but wants feminine care."

Clarissa looked over her shoulder at the man. With his looks, she was quite sure that feminine attention was not something he lacked. He was a most . . . rigorous-looking man.

"He looks very English," Clarissa said instead.

Jane smiled and arranged her shawl over her shoulders. "As do we all, I would say. It will be a fault most difficult to cure."

"Impossible, you mean to say," Clarissa said. "Would that there were a single Irishman in the room. I would happily give myself into his keeping."

"And into his small cottage?" Jane said. "You know Lindley spoke only the truth. Who among the native Irish owns a fine Irish estate? To have the life to which you have been born, you must marry a man as English as yourself."

Clarissa tried not to bristle at the insult, for she saw it as nothing less. Jane meant well and, as far as she was able, spoke the truth.

"I do understand your fascination with the Irish," Jane continued, looking down at her hands, "for during my own come-out, I developed a fondness for an Irishman who spoke tenderly and beautifully to me. I would have married him and even believe he would have asked, if not for my father's blunt refusal to have any part of him. So you must see, I share your frustration in being urged to marry against one's heart. But cannot the heart learn to follow where the mind has led?"

Perhaps. Perhaps the mind could lead the heart. She had a good mind; it should not be terribly difficult to command her heart to follow where reason led. Yet Jane had never married, never followed her own counsel. And perhaps she was warning Clarissa against making the same choice. Was the life of a companion to a distant relation really the life she sought for herself? It was clear Jane did not want it for her.

Clarissa looked at Jane with eyes full of gratitude at baring her soul in a heartfelt attempt to keep Clarissa from making the same misstep that she had made long years ago. The attempt had succeeded. She would rather marry than remain a spinster, even if that meant marrying an Englishman. Her head would rule her heart; she would become the buyer in this game of matrimony and find herself the husband who best suited her, Englishman though he be.

But certainly in all of London she could find a man who owned property in Ireland.

"Any progress?" Dalton asked.

Beau greeted Dalton with a grunt and a half bow of recognition.

"I thought to find you well engaged, with perhaps half a dozen women simpering at your elbows by this hour. What have you been up to, to be standing here alone?" Dalton persisted.

"Alone? I am hardly alone. I have my thoughts, my speculations, my plans to abide with me," Beau answered.

"Better than a wife, I daresay. Smart man. Keep marriage as a speculation and all will be well."

"Can't," Beau said. "Must get myself an heir. Family duty requires it."

"Not such an onerous duty, when it comes to that." Dalton grinned. "Have you found any takers?"

"I am rather taken with her," Beau said, looking across the room. "Why didn't you tell me that you had such a fine-looking sister? Lindley was more than happy to point her out to me."

"Lindley would be," Dalton said. "He's been made to take the plunge and is grabbing for any and all to get wet with him. I wouldn't fall for it, were I you."

"I must marry," Beau said easily, still looking at Clarissa. "Your sister has a look about her. . . . Will you make the introductions? I've looked enough; 'tis time to take the first step."

"I will not," Dalton said stiffly. "You and Clarissa would not suit at all. I'm surprised you would suggest it, even more surprised that you can't see it for yourself."

"I beg your pardon?"

Beau looked stupefied. Dalton couldn't have been happier.

"She's a sheltered girl, hardly out of the country, and as innocent as rain. A man as experienced as you with a girl like that? You'd have nothing to say to each other inside of five minutes. Besides, as you said, she's a fine-looking girl; she could do quite well for herself this season. Isn't Halston looking for a bride this year? He's got Haverly to offer. Must be worth more than—"

"Montwyn Hall is no shabby cottage on the edge of a field, Dalton," Beau cut in. "And Halston is almost forty. You'd encourage a match with a man twice her age?"

"And why not? He would be a stable, solid man for her." He ended the sentence there, but both heard the unspoken insult to Beau's maturity, solidity, and stability.

"I'm certain he would be," Beau said coldly. With a bow, he excused himself from Dalton's company, his anger plain.

Dalton watched him go with the faintest of smiles. Leave it to Lindley to play his hand openly, boldly encouraging Beau to offer for Clarissa. He pursued a darker course, one less plain. Nothing would set Beau after Clarissa like opposition; the man was as bored as he was himself in a sea of smiling and submissive girls. A squall would make him sit up and check his ropes. Dalton had stirred the breeze, and if he knew Clarissa, which he did, she would do the rest. If all went well, not only would Beau offer for her, he would be fairly determined to have her and none other.

Dalton smiled again at the thought of the two of them together and ducked his head until he had composed himself. He liked Beau, he truly did, and he would be a splendid match for Clarissa. Beau had an estate in Ireland, after all.

Determined not to indulge her sense of injustice and outrage about her inescapable fate as the wife of an Englishman, Clarissa decided to enjoy herself as well as she might in such company and circumstance. She had much to do if logic was to triumph over sentiment. With Jane beside her, they circled the room, mingling.

"He was rather . . . moist, was he not, Jane? I do not think that I should have to tolerate a damp husband. All the upholstery would be ruined in a month," Clarissa said softly as they moved away from Lord Dalrimple and his sister.

"Clarissa!" Jane gasped.

"What?" she replied.

"It is not seemly to say—"

"He cannot hear me, and I do say that I should be allowed my own opinion on the matter of my husband and his odors," Clarissa said. "Now, shall we join Lady Wolling and her son? He looks a likely sort, though a tad small for me. I should hate to outweigh my husband. Most difficult. I foresee very small and fragile children, and if they are boys . . . Well, perhaps we should simply bypass Lady Wolling altogether."

Jane nodded to Lady Wolling as they passed, her eyes alight with embarrassment and horrified humor.

"Although, now I do ponder it, I do not think that man capable of siring boys. Oh well," Clarissa said cheerily, "on to Miss Warthom and her sister, Eliza. No, never mind, I cannot stop to mingle with mere ladies. I must be about my duty to find myself a husband whom I can tolerate. A most difficult dilemma, is it not?"

"Really, Clarissa," Jane began, her cheeks flushed and her brow as white as chalk.

"Ah, but who is that in the corner with Perry? He's a likely looking young gentleman. Tall, well dressed, *dry;* why, he may be the very thing."

"Good evening, Lady Jane," he said with a bow.

"Good evening, Lord Stanson," Jane said.

Perry said, "May I introduce my sister, Lady Clarissa Walingford, to you? This is her first trip to London this season."

"My lord." Clarissa curtsied modestly.

"Lady Clarissa," Stanson answered. "Your first London season? And how are you finding it? An amusement, one hopes."

"Oh, yes, I have been often amused," Clarissa said, smiling. Stanson spoke with a slight lisp. Really, she had never heard her name pronounced so . . . delightfully in her life.

"How lovely," he answered. "And what sights have you seen thus far?"

He was not bad to look upon, though he had a mole near his nose and, of course, that lisp.

"Only the dressmakers thus far, my lord, and whatever amusements can be found within this room," she answered.

Perry grinned and took a quiet sip of his drink. Jane coughed and fussed with her shawl. Clarissa stood with complete composure, looking up at the Lord Stanson and all the amusements he offered her.

"She only came down last week," Perry offered into a silence that was stretching out uncomfortably. "I imagine that she'll be out more now that her wardrobe is set."

"Perry, a woman does not care to have her wardrobe deficits discussed in public," Clarissa said, "even if those deficits are now canceled. London has so much to offer, does it not, Lord Stanson?"

"Yes, the best shopping in all the world, I daresay. Have you tried Lackington's shop? The best bookseller in the city. He even carries the most popular novels, which are an especial favorite with my own sisters," Stanson said.

"Really?" Clarissa smiled too sweetly. "I shall stop there tomorrow."

"If you will excuse us, Lord Stanson?" Jane said, steering Clarissa away. "I see Lady Morland and must compliment her on the sweetness of her tarts."

"It is not her tarts that concern you," Clarissa said when

they had left Stanson behind to resume his conversation with Perry.

"No, it is the tartness of your tongue. Were you going to tell him that you do not read novels?" Jane asked.

"Why would I be so rude when he was only trying to help me find proper London amusements?" Clarissa asked in return. "Really, Jane, you must think me a horrid child to have such fears concerning my deportment."

"Well," Jane huffed. "I do apologize. It is only that you do seem to be possessed of an uncertain temper tonight, when the evening is so lovely."

"Temper? I have no temper," Clarissa said somewhat stiffly.

"And the scar on Braden's hand did not come from the cup you threw at him?"

Clarissa lifted her chin in annoyance. "If all my childhood indiscretions are to be laid at my feet, I shall surely stumble. But do not all children fight?"

"Clarissa, it was but two years ago," Jane said dryly.

"And I was sorely provoked, if you will also recall," Clarissa defended.

Braden, home on leave from his regiment, had thrown her cat out of the window for making a bed for itself on his sleeping face. And she was the one accused of having a temper?

"Your pet was fine. She landed on her feet, as cats will do."

"I do not see how it pertains. It was most unreasonable of him to react so violently to a sleeping cat."

"Ah, Fanny," Jane said, ending the budding argument, "what a lovely evening. You have made us all, each one, feel so very welcome."

"You are most kind, Jane," Fanny replied with a genuine smile. Hostessing was so very trying, and one had to think of so many details. Another guest had caught her attention and she drifted over to smile with warmth and welcome.

Perry quietly joined the ladies of his house and whispered to Clarissa, "You're fortunate. Stanson did not realize that you mocked him."

"If he is as obtuse as all that, then I am fortunate in finding out so soon. I will not wed a dullard."

"You will not wed at all, if you follow your inclinations."

"But I am not following my inclinations. I am following the course of familial duty. And I will marry, Perry. You may rely upon it," Clarissa said firmly.

Perry smiled and bowed to her. "Rely upon it I will. How do you progress?"

"Not well," she said bluntly. "But it has been only an hour and I am not discouraged. I never buy the first hat I try, and I don't imagine shopping for a husband to be a matter of less consequence than a hat."

"Clarissa!" Jane remonstrated.

"Well spoken, Clarissa," Perry said, laughing.

"Excuse me," Fanny said, rejoining them, "but I don't believe I've introduced Lord Montwyn to you."

Clarissa turned and faced the man whom she had observed speaking to Lindley earlier in the evening. He was more forbidding when seen at close quarters, and more handsome. He knew it, too, and such arrogance, such pride, was more tempting a target than she could bear to turn from.

He bowed. She curtsied. And she waited. Such a man would feel it his right to speak first. She would allow him that, for it was she who would have the last word.

"You are new to London, Lady Clarissa," he said.

"I am. Does it show?" she answered.

Perry snorted in amusement while Jane gathered breath to fuss and apologize.

"Actually, yes," he answered, his smile as light and bright as a rapier.

Looking up at him, at his dark brows and his deep green eyes, his very unrepentant eyes, Clarissa felt herself smile. Finally, a worthy adversary.

"Really," she responded. "Would it be terribly gauche of me to ask how I have . . . exposed myself?"

"If you will excuse me, Lord Montwyn, Clarissa," Jane said, "I will visit with Miss Walburn."

Montwyn bowed at her departure and then turned back to Clarissa and Perry.

"Let us not say 'exposed,' but rather 'revealed.'"

"Really, I cannot say I approve of this conversation," Perry interrupted.

"I'm certain that Lord Montwyn would not 'expose' me to any conversation not within the bounds of correct London etiquette. Would you?" she said.

"The bounds of etiquette shall be observed, naturally. I would do nothing to damage your reputation, Lady Clarissa."

"My brother will be relieved to hear it," she said.

"But not you?" Montwyn asked.

"I guard my own reputation, Lord Montwyn."

"And she does a fine job of it, too," Perry added.

"But this is London, Lady Clarissa," Montwyn said, his eyes twinkling, "and you are inexperienced."

"Rather say I am new to London, sir. I am not inexperienced."

"No?" He smiled. "But that is how I knew you were new to town. Your naivete lights you like a candle."

Clarissa took a breath and felt herself grow still at the raw sting of his insult. This man was different, and it was not London that made him so. His pride lit him like a bonfire, and while the light drew the eye, the heat of him was oppressive.

"I am certain you are mistaken. My education has been most complete."

"Yet how else to explain my knowing that you were new to town?"

"Perhaps"—she smiled—"because you visit every house that will open its door to you. You *were* invited to Lord and Lady Morland's tonight, were you not? I am certain that Lady Morland is too refined to have anyone thrown out. She is a most welcoming hostess."

"Well done, Clarissa," Perry chimed. "Not many can stand against my sister in verbal warfare, Lord Montwyn. I commend you for your bravery."

"Is that what this is?" Montwyn asked calmly, studying her boldly.

Most aggressive, even for an Englishman. Not appealing at all, but . . . compelling. A most disturbing thought—she would not tolerate it or him.

"Hardly," Clarissa said, affecting boredom with Lord Montwyn and his superiority. "I am looking for a husband tonight. Tomorrow I shall shop for books and a new pair of boots."

"A shopping trip to London," Montwyn summarized.

"Precisely," Clarissa said, looking him in the eye, communicating her disdain.

"Really, Clarissa," Perry sputtered. "I apologize, Lord Montwyn, for my sister's—"

"Unnecessary," Montwyn cut in. "I am here for the same reason. I need a wife."

He looked down at her while he said it, and she felt the weight of his words and his intent hit her like a stone. He was not put off. He should have been. He was not the sort of man she was looking for, though her eyes continued to look.

Masculine power emanated from him with every breath, confusing her purpose. She searched for an acceptable husband—Montwyn commanded a response from her heart that was completely unacceptable.

"Then you'd best circulate and find one," Clarissa said sharply.

"I am not an impulsive shopper. I like to take my time over my selections," Montwyn said, holding her eyes.

"How odd," Clarissa spat. "I can tell at a glance if a smock or even the merest bit of embroidered linen will suit. I know my own tastes and inclinations. Good evening, sir," she said, and turned to go, her arm resting on Perry's. Call it not a rout, but a wise retreat; she had to put distance between herself and Montwyn.

"But I am shopping for more than fripperies," Montwyn said to her retreating back. "Or would you disagree?"

Clarissa turned and said over her shoulder, "Only you can know your own intent."

"I would share it with a willing ear," Montwyn said with a smile.

"Again I say circulate, sir, to find what you seek."

Beau, Lord Montwyn, watched her walk away, her bearing regal, her head proud and high, the long line of her torso as graceful as a sapling in the wood.

"No need, miss," he said softly to himself, "for I've found what I came to London to find."

✳ Chapter Two ✳

"$\mathcal{I}$t was a complete waste of time," Clarissa said to Albert the next morning while helping herself to a cup of tea and a scone.

Albert sat up straighter in his chair and tugged at his waistcoat. "Kindly explain yourself, Clarissa. Do you mean to tell me that Lord and Lady Morland invited only women to their party last night?"

"They may as well have," Clarissa said over her cup, "if what I saw last night represents the best England has to offer. I will not marry either a runt or a sweaty, odorous beast to fulfill my family obligation, and if you were a loving brother you would not ask it of me."

"Since Henry Wakefield, Lord of Montwyn, is neither a runt nor odorous," Perry said, coming into the room, "I would hazard that you have not made mention of your meeting with him."

"No, I have not. Let me add him to the list: he is a boor."

"You seemed to be enjoying your conversation with him last night," Perry said. "At least, I was. Most entertaining."

Most entertaining, indeed. At first, yes, she had thought so, but then his countenance had seemed to her to be so proud, so overbearing. Such a man, no matter his fine form, would not do. He was a bear of a man who would crush her for his own amusement; or perhaps it was better said that he would try to, for she would not be cowed so easily by mere rudeness, no matter the level of his offenses. Or attraction. He had been attracted to her, that much was obvious, and perhaps she could even find something admirable in his boldness. She had not frightened him; he had made that plain enough. But he was not the sort of man she had in mind, and it was her mind that would decide her future, not a pair of shining green eyes.

"You at least were entertained," she said to Perry. "I was not. He will not do."

"How is it that an earl will not do?" Albert asked, rising from his chair.

"Oh, he would do," Perry chuckled, "if Clarissa had not prodded him unmercifully. She baited the man and then ran from him when he growled back."

"I did not run. He did not growl," she snapped.

"Good heavens, Clarissa, do not tell me that you have made a spectacle of yourself in London society," Albert said sternly. "You will not take that way out of your proper duty to marry and marry well. A union with Montwyn would be most advantageous to this family."

"And would it be advantageous to me, Albert?" she asked. "Besides, we would not suit. His temper is uncertain."

"Oh, I would say his temper is most certain, most predictable," Perry said with a smile.

"Oh, Perry, do keep your remarks to yourself!" Clarissa said.

"Do not say that you antagonized Lord Montwyn," Lindley said, coming into the room.

"I say no such thing," Clarissa said.

"'Twas I who said it." Perry grinned.

"Couldn't you have been civil to the man?" Lindley grumbled, fetching himself a plate.

"I was more than civil."

"She was," Perry agreed. "She was blatantly entertaining. At least, I was entertained."

"And Montwyn? Was he?" Lindley asked.

"I thought he was, when she said she was in town shopping for a husband," Perry volunteered.

Albert and Lindley were silent, their faces as dark as gloom. Dalton, having just come in, laughed. Clarissa was not grateful for it.

"Well done, Clarissa," Dalton said. "If a man can't stand a little ribbing, he'll make a sorry husband."

"I shall remind you of that sentiment when you are shopping for a bride," Lindley said, his dark eyes glowering at Dalton.

"Do you think you can remember it for that long?" Dalton smiled sharply at Lindley. Dalton would not be pushed into marriage, no matter what Albert threatened.

"Enough," Albert said. "It's past now, and nothing to be done but put a brave face on it. And try to make amends in your next encounter," he said, looking censoriously at Clarissa.

"Russell!" she said to her brother as he came in, refusing to answer Albert and all the rest. The best path for her at the moment lay in a controlled retreat. There seemed to be too much of that in her life of late, and Montwyn was ever the cause. "Will you please accompany me to Lackington's? I am book shopping today."

"Of course, Clarissa," he said agreeably. She knew beyond a doubt that he had been out all night and had just had time to change out of his evening wear; Russell would not want to stay and risk his own encounter with Albert's censure.

At her departure, the room broke up quickly, for none cared to stay and face his own comeuppance with Albert. If he had been a man of milder and softer temperament, he might have evoked pity, but he did not. He had been the head of the family—a family that consisted of nine younger brothers and Clarissa—for ten years. It was a burden he was accustomed to, one that he had been trained for all his life. If only his siblings would take to their traces as he had taken to his.

Jane entered as he stood in silent contemplation, his dark eyes studying the view of the garden through the glass. All was cold and gray and wet, yet the sundial gave the garden form and weight when all was leafless and bare. He had once enjoyed planning gardens, before he had been required to oversee the lives of his brothers. And Clarissa. Wild, impetuous Clarissa.

"Tell me your thoughts, Jane," he said softly, his face still to the glass. "What of Montwyn?"

Jane shrugged, and he saw the faint reflection of the gesture in the wavering glass. "You are worried. You need not be."

"You heard what she said to him?"

"No," Jane said cautiously. "But I did observe them from my place near the fire, and the air between them did not seem hostile."

"Not hostile? When she blatantly told him that she was shopping for a husband?"

Jane swallowed before she answered. "Lord Montwyn seems a capable, forthright man. I do not think such bantering will dissuade him."

"Dissuade him?" Albert turned to her. "Was he that interested, and so soon?"

"Let me not misspeak," she said softly. "I think him a man of firmness, of maturity. I think that if Lord Montwyn is at all interested in Clarissa, a few thoughtless words from her will not subdue that interest."

"You have always been observant," he said. "Let us hope you are right. I would not have her season so quickly spoiled."

"Nor would I," she agreed.

With a nod, he gazed back out at his frozen garden. Jane, without another word, left him to his contemplation.

In Lackington's, Beau spotted her immediately. Her dark red hair shone like bright embers against the dark green of her coat. But it was not her hair that drew him; it was her manner. Bright and sharp, feminine and soft, quick and proud—all mixed and blended to such confused refinement that he was able only to smile in bemusement at the contradiction of her.

He wanted her.

It was too soon for such a conclusion, yet it was no thoughtful, logical, intellectual process that brought him to the knowledge. It was instinct. Desire. Passion.

Poor yardsticks when choosing a wife. Yet so he found himself. He wanted her. With such a woman, having her required marriage. For her he was willing to pay the price, though it was high.

Propriety demanded a lengthier involvement before pronouncing his intent. Propriety demanded that he proceed slowly. Propriety demanded that he appear reasonable and methodical. He had never once considered the demands of propriety, and he saw no reason to begin now. The choice was made. Clarissa Walingford would be his wife, and the sooner the better.

He could not help wondering if she knew of their inevitable union as certainly as he did.

She did not.

She stood alone, Russell having taken himself off to another part of the shop while she conferred with the clerk. She felt his presence before she saw him, her breath quickening to match her pulse. It was a most inappropriate response to a man her logic had rejected. His arm appeared over her shoulder, and in his hand he held . . . a small square of embroidered linen.

"Do you like it?" he said, his words warm and soft on the back of her neck.

She turned to face him and held his green eyes with her gaze. She would not run from Lord Montwyn again, of that she was certain, though the urge to retreat from his proximity was strong. He was so very tall and broad, the shadow of his dark beard leaving a clear outline underneath his skin. She could see all so clearly, so intimately, and her heart raced. Against all logic her heart raced. But she would not run; she would instead compel him to run from her.

"A trifle ornate for my tastes, but then, it probably suits you."

He smiled and tucked the bit of linen into a pocket in his coat. "Searching for a book on embroidery?"

"No. I am not," she said, turning back to the clerk.

Montwyn moved to stand beside her and took the book she had been considering from her hands. His hands were large, his fingers long, his nails squared and clean. She looked away from his hands.

"*A History of the Peloponnesian Wars*," he quoted. "Not in Greek?" he asked.

"No," she said, lifting her chin.

"You disappoint me, miss."

"With pleasure, sir," she said with a sharp smile. "I'll take it," she said to the clerk. She had been debating choosing lighter reading; the debate within her ceased upon the arrival of Henry Wakefield. Where was Russell?

"Any more shopping to do?" Montwyn asked as the clerk wrapped the book and tallied the bill.

"Yes, but only for husbands," she said, watching the book being wrapped, not watching him. But she could feel him, feel his strength, the power of his personality. He was most unwelcome. If only he had the sense to realize it.

Montwyn laughed with genuine pleasure. The man was an obvious imbecile.

"You think to shock me," he said.

"Only if you find the truth shocking," she answered.

"Never." He smiled.

Even his smile was powerful. He was overwhelmingly masculine, a most unwelcome man.

"The truth," he continued, "is always delightful and precious for its rarity."

"That statement speaks volumes about you, sir. The truth is not rare, in my experience."

"And that, miss, speaks volumes about your innocence."

"I can only think you mean to insult me," she said.

"Never," he replied.

If not for his arrogance, his insults, his bone-deep Englishness, she might have found him attractive. But she did not. She would not. Where was Russell?

"Has your escort gone missing?" he asked, seeming to read her.

"My brother, Russell," she answered, taking the package from the clerk and nodding her thanks.

"A Walingford I have yet to meet, and I have met so many."

"Have you?" She smiled. "I rather doubt you have met us all. We are a rather large clan."

"Clan? An odd way of putting it."

"Not if one is Irish," she said, walking away from him. He followed. He was either more arrogant than she had thought or more unintelligent. Perhaps he was both.

"And your being English is then what makes it odd. Is that not so, Lady Clarissa?"

Russell's arrival, late but welcome, kept her from having to make a response to his most uncomfortable question and his most impertinent address.

The introductions were brief and cordial, both men seeming to take a liking to each other almost immediately. It was most irritating. They knew some of the same people, even shared common friends between them; when the conversation strolled in the direction of hunting parties, she loosed the reins on her strict and composed silence. Russell would no more build a friendship with this man than she would be ignored by him.

"I am certain that with all of your mutual acquaintances, there must be one among them who has a sister or a cousin of marriageable age who would be more than pleased to welcome Lord Montwyn into their company. I feel that his time would be so very well spent in such a gathering," she said.

Russell, dear Russell, could only blink in shock.

Clarissa smiled, awaiting whatever answer Montwyn could think to give, oddly gratified to have his full attention once more. That was odd, was it not? That she should so want those green eyes of his to be looking fully at her? It was not the way of a woman who disdained a man, and she was too honest not to see the truth in herself. She did not like Lord Montwyn. No, she did not. But . . . she did enjoy the time spent in his presence. He excited her as did no other. And that was something to ponder.

Montwyn smiled in the face of her challenge and her dismissal while she awaited his reply.

"I can only be eager to meet any woman of fine family and good name. Thank you for your avid attention to my needs; it speaks . . . volumes," he said with a knowing smile, and without taking another breath he excused himself and left the shop.

Which only irritated her. She was to have made her exit first, leaving him behind, leaving him defeated. It would not happen again, of that she was determined.

"What were you thinking to speak so to Montwyn, Clarissa? I hope you haven't offended him. He seems a likely chap, after all," Russell said, taking her arm and guiding her out of Lackington's.

Clarissa smiled and said with rueful respect for such a stellar exit, "Worry not, Russell. Lord Montwyn will be smiling for an hour."

Dalton happened upon Beau in the glove maker's shop. Montwyn was wearing an odd sort of half smile, which Dalton took note of but could not decipher. Whatever it was, Beau looked well pleased with himself and, knowing Beau as he did, Dalton could only conclude that Montwyn thought he had Clarissa well in hand. Such a conclusion would not do. An easy victory would only bore him, of that he was certain. Clarissa, nobly doing her part to cause Beau to trip at every turn, needed his help. He was only too glad to give it.

"You know, Beau, Kilworth's cousin is out this season. A fine-looking girl with a pleasing countenance and gentle manner. Blond, I've heard, but whether the curls are natural, no one is offering. She would do for you, I think," Dalton said, looking over Beau's selection. "This gray pair doesn't suit you, Montwyn, too pale."

Beau looked at him askance and tossed the gray to the clerk with a nod, making his selection. "You know that I've been rather taken with your own sister, Dalton. Why fob off Kilworth's cousin on me?"

"Just hate to see you settle in so soon, that's all," Dalton said. "Plenty of girls out this season. Clarissa isn't right for just any man."

"I am not 'any' man," Beau said, selecting a bloodred pair of gloves.

"No, of course not," Dalton said, holding up a pair of parrot green gloves and shuddering mildly before tossing them down. "But perhaps a girl of more . . . delicacy . . . would better suit. Marriage is a serious step. One must be certain of eventual contentment."

"I am content with Clarissa."

"But Clarissa is hardly likely to be content with you," Dalton said, choosing a dark brown pair of gloves and nodding his decision to the clerk.

"I beg your pardon?" Beau asked, his voice as rigid as his posture.

"No insult intended, naturally," Dalton said casually.

"Naturally," Beau repeated with a stiff smile.

"For some strange reason, Clarissa has determined to marry only a man with Irish property. And you have nothing there, unless I am mistaken?"

"That's blatantly ridiculous," Beau grumbled, making a mess of the clerk's carefully arranged selection. "Petulant. Outrageous."

"I agree completely, and that is only another reason for you to discard Clarissa from your consideration, as fond as I am of her—"

"It so happens that I *do* hold an estate in Ireland," Beau bit out, both angry and proud, it seemed to Dalton.

Dalton did an admirable job of appearing shocked. They really would have to get up more private theatricals to stretch his skill and give him the proper acclaim for his talent.

"Wouldn't tell Clarissa 'bout that. Would put you square in her sights," Dalton said in grim warning.

Beau merely scowled at him.

Really, Beau was a most unsatisfying audience.

She'd consider him because he held Irish lands? Ridiculous. Absurd. She'd consider him—by God, she'd *have* him—for more reason than that. He had lands, yes, and income, and title—all important when making a match, and there was no shame for it to be considered bluntly and in the bold light of day. But for such a girl to weigh him on the scales of matrimonial worth and find him *acceptable* because of Irish lands and nothing more was . . . insulting.

He knew his worth. He was a well-built man with regular features and a not unpleasing manner. He'd had his share of victories with women, broken a heart or two when all was said and done; he'd be considered for more than his *land*. She'd *take* him for more than his land. And what was more, she'd admit it. He'd not have her marrying him with Irish lands in her thoughts.

231

If she married him. Beau frowned and silently cursed Dalton and his serpent's tongue. And when he had calmed himself, he cursed Dalton again. It wouldn't do for a brother of hers to be against the match; it was hard for a girl to go against her brother, though Clarissa looked the sort to do as she pleased when it pleased her. That stood in his favor. She was pleased by him, hide it though she would. He was not so dull as not to sense a woman's interest in the very texture of his skin, and when he was near Clarissa Walingford, his skin very nearly burned. There was more to that than Irish lands.

Beau grunted and tugged at his cravat. Were all the brothers against a match between Walingford and Montwyn?

"Beau," Lindley said, interrupting his thoughts. "Didn't think to see you today," he said, stopping, urging Beau to stop his striding walk. Beau stopped. Lindley looked eager to see him. Lindley looking completely eager *was* something.

"No, well, I was out . . . shopping," Beau said with a tight smile.

"Yes, well," Lindley said haltingly, "I didn't know if you'd been invited to the Blakelys' tonight."

Beau said nothing; he merely waited, almost joyous at the look of eagerness on Lindley's face. Lindley was clearly not against the match, but Lindley might be alone in that.

"Should be an enjoyable evening," Lindley said. "Clarissa will be there. I hope to see you too."

"I haven't made my plans for the evening as yet," Beau said cordially. He would not so boldly reveal his interest in Clarissa, not with so many uncertainties. It would not do for word of his intent to get back to Clarissa, feeding a confidence he did not want her to feel. This matter of the Irish lands would be settled.

"Really?" Lindley said, his own irritation mounting and

displaying itself on his face. "I wish you a pleasant evening, whatever your diversion."

"Thank you," Beau said. "And you as well."

Both men parted, one newly frustrated and one with renewed confidence. Beau was more than happy to pass his frustration regarding Clarissa off to Lindley, old friend though he was.

Chapter Three

 $\mathcal{S}$ he would wear the lavender silk tonight, and for jewels . . . Perry came in as she was deliberating.

"What do you think, Perry? The amethyst necklace or the pearl? I cannot decide," she said, turning in her chair, her hands holding each selection aloft.

"I prefer the amethyst. All that sparkle," he said, sitting down on a chair near her dressing table.

"Yes, so much easier to attract a husband when one 'sparkles,'" she said, laying down the pearl necklace and arranging the amethysts around her exposed throat.

Another evening to be spent shopping for a husband. She sighed and checked the arrangement of her hair in the mirror. It was so much more pleasurable shopping for books. She had been reading her new book on the Peloponnesian wars all afternoon, and now her eyes were stinging with fatigue, but she had to go out tonight.

Actually, reading about battle was the perfect preparation for facing a roomful of Englishmen. Especially Montwyn. Would he be there? She smiled at her reflection, her brown eyes dancing with confidence. Of course he would be there. The idea of battling with him was the only excitement she would have all evening, and she was almost counting on him to make her night at the Blakelys' worthwhile. She could entertain herself with him while looking elsewhere for a husband.

"You sparkle enough without the aid of any jewels, Clarissa," Perry said. "Montwyn seems fairly dazzled."

He did, actually, and she hid her smile of satisfaction in the drawing on of a glove.

"Did you see him today?" she asked casually.

"Montwyn, you mean?"

She gave him a cross look for his clumsy attempt to rile her.

Perry shrugged and said, "Sorry. Yes, actually. Jane and I bumped into him on our way to the milliner's. Jane let it be known that you were at Lackington's—ridiculous if you ask me, since we weren't talking of Lackington's at all—and off he went. You saw him there?"

"Yes," she said, standing and smoothing her skirt. "He was at Lackington's."

"He must be interested if he ran off there on just a word from Jane."

"Of course he's interested," Clarissa said with a smile of satisfaction.

"But you're not," Perry said, standing with her, his face serious. "I think Montwyn rather rude and certainly inordinately proud."

"Inordinately? Oh, I think him proud to an uncivil degree, but his pride may be well deserved," Clarissa reluctantly defended.

"I've seen Montwyn Hall," Perry said. "There's enough pride for ten heirs in the Montwyn title. But there's more to a man than his house."

"Of course. There are his lands," Clarissa said firmly. "A man must have good land, good Irish land."

"And naught else?" Perry asked. "You seem interested in Montwyn, with or without Irish lands."

"I am *not* interested," she said, searching for a fan.

At Perry's skeptical look, she said, "I am not. Have more faith in me, Perry. I have more sense than to choose such a man. He is too—" she shrugged—"bold a man. I am looking for a man who'll burrow quietly in London and leave me contentedly in Ireland. There is nothing quiet about Montwyn, and he would never be able to content me."

"I agree with you," Perry said, standing near her bedroom door. "I wish I could believe you. You do sparkle when he's near, Clarissa, and I know that look in you. More, I think Montwyn to be a man attracted to bright resistance. And you are just that."

"I fear I have not been complimented," she said.

"Smart girl," he said with a grin. "Sparkle all night, dear, for I will be at your elbow throughout the evening. Montwyn shall not have you to himself."

"Thank you for that, Perry," she said. "Now I must do the final touches to myself. I'll meet you downstairs."

Perry left, but he did not like the glitter in Clarissa's dark eyes whenever Montwyn's name was mentioned. And she had fairly glowed when she had learned that Montwyn had followed her to Lackington's. She was a sharp girl, quick in both thoughts and actions, but she might have come up against her match with Montwyn. He was a formidable man, experienced, proud, determined. It was an uncomfortable contemplation that Montwyn might have determined to have Clarissa.

Russell was just coming up to change for the evening as Perry was going down.

"You going with us?" Perry asked.

"Yes, I thought I would," Russell said, his tone more serious than usual.

Stabbing in the dark, Perry said, "You saw Montwyn today?"

Russell looked startled for a moment and then nodded, "I did. When I was with Clarissa at Lackington's. Odd the way they spoke to each other. Rude. But they seemed to like it."

Perry, only a year younger than Russell, nodded and then shook his head in worry.

"What do you make of him, Russell?"

Russell rested his hand on the banister and studied the ceiling plaster. "I've made discreet inquiries. He's a bit wild, or was until he came into his title. Gets out a bit. Travels. Has seen hard duty in his regiment, but Lindley could tell you more, since they met when they both wore the uniform. Not quite a regular man, they say. Harder. Prouder. Perhaps even fierce, in a quiet sort of way."

"Not the sort I'd choose for Clarissa," Perry said.

"Nor I," Russell agreed. "It's that wildness that concerns me. Doesn't do for a man to leave his wife at home while he carouses."

"But he's not married yet," Perry said, "and you know him from your own carousing."

"True." Russell grinned. "But would he want me to marry his sister, if he had one? Probably not."

"You've seen them together," Perry stated. "She's different with him."

"No, I don't agree. She's completely herself. Completely Clarissa."

"Exactly," Perry said. "Why? She hardly knows him. Why

would she be so bold with him, unless she's drawn to him, feels something—"

"Not all bad to feel something for the man she might marry."

"Marry Montwyn? I don't think so. Steel against steel, the two of them. And I think he may be scaring off other suitors, leaving her with little choice but him."

"He's scaring off the suitors she's not scaring off herself?" Russell laughed.

Perry shrugged and said reluctantly, "Point taken. She is not showing her best to the London lads, as she calls them."

"Yet Montwyn—"

"Montwyn isn't put off by her manner at all," Perry finished.

Perry and Russell looked into each other's eyes in full comprehension—and with no comfort.

The evening's entertainment was a ball and it was lovely. The music, the candlelight, the colors of gowns and jewels and bouquets, were all lovely. Memorable. A sweet winter's night for a maid to cherish when she was old and fragile and lounging on her chaise in some cold and distant future. Clarissa knew it would be so. She would remember this night, this beautiful night of dancing and music, for years.

It was so sad that upon such an evening she was compelled to shop for an English husband.

Dalton had disappeared almost upon their arrival, Perry was whispering with the niece of their host quite a distance from her side, Russell was caught in what appeared to be a serious game of cards, and Lindley was at her side, his vigilance as constant as his advice.

"If you would only restrain your temper and be civil, you

would make much headway," he said, not bothering to disguise his exasperation.

"I am always civil," Clarissa said, her eyes glittering more sharply than her jewels. "What I will not do is fawn over these English fops."

"*You* are English, as English as any in this—"

"What sort of children would I be forced to bear if married to that?" she said in a hiss, cutting him off. She used her fan to indicate Lord Darnell, as fat as always and in need of a hair trimming. "Has any one of you considered that?" Darnell was all jowl and bristle—revolting. "I could do little worse in the barnyard."

"And does the ram bring in twenty thousand pounds per annum?"

"He is no ram, Lindley," she said bluntly. "Would you bind me to a porker for even half that amount?" she rejoined angrily.

"Shall we speak of the kitchen mouse to whom I have pledged?" Lindley said in a growl, his eyes as fierce and as bright as hers.

"Miss Brookdale is no mouse!" Clarissa protested.

"With Ridgehaven in tow, no woman is a mouse," he said, calming himself. "At least it shall not be admitted aloud."

Clarissa felt guilt tugging at her heels and could not run fast enough to escape its touch. She was churlish. Everyone married for money and position; she was not the first, nor would she be the last. It was childish to be so contrary. Lindley had done his part for the family, and she could do no less.

"Is it the porker you have in mind for me?" she asked with a wry smile.

"Never." He smiled back, their argument over and done. "Do your own choosing. But *choose*."

"Very well," Clarissa said, taking a deep breath. "I shall. Tonight."

"There is no need for such haste. The clock does not tick so loudly as all that," he argued. Lindley never could enjoy a period of calm for more than a moment.

"I am not of a disposition to dawdle," she said, drawing herself up and surveying the room. "What matters one man over another when they are all so confoundedly English? A length of bleached linen is a length of linen, is it not? What possible reason for confusion or hesitation? I shall make my decision tonight and will have the goods delivered next week."

"Confound you, Clarissa! You know there is no such need—"

She laid a hand upon his arm and looked up into his eyes. "I would rather have it behind me, Lindley. The matrimonial blade gleams quite wickedly over my neck. I would the sooner have it drop."

Now it was guilt that dogged him; she could read it in his eyes. But she had spoken truly; she had no will to delay what she knew was her family duty. To delay meant to feed the illusion of choice, and she had no choice. She must marry and marry well.

Lord Montwyn, joining their company, ended the argument, which was just as well.

"Good evening, Beau," Lindley said with a bow. "A pleasure to see you, as always."

"Good evening." Montwyn bowed, his eyes lingering on Clarissa. She returned his look after her quick curtsy. "I had hoped to see you tonight," he said.

Of course he had. He was behaving very much like a man who had made up his mind as to the woman of his choice; she knew enough of men to know that. And she knew Lindley well enough to know that her blatant perusal of Montwyn was making him uncomfortable. That was a pity—for Lindley. Henry Wakefield, Lord Montwyn, was not discomfitted at all, that she could see. She was quite certain that, having made the ill-guided decision that she was to be the future Earl of Montwyn's mother, Henry Wakefield expected her to be honored and flattered. He truly was an imbecile.

"You are called Beau, Lord Montwyn? I was told your given name was Henry," she said.

"Beau, for Beauford, another of my names. A childhood name that has stuck with me," he answered, holding her eyes. His eyes were the most intense shade of green. . . .

"I should think that few men would be so mild as to keep a childhood name alive into adulthood," she said, breaking contact with his eyes and looking down at her fan. What was behind his eyes? Something that called to her heart and not her head; she would ignore it.

"Yes, I suppose I would feel so if my nurse had taken to calling me Puddles," he said, grinning.

His face was transformed when he grinned. Oh, he was still formidable, but now he also seemed playful, boyish. He must have been a wild youth. She did not know but that he was a wild man. And, foolishly, the thought did not dismay her as it should have. He was bold, yet she could be bold as well.

"Did you make any other purchases at Lackington's today, Lady Clarissa?" Montwyn asked.

"Didn't you watch?" she said. Yes, she could be bold and would be. It delighted him, she knew, and delighting him, just for the moment, amused her.

"Please excuse my sister—" Lindley began, his cheeks red with fury. She knew she had pushed him past mere embarrassment.

"There's no need," Beau interrupted. "She's quite right. I did watch. One book. No—"

"Husband," Clarissa completed for him, smiling up at him. His eyes were like emeralds, deep and sparkling, almost blue in the candlelight.

"Come, Lindley," Jane said, approaching and drawing Lindley off. "Miss Whaley insists on hearing of your exploits with your regiment. It seems her cousin has just bought himself a commission. . . ."

Lindley let himself be taken off, for the most part because Clarissa made it clear that she wanted him to go.

"You enjoy embarrassing him?" Beau asked when they stood alone.

"Not at all. I simply enjoy speaking my mind," she said, still holding his gaze.

Beau studied her, this bold girl, and decided again that he liked what he saw. She had a tongue in her head, and he'd always had an appreciation for redheads. Good family, good name, good looks—and she was not immune to him. He could read her fascination easily enough, and none of it had anything to do with his Irish estate, not with that glowing eye and flushed cheek. A girl could well like Ireland and not have that sort of response. No, she had an affinity for him; that was plain. And she was not afraid of him. So many of these girls this season appeared overawed. But not this one, this girl who so boldly declared herself to be shopping for a husband this year.

Beau smiled deeply, and decided. She was the one. He'd make an offer for her tomorrow morning. It should all be settled by next week—by Christmas, in fact. Convenient, that. He liked to be at Montwyn Hall for the holidays. It would be good to get it all settled and behind him.

"And every Englishman has the right to speak his mind," he

answered. "You will find no hindrance here, Lady Clarissa."

She bristled as if poked. Had he insulted her somehow? Damned if he knew.

He had insulted her, the dolt. Instantly his facility at amusing her vanished. Really, there was so little logic in allowing herself to find enjoyment in the company of a moderately handsome man of marginal intelligence; her heart thumped an entirely different summation of the man, but her heart—and her eyes as well—had no part in this.

"Excuse me, but I have promised this dance to another. I should like to see you again this evening." He bowed, his eyes never leaving hers.

Arrogant fop. Words of insult crowded her tongue and threatened to smother her judgment. She had been better brought up than to bow to uncivilized urges.

"Enjoy your dance, Lord Montwyn," she said.

"Oh"— he turned to her—"but it is more than a dance, is it not? I am shopping for a bride."

"You attempt to shock me," she said, furious with him as completely as she had been delighted by him a moment before. "All you have accomplished is to illustrate the degradation of your manners and, perhaps, your morals."

"By speaking my mind?" he said with a smile, tormenting her with her own choice of words. "Good evening, Lady Clarissa. I hope to see you again. Soon."

He left her then, his smile as wide, arrogant as a fox. He was a boor. She hated him. He was the most arrogant and insufferable of them all. He was also the one her eyes followed. Stupid thing, eyes. One didn't need them to make a marriage contract. She forced herself to look away from him and survey the rest of the room.

He did cut a splendid figure, though, his height being an advantage few could lay claim to. She forced her eyes to obey her will and studied the other men arrayed for her consideration. What she needed was a list, a list of net worth, annual income, and, most important, Irish holdings. *That* would be the measure of the man she chose, not green eyes and a devilish manner, for she would return to Ireland as mistress of her own domain and destiny. Let her husband, whomever he was, wallow in London. In fact, she would prefer it.

Chapter Four

The next morning, in the privacy of her room, with a cup of chocolate to sustain her, Clarissa sat amid a haphazardly organized pile of papers and lists—all necessary research materials in her attempt to compile her list of men suitable to fill the position of husband.

Naturally Jane was horrified by the cold-bloodedness of it, but Jane had a strong leaning toward sentiment and romance. Clarissa was going to be ruled by her head and the sense that God had given her; she was going to be logical and she was going to be efficient. And she was going to be quick.

"But Clarissa," Jane pleaded, clasping her hands before her, "there is more to marriage than contracts and obligations."

"Is there? I fail to see it. What is there of sentiment in arranging a marriage anyway? Albert would scoff at you, Jane."

"But sentiment should grow in such a union. What chance is there for warm sentiment with such a cold beginning?"

"Let him have lands in Leinster and I shall have sentiment enough," Clarissa said, taking a healthy swallow of her morning chocolate. "If he has lands in Wexford itself, I shall love him unreservedly . . . from Wexford. Let him occupy himself in London or even Dublin."

"Clarissa," Jane said, trying for severity.

"It is no use your trying to dissuade me, Jane. I am quite determined and have even given Lindley my pledge that all will be settled by next week. I do so want to enjoy the Christmas holiday without this hanging over me. Now, help me with my list if you would help me."

"I shall help," Dalton said, coming into her room, "and gladly. What is it you wish to know?"

"Oh, Dalton, just the one I need," Clarissa said, laying aside her shawl. "You know everyone in society. Just who has Irish lands?"

"Irish lands, is it? Well, I suppose I'm not surprised. You will have your way and go back, and if it takes an aging husband to get you there, then you're hardly likely to balk."

"Of course not," she said, hesitating only slightly. "If you'll only help me compile my list?"

"Yes, of course," Dalton said with a slight smile.

"Dalton, you're not to encourage her," Jane said.

"But how can I not, Jane, when she is being so very reasonable, so extremely logical?"

"Exactly," Clarissa said with a nod to Jane.

"Well, then, you must have Lord Benson on your list. He has a prime estate in County Wicklow."

"Lord Benson," she repeated, forcing herself to add him to her list. Benson was past fifty and had a small pastry for a nose.

"Then there is Lord Esherton, recently available, with an estate in Waterford much talked of."

She had already met Lord Esherton; he was without a single hair on his head, and he had a most peculiar odor about him. His first wife had most likely died of asphyxiation. Still, Waterford was so very near Wexford, the place of her youth. Esherton was added to her list.

"I almost hesitate to mention . . ." Dalton said leisurely, "but you did ask for my complete help."

"Yes, who is it?" she said sharply, redipping her quill.

"There is Lord Montwyn, whom I know you have met. He does have an estate of some merit in County Meath, I think it is."

"Ah," she said, trying not to smile. And failing.

"I thought you'd be glad to add Montwyn to your list," Dalton teased with a chuckle.

"Don't be ridiculous, Dalton," she barked, laying aside her quill. "If I must shop for a husband, I would be rather stupid not to have a shopping list from which to make my selections."

"And you are certainly not stupid," Dalton said merrily. "Tell me, what exactly is on your wish list for a future husband?"

"Irish lands, of course. That is of primary importance."

"And of secondary importance?"

"His annual income."

"A most practical list," he said, smiling.

"For a most serious purpose," she said with a small scowl.

"Assuredly. Shall I inform Lord Montwyn that he is on your list?"

"Don't be an imbecile, Dalton," she snapped. "It would be so like you to do it, just for a laugh. But tell him, if you must. I'll wager it will matter little," she said, grinning.

"That confident, are you?"

"Not another word from you, Dalton," she said, turning her back to him and sipping her chocolate most delicately.

Dalton limited his response to a bark of laughter, and then left her room with Jane at his elbow, whispering words of wise counsel, no doubt. It was unfortunate for Jane that she was hampered by an obstinate family, ruled for the most part by their own stubborn ways.

But not Clarissa. She was proceeding wisely and most cautiously. Did she not have her list? And what a welcome addition Montwyn was to that list, especially when compared to his competition. But really, to be honest with herself, he had no competition. With Irish lands behind him, he became just possible for consideration as a husband. He was still rude and overbearing and proud, yet he was compelling in a blatant sort of way.

He just might do.

He was certainly a more attractive candidate than Esherton. All that was lacking was the certainty that she could manage him. Yet if she was able to manuever him into making an offer for her, it would be no great task to softly manage him during their marriage. She was almost certain Montwyn wouldn't present too much of a problem.

Let Dalton spill the truth about her list to him; she just hoped he would. If she knew men—and she did, with ten older brothers to instruct her—his knowing she had compiled a list with his name on it would fire both his anger and his interest. His pride would be pricked, as would his manly desire to win at any game, any competition. And so he would compete—to be her husband. She would have her Irish estate and, if Montwyn did as she expected, a husband who didn't smell like a dirty dish.

* * *

Dalton met Lindley in the foyer as he was pulling on his new gloves. He was in fine mettle and it showed.

"Rest easily, Lindley; I'd wager Clarissa will choose Montwyn within the week, if Montwyn can be properly encouraged to offer for her."

"Really?" Lindley asked, trying to decide just when this decision on Clarissa's part could have taken place. Of course, there was Beau to entice to the altar as well. If Clarissa was of a mind to accept Montwyn, there was no time to waste in getting Beau to offer for her. She was so changeable lately that any delay could ruin the whole arrangement.

Dalton hurried out, every item of clothing in perfect place, to find Montwyn and do his cheerful best to push him into matrimony.

Lindley, unfortunately, did not know this and left hurriedly on exactly the same errand.

Only Russell, who had heard the short exchange from the study, was of a different mind. It was obvious to him that both Dalton and Lindley were well-disposed to having Montwyn a part of their family. He, however, was much less certain of the man's worth as Clarissa's husband. Montwyn had a reputation as a hard man, and Clarissa, with her outspoken ways, would have an easier time of it with a milder sort of fellow. Certainly Clarissa could be convinced of this bald truth.

He approached her door quietly, only to hear her talking softly with Perry. It didn't sound the sort of conversation one intruded upon, and so he left to make his way to Montwyn, to put him off Clarissa, by whatever means he could find, and onto another girl. Young Mary Beckham was a lovely girl of sweet temperament and radiant complexion. If he were in the market for a wife, he'd be easily induced to look her way. He could not imagine that Montwyn would see her any differently.

He had forgotten completely how blind a brother could be to his sister's appeal.

"Is it possible that you are unaware how completely ridiculous the entire idea is?" Perry asked, as close to fury as he had ever come. "You've made a *list*? That is absolutely not the way to choose a husband. What if none of the men on your list offers for you? What good then, Clarissa?"

"Not offer?" She laughed. "They'll *all* offer for me. What is wrong with you to have so little faith in me?"

"And if they do, then whom will you pick if all are equal upon your list?"

Perry reached over and took the list from the table, reading aloud.

"Benson, Esherton, and *Montwyn!* They're all impossible; surely you can see that, Clarissa. How have you compiled this list, for such unsuitable men to be grouped together so cozily?"

"They are not unsuitable," she snapped. How could he put Beau in with Benson? Was it possible that a man did not see a suitor in the same light as a woman would? Could any man, even Perry, be that blind? "And I've compiled my list by priorities. My priorities. Land in Ireland is my first concern. His owning an estate in Ireland is more important than anything."

"It must be for Montwyn to appear on your list."

"Why else would he be there?" she said stiffly. "I simply must return to Ireland, Perry. You, of all people, should understand that."

Perry sat down next to her and took her hand in his. "I don't want you to go back," he said gently. "I don't want it to be so important to you."

"But it is," she said, stroking his hand. "I must go back."

Perry dropped his head and sighed. "Are you still having the dream?"

Images jolted into her mind's eye at the question, unwelcome images of red coats and bright blood and blazing fire. Swirling and unwelcome shades of red burned behind her eyes. And then screams and gunfire and explosion; the sounds of war and battle and pain. All were viewed from above, as if she had no part in it. But she was a part, had been a part, could not forget. She would never forget the screams of a dying man, the eyes of an English soldier.

She forced herself to keep her expression calm as she answered, "Not as much."

Perry, it seemed, was unconvinced. "You should stay here," he pronounced, and not for the first time. All her brothers were in agreement on that: keep Clarissa out of Ireland.

"If I am in Ireland again, the dream will leave me," she said, standing and escaping his touch. She felt trapped and hated it; she should not feel trapped by Perry. He loved her.

"I don't know why it would," he said, his eyes never leaving her.

"It just would," she insisted. "I must go back."

"Albert will never allow it."

"It will no longer be Albert's decision," she said softly, hiding her triumph.

"Your husband will leave you in Ireland while he lounges in England?" Perry asked mockingly. At her nod, he said, "It is at moments like this that I wonder how well you truly understand men, Clarissa."

"I understand them well enough," she said, and then laughed, breaking the somber mood. "Each one of these men will offer for me by year's end." And at that she was being conservative. She doubted it would take even two weeks. She would be married by Christmas.

"Even Montwyn?" Perry asked.

Clarissa smiled. "Even Montwyn." *Especially* Montwyn.

Lindley called upon Beau at his home on Grosvenor Street and managed to catch him in.

"Well done, Beau," he greeted upon being directed into Beau's handsome library.

Beau rose from his chair at the greeting and said, "While I enjoy praise as earnestly as any man, for what am I being congratulated at this hour of the day?"

"Why, for your success with Clarissa," Lindley said, a scowl just beginning to form at the evidence of Beau's ignorance. "Whatever you have done must be working quite to your advantage, because she is more than half prepared to accept an offer of marriage from you."

"Really?" Beau said with a bemused smile.

She was prepared to accept him? She'd be a damned fool not to, by his reckoning. He was quite aware that she was attracted to him; she hadn't been adept at hiding that from him, not that he cared, in any regard. Still, Lindley had a right to be pleased; it would be a good union for all concerned. He was more than a sight pleased himself. He had come to London to find a wife, and he had done so rather expeditiously, not wasting time when his duty was to get an heir at all speed. Perhaps he'd have a son by Christmas next.

Yes, he was quite pleased with the way events were progressing. Lindley had an air of being almost relieved to have the matter of Clarissa settled, and well he should be; Clarissa was ravishing, true, but she was a bit of a scold. Not a proper sort of wife for every man, but he was more than certain that he would manage her most efficiently.

He had almost reached the stables when Russell Walingford greeted him. Truly, London seemed awash in Walingfords since Clarissa had come to town to find a husband. Beau greeted him cordially, as befitted a future brother, and waited civilly while Russell came to the point. He was beyond certain that Clarissa would be mentioned.

He was wrong.

"I noticed how prettily Miss Maria Belgrave played. Did you not also make note of it? A lovely young woman, is she not?"

"I would not disagree," Beau said with a mental shrug.

"So many young women to meet this season, Lord Montwyn," Russell said, pressing the point. "Delightful parties and splendid dinners abound, wouldn't you say? A shame for a man to cut himself off, so to speak, so early in the season."

"Cut himself off?" Beau repeated heavily. "I do not comprehend you."

"Have you not met Lady Mary Beckham? A most delightful girl. She is to be at the Mongrave dinner, to which I am certain you have received an invitation."

"Is that where the Walingfords will be spending their evening?" Beau asked.

Russell cleared his throat before answering, "I do not believe so, but you should avail yourself of the invitation. Mary is a stellar woman of rare beauty and pleasing deportment."

"Then allow me to encourage you to attend the Mongrave dinner, so that you may better enjoy the company of Lady Mary," Beau said, striving to maintain his cordiality.

"It was your own enjoyment that prompted me, Lord Montwyn," Russell said. "You would be rewarded in pleasure by spending time in Mary's company."

How much more pleasure he would have received if he had not understood Russell's intent; he was obviously trying to dissuade him from Clarissa by throwing Mary Beckham, or any other young woman, in his path. What to make of this state of events when Lindley, not half an hour since, had hailed him on, encouraging him to finish the task he had started when first he came to London and beheld Clarissa?

According to Lindley, Clarissa was his. According to Russell, he should look elsewhere. But perhaps Russell was not privy to Clarissa's thoughts . . . and perhaps Lindley was not either. Perhaps it was only that Lindley voiced his own wish. *Blast!* These Walingfords were a bedeviling lot, Clarissa the worst of all with her bold talk and mischievous air. He should forget her and give Mary Beckham a look, find a wife of a more demure nature and submissive demeanor.

He should, but he would not.

How could he, having met Clarissa?

He had excused himself—rather abruptly, if he must admit it—from Russell and proceeded to the stables. A good ride in the park was just the thing to clear his head and illuminate his resolve. His mount was reliable and of an easy temperament and just as eager for a run in the cold winter air as his master. Beau gave him his head and threw out all thoughts but the pure joy of riding a good horse. Clarissa and her brothers would be managed in their own time. For the moment he wanted to be free of the responsibility of making a good marriage and the necessity of producing an heir to secure Montwyn for future generations.

It was a burden that had belonged to his older brother, William, and William had borne it cheerfully. But William had died of a fever without issue, his widow had remarried, and now it fell to Beau to carry on. He had never wished for the duty. He had taken up a commission in the regiment and found joy there. He had resigned his commission and taken up a life of gaming and women and found joy there. He was now called upon to resign his life of decadence and assume the role of Lord of Montwyn. He only hoped he could find some small measure of joy in it.

Meeting Clarissa had given him hope. He had to marry and to marry a certain type of woman, of certain family and certain position, and such women were generally of the same type: quiet, demure, and biddable. Certainly there were benefits to having such a woman in a man's life, but the drawbacks gleamed more brightly. He did not want to share his life with a woman of little more spirit and fire than a babe. He suspected that such a woman would drown a man with her constant need for guidance and direction. And, for all that it was unfashionable, he wanted a wife with whom he could converse.

Clarissa had a tongue in her head and the brain to wield it in a most entertaining manner.

He did not think he would ever grow bored with Clarissa.

He was certain Clarissa was the ideal choice.

He was equally certain, most of the time, that Clarissa saw him in the same light.

Of what could she complain? He was well propertied, well titled, well fixed, and . . . he did not want her to want him for those reasons. Blast, but he would have her wanting him for himself and not what he brought to the union, though it went against all logic for him to wish it. Should he even want a woman who would throw all sense aside to listen to her heart? No, and yet he did.

And no matter what Russell said, he was certain that she wanted him for those things that could not be listed on a clerk's ledger. That is, he was certain most of the time.

All good intentions aside, he had not been able to leave Clarissa and her brothers behind him on his ride. Still, it had been good to get out into the air. He felt better for it.

Until he saw Dalton waiting for him at the stable as he returned his mount.

"I hate to say it, since I consider you a friend," Dalton said with a huge grin, "but you seem to be something of a fool, Beau."

Beau dismounted and handed the horse off to the groom.

"In the name of that friendship, I will refrain from calling you out," Beau said with the barest hint of a smile.

Dalton bowed. "Thank you, Lord Montwyn. But you have been fool enough to let it be known that you were in the possession of an Irish estate, and that has put you firmly on her list."

"List?" Beau said as he walked out, Dalton matching his stride.

"Oh, yes, let me inform you of the method that my darling sister is implementing in her quest to obtain for herself the ideal husband."

"You mock her, yet it shows sense," Beau said. Perhaps his personal attributes were mentioned on the list.

"Oh, good sense, I will agree," Dalton said, laughing. "At the top of her list is the necessity for her future husband to be the lord of an Irish estate. The second requirement, which naturally follows and which you can hardly debate the wisdom of, is an annual income of not less than thirty thousand pounds a year, for how can an Irish estate be maintained for less?"

"In addition to a home or two in England," Beau added calmly. "She shows a rare inclination for management. You must give my compliments to your sister."

Dalton merely smiled and kept walking, swinging his stick most irritatingly.

She wanted him; that matched with Lindley's impression. But for his Irish lands? He would not believe it. He had seen her eyes when she looked at him and watched the thrumming of her blood in the slender stem of her throat; she wanted him. Let her tell her brothers that it was his Irish lands that compelled her to him, if it suited her, but he knew the spark of female interest when it landed in his lap, so to speak. She had him on her shopping list of possible husbands for more flattering reasons than property and income.

"Our Clarissa," Dalton said, "is a very clever, very level-headed girl. No limp sentiment for her. I will deliver your compliments to my sister, Lord Montwyn."

Dalton bowed and left Beau at Grosvenor Place and Piccadilly. Beau did not return the bow; he walked on, more determined than ever to prove, at least to himself, how very wrong Clarissa was if she thought to have him for his property alone.

Another evening's entertainment to be readied for. In truth, she found she was looking forward to it. She was more than certain that Beau would be there, and the knowledge made her preparations all the more enjoyable. Tonight she would wear the pale green gown with light pink and wine red embroidered blossoms strewn about the neckline; the ruby necklace from her mother would do well with it.

Albert requested entry as she was choosing her gloves and fan; she kept her manner light, though she could feel her heart sink within her chest.

"Good evening, Clarissa," Albert said, choosing to remain standing though Clarissa had offered him a chair. "I don't mean to interrupt, but have you met anyone who might be suitable?"

Uncharitable thoughts and hard words rose in her mind, but she subdued them. Instead she tossed him her list with a carelessness she did not feel. Let her list speak for her. He would see how far he had pushed her. He would see to what lengths she had been driven in the name of familial duty and feminine submission.

She regally pulled on a glove as she awaited his declamations of sorrow, regret, and guilt.

"I commend you, Clarissa," Albert said. She turned to face him. His face was radiant with joy and pride. "You display a level of intelligence about the whole matter of choosing a spouse that I find wholly admirable. If more young women were of your caliber, Britain would have more productive marriages. In fact, I can think of a few names you may have overlooked in ignorance. You will allow me to add them?" Clarissa nodded dumbly. "Lord Chister has a lovely park in Tipperary as well as a small manor in France, now under dispute, of course, but that may right itself and must be considered, don't you think?"

"Naturally," Clarissa managed stiffly. "A manor in France would be delightful."

"And then there is old Lord Baring, who is of an age to need a nurse more than a wife, but one cannot ignore the fact that he is in possession of the finest estate in Kildare. I can see you now in his yellow salon . . . a striking portrait, if I do say. You are a clever girl to keep your head about you so well when so many girls flit off with the first pretty man with curling hair who happens to bow before them. Well, I won't detain you, seeing that you have the matter so well in hand. Given your abilities, I should not be surprised by a Christmas wedding, I tell you. Well done, Clarissa!"

He strode to the door of her chamber, and she could hardly find the words to bid him good night.

"You are satisfied, then?" she managed to say.

Albert turned at the door and considered her. She looked as forlorn as a pup in the rain, though he knew she was unaware of it. "More than satisfied—proud, if you must know. You are being remarkably reasonable about the whole business. Most gratifying. Shows the makings of a splendid wife." And he turned and left.

Once in the privacy of the hall, Albert gave in to the laugh he had been swallowing for the past ten minutes. *Gad, that should do it.* She'd drop the whole notion of the list now that she had been commended for it.

He hadn't missed the significance of Montwyn's name appearing with the rest. Oh, yes, the man had an Irish estate, but he was also well titled and of a firm and unyielding temperament: perfect for his young sister. That was a match well made; he could hardly have done better himself for her.

Resuming his characteristic stoic demeanor, Albert retired to his study to await the eventual—one could almost say inevitable—arrival of Lord Montwyn. One truth he had spoken: he anticipated a Christmas wedding. To be sure, Montwyn, from all that he had heard of the man, was not one to dally.

*
Chapter Five
*

The dinner was sumptuous, the company pleasing, the house spectacular, and Clarissa was trying very hard to appear to be enjoying herself. It did not help that the man seated to her right was Lord Baring, who was not only the possessor of the finest estate in Kildare, but of a very poorly designed set of false teeth. He was making quite a mess of his capon. She was trying desperately not to hear him wetly gumming the small bones of the bird in his mouth. Most unappetizing, even if his estate was glorious.

Matters were not helped in that Beau was seated halfway down and across the table next to a very pretty blond woman, Lady Elena Montaine, who appeared from this distance to be absolutely captivated by every utterance of Lord Montwyn. And Lord Montwyn appeared most gratified by her blatant attentions.

Clarissa felt the beginnings of a headache behind her right eye.

Small wonder.

Each of her brothers in residence had felt it imperative to impart special instruction, counsel, and advice into her ear before she left for the evening. Lindley had urged her not to be a lackwit and let Montwyn slip by her. Dalton had stopped her to point out that Montwyn's Irish lands were very fine and that she wasn't the only young woman out for her first season who would enjoy an estate in Ireland, or Montwyn himself, for that matter. Russell had been considerably gentler when he had reminded her that Montwyn was well known as a guest at some of the more questionable house parties, in season and out; something he well knew, as he was often at the same parties. Perry, her most devoted brother, had warned her not to allow Montwyn to get so firm a hold on her attentions that all other possible suitors would bolt before the game had been played out. Though each bit of advice was as different as her brothers were different, the common thread was Montwyn himself.

Had the field narrowed so drastically and so soon, then?

Had it really all come down to Henry Wakefield?

Past the slippery sound of Lord Baring's crunching, she watched Beau. His dark hair was thick and shining, his brow noble and high, his eyes intelligent; he was a most handsome man. Tall, broad in the shoulder, trim in the waist, and powerful. He was a most powerful man. He was magnificent, and, of course, he had those very necessary Irish lands.

Lady Elena, rapt at his side, laughed sweetly at something he said, and Beau smiled his response to her.

Awareness surged through her as completely as a shiver. She wanted that smile to be for her. She wanted those eyes to look only at her. She wanted his attention and his conversation and his regard.

And as she was filled with wanting, Beau looked away from his dinner companion and stared straight into her eyes. Unerringly, he pinned her with a look. Unreservedly, she returned it.

Feminine awareness took hold and set its roots deep within her for the first time in her life. She understood his look, understood the wanting behind it, the power that drove it, the determination to fulfill its demands. Such a look, a look of hunger for her and recognition that it was she and she alone who could meet his need, filled her with a sense of joy and power such as she had never known. She held his look, wanting it. Wanting the desire she saw glimmering just beneath the surface, understanding that she aroused him. Glorying in the knowledge.

And then the look was broken. It was just a glance, really, nothing more, yet she had read all that in the short moment it took for a brief meeting of their eyes.

She had read something of his heart in that glance.

The list could be burned. Montwyn was her choice. The only thing left to do was let him know of his good fortune.

Their after-dinner entertainment was supplied by Lady Elena of the sweet smile. She played the pianoforte and she played it very well. She would make someone a very pretty wife. But not Montwyn. Montwyn was to be hers.

She could not see him from her position on the couch, but she knew that he was somewhere behind her. Where behind her? Looking fondly at Lady Elena, imagining her playing the pianoforte in Montwyn Hall?

Clarissa turned her head as casually as she could manage in order to look into the dim corners of the capacious room. She did not have to look so far as that, for Beau stood just behind her and met her eyes as she turned. Green eyes sparkled into deepest brown; she did not look away, but took in the sight of him, knowing that he had been looking at her and not at Elena.

The glance, growing into a stare of awareness, did not break. She could feel the power of him through his eyes. She could see him smile in self-satisfaction.

Oh, yes, that was what it was. She had ten older brothers; she knew the look well.

Clarissa turned away and fanned herself gracefully, pretending to listen to the crescendo of Elena's piece. Beau grew more confident by the hour, and such confidence, since it was directed at her, did not sit well. It was stupid to delay the inevitable when it would only gratify his arrogance. She would not be coy or flirtatious with the man she had chosen to marry. To what purpose to pretend hesitation or uncertainty? She had made her selection—all that was left was to pay the bill.

Elena concluded to a round of warm applause at her skill and her general prettiness. Beau left his position at Clarissa's back and went around to the pianoforte, bowing low over Lady Elena's hand and murmuring words that only she could hear—and that caused a most delicate blush to rise in her cheeks. Clarissa watched all with a cold eye and a trim smile of amusement. Let him play at seduction; he was already hers. She was certain he knew that as well as she, for she would never have chosen a man of low intelligence or dull sensitivity.

After escorting Elena back to her seat, Beau approached Clarissa. She rose so as to meet him standing. She had known he would return to her; it was inevitable.

His eyes searched hers again, and again she held his gaze. She was not insensible to him—hardly that, for he made the blood grow thick in her bosom and her legs felt as soft as pudding—but she would not be the timid miss for him; he would not want that, and she did not want it for herself. Let them meet as equals in this matrimonial excursion, and let them both willingly and openly pay the price of union.

"You've made your selection," she said softly, her bosom heating as she said the words. "Why encourage her to think otherwise?"

"Have I?" he whispered, staring down at her.

He was such a tall man, so broad, with such bearing; it came to her mind that she should be the slightest bit in awe of him. She rejected the thought as illogical.

"You would like to play out the farce?" she asked. "When we both know the finale?"

"Are you as bold as you seem?" he said, almost in an undertone for his own ears.

"Is it boldness you see in me?" Clarissa asked, wanting him to see more.

"Assuredly," he said.

"Not astuteness? Not discernment?"

He took her arm in answer, and they left the light and noise of the salon behind them. Lord Wingate and his sister were being encouraged in a duet. Beau closed the door behind them and led her into the wide central hallway. It was well lit, with the noise of the party and the bustle of servants surrounding them, yet the quiet and seclusion, the intensity of his presence, made all seem intimate and clandestine. She felt, somehow, that it was intentional on his part—that he was testing the degree of her temerity. She did not care. He was her best choice, and, without undue pride, she determined that she was his.

"Because you are an astute shopper?" he asked, his eyes

intent upon her face. "Able to choose the finest lace at the most reasonable price?" He moved closer to her, just a step, but she felt her breath catch and moved away from him.

"I *am* a good shopper. Your vanity must compel you to agree. And there are worse attributes in a wife."

"And what woman, maid or matron, shops without a list?" he said abruptly, hoping to catch her in an embarrassment.

"Not I, surely," she said, chin up and eyes clear as fine wine.

Yet she, impossible woman, would not be pricked by so small a thing as shame. She did not bleed from the wound his words had attempted. She *was* bold, no matter her claims to be discerning. What woman on the marriage mart would be so obvious, so blatant, so without feminine guile in her matrimonial pursuits? Was it a game she played to catch his interest, for she surely had, or was she truly as bold as she appeared?

He pressed closer to her, his hand upon her arm, and forced her to promenade the hallway with him; he would not compromise her, for he did not want her by that route, and he would not give her the chance to catch him with that old ruse. No, all would be proper, if a bit irregular.

"What was the body of your list? How was it compiled?" he asked.

"By priorities, my lord, how else?" she said, and then smiled. "Surely Dalton told you as much."

He smiled down at her, amused and engaged. She *was* astute. And a beauty. If he had bothered to compile a list, certainly it would have featured those two attributes. Rather call them necessities.

"I was informed only of a list in the making," he quibbled. "I am . . . honored? . . . to have been included."

"You are not sincere, but I am," she said, her hand light upon his arm. She did not tremble. He was impressed. "You are on my list of possible husbands. If the truth be told, I am quite certain that you are on many similar lists throughout London. I'm sure your dining companion who plays the pianoforte so sweetly will add your name to her list before she retires."

Her boldness went too far, straying into vulgarity. "You show only boldness and no discernment in making such a remark," he said with tight anger.

"You are right. I apologize," she said quickly enough. "But it is the truth."

It may well have been the truth, but he was both appalled . . . and flattered. She could read it in him, he knew.

"The truth is delightful, is it not?" she said, laughing lightly.

He had never found being laughed at to be even remotely tolerable. Until now.

He wanted to tell her that *she* was the rarity, the delight. He didn't know there could be such a woman as Clarissa Walingford seemed to be. But perhaps she only *seemed* to be.

"Shall we test it?" he challenged. "A conversation of truth, only truth, with none of the layered shadings of practiced civility? Do you dare it, Clarissa?"

"Truth need not be uncivil," she said, her manner quietly cautious. He silently applauded her: bold but not reckless.

"Then a civil truth. Shall we try?" He grinned, pressing his hand over hers as it lay upon his arm.

Clarissa smiled up at him, her expression playful, and said, "Yes. I would enjoy it."

"The first truth. And a truth most civil," he teased. But he wanted more than careful, polite truths from her. He wanted to see into her heart. "How real is your list?"

"Quite real. I held it in my hand but hours ago," she said.

"And my name was on it, held between your hands?"

He did not touch her hand, but his eyes went there, and she clenched her hand upon his arm to keep him away from the vulnerability of her palm.

"Yes," she said softly, averting her eyes. He was so overwhelming at this proximity. It was becoming increasingly difficult to maintain her composure.

"Why am I on your list?" he asked.

She could only look at him, feeling his nearness and his strength, feeling that she should take care and protect herself, but she could not. She stood, immobilized by his touch and by the impossible nature of his question. Why was he on her list? She would not tell him that he was handsome. She would not tell him that he amused her. She would not tell him that he drew her in when all of London seemed closed to her Irish heart. She would not tell, for she would not allow those words into her thoughts. She could only want him for what he could give her, not for what he could inspire in her. That was all she would allow herself.

"What is it about me that has made me so profoundly eligible?" he said.

Ah, he wanted compliments, as all men did. That, also, she would not do. A man never appreciated the giver of the compliment, but only the compliment itself, hugging the words to his chest as he strolled off in self-congratulation. She had not needed ten brothers to teach her that basic truth.

"You have a wonderful . . . estate in Ireland," she said casually.

It was not what he had expected to hear. It was not what he *wanted* to hear. He was titled, well regarded, fit, and not unpleasant to look upon. All for naught if his Irish lands were forfeit? Impossible. No truth could have so much folly in it. She *wanted* him; he knew that for a truth.

"Dalton mentioned as much to me. I assumed in jest," he said, turning her for the walk back down the hall. It was much quieter here, which did not suit him at present, as it made the sound of his shattering vanity ring more loudly in his ears.

"It is no jest."

"I can see that it is not. Why Ireland?" he asked. He *had* been wondering. It was a strange prerequisite for a betrothal.

"Ireland is home," she said in all simplicity. "I want to go home."

"Ireland is home? When were you last there?"

"Ten years or so. I miss it very much."

"I would say that you could hardly remember it."

"Then you would be wrong. I remember it well," she said, her voice firm and strangely resolute.

He doubted the truth of that statement. She must have been a young girl when she had left, not above ten years. But he could see that she believed her words. As it was to be a discussion of civil truths, he would not argue the point with her.

"Why do you want to marry me?" she asked into his silence.

"Have I said I do?" he replied, just a bit flustered. What sort of woman asked such a question?

"Is this not to be a conversation of truths?" she asked, her words biting into his manhood. "Were the truths all to be my own?"

"I blush," he said almost comically. "You shame me." He grinned and granted her a brief bow. "Very well. I do want to marry you. Have I just proposed?"

"If you need to ask me, then no, you have not. I would not be so unfair."

But he would not call it unfair to achieve union with such a woman. She was enchanting, completely out of his experience, delightful. He was more than ready to ask her for her hand.

He was not to have the chance that evening. Perry and Jane, obviously concerned over her lengthy absence and not put at ease at finding them in such relative seclusion, interrupted their conversation. It would not be resumed that night; he was to have no such liberties with Lady Clarissa again. His eyes followed her throughout the remainder of the evening; he could not even think to play at his amusement with Lady Elena. In all the room there was only Clarissa.

They had not finished their conversation, not yet. Tomorrow . . . tomorrow he would call upon her. The thought was a fever in his blood that he welcomed as warmly as a brother.

"Has he proposed yet?" Jane whispered as they donned their cloaks.

"Tomorrow," Clarissa said softly, with a smile of pure anticipation. "He will tomorrow."

At the hour of three, which was when Beau felt it appropriate to make his appearance at the Walingford town house, everyone in the house, including the pastry chef, knew he was there to propose marriage. Her brothers were especially jubilant; after all, Clarissa might have an imperfect understanding of politics, but she understood the way a man's mind worked well enough. With ten tutors it was hardly likely that she'd be less than proficient at it. They were damned proud of her, too. Montwyn was a good match for them. She'd done well. For privacy, it was agreed that they be allowed to stroll the garden together. Clarissa looked fetching in a lilac pelisse with a matching bonnet. Dalton, watching from a third-floor window, could only smile. Montwyn had been spoken for. One could only wonder if he realized it yet.

However, the more interesting question was whether Clarissa understood that Montwyn would never let her plop herself down in Ireland without him.

The garden was barren of leaves, but the privet hedge provided structure, as did the stone bench on the back wall. It was a pretty garden, the bricks laid in a herringbone pattern around a sundial that amply demonstrated how cloudy a day it was. Fortunately there had been no rain for a week. It was a pleasant place to linger, even in December. And they had all the privacy they could wish.

"Shall we continue?" Beau asked, looking larger than usual in his greatcoat and hat.

"You like truth very well, it seems," she said, smiling at him.

"I do." He nodded with a smile. "I may well have contracted a daily need for it."

Clarissa held her tongue. She would not put the words in his mouth to spit back out at her. He would do this on his own.

"Do you play coy now?" he asked.

"No," she said pleasantly. "Let us return to my question of last evening. Why do you want to marry me?"

"Why?" he blustered, clearly taken aback. It was most amusing. "Why does any man want to marry?"

"For heirs?" she said. "Any woman could do that for you."

He really was blushing now, but she would not relent. She would not bind herself to a man because he found her amusing or entertaining. Let there be more to their union than that, even if she dwelled in Ireland alone. But with this man, would she be left alone?

"You are the most confounded woman," he grumbled.

"I suppose I am, and it's best you know it now. Perhaps if you ask me to marry you, our conversation will progress more smoothly," she suggested, giving up her earlier transigence.

He turned to face her, stopping them on the path. Her feet were cold. It didn't matter. He was the most beautiful man she had ever seen, the most masculine, the most marvelous. His eyes, so green in the gray world of winter, demanded something of her. Pity, she supposed. He looked a man beset and just a bit bewildered. A man on the brink of matrimony would have such a look; Lindley had looked so when he had offered for Miss Brookdale. It must be the way of men to have to be hounded to the altar. She felt completely calm. She knew what she wanted. She only waited for him to say it.

"Let me ask you instead why you so clearly want to marry me," he said, adjusting his hat when it was already set perfectly upon his head. When she paused, he crowed, "You see? It is not so simple a question to answer. No one should be put in such a position. I withdraw—"

"No," she interrupted him. "I want to answer you. This is more in the matter of a practical arrangement, and I believe we should be truthful about both our purpose and our expectations."

"Come now. I expect no such answer. This borders on incivility—"

"I disagree. Let us be honest with each other at the very least; even if this is to be our last conversation."

At his silence, she only smiled. He had not liked hearing that gently voiced threat.

"I have come to the point in my life when marriage is expected," she said, her voice grave. "I have a duty to my family to marry well. Your title and your income make you quite desirable."

"High on your list, you might say," he interjected curtly. He looked irritated. It didn't alarm her, as it didn't signify; men were so easily irritated.

"I do say," she said brightly. "You are my first choice, most especially because of the desirability of your Irish estate. You are in a county I particularly admire, and all agree that your house is outstanding."

"To hell with all that!" he roared, obviously pushed beyond his endurance for honest communication.

Oh, he was definitely angry. And he had used foul language. If he thought to shock her into silence or submission he had calculated poorly; she had ten brothers, three of them in the army.

"My lord? I am not accustomed to such speech," she said tartly. "Can you not refrain? This is a point I had not considered; is such intemperance a permanent feature of your character?"

Apparently it was.

Beau, his face a mask of barely controlled frustration, pulled her into his arms. He was not gentle. She was not afraid. She felt lost against the size of him—lost and then found.

"There is more to me than my estate, Clarissa, and more between us than titles," he said in a growl, his mouth bare inches above hers. "That is a truth you shall not deny."

He kissed her then, and, bold as she was, she welcomed it. It was a hard kiss, an angry kiss, a kiss of threat and promise. She felt only the promise.

His mouth was hot and heavy upon hers, yet she did not

turn from it, for there was passion, too, and she was hungry
for his passion. She knew the truth of his desire for her in his
kiss. She could not—would not—turn from that.

Dalton, appearing at the entrance to the garden, ended it.

Beau lifted his head from hers, his eyes green points of fire
in a face chilled by winter. She felt burned, and shivered.

"I'm afraid I'll have to insist that you marry her now,
Beau," Dalton said, cheerily enough, all things considered.
"You certainly have fixed yourself." He almost laughed.

"I had already asked your sister to marry me," Beau said,
pulling Clarissa to his side and holding her there. "This was
her answer."

"Ahhh." Dalton grinned.

He didn't believe a word of it.

The marriage took place on Friday of that week, a small
affair of family only. Still, they filled the salon. Chadwick
and Braden, both in the army, were unable to attend.
Leighton was busy in Ireland and couldn't make the crossing in time, and Alston and Harden were touring the conti-
nent, trying to avoid trouble, they wrote. So only Albert,
Lindley, Jane, Dalton, Russell, and Perry attended the ceremony from her side. All wore smiles. On Beau's side was his
paternal grandmother, Lady Claire, a delightful woman with
the same green eyes as her grandson.

Beau still looked a trifle angry, which puzzled Clarissa
completely. Oh, well, that would pass. He had the wife of his
choosing. She had done her duty to her family and married
well without a whimper of complaint. At least not in the last
week.

During the wedding breakfast, she sat quietly congratulating herself as the conversation flowed around her. Beau was

oddly quiet as well; perhaps he was equally self-congratulatory. They had made a good match, each of them, and deserved a small moment of victory. Before the breakfast was quite over—she had hardly finished her tea—Beau announced to the room that they would be leaving immediately on their wedding trip. It seemed a bit precipitous to her, but she was not of a mind to cause any commotion over it. She *was* eager to see Montwyn Hall.

Naturally Jane would accompany her.

Naturally Albert had to stop her as she was entering the coach to congratulate her once more on her excellent judgment. And again, as it had the last ten times he had offered such words of praise, the compliment rankled. It should not. She *had* made the best match of the season. She *was* on her way to Ireland even now, for that was the final destination of their bridal itinerary. Ireland. She would be in Ireland again. Home. Once she was settled, Beau would return to England. Which was where he belonged, being English. She would remain in Ireland, alone.

The thought brought less pleasure than it had even a week ago. *Alone* was such a lonely-sounding word. Would he really leave her alone? Pish, she would have Jane . . . and Ireland. She would not be alone.

But she would not have Beau.

Did he honestly mean to leave her alone?

At present, he did not. Beau had her bundled into the coach with Jane snug against her side before she had quite finished her farewells. Beau sat across from them, warm in his greatcoat, solemn and silent.

And so he remained throughout the day; even Jane with her pleasant and hopeful nature could not stand against such a wall of silence.

Clarissa had no energy to make the effort. All her thoughts

were of Ireland; the man who had made it possible, her husband, she barred from her thoughts. Though it was a most difficult thing to do with him sitting just across from her, his knees brushing against her skirts, his green eyes studying her. Still, she persevered. It was to be only the first of many barriers she would set between them, because, ultimately, she would bar him from her life. She had married well, done credit to her family, acquired access to an Irish estate, and, once she'd produced a child or two, giving him his heir, their paths would hardly cross again.

Just what was required to produce an heir she did not dwell upon.

And so the journey was spent in silence, a silence as heavy and cold as winter itself.

They arrived at Montwyn Hall just at dusk. It was impressive. *Most* impressive.

Manicured woods, bare now, limbs reaching toward the growing darkness, lined the gravel drive, which swept in a graceful arc to the front of the hall. The hall itself consisted of a massive central building surrounded by four pavilions linked by quadrant colonnades, all perfectly symmetrical, perfectly grand.

Jane looked suitably impressed. Clarissa could not have been more pleased.

"So you're happy with your bargain?" Beau asked as the coach stopped in front of the portico. It was the first sentence he'd spoken to her all day.

He sounded insulted, yet why should he be? Why should he not be flattered and pleased that the legacy she had married into was grand? She was expected to marry well. Should she be derided because she had? Obviously not. Her only recourse was to ignore him, since he was being so contrary.

But he was very difficult to ignore.

*   *   *

He knew that well enough.

Beau was perfectly aware that Clarissa was doing all in her power to ignore him, as if he were an unnecessary accessory to "her" Irish lands. She had been clear in her purpose from the start and equally vocal. What cause had he to complain now?

What cause? Because he had believed her to have some kindred feeling for him. Because he had wanted her with the first look. Because her odd honesty had beguiled him as surely as her beauty.

Beguiled but not blinded. He was no fool; he would not have pursued her if he had not felt some shimmer of attraction in her. She wanted him, and for more than his title and lands. She had to want him. No woman could be so cold and . . . practical. It was only left for him to prove it to her. He was not a pair of gloves purchased for her convenience. He was her husband. If she did not understand the difference, she soon would.

The house was entered through the marble hall, and he could hear her intake of breath; it was breathtaking. Corinthian columns of pink Nottinghamshire alabaster made up the colonnade. The ceiling was frescoed and lit by circular skylights. The floor was buff marble inlaid with curls and circles of white marble. It was most impressive entry.

"A most beautiful hall, Lord Montwyn," Jane offered.

Beau nodded at the compliment, graciously accepting it from her.

"Shall we have a tour?" Clarissa said, her priorities clear, as always.

"Not tonight," Beau answered. "Moresby has prepared a light supper for us. We shall dine and then retire for the evening. It has been a long and tiring day; I am certain a good night's rest must head our list of priorities."

Clarissa swallowed her argument and smiled her acquiescence. Most reasonable of her, especially as he had not given her any choice but compliance. Moresby, the head butler, was introduced to them, and he led the way to the dining room, where they ate sparingly. It had been a long day, and Jane, if not Clarissa, was most fatigued.

"I do think I could look at the ground floor," Clarissa said as the plates were being cleared. "What was beyond the marble hall?"

"The salon," Beau answered, rising from his chair, "and you shall see it tomorrow. Good night, Lady Jane," he said. "Moresby will conduct you to your chamber. Have a most restful night."

Jane left without a murmur of protest or even any hesitancy of step.

"That was most rude of you," Clarissa said as they proceeded up the stairs. "Jane would have enjoyed a tour of Montwyn Hall very much. You gave not a thought to her pleasure."

"I do believe that Jane is more attuned to my pleasure than my own wife," he said. "Should we not hasten to the bedchamber and conclude our transaction?"

"I believe I quote your sentiments when I remark that you are delving into the vulgar in your attempts at truth telling," she said.

"Perhaps the fault, if there is one, is that I lack your practice at speaking a civil truth. Perhaps I can phrase it better." He pondered, leading her on down a wide hallway ornately littered with oil paintings and mahogany chairs. "Ah, let's try this." He smiled. "I want to sample the goods I have paid for. Better?"

"I should have paid more attention to your outburst in the garden. You *are* intemperate," she said stiffly. Her stomach dropped into the cradle of her hips to wiggle there in a most distracting manner.

Beau merely smiled and opened the door for her. The chamber beyond was sumptuous, large, and well lit by fire and candle. The room was done in green, buff, and gold, the furniture Chippendale, the hangings silk. The bedcover had been turned down. All was ready for his "sampling."

"Perhaps," he said, closing the door behind them. "I would have said eager, but the best word may be *curious*."

"Curious?"

"To see if your boldness was a ploy. I often wondered if you were as bold as you seemed. It appears I am soon to have my answer."

"I understand the transactions of the marketplace as well as you," she said coldly. "Let a servant attend me. I will present myself to you shortly, and then the bargain we have struck will be well and truly sealed."

"No servants," he said. "Just us. And this bargain, this union, is already sealed, Clarissa. All has been signed, our words have been spoken, our families have borne witness; we are wed, and not intemperately. We knew what we were about, did we not? Did you not know that when you shopped for an Irish estate, a husband came with it? Surely a great bargain for such an astute shopper as you."

She stood speechless as he began to disrobe. He moved quickly. He showed no embarrassment at the revelation of his skin. She dared show none, though it was not embarrassment she felt but fear. Now came the moment when the bill must be paid. An heir must be conceived. She would have to couple with this man, this husband of hers, until her duty had been accomplished.

If he had looked powerful in cravat and coat, he was a hundred times more so bared to the waist. Muscle gleamed in the firelight, rippling with each movement of his body, proclaiming his raw masculinity loudly to her eyes. Her heart jumped into her throat to almost suffocate her. He stared at her; his eyes were intense and discerning, reading in her what she most wanted to hide.

She wanted him.

Yet wanting to touch and be touched by the man before her could have no part in a rational mind; it was all blind desire and need. Such a response shamed her. She wanted him and . . . she thought she might love him.

She could not love him. She could not want him. She could not need him. Because she would leave him when she went home to Ireland. She would leave and he would stay; his duty would require it. Her heart would call her to Ireland; she would not leave it again.

"Come, Clarissa," he said, clad only in his tight buckskin breeches. "I will not hurt you and I will not provoke you further."

Not provoke? He truly had no skill at speaking honestly. He was broad and hard, his muscles sculpted by flawless skin. His chest was lightly furred with black hair, and his eyes shone green as spring growth.

"Thank you," she said, turning her back on him. "Is there no one to assist me? No screen—"

"I will assist you, if you have need, and there is no need for a screen. Delay is not to your advantage, my dear. With a bold stroke, the matter is behind us."

"I wish you had used a different expression," she said with an uncomfortable laugh.

"I apologize," he said, grinning. "Do not rebuke me for my lack of skill in truthful communication; I will learn.

Now, if you had been a different sort of woman, I would have resorted to my old ways of sparkling civility and polished pretense."

"Really?" she asked, sitting to remove her shoes. "And what would you have said?"

He knelt at her feet and removed her shoes for her, his hands on her feet and ankles, his position submissive, his manner valorous. "I would have told you that since I first beheld you, with your vibrant hair curling around your face, I was captivated. I needed no brothers to commend you to me; my own eyes would have borne the task lightly."

Her shoes were removed. With a gentle and subtle hand, he inched his way up to the top of her stocking. Her limbs shook and she could not stop her trembling. His eyes held hers, green as the darkest yew branches. She could not look away and could not find a reason to want to.

"I would have told you that, having seen you, I was halfway to offering for you. Hair as red as embers, eyes as deep and lustrous as a doe's, skin as flawless as satin; what man would not want such a woman for his own?"

His fingertips touched her thigh, his skin cool next to her heat, and very gently he slipped her stocking down to her ankle. Over her foot he slipped it, his fingers caressing her arch and the delicate back of her ankle. She shivered and looked down into her lap.

"But what you speak is pretense, is it not? We have agreed upon that," she said, not looking at him.

With bolder hands, he reached up and carefully slid down the other stocking. She felt strangely nude, yet she was fully covered.

He touched her face with the tips of his fingers, tracing her. "You taught me that truth need not be uncivil. I teach you now that civility need not be pretense."

He raised her to her feet and stepped behind her, loosening her gown. He did it without an overt air of seduction, yet it was seductive simply because it was Beau. Just knowing he was in the room made her heart pound erratically. To know that he was disrobing her . . . she felt light-headed, and her vision blurred.

"And when I spoke to you," he continued, slipping her dress down to her feet, leaving her in her tissue-thin undergarments, "when I first understood that you had a tongue in your head—"

"Of course I have a tongue," she interrupted, crossing her arms over her breasts and moving away from him. "What did you expect?"

"I can see that you have not been shopping for a bride, lady, or you would not ask," he said with a chuckle.

"Not lately," she said, turning to him again, her smile soft. He had not taunted her for her retreat from him, and for that she was grateful. He had every right to see her, to touch her; the deal had been struck. "I have been rather busy shopping for a husband. Tell me, what is the market in brides like this season?"

"Grim, lady," he said, sitting on a chair by the fire to pull off his Hessians. "Silent and still when it is known you are looking for a bride. The women are demure and submissive, showing their best qualities first, I suppose, and then, when the dance has been shared and the turn in the garden has been taken, the truth comes out."

"Truth is always good," she said, kneeling before him to help with his boots. She would be logical and not fearful. The marriage must be consummated.

"Not in my experience," he said. "For the truth is . . . they have nothing to say. Demure silence is their only recourse when nothing intelligible comes forth."

"Perhaps they are overawed by you," she said, succeeding with one boot.

"Undereducated and lacking spirit, rather," he argued, succeeding with his second boot.

He should have looked rather harmless sitting in a chair in his stockinged feet. He did not. Beau Wakefield was not the least bit harmless, sitting or standing, naked or clothed. Naked . . . they were almost naked.

Clarissa shot to her feet and stood by the fire, logic deserting her.

"You, my wife," he said, rising to stand near her, "never lacked for spirit."

"I may disappoint you," she said on a whisper. His mouth was just above hers, his body massive and pulsing with heat. He would kiss her, she knew, and it would be a kiss nothing like their winter garden kiss. There was no anger in Beau now, only desire.

She was more comfortable with his anger.

"You will never disappoint me," he said softly as his mouth took hers.

He was gentle when she had expected raw passion. She was grateful, for bold he might call her, but she was afraid. His arms wrapped around her and held her tenderly, warmly, welcoming her into his embrace. She sighed away her tension and her fear as his kiss lifted her up to meet his desire.

With ease, he held her in his arms, kissing her face, her throat, her mouth, murmuring words she could not understand beyond his intent; he wished to soothe her, to arouse her. He was succeeding.

And with that thought, she realized that she wanted him to succeed. His success would be hers. She wanted his arousal; had she not realized that before? She wanted him to want her, and he did, and in wanting her, he fed her own desire for him. For she did desire him.

Bold as she was, she let him know it.

"I want you," she said against his throat, her arms wrapping themselves around him, her mouth hot against his skin.

He could feel her nipples pushing against the thin lawn of her undergarment, feel the tension of fear leave her to be replaced by the tense demands of passion. She wanted him. The words settled upon him like golden netting. She wanted him for more than his Irish lands, and her decision to wed him had been grounded in more than hard practicality. In his heart he had known it. But how sweet the words.

"Good," he said to her, laying her upon the bed and lying atop her. She was soft and firm and willing; praise God for a willing virgin on the bridal bed. But he had not expected less from Clarissa. Fear and timidity would never rule her.

He cupped her through her gown and she spread her legs wide for him, moaning her willingness. She was already wet, but he would not rush her. Her skin was white as cream and as smooth, her eyes dark and full in the flickering light, her mouth open and panting.

"Bare yourself to me, Clarissa," he commanded, sitting back from her.

For a moment she paused, and then she smiled. "If you'll do me the same courtesy, my lord."

With quick hands they slid off their remaining clothing. Naked on the bed, they studied each other. He was darkness to her fire and light, and they wished only to combine and consume each other.

"Beautiful," he said softly. His eyes scoured her and she shivered in response. He reached for her, pulling her to him by the back of her exposed and slender neck, and then urged her down at the foot of the bed.

"Do it quickly," she whispered.

"I don't want to hurt you," he said, looking into her eyes.

"Don't hurt me," she said, "but do it now. I cannot bear the waiting."

No, that would little suit her. Bold action was her way.

Hands on her breasts, he touched her, arousing her, pleasuring her, thinking only of bringing her to such need that his taking of her would be a release and not a fear-filled memory to cloud their future together. His mouth moved everywhere upon her. Her skin was hot and soft, her limbs twitching with flares of passion as they surged through her. She was a most willing bride, trusting him to protect her and please her. He would. He would do nothing less.

He spread her and she sighed. When he touched her, she groaned and pulled him to her breast. His mouth found her nipple and he teased her to the next level of desire.

"Please. Hurry," she said in a moan, thrashing beneath him.

"A truth I was most anxious to hear," he murmured against her skin. "It will be uncomfortable at first," he said. "I will do all I can to keep you from pain."

"Yes. Do it," she said breathlessly.

She was wet and ready, and he slid just the bare tip of himself into her.

"Oh." She grunted, her limbs tightening against him.

He kissed her mouth, his tongue gliding over hers, learning the inside of her. With his finger he pressed into her, widening her slightly. She was very tight. He did not know how to keep her from the pain of lost virginity.

She pulled her mouth from his. "It's going to hurt, isn't it?"

Her brown eyes were full of fear and trust. He did not know what to tell her that would ease her.

"Tell me the truth," she said.

"Yes," he said.

"Then do not hesitate," she begged. "Let me get beyond it. Help me to be past it."

Yes, he understood her. And he marveled. She was a remarkable woman, as bold and astute as she had appeared. He could only do as she asked, though it pained him more than it would her; he did not want to hurt her, yet delaying the pain she knew was to come was a torture of its own.

Staring down into her eyes, he thrust. She cried out and closed her eyes, thinking it accomplished. He was only halfway there. Waiting for her to soften around him, he thrust again. Home. She choked out a smothered scream and then instantly was still. He looked down at her, at her tense and expectant face, at her eyes pressed shut, and felt her soften around him still more.

Home at last.

"'Tis done, Clarissa. The worst is done," he said, kissing her mouth softly.

"Good," she said. "Is it over now?"

Beau smiled. "No, not yet."

"Oh." She frowned slightly.

"It gets better," he said, poised above her, holding himself still.

"Oh," she said, trying to look hopeful.

Beau smiled and slowly withdrew. He ignored her look of relief and pumped back into her. Again. She was soft and wet. Again.

"Oh!" Clarissa said, her hands clenching against his back.

Beau grinned in male satisfaction and bit her throat gently.

He reached down and fingered, her pleased to hear her gasp at the contact, more pleased when she groaned and strained against his hand.

Again he withdrew, and again he plunged into her, harder now.

She met him, her hips lifting.

Again.

And again.

He wrapped her legs around his hips, opening her further, plunging deeper. He kissed her, stealing her breath, breathing her scent and her cries until he merged with her completely.

His hands roamed her breasts as he thrust into her, holding back his release until desire consumed her.

"Hurry. Harder," she cried, panting. "More."

He gave her more.

With a scream, she shattered and he fell against her, breaking, feeling her release, pulsing against her spasms of fulfilled desire.

Slowly she put her arms around his neck, and her breathing slowed. With a sigh of surprised contentment, she kissed his cheek. It was the sweetest kiss in all his life.

"Thank you," she said into his ear, and then she softly bit him on the lobe.

He chuckled and said, "Did I manage to drive all thoughts of Ireland from you tonight?"

"Stop talking," she said dreamily, still managing to scold. "You'll ruin it."

He laughed and slid out of her and then nestled her into his arms. They lay in a tangled and easy embrace, content. He ran his fingers through her hair, red even in the dim light of the curtained bed.

"We'll go soon." He knew no explanation would be necessary. There was only one place she wanted to go, and all the world knew of it.

"Good," she said. "But I want to see Montwyn Hall first. All of it."

"You shall. Let's spend Christmas Day here—we'll invite your brothers if you like—and then we'll go to Dantry House, which I think should please you, for the turning of the year. It will be a rough crossing, but as eager as you are, I don't think you'll mind it."

"Mind? I would fly there if I could," she said.

"Not necessary. We'll sail, thank you," he said lightly.

"Thank you again," she whispered, squeezing his hand.

"You are most welcome," he replied. "Consider it a Christmas gift. I shall be giving you the first item on your wish list of husbands: a fine Irish estate."

"It's a home you've given me," she said, "and nothing less."

"I think you'll love it," he said softly, feeling her begin to fall asleep in his arms.

"I know I shall," she murmured on a sigh, slipping into sleep, thoughts of Ireland accompanying her into the darkness.

Her skirts were dirty, her shoes muddy, her bonnet hanging down her back held only by the ribbons at her throat. She could feel them pressing against her throat.

She was not supposed to be here. Her father had forbidden it. But she was with Perry. It was all right if she was with Perry.

The smell of burning was strong, and she wanted to press a hand to her nose to keep out the smell.

The sound of gunshots ripped against her ears, and she had to press her hands there to deaden the retort.

Sobs came at her through the air, but she could not see for all the smoke.

She was high in a tree. Perry had pushed her into the tree and he stood at the bottom, crying. Crying surrounded her from all sides.

A cold wind swept by her, making a path through the smoke, and she could see.

She did not want to see, but she did not know how to keep from seeing.

She should not be here.

Red cloth, soldiers' coats, fire, and smoke. Redcoats and fire. A man, an Irishman, his head coated in pitch, was lit on fire by a British soldier. Pitchcapped. He ran, screaming, tearing at his skull. His only salvation was to tear off his own scalp. He tried. He screamed.

She watched.

Where was Perry?

Redcoats came toward her, shouting. One soldier saw her.

Perry was beneath her, pulling at her foot, shouting at her. Shouting something.

She should not be here.

The soldier who'd spotted her shot the Irishman who had been lit like a torch. He fell. He stopped screaming.

The soldier ran toward her. He did not shout. He was quiet. She could not move, even with Perry's pulling.

She should not be here.

The soldier grabbed her and lifted her in his arms. He pulled Perry behind him and then they ran to a stone wall that contained a field. The field was empty. The stones held nothing.

Nothing.

Only the sound of crying.

✳   ✳   ✳

She awoke with a cry that strangled itself before it was fully born. Beau jerked upright beside her and reached for her. In the firelight, she looked into his eyes, the dream still as real as her last heartbeat.

And when she looked into his eyes, so green and so full of concern, she recognized him.

He was the one.

"You," she squeezed out past lungs still choked by remembered smoke and fire.

"What is it? You were crying," Beau said, folding her into his arms.

"You!" she repeated, jerking away from his touch. "You're the one."

He was the one. The monster from her nightly torture. He'd haunted her for ten years, and now she shared his bed. It could not be.

"Clarissa," he said slowly, not touching her. "Have a sip of wine. Calm yourself."

"It was you; don't deny it. I recognize you now," she said, the tears starting to press at the backs of her eyes. "You were there. You were in the regiment."

"Yes, with Lindley," he said.

"Lindley wasn't there!" she shouted. He would not make Lindley a part of this. Lindley had no part in it. Only she.

"Where, Clarissa?" he asked.

Where? Where her dreams took her almost nightly. Where *it* had happened. "Wexford," she murmured. It was like saying the name of a demon in the dark of hell.

At the name, his eyes went carefully blank. He knew what had happened in Wexford.

"I was there. I saw you," she accused, sounding like the eight-year-old girl she had been and was again, every night, in the darkness alone. Logic had no place in this memory; all was pure emotion, catching her up and tossing her about like a storm wind, her only companion the terror she had known and still knew. Every night.

"You," he said, his face a mask. "You were the girl. And the boy . . . that was Perry? Yes, it would have been," he said carefully, all emotion bled from his voice.

"I saw you! You killed him. You murdered him."

"No!" he said, grabbing her by the arms. She jerked away from his touch, but he would not let her go. Just like before. He would not let her go. "He was dead already. Do you think he wanted to die like that? Burned and mutilated? I showed him mercy; that was all."

"You killed him," she said, her voice as hard as stone. "You wore the coat. You're one of *them.*"

"Who?"

"The English! The English did it."

"Clarissa, you're English."

"*No!* I'm not! I'm Irish! I'm not like that. I can't be like that."

Beau jerked back the blankets and dragged a resisting Clarissa out of bed. He put her in one chair by the fire and seated himself in another. Naked, they faced each other, the glow of the fire lighting only half their faces, leaving the other side in deep shadow. But for the first time he saw all of her. And understood everything.

Ireland was home because she had to be Irish. Because she could not bear to be English. The English pitchcapped. The English murdered. The English set ablaze the houses of the innocent. She could not be part of that, and so she renounced her culture and her race, seeking an innocence she did not feel.

But the Irish were not innocent, not as she thought.

Wexford had been a nightmare of careless cruelty.

But what of Enniscorthy, where Irish Catholics had burned Irish Protestants by the hundreds? None had been innocent in the events that led to the union of Ireland with England.

What could a girl of eight know of that? A woman sat before him, her face set and angry, but in her Irish heart she was a child still. A child scarred by what she had seen; a woman tortured by memory.

Yet he had faith in the ultimate strength of Clarissa and her practical mind; Clarissa would not be ruled by the tyranny of raw emotion, not willingly. He had only to convince her to let go the pain of memory and grasp the cool peace of reason.

"Clarissa, you did nothing wrong. The man who set the pitchcap was wrong. He was drummed out; I reported him myself. I did nothing wrong when I shot that man. I do not know if he was innocent of wrongdoing or guilty, but I know that I shortened his suffering, and I am not sorry." When she would have spoken, in protest and argument, he was certain, he continued. "What of what I, an English officer, did for you? I was trying to save you. I saw a small girl and her equally small brother in a place where no child should be. I took you away. I kept you safe. I did not know you. I did not know that one day I would see you again as the woman you are."

He stopped and studied her face, delicate and stubborn and pulled into a frown. He had known it from the start: she was soft femininity and strong determination rolled together. He had known he loved her at her first volley of smiling insults. There was no one like her.

"I did not know that I would one day love you."

"I don't believe you," she said coldly.

"Which part?" he asked, smiling.

"Any of it. All of it," she said. "You are just trying to soothe me."

"Yes, I am trying to soothe you, but that does not mean that I am not being truthful. How much truth is there in you, Clarissa? You are English, whether you want to be or not. And Lindley was a soldier and Perry is about to buy his commission. Of what are they guilty? Some Irish murder other Irish and some Irish never kill anyone. It is not nationality that determines a man's acts, but the man himself."

"But you killed someone," she whispered.

"And you watched," he said. "I am sorry for that. I was sorry then. But would I shoot him again? Yes. It is an uncomfortable truth, but it is the truth, and I believe that you want nothing less."

Did she? Some truths were very ugly, very painful. What sort of truth did she want? Only the truths that pleased her or served her? She would not be that sort of woman.

But this truth was very hard; it challenged all that she had believed for a lifetime. Yet if what she had believed was half lie and half childish terror, what was gained by clinging to it?

Yet what she felt in her heart was not so simple as that. Choosing a husband by cold logic was one thing; choosing a memory was quite another. And how much logic had there truly been in her choosing of Beau? She loved him, Englishman though he was.

"I do not think I can do this," she whispered.

"I know you can," Beau said, his voice warm with confidence.

"This pain is not so easily dismissed," she said, looking at the fire. "I think I may, after all, disappoint you."

"Never," he said. "Never."

And when she looked into his eyes, he smiled his belief.

"It will take time to forge a new memory and lay aside the

horror of that day, but you will succeed. You are a woman ruled by reason and not emotion. Does any other woman compile a list?" He smiled gently. "We will attack this together and we will win."

They looked at each other, hope beginning to reign over her features, confidence riding his.

"Do you believe me now?" he asked, reaching out his hand to hers. "Any and all of what I declare?"

His hands were large and strong, the fingers long and graceful. Those hands had carried her to safety when she was a child. They would not drop her now.

"I'm not certain," she said, slowly taking his hand, feeling the hard warmth of him. "You did, did you not, say you loved me?"

"I did." He nodded.

"Were you sincere or were you just hoping to calm me?"

"Clarissa, when a man tells a woman he loves her, he is not hoping to calm her."

He loved her. Was it as simple as that?

He loved her. There was nothing simple about it.

"When did you know?" she asked.

Beau collapsed in his chair with a groan and tugged her over until she sat on his lap. "Now is not the time for conversation, truthful or otherwise."

"But I only want to know—"

"And I want to know if you love me, my dear, or in this conversation of truths to which you are so addicted, are the truths to be all my own? I believe I have quoted you accurately? And I not only want to know if you do love me, but when you first realized it and what it is about me, exactly, that you find so admirable, beyond my Irish estate, that is." He grinned, awaiting her response.

Tell him she loved him this early in the marriage? Hardly

wise. His arrogance would be insufferable if he knew he had won her heart so easily. There was time enough to confess her love . . . perhaps in a year? Or two?

She grinned in return before saying softly against his ear, "You are so right. This is not the time for conversation."

"Really?" he asked, running his hand up her thigh to her hip. "Convince me."

All I Want

LYNSAY SANDS

Prologue

"A doll just like the one in Werster's window. That's what I want for Christmas."

Prudence smiled slightly at her sister's words as the younger girl hugged their mother and kissed her good-night. Charlotte had been making her wishes known for weeks now, and Prudence and her mother had been working very hard at making a similar doll for her for most of that time. The doll itself was finished, though not completely satisfactorily. They were not professionals at the job, but they had done the best they could. Charlotte was a good girl, though; she would love it no matter its imperfections. Especially since they were making tiny little dresses for the doll that matched each of the girl's own gowns. Prudence was positive the child would be pleased.

"Good night, Pru!"

She gave a grunt as her younger sister launched herself at

her, hugging her hard before spinning away to rush out of the room. Prudence watched the little whirlwind go with affection, then glanced at her mother, frowning when she saw the unhappiness on her mother's face as she peered out the window.

"What would you like for Christmas, Mother?" she asked after a moment, hoping to distract her from whatever thoughts troubled her. Meg Prescott remained silent, so Prudence moved to her side to peer out and see what distracted her so.

Outside, two men stood on the front stoop arguing with Bentley. The last of their male retainers, the older man served as butler, valet, stablemaster, and anything else that was required. His wife, Alice, was their last female servant. The two did their best to keep the house running as smoothly as possible, but if things did not soon change, even they would have to be released. Prudence watched sadly as the older man doggedly shook his head and finally sent the two men on their way.

"Creditors," she muttered with disgust as she watched them go, though who the disgust was for she couldn't say. She could hardly blame anyone for attempting to get funds owed them. If her father would just—

"All I want for Christmas is for your father to stop his gambling before he sees us in debtor's prison."

Prudence glanced at her mother's strained face. Apparently she had heard the question after all. Her gaze returned to the two men as they went through the front gate and pulled it closed with an angry clang. Creditors were starting to arrive at the door every day now. And there were a lot of them. Her father, of course, was never available. When he was home, he was sleeping off the drink from the night before. When he was awake, he wasn't home but off drinking and gambling them closer to ruin. Bentley had managed to turn away the creditors so far, but soon they would not be brushed off. Debtor's prison was becoming a very real possibility. Why could her father not see what he was doing?

She glanced at her mother again and felt her heart tighten at the weary grief on her face. Things had been bad since Pru's brother John had died in a carriage accident. He had belonged to the Four Horsemen's club, where the sons of nobility went to race carriages they really didn't have the skill to drive. He had died when his carriage lost a wheel and he'd been sent flying into a tree and broke his neck. That was when their father, Edward Prescott, had started to drink and gamble. He had taken the loss of his oldest child and only son poorly.

"That is all I want for Christmas," her mother said now. "And I pray to God for it every day."

For a moment Prudence felt sadness weigh her down; then she grimly straightened her shoulders. Her mother was of the old school, where a wife did not question her husband or his behavior. Prudence was of the firm belief that when the husband was destroying his family, someone needed to alert him to the matter. Besides, it had always been her opinion that God helped those who helped themselves. Which left it up to her to see if she could not help God wrap this Christmas wish up for her mother.

Chapter One

Prudence accepted the hack driver's assistance to alight, paid him, then turned to stare at the front of Ballard's. The building was clean and stately looking, with windows on every level. It looked like a home. No one seeing it would know that it was a gaming hell where men gambled away their lives and the lives of the family members they were supposed to love.

Prudence blew an irritated breath out as her conscience pricked her. She supposed calling it a gaming hell was not being quite fair. There were no Captain Sharpes here waiting to cheat the gamblers who frequented the establishment. This was, by all accounts, an honest concern. But it was not a private club either. Membership was not necessary to enter. However, it did only cater to better-quality patrons. Proper decorum and a certain caliber of dress were required to enter, as well as the desire to stay and gamble your life away.

Fingers tightening around the handle of her umbrella, Prudence scowled at the building, then glanced to the main door and the three men entering. Two men, she corrected herself. The third appeared to be the doorman. He nodded, held the door for the other two, then closed it and settled in, arms crossed over his barrel-like chest, an intimidating expression on his face.

Prudence felt her heart sink. She very much suspected that the man was not going to let her enter. It might not be a private club, but that didn't mean women were any more welcome. Except as servants, she amended. Prudence had heard that Lord Stockton, the owner, had taken the innovative step of hiring female servants to serve the food and drink that persuaded clients to stay longer and lose more money. But those were the only women welcome inside.

Nay, the man guarding the door would not be eager to allow her entry. To be honest, Pru wasn't enthusiastic about the idea herself. It certainly wouldn't do her reputation any good. Not that there was much to worry about. She, her mother, and her whole family had already been as good as ruined—or would be the moment it was revealed the depths to which her father's gambling had brought them.

It would be only a matter of time, she thought unhappily. The rumors and gossip were already beginning to flow. The difference in the way the *ton* in general responded to the Prescott family was already notable. They were starting to distance themselves, not shunning the family openly yet—that would wait until the rumors and gossip were proven true—but invitations to balls had all but stopped and no one spoke to them at those they did attend. Pru supposed that was why her mother now prayed that her father would stop before they were in debtor's prison and not before the family was ruined. It was too late for the latter.

Still, it was one thing for her father to see them ruined, quite another for Prudence to throw her reputation away, which was what she was doing with this visit. But this was the only way she could think of to get to see her father. Talking to him at home would have been easier, of course, but Edward Prescott had developed the inconvenient habit of leaving the house the moment he awoke each day, leaving his daughter little opportunity to speak to him. Perhaps that was why he did it.

The hack she had hired to get her here began to pull away, the clip-clop of the horses' hooves drawing her from her thoughts.

Standing about staring up at the building like a scared ninny would not get the task done, she reprimanded herself. Action was what was needed! Straightening her shoulders, she forced her chin up and marched forward.

Prudence hadn't really considered how she would get past the doorman zealously guarding Ballard's entrance, but taking him by surprise seemed her best chance. That being the case, she started out walking parallel to the building as if she meant to walk past it. She moved at a quick clip, as quickly as the slippery walk allowed. It had been unseasonably warm and had rained earlier, which was why she had her umbrella with her. But the temperature was dropping now that night had fallen and ice was forming, making walking treacherous.

She waited till the very last moment; then, when she was directly in front of the entrance, Prudence veered sharply to the right and straight for the doors. She nearly smiled upon seeing that the man was distracted talking to a new arrival and that her path was clear. Tasting victory, she picked up her speed and barreled ahead. That speed almost saw her tumbling backward onto her fanny when the doorman suddenly stepped into her path. He was a solid wall of human flesh, and Prudence crashed into him, the air rushing out of her with an "oomph," then bounced backward, grabbing frantically for something, anything, to keep her feet. She ended up with a handful of his shirtfront clutched in one hand, the other waving her closed umbrella rather wildly as she fought to regain her balance.

"Ain't no women allowed."

Prudence grimaced at the growled announcement as she found her footing. Releasing her hold on the man's shirt, she took a step back, tipping her head up. Way up. The man was huge. Unnaturally tall, she decided as her neck began to complain at the distance it was being forced backward. Finally able to focus on his face, she forced her prettiest smile.

"Good evening."

His already smallish eyes went even smaller, signifying unpleasant suspicion in his bulldoggish face. "Evenin'."

"I am sorry to trouble you, sir, and I do realize that ladies are not generally allowed inside. However—"

"Never."

"Never?" she asked warily.

"Ladies ain't *never* allowed. Never *ever*."

"Never ever?" she repeated dully, then scowled. "Aye, but you see, this is a somewhat urgent matter, so if you would—"

"What sort of an urgent matter?"

Prudence paused, her mouth still open and her mind blank. She really should have considered a handy lie with which to answer such a question, she realized with dismay. He began to nod his head knowingly.

"It ain't real urgent, is it?"

"Oh—I—But—" Feeling panic set in as her chances of entrance dwindled, Prudence let her reticule drop to the ground between them. As one would expect, the doorman bent to pick it up. Seeing the opportunity Prudence, quite without thinking, cracked her umbrella down hard over his big thick head. Much to her alarm, rather than bringing down her intended victim, the umbrella snapped in half.

"Now, what'd ye go and do that for?" the man asked irritably, scowling at her as he straightened.

Prudence stared wide-eyed from him to her broken umbrella, quite overcome with shame and horror. She had never, *ever,* used physical violence in her life. It only served her right that the first time she did, she'd broken her umbrella. Oh, this wasn't working at all! She would never convince her father to quit his gambling and drinking. They would all be in debtor's prison by Christmas, and would probably die there. She pictured her mother there, wasting away, her little sister's youth and beauty fading, her own hopes of a husband and children dying a slow, miserable death and, much to her horror, she felt her eyes brimming with tears.

"Oh, now, don't start crying. That won't work with me."

Prudence heard the panic that belied the man's words, and that only made the tears come faster. When he moved closer and began clumsily patting her, she turned instinctively into his chest and blubbered like a baby.

"Please stop now. I ain't angry with ye. Ye didn't even hurt me none, if that's what you're crying about." When that simply made her cry harder, the doorman began babbling desperately. "Ye can hit me again if ye like. I'll let ye inside, I will. Just stop your crying and—"

Pru's tears died abruptly. Her eyes shining with hope and gratitude, she peered up at him. "You will?"

"Ah, damn." The man sighed unhappily. "You're gonna see me out of a good job, aren't ye?"

"Plunkett! What goes on here?"

Hands whipping quickly behind his back, the doorman

stepped away from Prudence and whirled guiltily to face the owner of that commanding voice.

Stephen. Lord Stockton. Prudence recognized the man at once as she turned to see him stepping down from his carriage. Everyone knew Lord Stockton. The dashing man was rather infamous—a member of the nobility who was accepted only reluctantly by the ton. If they could, Pru felt sure society would have given him the cut direct and excluded him from the more elite balls and soirees. It wasn't that the man wasn't noble enough; his blood was almost bluer than the king's, and his history could probably be traced farther back. Unfortunately, the man had committed that dreaded sin: he worked for a living! If one could call owning one of the most successful gambling establishments in London working for a living, she thought with irritation. It was his club that made him both undesirable as far as most of society was concerned, but also made it impossible to cut him out. The *ton* could hardly exclude him and risk his calling in the many markers he had on the majority of them.

Prudence watched the man approach and silently cursed her luck. She was sure the doorman—Plunkett, as Stockton had called him—had been about to let her slip inside. She was also quite sure that Stockton's arrival would put an end to that likelihood. The blasted man, she thought now with annoyance. She had been so close!

Stephen approached slowly, his eyes narrowing first on his new doorman, then on the young lady the beefy employee had been mauling just moments before. The woman looked angry, but there was no missing the trace of tears on her face. As for the large man he had hired to replace his previous doorman, Plunkett stood with his hands hidden guiltily behind his back, a culpable expression on his face. He was also avoiding looking at the woman.

Pausing before the large man, Stephen snapped, "Explain yourself, Plunkett."

The doorman's round face squinched up in alarm, his eyes filling with panic. "I—She—You—" His gaze shot wildly from Stephen, to the woman, then to the door of the club before returning to his employer's steely expression. Finally his shoulders slumped in defeat, he rumbled, "I knew this job was too good to keep."

Much to Stephen's amazement, that seemed to upset the woman even more. A scowl covering her face, she turned on him. "You cannot fire this poor man. He did absolutely nothing wrong."

"He was mauling you just moments ago," Stephen pointed out quietly.

"Nay. He was attempting to comfort me. I had—" She seemed to struggle briefly, her gaze dropping to the mangled item in her hand before she visibly brightened and held it up as if in proof. "My umbrella! I had broken it and was quite distressed. He, kind gentleman that he is, was attempting to offer assistance." A cagey smile came to her face as she turned to the doorman and said, "So, while I thank you for your effort to assist me, it is completely unnecessary. Now, if you gentlemen will excuse me, I should be on my way."

Nodding to each of them, the lady started calmly forward, a pleasant smile on her face that died abruptly when Stephen caught her arm and drew her to a halt.

"My apologies, my lady. But your brief upset appears to have rattled your sense of direction." He turned her firmly away from the door to his club, unsurprised to see the vexation on her face as she found herself facing the street. For a moment he thought she would go about her business, but then she turned determinedly to face him.

"I realize that ladies are not generally allowed inside—"

"Never *ever*," Plunkett rumbled, shaking his head sadly.

The woman bent a brief, irritated glance at the doorman, then continued, "However, this is a somewhat urgent matter and—"

"What sort of urgent matter?" Stephen asked.

"What sort?" she echoed, looking annoyed.

"Watch out for her umbrella," Plunkett warned in an undertone, drawing Stephen's confused glance.

"Her umbrella?"

The giant nodded solemnly. "If she drops her reticule, watch out for that umbrella."

"I will not drop my reticule," the woman said through her teeth, making the man shrug.

"You did before."

"That was purely accidental," she told him firmly.

"Uh-huh. And I suppose breaking your parasol over my head was an accident, too," the larger man added. The accusation seemed to distress the woman further, and she began to twist the broken parts of her umbrella in agitation.

"It *was* an accident. It slipped." She was a poor liar, Stephen decided, and he nearly let the amusement building inside him escape in a laugh. The woman looked like she would like to hit his doorman again. She also looked vaguely familiar. He spent a moment searching his mind for where he knew her from while his doorman continued his argument with the woman.

"It slipped?" Plunkett said doubtfully. "And cracked in half over my head?"

"That is where it slipped to. It *was* an accident," she insisted.

But in the pool of light from the lanterns on either side of the door, her face appeared to be as red as a ripe cherry.

"Uh-huh." Plunkett nodded slowly. "Just like your getting inside is an urgent matter."

"It *is* an urgent matter," she said firmly. Then, looking unhappy, she added, "To me."

Deciding he had heard all he cared to, and that Plunkett could handle the situation well enough on his own, Stephen shook his head and turned to enter his place of business. He had barely taken a step in that direction when the woman grasped his arm and tugged. Her expression, when he glanced impatiently back, was imploring.

"Please, Lord Stockton. I beg you. It really is important."

Stephen hesitated briefly, then, wondering why even as he did so, turned back to face her. "So what is this urgent matter?"

He was more irritated than surprised when she looked hesitant and glanced uncomfortably toward Plunkett, then down at the freezing walk. Stephen opened his mouth to repeat the question, but paused impatiently as a carriage pulled up behind his own, spilling several young dandies out onto the street. As they headed for the entrance to Ballard's, he took the woman's arm and urged her away from the door. "Now, why do you wish to get inside my place of business?"

"I need to speak to my father."

Stephen blinked at her quiet pronouncement. "Your father is inside and you wish to speak to him?"

She nodded, her expression bleak.

"Why?"

"Why?"

"Why?" Stephen repeated firmly.

"My mother . . ."

When she hesitated again, he prompted, "Has she been injured? Fallen ill?"

The question seemed to startle her and she quickly shook her head. "Nay, she . . ." This time when she paused, he had the distinct impression she was mentally berating herself for not grasping at that excuse. Apparently deciding it was too late, she said, "Nay. As you might know, my brother died last year."

"I am sorry for your loss," Stephen said quietly, peering closely at the woman. Her words assured him that there was a reason she looked familiar. Apparently he *should* know her. Unfortunately he couldn't place her name or title. It was quite hard to tell what she looked like, too, with that prim little hat she wore and the way she kept ducking her head.

"Thank you. But you see, it hit my family hard. My brother was the only male child and it was an accident . . . unexpected, so . . ." She hesitated, head lowered, eyes fixed on the agitated movements of her hands. Then she took a chance. "My father took it poorly. He hasn't really recovered. In fact, he is drinking heavily, you see, and gambling—"

"I am sorry that your father is not dealing well with his loss," Stephen interrupted. He knew who she was now. The part about the accident a year ago and her father dealing with it by drinking and gambling had cleared up the matter. Her father was Lord Prescott, a regular at Ballard's. The moment he recalled the man, he recognized his daughter. This was Lady Prudence Prescott. "But you have yet to explain this urgent matter that—"

"It is all she wants for Christmas!" Prudence blurted over his voice, and Stephen frowned.

"Who?" Stephen asked in bewilderment. What was this lady blabbering about?

"My mother. She has been just as distressed by John's death, but is now troubled further by Father's behavior. He is gambling without restraint. The creditors have begun to visit daily and he is not even aware . . . or if he is, he does not care. He insists on drowning himself in drink and . . ." She paused, taking in what Stephen knew was an uncomfortable and even slightly embarrassed expression on his face at hearing such personal details, then forged ahead determinedly. "Several days ago I asked my mother what she wanted for Christmas. Her reply was 'For your father to stop drinking and gambling our lives away and come back to us before he lands us all in debtor's prison.' And I thought, well, the good Lord helps those who help themselves, and if I could just make him see what he is doing to us all, if I could just make him see . . . But he will not stand still long enough for me to approach him on the matter! He is out the door the moment he awakes. He heads straight here to gamble and . . ."

Her voice faded away and Stephen glanced reluctantly back to her eyes. He really didn't want to know all this about the Prescotts. He really didn't wish to become involved in their problems and had let his gaze wander, his mind searching for a polite way to excuse himself. Now he saw her disheartened expression and felt guilt prick him. The man was gambling his family's lives away while they stood outside in the cold winter air.

"Where is your carriage?" he asked abruptly, then cursed himself for the stupid question when her hands tightened on her broken umbrella and she blushed. He was surprised by the candor of her answer and admired the proud way she raised her head and the dignified voice she used to give it.

"It was sold for the creditors."

Nodding, he glanced toward his carriage, then took her arm and urged her toward it.

"What are you doing, my lord?" the girl asked, sounding more startled than alarmed.

"I am having you taken home." He paused beside his closed conveyance to open the door, then tried to hand her up into it, but she was having none of it. Digging her heels in, she turned on Stephen, her eyebrows drawing together in displeasure.

"I have no wish to go home. I need to speak to my father. He—"

"He is a fully grown man. And he is your father. He knows what he is doing."

"Nay," she said quickly. "That is not so. If he knew the effect his gambling was having—"

"He would give it up and return home to sit by the fire singing Christmas carols as a good man should," Stephen finished wearily, then glanced away from the stricken look on her face. After a moment of silence he peered back, a sympathetic expression on his face. "Nothing you say shall stop him, you know. You cannot change his behavior. He must do that on his own."

"I must at least try."

Stephen's mouth tightened at her determination. There would be no reasoning with her. She was desperate. "Then you shall have to try at home, Lady Prescott. Ballard's is no place for a woman."

"It is no place for a man either," she replied quickly, and he felt his guilt replaced by annoyance.

He was much less sympathetic when he said, "Ladies are not allowed inside Ballard's, and I shall not help you ruin your reputation by making you the exception. Now, in you get."

This time, when he tried to hand her into the carriage, she went. Reluctantly, but she went. He closed the door the moment she was inside, afraid she might change her mind, then asked for her address through the window. She gave her answer in such a low voice that he had to strain to hear it. Nodding, he tipped his hat the slightest bit in respect, then

311

moved to give the address and his orders to his driver. A moment later the carriage was away, and Stephen was left to watch her pale face grow smaller as she peered out the window of the departing carriage.

He was annoyed to find that the image haunted him for the rest of the night as he oversaw his club, mingled, drank, and gambled with his guests.

Prudence sat on the expensive upholstery of Lord Stockton's carriage seats, rage pulsing through her like a living thing. She was furious and frustrated, and knew exactly who to blame for it: one Stephen Ballard, Lord Stockton. He was the one who owned the club where her father was tossing his family's lives away. He was the one who wouldn't let her in to speak to her father and perhaps turn him from his destructive path.

"So ladies are not allowed in Ballard's. No exceptions," she said to herself as the carriage rolled to a stop before her home. "Then I suppose I shall have to go as a man."

✳ Chapter Two ✳

Tugging the carriage curtain aside, Prudence swallowed as she saw that they were nearing her destination. She had thought this such a good idea when she came up with it. Confronting her father in the club would have to be successful; Edward Prescott could not walk away and leave his daughter inside. He would not want the scandal. Prudence would finally get the chance to say what needed saying. But the closer the carriage drew to Ballard's, the more she was positive that this was a huge mistake. Terrible folly. And she had to wonder how Ellie could have possibly allowed her to go through with it.

Ellie. Eleanore Kindersley. Pru's tension eased slightly at the thought of her best friend. She had visited the other girl for tea that afternoon and proceeded to rant about her father's behavior, her fears about what it was doing to her family, and her failed attempt to get into Ballard's the night before. The other young woman had listened sympathetically, offering to help Prudence in any way that she could with the matter, and when Pru had revealed her plans to gain entrance to the club that night disguised as a man, Eleanore had applauded the "brilliant" idea and had even volunteered to accompany her. Prudence had quickly refused that offer—unwilling to risk the other girl's reputation—but had accepted the proffered use of her friends private coach.

Well, it was really Ellie's father's coach, she admitted, hoping that Lord Kindersley would not be too upset at his daughter for lending it out. Eleanore was always doing good and generous things like that. She was a dear friend.

Aye. Eleanore is an excellent friend. But really, she should have dissuaded me from this folly, Prudence thought with regret.

Realizing that she was terribly close to giving up and telling Jamison, the Kindersleys' driver, to take her home, Prudence released the curtain and forced herself to lean back on the plush, cushioned seats to take a deep, calming breath. Unfortunately she didn't feel much better when at last the coach rolled to a stop. Peering out the window to see Plunkett standing, grim-faced and arms crossed, before the door of Ballard's did not help much.

Feeling her courage dwindling further, Prudence pushed the door open and burst out of the carriage, coming up short as the Kindersleys' coachman came to an abrupt halt before her, his expression horrified. Pru heaved an inner sigh, but managed an apologetic smile. Eleanore, of course, would never have bustled out of the carriage before the man could open the door for her. But then Ellie was always a perfect lady. Prudence was not. Perfect ladies did not rush about in men's clothes, chasing their fathers out of gambling establishments in efforts to save their families.

314

Ah, well, she thought philosophically, *no one is perfect.* Besides, she had more to worry about than behaving like a perfect lady, especially while dressed as a man. With that concern out of the way, she straightened her shoulders, stepped around the disapproving driver, and started forth.

Prudence had barely taken half a dozen steps when her breeches began slipping down her hips. Slowing her step, she jerked at them under cover of the cape she wore. Both items were her father's, as were the shirt, waistcoat, and cravat she wore.

Unfortunately, when Prudence had devised this plan, she had not considered the fact that Edward Prescott was a jolly little man of about twice her width. Neither had she recalled that her mother had given her brother's vestments away to charity after his death. Not that John's clothing would have fit properly either. They, too, would have been large on her—but at least she wouldn't have been swimming in them as she was in her father's clothing.

Prudence had spent a goodly amount of time this evening tucking and pinning the breeches in the back in an effort to make them look more presentable, and she had succeeded for the most part. Well, they looked passable in the front. Unfortunately it appeared that her handiwork was coming undone. The moment she released the breeches they began to slip again.

Scowling in irritation, she yanked them up once more, this time anchoring them in place with a hand on her hip under the cape. Realizing how foolish she must look walking like that, she tried to add a swagger to her step to appear more manly, but found that the excessive activity made her head bob, sending the top hat she wore shifting forward on her head. It, too, was her father's and was too large for her.

At first, that had seemed something of a blessing, since it

allowed her to tuck her long chestnut hair underneath. Now Prudence found it more of a problem. She feared it might slide right off her head, spilling her hair and revealing her gender. With her father's old cane in her right hand, and her left hand needed to twist the breeches on her hip, she was rather at a loss as to what to do. After one frantic moment, she raised the cane she held and used it to push the hat back. Fortunately the action worked; the hat shifted into place and Prudence was able to continue forward. She did so much more cautiously, trying to keep her head steady as she approached Ballard's front door—and Plunkett.

Pru hadn't really plotted this part of her plan. She supposed she had just assumed that the man would open the door and step aside for her to enter. He, apparently, had other thoughts. He merely stood in place, his expression turning mean as he squinted at her approach.

"Pip, pip, cheerio," she tried in her deepest voice, hoping her mounting panic did not show as she attempted to maneuver around the man to get to the door. Her heart sank when he stepped sideways into her path, firmly blocking her entrance.

"You look familiar," he rumbled, making Pru's heart skip a beat.

"Aye, well . . . Undoubtedly that would be because I am a regular at this fine establishment," she forced out, following the lie with the deepest laugh she could muster. Unfortunately, the effort scratched her throat and sent her into a coughing fit.

Eyes rounding in horror, Prudence reached up quickly to anchor her hat in place with the hand that held the cane, nearly braining Plunkett in the process. The doorman managed to avoid the blow with a quick duck and feint that would have done any boxing teacher proud, then scowled at

Prudence, who, with both hands occupied, proceeded to cough rudely all over his folded arms.

Apparently deciding that holding her up was not to his benefit, Plunkett promptly opened the door, using the act as a way to step clear of her moist coughing.

"Thank you," Prudence rasped as she rushed forward, eager to get inside before the man changed his mind.

The door closed behind her with a snap, and Prudence had just begun to take a relieved breath when she realized that she had only managed to cross the first hurdle. She was not now in the gaming room; she was in an entryway with a cloakroom off of it. There was another door to get through, and two servants between her and that door.

Squelching the panic that rose in her as the two servants rushed forward, reaching eagerly for her hat and cloak, Prudence let go of her hat long enough to brandish her cane threateningly before her.

"I shall not be here long enough to have need of your services," she said quickly, then rushed between them. Pushing through the door, she raised her hand to moor her hat as she did. It worked.

The first thing to strike Prudence as she burst into the gaming area was the noise. There were well over a hundred men in the large room, and every single one of them appeared to be talking or laughing, each voice just a bit louder than the next in an effort to be heard. It appeared men were much noisier when women weren't around. Or, at least, when *ladies* weren't around, she corrected herself as she noted that what she had heard was true; Ballard's did have female servants. There were several moving through the crowd, carrying trays of drinks and various food items.

Prudence watched one such servant distribute drinks at a nearby table and paused to admire her outfit. The long, deep red skirt and snow white top were really quite fetching. Of course, it was nothing she herself would have dared wear. The skirt was just a touch short of being considered proper. Prudence even caught a glimpse of the girl's ankles as she hurried about. The scoop-necked top was a touch risqué as well, she decided critically, but all in all it was an attractive uniform. Since every woman present wore it, she decided that it had to be a uniform.

The entrance of new arrivals behind her forced Prudence to give up her consideration of the apparel Lord Stockton had chosen for his servants. Moving away from the door, she started through the room, her gaze shifting over the sea of men in search of her father. She had reached the back right corner of the club before spying Lord Prescott deeply involved in a game of cards at a table in the opposite corner. Spotting the pile of money in the center of the round surface, she wondered bitterly how much of it her father had added to the pile. The sum there would go a long way toward paying off their debts should he win, she could not help thinking. But that was the trick. He would not win. *She* would lay odds on *that*.

Determined that however much he had already gambled away, he would be losing no more, Prudence straightened her shoulders and prepared to confront him. She was about to stride forward when a cry of pain by her side made her hesitate and glance over at a dispute taking place. Nearby, a tall, hawkish man had one of the serving women by the arm and was shaking her rather viciously as he hissed into her face.

Frowning, Pru moved close enough to hear what was being said.

"You stupid, clumsy strumpet!" the man said snarling. "This waistcoat cost more than you will make in a lifetime!"

"I am sorry, my lord. I didn't mean to spill ale on you, but you bumped my arm and—"

"Are you suggesting that it is my fault?" the noble barked, giving the servant a bone-rattling shake that had Pru's teeth aching in sympathy. Putting aside the matter of her father for the moment, she slipped closer to the pair.

"I say there, my good man," she said lightly, doing her best imitation of her father's cajoling voice. "Surely the gel did not mean to—"

Pru's voice ended on an alarmed squeak as she found herself suddenly grabbed by the cravat and jerked nearly off the floor. Feet slipping in her father's overlarge boots, she was suddenly standing on the very tips of her toes and nose-to-nose with the hawk-faced man.

"Did I ask for your opinion?"

Wincing at both the pain he was causing in her neck and the cloud of whiskey fumes that spewed from his mouth, Prudence glanced from him to the serving girl, who had tumbled to the floor as he had abruptly pushed her away. The servant appeared rather relieved to be on the floor, and Prudence couldn't blame her. The wooden surface was looking a fairly comfy place to be at the moment, she thought, then noted the shocked horror now coming over the girl's face.

"A woman!"

Pru's attention jerked back to the hawkish man at that exclamation, only then noting that her head was feeling a touch cooler than it had moments before. Alarm rising up within her, she forgot about the cane she held and reached up instinctively to feel for the hat that should have been on her head, nearly knocking herself senseless in the process. Prudence actually saw stars as pain exploded through her head, but it might have been partially due to the fact that the man had lifted her higher in his surprise and she was now dangling off the floor, her cravat becoming a rather effective hangman's noose.

Struggling for breath, Prudence acted instinctively and brought her cane down square on top of Hawkman's head. Her tormentor released her at once. Sucking in great gasps of air, Pru stumbled backward, just avoiding the retaliatory fist the man sent flying at her face as she tumbled to the floor beside the serving girl. She wasn't terribly surprised that the man had tried to hit her despite knowing she was a woman. After all, he hadn't been treating the serving girl very well. Everyone was surprised, however, when the blow he intended for her landed squarely on the jaw of a large blond man who had apparently stepped forward to intervene. The blow was enough to send the man crashing to the floor, and Prudence bit her lip and winced in sympathy, but was more than grateful that she had not managed to stay on her feet for that shot.

Silence fell in a wave that spread to the far corners of the room as the blond shook his head and regained his feet. Then Hawkman, looking pale and frightened, blurted, "I did not mean to hit you. I was—"

It was as far as he got before the blond man's fist plowed into his face. Prudence almost cheered at the blow. She did hate cowards, and any man who was so vicious to women, then quavered when confronted with a man his own size, was definitely a coward.

She watched with satisfaction as Hawkman stumbled backward, then winced as he crashed into a serving girl who had just come through a nearby door with a tray of beverages. The tray upended, sending the drinks flying over a pair of men; then all hell broke loose. The two men promptly joined the fray and were quickly followed by others—everyone soon striking out at his neighbors. The violence moved in a wave much as the silence had a moment before, rippling out over the crowd until everyone seemed to be involved.

Pru pushed herself up to a sitting position and gaped at the riot breaking out around her, then scrambled up to rescue her father's second-best top hat from between two combatants' feet. Unfortunately she was too slow, and the hat got slightly dented and compressed. Prudence scowled at the damaged item, then glanced to the side a bit wildly when someone tugged at her arm.

"Come on," the serving woman cried, then promptly shifted to her hands and knees and began to crawl away through the legs surrounding them.

Pru stared after her in amazement for a moment, then, afraid of being left to fend for herself in the midst of the mob, shifted to her hands and knees and scrabbled after her. She started out trying to crawl while holding her father's cane in her hand. That was a painful endeavor, as she found herself grinding her fingers between the hard object and the floor with her weight on it. Leaving the item reluctantly behind, she found it easier going and was able to make much better time, despite having to pause every few feet to yank up her breeches—crawling about left her with no hands to hold them up, and the activity seemed to drag at them.

"Do you not think we would move faster on our feet?" she asked breathlessly, dodging between a couple of flailing legs to catch up with the woman, whose path was blocked by a pair of men rolling on the floor, fists flying.

"Sure, if you don't mind a fist to the face," the servant answered over her shoulder as she changed direction to crawl around the battling pair. The words sounded practical enough to Prudence, but she couldn't help thinking that she might prefer a fist in the face to a boot in it.

Pru had barely had that thought when she got a boot to the stomach as someone tripped over her. It was more a knock than a kick, but was enough to startle an "oomph" out of her and make her decide she would risk the fists. Pausing, she started to draw her knees up to rise, only to find herself assisted to her feet by someone grasping the back of her collar and jerking her upward.

Closing her eyes instinctively, Prudence clutched at her drooping drawers and winced against the blow she felt sure was coming. She was spun on her feet to face her assailant.

"You!"

Opening one eye cautiously, Pru nearly groaned aloud—Lord Stockton. She silently cursed her luck. Then, deciding that bravado was her best option in the situation, she beamed at the man as if he were a dear friend she had run into unexpectedly in the middle of a crushingly overcrowded ballroom.

"Oh! Good evening, my lord! What a pleasant surprise. And how are you this evening?"

Watching the red suffuse his face, darken, then turn to purple as his mouth worked silently, Prudence considered that bravado might have been the wrong choice.

"You!" This time the word was not shocked so much as a long, drawn-out, frustrated and furious sound. Yes, she had definitely made the wrong choice with bravado. Perhaps throwing herself into his arms with relief and pretending to desire his protection from the mad horde around them would have been a better approach. She almost carried that thought through to action, but was denied the opportunity when a pair of struggling combatants suddenly rammed into her captor, sending him reeling. Prudence actually almost rushed forward to catch him and help him regain his balance, then realized that she would hardly be doing herself any favors and decided that fleeing was the better option.

She whirled away and started to try to fight her way through the crowd, only to quickly understand what the serving girl had meant. Not only were fists flying, but elbows were thrusting, and bodies were banging. It was almost impossible to get through the men on foot. Glancing over her shoulder in a purely panicky action to see that Stockton had regained his balance and was now fighting toward her, Prudence returned to her hands and knees and began to scramble past, around, and even sometimes through the pairs of legs shifting and stumbling around her, sometimes hopping along like a three-limbed dog as she was forced to yank at her damned breeches. Still, she was able to move much more swiftly like this, and she was just congratulating herself on the maneuver when she was collared again, dragged to her feet, then hustled through the crowd.

Stockton had pushed his way through the fighting men much more effectively than she had managed, she admitted unhappily as she was half pushed and half dragged through a door. Finding herself in the kitchens amidst the culinary staff and few servers who had managed to reach the relative safety there, she forced another smile to her face and tried to turn it on Lord Stockton. It was no easy task, with the way he still grasped her by the neck of her cape. She ended up smiling into her collar as she offered a cheerful "My goodness! I am forever in your debt, my lord. I was finding it nearly impossible to make my way through that mob."

She did not think it was a good sign when he merely ground his teeth a little harder than they had already been grinding and jerked her along, ushering her through the kitchens to another door. It turned out to lead to an office. His, she supposed as he pushed her inside and slammed the door.

She glanced briefly over the small, neat room with its sparse furnishings of a standing cupboard and a desk with one chair behind it and one in front, then turned to eye the man standing statue-still before the door. "I—"

"Do not say it!" he interrupted harshly, beginning to pace.

"But you do not even know what I was going to say!" Prudence protested.

"I do not care. Do not say anything. Anything at all," he snapped.

"Oh, now surely—" Her words ended on a startled gasp when he suddenly whirled and strode forward with an expression that did not bode well.

Alarm coursing through her, Prudence lurched back, only to come up against the chair before his desk. She opened her mouth desperately, ready to babble that she was sorry and would remain silent, only to have his mouth close down over hers as he paused before her. Eyes wide open, she stood completely still as his mouth moved over hers, her heart seemingly dead from shock in her chest. Then she felt the first smoky tendrils of passion stir to life within her and she softened under the kiss, only to be left gasping when he suddenly tore his lips away.

She started to lift one hand to her lips, but he had grabbed her by the upper arms and still held her.

"You kissed me," she said in a gasp. His mouth twitched at her startled announcement, then twisted when she added, "Why?"

"To silence you," he answered abruptly.

"Oh." She heard the disappointment in her voice and nearly winced at the softening it caused on Stockton's face, positive he would now feel pity for her. Prudence wasn't left to worry over the possibility long. Despite his claim that he had kissed her to silence her, and the fact that she had finally fallen silent, he suddenly covered her lips again, his mouth moving warm and firm over hers. Pru tried to resist the feelings the kiss stirred in her. Well, all right, perhaps she didn't try very hard. It wasn't more than a moment before she gave in on a soft sigh and let her hands slide up around his neck as she kissed him back.

He had opened his mouth over hers, prodding gently at her lips with his tongue to urge them apart, turning the kiss into a terribly interesting experience for Prudence, when a knock at the door interrupted them. Breaking away, Lord Stockton moved a couple of steps away and turned to call out for the person to enter.

Pru sucked her lower lip into her mouth, tasting him on it as she watched the door open to reveal Plunkett.

"I put an end to the fighting, my lord, and—" The large man's words died as his gaze slid to Prudence. Seeing the shock on his face, Pru grimaced, knowing that the large man no doubt now recognized her and understood why she had seemed so familiar. But then Stephen frowned and followed the man's gaze, his expression changing to one of consternation. When he quickly stepped in front of her, sheltering her from view, she had the most horrendous idea that—

Glancing down, she cried out in horror. Her father's breeches were lying in a pool around her feet. She had given up her hold on them to put her arms around his neck, and apparently the kiss had been sufficiently distracting that she hadn't noticed when they glided down her legs. Only her father's overly large shirt was left to cover her where the cape was open, and that reached only partway down her thighs.

Her face burning with embarrassment, Prudence bent quickly to pull the trousers back up, not even hearing Stephen's babbling excuse. She pushed past both men and fled as fast as her feet would carry her.

*   *   *

Stephen took a step forward, intending to chase after Prudence, then caught himself with a sigh. The poor girl had been thoroughly humiliated. His chasing after her would achieve nothing more than to embarrass her further. Besides, he had already proven that he couldn't be trusted around her. He had been enraged when he had spotted her there in his gaming room, shocked that she would dare enter—dressed as a man no less—and furious that she would risk her reputation so. But all that shock and fury had quickly turned to a different sort of fire the moment he had gotten her alone. And hadn't that been a brilliant idea? He took a moment to berate himself for treating her so cavalierly. At the time, kissing her had seemed an acceptable alternative to the throttling she deserved. Obviously he hadn't been thinking very clearly. No lady deserved to be treated as thoughtlessly as he had just done.

Not that she had fought him off, he thought, enjoying the memory, then gave himself a shake. The girl was obviously as innocent as a babe. She had probably been overwhelmed by his attention. Hell, he had been overwhelmed himself. But his behavior had been simply unacceptable.

A quiet shuffling drew his attention. Plunkett still stood just inside the door, but his stunned expression at the sight of Prudence with her drawers on the floor had turned to grim disapproval that the man was directing straight at his employer. Stephen felt himself straighten defensively.

"I had nothing to do with her trousers falling down." The words came blurting out without his volition. He really had no need to explain himself to his staff. Still, the words came out, and when Plunkett looked doubtful—as anyone would after seeing the red, swollen, obviously just-kissed state of

Prudence's lips—Stephen felt compelled to explain further, "Well, I did kiss her, but . . . it is not as if we have not been introduced. We have met at various balls."

That wasn't strictly true. Stephen had attended several of the same balls as the Prescotts and always noted their daughter's presence. Prudence was a lovely woman. Her beauty was the sort that shone through like a collection of snow white daisies in a mixed arrangement, not screaming for first attention like a red rose with its hidden thorns, but subtly drawing the eye with its soft loveliness. Of course, with his precarious situation in the *ton*, he hadn't ever approached the woman until just recently. It was only when the rumors and gossip had begun to circulate about the state of the Prescott finances, when the rest of the *ton* had begun to draw away, that he had dared ask for a dance or two. He had not wanted to sully her with his reputation.

But with the *ton* acting as they were, it had given him the perfect opportunity. He had approached under the guise of saving her from being a wallflower, something he had done in the past with other shy young ladies. That had been the ruse under which he had made his polite request, and he had found himself drawn to the girl with her soft voice and quick wit. The only reason he hadn't recognized her right away that first night outside his club was because of the darkness, the unexpectedness of her presence there, that silly hat she had been wearing, and the way she had been bundled against the cold.

Aware that Plunkett was still glaring at him like a father who had caught him mauling his daughter, Stephen shifted impatiently. "You say the fighting has ended?"

Plunkett spent another moment looking down his stub of a nose at Stephen, then nodded slowly. "Had to clear out the club to do it, though. The place is empty and the doors locked. Should I open 'em up again?"

Moving behind his desk, Stephen made a face and shook his head. He dropped wearily into his chair. "No. That was enough excitement for one night. Is there much damage?"

"A couple tables broke and a couple of the serving girls got roughed up. Sally took a nasty poke to the eye. It's swollen shut and blackening bad, and I think Belle's got a cracked rib or two."

Stephen scowled. For all that he had been in this business for years, it still startled him to see how a little drink and a game of cards could bring out the worst in these supposed "men of nobility." Some nights he was ashamed to be counted a member of them, and those nights were coming more and more frequently. Stephen had always loathed the weakness that shone through as he watched desperate men gamble away what little they had left in the hopes of making a fortune. But more and more often of late, he was also bearing witness to a cruelty hidden beneath some of those men's suave exteriors. It wearied his soul and made him think that perhaps it was time to get out of this business. He had even looked into several alternative ventures, but had not struck on anything as lucrative yet. Once he did . . .

Shrugging his thoughts away, he turned his attention to the matter at hand. "Take Sally and Belle to be tended; then see them home. Here." Unlocking the drawer of his desk, he retrieved a sack and tossed it to his doorman. "Split this between them and tell them not to come back until they are recovered."

Nodding, the large man turned and left him alone to his thoughts, which promptly returned to the woman he had been kissing only moments before. Damn, she had looked fine in breeches. Even sagging, baggy breeches. But, he thought with a small smile, she had looked even better with them pooled around her ankles.

✳ Chapter Three ✳

"Oh, dear."

"'Oh, dear' is right!" Prudence quit her pacing and dropped glumly onto the settee beside Eleanore. The Kindersleys' town house was where Prudence had taken her father's clothes to change into them before attempting her infiltration of Ballard's. After fleeing the scene of her humiliation, she had been forced to return to change back into her gown. She would have preferred to have Jamison take her straight home, where she could weep over her humiliating failure in private, but, dressed as she had been, going home had been impossible. Meg Prescott was not aware of what her daughter was up to. It was her Christmas wish, after all. Besides, she probably wouldn't have approved.

Now that she was here and had revealed the humiliating results of her venture, Prudence found that she did actually feel a touch better. Eleanore's sympathy was a soothing balm.

"What was it like?"

Pru turned a confused gaze to her friend. "What? Realizing that I was standing there with Father's breeches down around my ankles like some—"

"Nay."

The other woman started to smile, but bit it back quickly, Prudence noticed.

"Nay," she repeated. "I meant the kiss. What was his kiss like?"

Prudence glanced away, her mouth twitching and twisting before she could control it. She wasn't at all surprised to find her friend curious about *that*. They had often talked about the members of the *ton*, discussing the men they found attractive and such. Stephen had been one of them.

He was terribly handsome and debonair. And she and Eleanore were not the only ones who thought so. The older set among the *ton* might have resented having to admit him to society, but the younger ladies were more than happy to have him around, and they often vied for his attention. Eleanore and Prudence had never been among those who vied, but they had certainly noticed the man and would not have said nay had he asked for a dance, or the opportunity to fetch them a refreshment.

It wasn't just that he was attractive, but he had shown his kindness on several occasions. It was well known that he had a tendency to befriend those the *ton* saw as just barely acceptable, and there was never a wallflower so long as he was in attendance. He made a point of being introduced, and of making everyone feel included. Pru and Ellie had both appreciated that. Especially Prudence, who just lately had found herself in need of being rescued from being a wallflower. She rarely attended social functions, but had on one or two occasions under pressure from Eleanore. Unable to afford a new gown, she had been forced to wear last season's fashions. The fact had been recognized at once by all, and the fact that it meant that the family's wealth was now failing had been understood. There was nothing the *ton* fled from faster than those whose wealth was dwindling. Prudence had found herself in the uncomfortable position of being avoided by most people as if she had the plague. And absolutely no one had asked her to dance—except for Stephen, once, at each of the events. No, he might not have recalled her upon their meeting, but she had had no problems remembering him.

If she were honest with herself, Prudence would admit that after each affair she had wasted several minutes lying abed at night fantasizing that they had shared more than a dance. She imagined that she had seen a certain something in his eyes as they had moved about the dance floor, and that he would someday sweep into her life and save her from the embarrassing situation her father was dragging them all into. But that had been before she learned that he actually owned the establishment her father favored for his destructive behavior. Oh, she had known that he owned some sort of hall, but she hadn't realized it was one where gambling took place—or that it was the exact one her father spent most of his time at. Prudence had stopped fantasizing about the man the moment she had learned that. Well, all right. So she hadn't stopped fantasizing about him, but she had taken to berating herself most firmly afterward for doing so.

"Well?"

Pru turned her attention back to Eleanore at her friend's impatient prompting and shrugged. "It was a kiss, Eleanore. Just a kiss."

"Uh-huh. Just a kiss that distracted you enough that you did not even notice you were losing your trousers."

Prudence felt her face flush with remembered embarrassment, then shifted impatiently and got up to pace again. "Can we not concentrate on my problem? What am I to do now? Plunkett will not let women in and would not be fooled by my being disguised as a man again. I must find another way to get inside."

"Can you not just confront your father at home, Pru? Surely that would be easier than—"

"Nay. He leaves the moment he arises."

"Catch him on his way out then."

"I have attempted to do so, but he continually evades me. Yesterday I waited outside his door for two hours. I left to visit the privy—for just a minute, mind—and he slipped out while I was gone. I think he must have been watching out his keyhole and waited for me to leave."

"Hmm." They both fell silent as Eleanore pondered this news; then she murmured, "Perhaps you should try a different approach."

"What do you mean?" Prudence stopped her pacing and turned to eye her friend with interest.

"Well, you have said that he drinks first, then gambles?" When she nodded at that, Ellie suggested, "Well, if you could prevent his drinking, he might stop gambling."

Prudence considered that briefly. "Think you that would really work?"

"Well, the one does seem to follow the other. Does it not?"

"Aye."

The other girl shrugged. "So if you stop him from drinking, mayhap the gambling will seem less appealing."

A smile slowly blossomed on Pru's face at her friend's logic. It seemed sound to her. "Eleanore, you are brilliant!" she pronounced at last, making the other girl flush with pleasure. "But how?"

"How?"

"How am I to prevent his drinking? He does most of his imbibing out of the house."

"Oh." Eleanore fretted over the problem briefly, then suddenly got to her feet and hurried from the salon. Prudence watched her go with confusion and even stood, uncertain whether to follow her friend or not. But before she could reach the door, Ellie was rushing back into the room, a book in hand.

"What is that?" Prudence asked.

"One of my mother's books of general advice. It includes a medical dictionary. I thought to see what it advises regarding imbibing intoxicants." Leading Prudence back to the settee, Eleanore settled there, waited until Prudence had arranged herself beside her, then held the book between them and began riffling through the pages, muttering under her breath. "Intoxicants, intoxicants, intoxi— No intoxicants, but they do have intoxication," she said with quiet excitement, and lifted the book closer to her face to read. "'Although literally meaning "poisoning of the blood by alco—'"

"Skip over that part, Ellie, and find what they suggest to rectify the problem," Prudence urged impatiently.

"Suggestions." Eleanore scanned the long paragraph, reading various words aloud as she went. "'Imagination is excited'... 'symptoms'... 'delirium—'" She scowled impatiently. "Nay, all they say is that 'in cases of poisoning, vomiting should be induced by a subcutaneous injection of apomorphine.'"

"Apomorphine?"

"An emetic," she explained.

"Oh."

"But your father hardly drinks to the point of poisoning himself."

Prudence snorted. "Nay. Not himself, just our lives." She was silent for a moment, misery making her slump; then her head slowly lifted, scheming obvious on her face.

Eleanore eyed her warily. "I know that look. It usually precedes trouble. Prudence, what are you thinking?"

"Think you that there are such things as oral emetics?"

Ellie slammed the book closed, alarm clear on her face. "Prudence!"

"It is perfect!" she cried excitedly. "A bout or two of drinking that leaves him hanging over the chamber pot ere he gets too sotted might cure him of any desire to drink and thereby end his gambling!"

"Pru!"

"Oh, do not look at me like that, Ellie," she snapped with irritation. "I am desperate. I no more wish to end up in debtor's prison than you would. He will ruin us with his drinking and gambling. He has been doing both steadily since John died. I am sure that if we could but keep him sober for a day or two, he would regain enough of his wits to realize what he is doing to our family."

"But—"

"How would you feel if it were *your* father?"

Eleanore fell silent. Prudence watched several expressions flit across her friend's face until resignation settled there. Placing the book on the settee between them, the girl stood and silently left the room.

Prudence promptly picked up the book she had left behind and leafed through it, looking for *gambling, betting,* and *excesses,* but none of those terms were to be found. It seemed such was an ailment of the soul, not the body. Sighing, she had just set the book aside when Eleanore hurried back into the room, a large bottle gripped tightly in her hands.

"What is it?" Prudence asked curiously as her friend handed it to her, her lower lip caught between her teeth.

"Do you recall when Bessy had a sour stomach?"

"Bessy?" Prudence shook her head with confusion. "Your horse?"

Eleanore nodded. "At the time the stablemaster was sure she had eaten something she shouldn't have. He procured this to help her remove it." When Prudence stared at her blankly, she sighed and elucidated. "This concoction encouraged her to bring it back up. It is an emetic."

Prudence's eyes widened incredulously. "You think I should give my father a horse emetic?"

The other girl hesitated, looking uncertain. "Perhaps it is a bad idea."

"Nay!" Prudence stood and moved swiftly out of reach when Ellie tried to grab the bottle back. Crossing the room, she peered at it with fascination. "A horse emetic."

"Prudence, I do not think . . ." Eleanore trailed her across the room anxiously.

"But it is perfect. It should have the same results with Papa, do you not think? How much did your stablemaster give Bessy? And how long before it took effect?"

Ellie grimaced. "A couple of spoonfuls. It took effect immediately, but a man is much smaller than Bessy. I do not think more than a drop or so should be used. I— Oh, Prudence, I do not think it should be used at all. This was a terrible idea. Please just give it to me and let us forget this."

"And shall you visit me in debtor's prison?" Prudence asked quietly, turning to face her friend. Eleanore paused, a struggle taking place on her face, until she gave in with a sigh.

"How will you administer it? For your plan to work, if it is going to work at all," she added dryly, "he must receive it while he is drinking. He does that at the club, for the most part. You just finished regaling me with your last foray into Ballard's. After tonight Plunkett will be on the lookout for you. Disguising yourself as a man will not work."

"Aye," Prudence murmured thoughtfully, then slowly smiled. "Plunkett will never again let me through Ballard's *front* door."

Turning away from the ale barrel, Prudence took a few steps, then paused to scowl down at her chest. Muttering under her breath, she balanced the tray with the single mug of ale in one hand, using the other to tug uselessly at the neckline of the white top she wore. Honestly, it was as indecent as could be, she thought impatiently, and wasted a moment wishing she had worn one of her own gowns. Of course, that was impossible. She had seen for herself that all the girls wore the same costume: the red skirt and rather blousy white top with a scoop neck. But this one seemed extremely scooped to Prudence. Her nipples were nearly showing!

Realizing it was a wasted effort, Prudence gave up tugging at the top. She had had to work hard for the use of the indecent outfit for the night. Well, not the whole night. Pru had assured the girl she would need to take her place for only a matter of moments, just long enough to get a message to the man she loved. That was what she had told the girl. Of course, the truth was that she wanted a way to deliver the emetic to her father, but she could hardly have told Lizzy that. The servant's gratitude for Pru's intervention with the hawk-faced man had stretched far enough for Lizzy to agree to loan her gown to Prudence and let her briefly take her place as a servant inside Ballard's, but she suspected it would not have done so had the girl known Pru's true intentions.

Prudence had salved her conscience about the lie by telling herself that it wasn't a complete falsehood. She *did* love her father, and the emetic *was* a message . . . of sorts.

Deciding it was a sad day indeed when a woman began lying to herself, Prudence moved out of the kitchen, then paused to peer around the club proper. She had waited outside the back entrance of the establishment the night before, doing her best to ignore the fact that she was standing in a dark, stinking alley as she had waited for the place to close and the workers to leave. Most of the women had left in pairs or groups. At last Lizzy had straggled out, all alone and one of the last to leave. When Prudence had recognized her as the serving woman that the hawk-faced man had been manhandling, she had pulled her cloak closer about herself and proceeded to follow. Trying to move silently, and staying in the shadows as much as possible, she had trailed the girl up the alley leading from the back of the building around to the front. She had followed Lizzy along several roads, grateful to know that Eleanore's driver was following her for protection—even more grateful that her friend had insisted she use the coach and the family's discreet driver for the excursion.

Once far enough away from the club that she thought no one from it would witness the exchange, she had approached the girl with a story of true love hampered by disapproving parents and her need to get a message to her lover. Lizzy had been sympathetic, but the girl was also the pragmatic sort and hadn't been willing to risk her job to aid in the escapade. Prudence had been forced to resort to bribery, doing her best not to wince as she had bartered away a necklace of some sentimental as well as monetary value. It had been a gift from her grandmother when she was still alive. But if the plan worked, it would be well worth the sacrifice, she assured herself. And she was determined that it would work. Of course, Ellie was positive that it would not. She felt sure that Prudence would be recognized and escorted from the property. But Prudence was of the opinion that no one paid any attention to servants. Neither Stockton nor her father would give her a second glance—she hoped.

There would be no negative thinking now, she remonstrated herself. So far everything had gone without a hitch. Lizzy had met her as promised, entered Eleanore's borrowed carriage, switched clothes with Prudence, and told her, *Just walk in like ye belong. Grab an ale, so it looks like ye're working, find your lover, give him the message, and get back out here so I can get back to work. And don't get caught. I could lose me job if aught find out about this.*

So Pru had walked in, doing her best to look as if she belonged there, grabbed an empty mug, then slipped back outside, where she had carefully administered a couple of drops of Bessy's tonic to the empty mug from the bottle presently strapped to her thigh. She had worried over that part. The bottle Eleanore had given her had been rather large to cart around unnoticed, so she had had to find a smaller one to place the liquid in. Then she had suffered a quandary about where to keep it. It had to be somewhere within easy access. Tied tightly to her thigh, upside down with two pieces of cloth, had seemed the safest place, which appeared to be working. She had doctored the empty mug, replaced the bottle, and slipped back inside, walking boldly up to the open ale barrel to fill the mug with yeasty brew.

"Well, now, what have we here?"

Prudence had just spotted her father at one of the tables when her view was blocked by a rather large, leering man. Forcing a smile, she tried to step around him, only to find her path blocked and herself maneuvered up against a wall.

"You must be new. I do not recognize you."

Prudence nearly groaned aloud, but caught herself. She truly did not need a half-drunk lout to pester her. "Excuse me, my lord, but I must deliver this drink."

"Ah, now, don't be so unfriendly." The man gave her a smile that Prudence forced herself to return, but then he moved in and reached around to grope her behind in far too familiar a fashion. A squeak of alarm slipping from her lips, Prudence immediately grabbed at his hand.

"I just happen to be in need of a drink myself."

She glanced at him, her mouth open to demand he unhand her, when she realized he had taken the mug from her tray and was lifting it to his lips. "Oh, no! Do not—"

Prudence paused, her mouth agape. The irritating patron had poured the drink down his throat with one gulp.

"Mmmm." He wiped his mouth with the back of his hand and smiled at her. "That was refreshing. Thank you, luv."

Pru snapped her teeth closed with vexation, then snatched the empty mug from him. "You are not welcome. Now I shall have to fetch another." She tried to step around him, but found him immediately in her path again.

"Now, now, none of that, Lord Setterington," a deep voice said quietly nearby. "You know patrons are not allowed to bother the girls."

Recognizing the voice, Prudence stiffened. Lord Stockton. Panic rising within her, she stiffly kept her face forward and moved around the man Stockton had addressed. This time the odious man did not try to prevent her, and Pru was able to rush back to the safety of the kitchens. Once there, she frowned at the sight of how busy the ale barrel was. There were three women awaiting their turns at it.

Unwilling to risk one of the other servants recognizing that she didn't belong, Prudence turned back and cracked the door open to peer out to where Lord Stockton and Lord

Setterington were still conversing. The two men seemed rather chummy, which didn't bother Prudence as much as the fact that Setterington didn't appear the least bit affected by the tincture she had put in the ale. She watched for several minutes, turning her head away and moving to the side occasionally as servants entered and left the room. Members of nobility might not deign to notice servants, but servants surely noticed each other. After several minutes she gave up waiting on her unintentional victim to show signs of taking ill, and glanced back to the barrel. There was no one by it. Even the cooking staff was gone. But, then, they had finished their shift and left before she had arrived. Prudence had planned it that way, finding out what time the kitchen staff finished, and arranging to meet Lizzy after that.

Reaching down, she felt along her upper leg for the bottle holding the emetic, then glanced out the door again. Setterington and Stockton were still talking, and no one appeared headed in the direction of the kitchens. It seemed safe to fill the mug again. Letting the door slide closed, she turned and hurried to the ale barrel. She started with the drops first, for fear that someone might interrupt if she did it the other way around.

Setting the mug on the half lid that had been left on the barrel, she quickly rucked up her skirt and slid the bottle out. Letting her skirt fall back into place, she undid the bottle, held the lid between thumb and finger, and slid the other three fingers of that hand through the handle of the mug, lifting it to put in a couple of drops of the potion. She hesitated a moment, then dumped a good splash of the liquid in. The two drops she had put in the other drink were taking too long to work—if they were working at all. Obviously more than that was needed to affect a body properly.

Prudence started to try to put the lid back on the emetic

then, but with the mug, lid, and bottle all in hand, it was awkward, and she ended up dropping the lid. Clucking her tongue in disgust, she set both the mug and the small bottle on the barrel and knelt to look for her missing lid. It, of course, was nowhere in sight. Thinking that it must have rolled into the shadows against the wall behind the barrel, Prudence shifted to her hands and knees and crawled around, then swept her hand over the dark floor between barrel and wall.

She heard a deep male voice say something, but didn't really catch what it was, so was wholly unprepared for the sudden slap on her backside. Squealing, she jerked to the side, crashing into the barrel, then straightened on her knees and peered around in time to see one of the male servants swaggering out of the room through the door that led to the alley behind the building.

"Men!" she muttered with agitation, then grasped the lip of the barrel to get back to her feet. Once there, she saw that while the mug was still in place, the bottle of emetic was gone. She glanced around briefly, but it was nowhere on the floor. Either it had rolled into the shadows as the lid had done, or the male servant had absconded with it.

Her gaze slid to the door leading to the alley, and she took a step toward it, then changed her mind. The fellow was probably on a break and thought he had stolen her private stock. He was doubtlessly gulping the sweet-smelling liquid down at that very moment. She hoped it was a big swallow, for one was all he would probably take, and Prudence rather hoped he downed enough of it to end up retching for hours. It served him right for touching her behind!

Smiling to herself at that thought, she dipped the already-doctored mug into the ale barrel, then turned back to the door to the gaming room. Cracking it open, she saw that

Stockton and Setterington had moved away. In fact, neither man was in sight.

A sudden excited outburst at the center table drew her attention. One man was laughing happily as he scooped up a rather large pile of money. Everyone else at the table looked decidedly unhappy, though they were doing their best to hide it as they slapped the man on the back in congratulations.

"Here!" the winner suddenly called out to a nearby servant. "A round of ale for everyone in the club to celebrate. On me!"

Pru's eyes widened as every single servant in the club made a sudden exodus toward the kitchen doors. Deciding that it was time to move now or risk being discovered as an impostor, Prudence scampered determinedly out of the kitchens and straight to the table where earlier she had spotted her father playing cards.

Her eyes darted nervously about the room with every step she took, watching warily for Stockton, or for anyone who might intercept her and steal her precious drink as Setterington had done. She was nearly at the table where her father was playing cards when she spotted him. The gray-haired fellow who had been seated at the card table next to her father had apparently left, and Stockton sat there now.

Prudence nearly turned on her heel and fled for the kitchens again, but then she caught herself and forced her feet to continue. Stockton would not notice her, she assured herself firmly. She would keep her face averted, approaching with her front to her father and her back to Stockton. She would slide in, set the drink down, and leave. The man would see only the back of her head, and her father wouldn't even glance at her. Members of nobility *never* looked at servants, or if they did, they rarely saw them. And her father was no exception. *Dear God, please don't let Father be the exception*, she prayed as she turned to slide between the two men, her back to Stockton as she set the drink at her father's elbow. He did not glance up from his cards, at least no further than to notice the drink and cluck his tongue in annoyance.

"I didn't order that," she heard him grumble as she quickly started to slide out from between the two chairs, but she kept on going, hoping that if she left it there, he would drink it anyway.

"Girl!"

"'Tis all right, Prescott," she heard Stockton say. "I shall drink it."

It made Prudence pause. Swinging back in alarm, she saw the establishment's owner pick up the mug and swallow a good quantity of its contents. She didn't say anything—at least nothing comprehensible. Instead there came more of a squawking sound that slid from her lips as he lowered the drink and she saw that more than half of it was gone. It was enough to draw Stockton's gaze to her over the rim of the mug he was again lifting to his lips. Prudence nearly stopped him, but realized that there was really no use. He had already downed enough of it that there was no way he could avoid reacting. Especially since she had put in such a large amount.

Oh, he was not going to be happy about this at all, Prudence thought faintly, and took an unconscious step backward. She was paling and knew it. She could feel the blood drain from her face as the man's eyes narrowed on her. She started to back away faster, wincing when his eyes suddenly widened in recognition. She gave a gulp as he excused himself from the game and started to his feet, and she whirled away, heading for the kitchens at a dead run.

She had reached the kitchens when he caught up to her. In

fact, she had pushed her way past the half dozen servants around the ale barrel and nearly made it out the back door into the alley, but he caught her hand and drew her to a halt. Prudence whirled, mouth open to demand he release her, but he was already starting for his office, pulling her behind him. Catching sight of the curious servants, she decided not to cause a scene and allowed him to drag her where he would.

Tugging her inside the small, cramped office he had taken her to the last time, he released her abruptly, slammed the door, and leaned his back on it to glare at her. "Why are you back? To work? Surely your family's situation has not deteriorated to the point that you have actually been forced to seek a paid position?"

It was the way he said the word *work* that suddenly calmed Prudence. It sounded sarcastic and bitter on his lips, reminding her of the snubs and insults he had suffered for having to make a living in the world—a torment she would not wish on anyone. Her annoyance at his drinking the potion meant for her father was briefly forgotten and she said gently, "There is nothing wrong with earning your living."

He gave a disbelieving laugh. "Certainly there is. Just ask anyone and they will inform you of it. Every one of them thinks I am beneath them because—"

"I am not everyone," Prudence interrupted, bringing what she was sure would have been a long rant to an end.

He eyed her speculatively for a moment, then said, "I personally choose my workers. You are not employed here. You also made no attempt to talk to your father, which was the reason you gave for wishing to get inside Ballard's. You did not say a word to him when you had the chance. So, my lady, why are you here?"

"I did not come here this evening to talk to my father," Prudence answered evasively.

He stared at her for another moment, then said, "Perhaps you came here to see me?"

Startled by that suggestion, Prudence was slow to notice that he was moving forward. Backing nervously away, she shook her head. "Nay, I—"

Her words died as he slid his palm gently against her cheek. His voice was husky when he spoke. "Nay?"

Prudence started to shake her head, but paused and swallowed when his other hand trailed lightly down her arm. It was as if one of her fantasies had come to life. Not that she had ever fantasized quite this situation, but the look in his eyes was quite the same. A little more heated than adoring, perhaps, but . . .

"I am sorry for that unfortunate incident the other night. I would never have allowed Plunkett to enter had I realized—" He cut himself off and grimaced when Prudence suddenly flushed bright pink at the reminder of her humiliation.

"I *am* sorry," he repeated. Then she watched wide-eyed as his lips lowered toward hers. Her breath caught in her throat and her eyes slipped closed as she waited for the soft caress of his mouth on hers . . . and waited. And waited.

He had never taken this long finding her lips in her fantasies. Frowning, she popped her eyes open. His face was a mere few inches away, but it was no longer moving closer. He appeared to be almost frozen, and he had the oddest expression on his face.

"Is there something amiss?" she asked with concern.

Lord Stockton heaved. Recalling that he had downed her father's dosed ale, Prudence watched in horror as Stephen clapped his mouth closed. His cheeks bulged and his eyes were huge in his face as he whirled away. After a brief but frantic glance around, he rushed for the window.

"Oh, dear," she murmured as he threw it open. The next moment he was hanging over the ledge, being ill.

Biting her lip, Prudence shifted on her feet, unsure what to do; then she moved forward and patted his back rather limply. He straightened.

"Feeling better?" she asked hopefully.

He started to nod, then whirled back to hang out the window again.

"I guess not," Prudence muttered, wondering how to help. Were she home and he Charlotte, she would have wiped her younger sister's forehead with damp cloths and murmured soothing sounds. Her gaze moved to the office door, and she had an idea. She left him and hurried out to the kitchens. There had to be water and cloths somewhere. This was a kitchen.

Unfortunately it was a rather large kitchen, and empty again, so that there was no one to direct her to find what she sought. She searched for several minutes before coming up with a cloth clean enough to suit her, then wasted several more looking for water. She was wringing out the damp cloth when she became aware of the assorted sounds coming from the next room.

There came a rather loud screeching of chair legs on the wooden floor and the panicky shuffling of feet, and it drew her to the door. Cracking it open, she peered out curiously. Nearly every single man in the club was on his feet, darting madly about—some rushing this way, some rushing that. Prudence gaped at the madness briefly; then a noise behind her made her turn. Lord Stockton stood leaning weakly against the doorway to his office.

"Are you feeling any better?" Pru asked with concern.

"I thought you left," was his answer, and there was no mistaking his relief that she hadn't. Prudence smiled softly and held up the bit of wadded material in her hand.

"Nay. I thought to find you a damp cloth," she explained, then glanced toward the door as the sounds in the next room changed to guttural noises.

"What the devil is that?"

Prudence stepped aside as Stephen moved to the door and tugged it open. She didn't bother to look out. She had finally deduced what the mad behavior she had been watching was about. The sound she was now listening to was the almost symphonic noise of nearly a hundred men being sick. The club was full of vomiting patrons.

"Dear God!" Stephen said faintly, then shouted, "Stop, man! What the hell is going on?"

"I don't know, milord," someone answered—probably a servant, Prudence decided, since the voice sounded hale and heave-free. "Everyone is tossing their innards out. Bad batch of ale'd be my guess."

"Well, find out, damn it!" Stephen said in what was probably supposed to be a roar, but came out too weak to be considered one. Prudence bit her lip guiltily as she watched him sag against the doorjamb. Then he turned and gestured for her to follow him as he staggered back toward his office.

Pru hesitated, her gaze going to the door to the gaming room, then to the barrel of ale. She understood what had happened, of course. The bottle of emetic had not fallen on the floor or been stolen by the male servant who slapped her behind. It must have fallen *into* the ale, probably knocked there when she crashed against the barrel. *She* was what had happened to Ballard's patrons. Fortunately Lord Stockton didn't appear to be aware of that. He was putting it down to a bad batch of ale. She was relatively safe if she stayed for a bit. Which she wanted to do—purely to be of assistance while he felt so poorly, she assured herself. After all, she was the reason he was sick. She really should do what she could for him.

Having reasoned the matter out thusly, Prudence gave up her position by the door to the gaming room and followed Lord Stockton. He was slumped in the chair behind his desk when she stepped into the office. Moving to his side, she peered down at his closed eyes, then gently began to mop his face with her now warm, but still damp cloth, cooing soothing noises as she did.

His eyes flickered briefly at her touch, but they remained closed, his face slowly relaxing. She was beginning to think he had fallen asleep when he suddenly caught her hand in his. Prudence found herself blushing when his eyes opened and peered into hers.

She tugged her hand free after a moment of silence had passed, then turned away. "I shall fetch you a drink."

"Not from out there."

Pru hesitated at the door and glanced uncertainly back to see him gesture to the cupboard along the wall. "There is whiskey in there."

After a moment, Prudence nodded and moved to the cupboard. Opening the door she found a bottle of whiskey and two glasses inside. She took one and filled it, then carried it carefully back to the desk.

"Thank you." Stephen accepted the glass, took a mouthful of the golden liquid, swished it around, then stood and moved to the window to spit. He did that twice more before allowing himself to swallow the next drink. Then he glanced at Prudence and smiled.

"Thank you." His voice was raspy, but still soft as he raised a hand to caress her cheek. "I appreciate your care."

Prudence felt her face flush. She was not sure herself whether it was with pleasure at his touch, or with embarrassment at being praised when she had been the cause of his ailment. She *did* know she was disappointed when his hand slipped away from her cheek and he turned to pick up his glass again. He had just taken another swig when a knock sounded at the door.

Swallowing, he set the glass back on his desk, then moved around her to shield Prudence from view. "Enter," he called out.

Prudence heard the door open; then a male voice announced, "This was found floating in the ale barrel."

By lifting up on her tiptoes, Pru was able to just see over Stephen's shoulder and glimpse what was held out by the man in the doorway. Her bottle, she saw with a wince. The man added, "It looks a deliberate attempt to poison our patrons."

"What?" There was no mistaking the shock in Stephen's voice. "Why would anyone wish to poison our—"

Prudence backed away as he suddenly spun to glare at her. Forcing a smile, she exclaimed, "I am *sure* whomever it was had no intention of poisoning your patrons. They most likely meant to—"

"To poison one particular patron?" he asked coldly. "Such as your father, perhaps? That mug I drank from was meant for him, after all. You poisoned my ale!"

He moved toward her, his repressed fury evident, and Prudence did the only thing she could think to do; she made a run for it.

"Do not let her get away!" she heard Stephen shout, but at that point the devil himself couldn't have caught her. Propelled by fear, Pru was running so fast she wasn't even sure her feet were touching the floor. She was out the door and racing along the alley to the front of the building in a trice. Jamison, bless his heart, either heard the rapid *tap-tap* of her feet, or saw her approaching. Whatever the case, he was off his seat and had the door open when she got there.

"Get us away from here, Jamison. Quickly!" she cried as she lunged into the carriage. The door was closed behind her before she even landed on the seat.

"What happened? Ye haven't lost me my job, have ye?" Lizzy cried as the carriage shifted under the weight of Jamison remounting the driver's bench.

Prudence grabbed at the seat and waited until the carriage had lurched forward before answering.

Chapter Four

"*P*oisoning the punch, are we?"

Dropping the dipper in the punch bowl, Prudence whirled to find the owner of that silky voice, eyes wary as she met Lord Stockton's mocking gaze. She hadn't seen the man since the night of the little accident at his club. Well, all right, the night she had poisoned his patrons. Which had been two nights ago. Pru had considered sending him a letter of apology explaining the situation, but had decided against it, thinking that such an apology really should be given in person. But here was her chance, and she wished she had sent him a letter. Or that she had refused to allow Eleanore to talk her into coming tonight. Forcing Prudence to attend her mother's ball had been Ellie's attempt to cheer her friend and distract her from the Prescott family's mounting bills.

Prudence was neither distracted nor cheered. She was terribly conscious of the fact that she was wearing a borrowed gown, and nothing could make her forget the subtle snubs she was receiving, or the fact that no one had asked her to dance.

"You have yet to answer my question," Stephen said, drawing her attention back to him. "Are you poisoning the punch? I ask only because I should like to know if you are out to torment *all* of the *ton* for your father's misdeeds, or are concentrating solely on ruining *me*."

Catching the startled glances being cast at them and the way people around the punch bowl were suddenly setting down their empty glasses, Prudence forced a stiff chuckle. "Oh, my lord, you are such a wit. But you should not jest like that or people might truly believe that I would do such a thing."

"The ones who suffered so foully at my club the other night, thanks to your poisoning, would have no trouble believing—"

Prudence cut him off by grabbing his arm, jerking him away from the table of refreshments and toward the balcony doors. She had no delusions about her strength. The only reason she managed to drag him out of the ballroom was because he let her. Since it suited her needs at the moment, she could only be grateful for his docility.

Prudence pulled him outside, shivered as the winter chill struck her skin, then led him along the wall of glass doors until they reached those leading into Lord Kindersley's office. Ellie's father didn't like anyone in there, but it was too cold to stay outside, and she needed privacy for this confrontation.

"So, what plans have you for tonight?" Stephen asked as she entered the gloomy room and turned to face him. "You have already both started a riot and poisoned a large crowd. Perhaps you intend to start a fire to roast all of—"

"Please stop," Prudence said wearily. She was not surprised by his irritation, but with all the troubles plaguing her, did not have the energy to fend it off. "I did not intend to start that riot. I was attempting to protect one of your serving women from a rather nasty client of yours."

"I know." Stockton's mouth was a bit tight, but some of the tension had left his body. Prudence felt some relief at that. She was even happier to see the last of that tension leave him as she explained, "Neither did I intend to poison your patrons. The bottle of emetic must have fallen into the barrel while I was searching about for the lid on the floor. I did not realize that it had or I would have warned someone. . . . Probably," she added, because she wasn't at all sure she would have. She had been so determined to see her father out of Ballard's. She still was, for that matter.

"Emetic?" He grimaced with distaste at the realization of what had forced him to hang out his office window. "I take it the emetic was meant for your father?"

"Aye. Ellie suggested that perhaps getting him to refrain from imbibing would put an end to his gambling as well. It seemed plausible, so . . ." She shrugged.

"Ellie? Eleanore Kindersley?"

"Aye." She brightened slightly. "Do you know her?"

"She is the daughter of our host," he pointed out gently. "And I do know that she is your friend."

"Oh." Prudence accepted the information, then, recalling a suggestion Eleanore had made earlier that day, managed a pleasant smile and raised her hand. "Well, I vow here and now, my lord, that you need no longer fear my disrupting the workings of Ballard's. I will not attempt to gain entrance again."

"Hmmm." He considered her doubtfully. "Never again, eh?"

"Never *ever*," Prudence teased lightly, mimicking Plunkett's deep voice, and felt optimism rise within her when a reluctant smile began to pull at the corners of his mouth. Then he forced it away, a scowl coming in its place.

"You do realize that you have caused me a good deal of trouble?"

"I am sorry for that."

"That may be, but my clientele has taken a dip."

She peered repentantly down at her feet and waited, relieved when at last he sighed.

"Well, I am sure business will pick up again soon enough. And I realize that you did not mean the harm you caused. At least not on the scale you managed. Besides, I tried a similar trick or two on my own father when he was gambling us to ruin. But I feel I should tell you that such tricks will not work. Your energy would be better spent picketing to get the laws changed and all gambling establishments closed dow—"

"Your father?" Prudence interrupted him.

His mouth turned down in displeasure and he moved away. Realizing that it was likely a sensitive issue, Prudence gave him a moment to compose his thoughts and glanced around the darkened room. The remains of a dying fire smoldered in the fireplace. That was the only light. Obviously guests were not intended to be here, and she felt slightly guilty. She knew Lord Kindersley was so jealous of his privacy that he did not even allow servants in here to clean. Had Ellie not told her that, the layer of dust and many cobwebs would have. Thinking of spiders and shuddering, she followed Stephen to a large statue in the corner of the room. It was in the Greek style, a seven-foot woman in a toga reaching toward the sky, her arms turning into the branches of a tree over their heads. Deciding that Lord Kindersley had atrocious taste, Prudence turned her attention to Stephen as he brushed at a spiderweb spun between two of the marble branches and finally spoke.

"My father did the same thing your father is now doing. He drove us to the edge of ruin with his gambling. He did not drink, however. Just gambled. And he did not start suddenly, as a tonic to distract himself from the death of his son and heir; he was always a gambler—but the longer he did it, the worse it got. I used to—" He paused abruptly, and Prudence moved a step closer, laying her hand gently over his now fisted one in a silent effort to soothe him. He glanced down with surprise; then his expression softened and his hand opened under hers, moving to gently clasp it.

"How did you convince him to stop?" Prudence asked after a moment of silence.

A harsh laugh burst from his lips, and his fingers tightened around hers. She didn't think he realized that he was crushing her hand, but she hesitated to draw his attention to the fact, because she desperately wanted to hear the answer to her question. If he had managed to make his father stop, perhaps she could save her father the same way.

Those hopes were shattered when he said, "He stopped himself. He gambled everything away but the Stockton estate. He could not touch that. So he came home that night, after gambling the last of everything else away, and shot himself."

Prudence flinched at his cold admission, horrified. She had a sudden vision of her father taking one of grandfather's old dueling pistols and—

"Do not look like that. I should not have told you. I am sorry."

Prudence focused on his troubled expression, only then becoming aware of his hand on her cheek. "I—"

He smothered whatever she would have said by covering

her mouth with his lips. Prudence stayed still for a moment under the assault—a variety of unexpected responses rushing through her—then kissed him back. She told herself that she was doing so just because she was eager to erase the image of his father's death from her mind, but she knew she was lying to herself. She had wanted him to kiss her again ever since that first time in his office. Perhaps she had wanted him to kiss her even before that. She had fantasized about him sweeping her up at some ball and rescuing her from her troubled life since that first time he had saved her from being a complete wallflower. Since the first time she had seen him, really. He was terribly handsome, and his basic kindness showed through his dissolute air. That, she was sure, was only a defense against the cold cuts society directed his way. She had always seen him as some sort of martyr, for she had never seen anything truly wrong with the fact that he chose to run a gambling establishment . . . well, until she had seen how the vice affected her family.

"Oh, Pru," he breathed against her cheek.

Surprised by his familiarity, but warmed by it, Prudence moaned as his lips trailed down her throat, leaving a blistering trail. She leaned in to him, her hands sliding over his shoulders, then into his hair. It felt so good to be held like this. To let go of the constant tension of her worries and let passion carry her away. For a few moments, to just feel. His hands clasped her breasts through her gown, squeezing gently, and for a moment it felt as if all the air had left her lungs. She was left gasping and arching, little sounds of excitement slipping through her lips, until he muffled them again with his mouth. He kissed her almost violently, and slid a knee between her legs, drawing the material of her borrowed gown with it.

Borrowed gown. Eleanore's gown. Eleanore's advice. As

quickly as that, Prudence's troubles crashed back down around her, abruptly dampening her ardor. Recalling what she had intended to do, she clenched her fingers in his hair and tugged urgently at it, trying to pull him away. "Wait. Wait, my lord, I—"

His soft chuckle made her hesitate and peer at him uncertainly as he eased their embrace enough for her to slip her arms between them.

"I think you can call me Stephen now, my lady." His voice was husky with passion as he peered down at her through the dim light. "I believe we are beyond formality."

Prudence offered him a strained smile. "Aye. Well." Reluctant to escape his embrace, she began to play with the front of his shirt, keeping him near, yet far enough away that he couldn't kiss her again and muddle her thinking. "I . . ."

His eyebrows rose at her hesitation. "Aye?"

"I wished to ask you . . ." She got further that time before faltering, then forced herself to continue. "To ask if you would please refuse him admittal?"

She said the last with her eyes shut, horrified at how the request sounded. It had not seemed a bad suggestion when Eleanore had made it. *If you cannot keep him from going to Ballard's the owner can. Mayhap if you ask nicely, Lord Stockton would do that for you,* she had said. Of course, Prudence supposed her friend hadn't imagined Prudence being in his arms when she made the request. Stephen certainly didn't appear as if he was reacting well. His arms tightened around her, his face becoming expressionless. She could feel his emotional withdrawal from her like a physical tearing.

"I see. Well, I imagine it could be arranged. It depends."

Prudence swallowed at the unpleasant undertone to his voice. "Depends on what?"

"How much more of this might I get should I do so?"

Her first reaction was a backward jerk of her head, as if he had slapped her. It couldn't have hurt her more had he actually done so. But her second reaction was chagrin. What could she expect him to think? She had certainly done everything else she could to save her family, much of it likely illegal. Unquestionably it was all improper behavior for a well-bred young lady of the *ton*. And she had also never made any attempt to hide her desperation. She shouldn't be surprised that he had jumped to such a conclusion.

"My allowing you to kiss me has nothing to do with this," she said with quiet dignity. "As a point of fact, I brought a halt to the kiss because I was becoming rather . . . er . . . distracted and feared forgetting to make the request at all." She could feel her face burning with embarrassment as she made the admission, and was grateful for the concealing darkness.

Stephen considered her through the gloom, then said, "So you like my kisses? This is not some new scheme? This is not some way to pay me back because your father loses money in my establishment?"

Prudence frowned, trying to find an argument in her mind to prove that she enjoyed Lord Stockton's kisses, then brightened. "Surely you can tell if a woman is enjoying your kiss? Does it not show?"

"Aye. Unfortunately I was rather distracted with my own enjoyment and did not—" His words broke off on a surprised gasp when Prudence suddenly stepped closer, reached up on tiptoe, and pressed her lips against his.

He did nothing at first to make the kiss easier for her, but as she felt the tension in his arms ease, his hands began to move over her back and his lips moved with true passion. Prudence let a little sigh slip out as her mouth opened under his, her toes curling in her slippers as she arched into him, putting all she had into the kiss. Following his lead, she ran her own hands over his back, enjoying the solid feel of him beneath her fingers. She gasped and lifted further up on her toes when his hands slid up over her rib cage to cup her breasts; then he broke away and trailed his lips over her cheek.

"I believe you," he said softly after several heated moments.

"Aye." Prudence kissed his ear eagerly when it came within reach.

"We should stop, else I cannot promise—"

"Nay." Prudence moaned, biting his chin at the very suggestion.

"Nay?"

"Aye."

A chuckle rumbled from his mouth, reverberating against her throat and making her squeeze her legs together in excitement. "Aye or nay?" he asked, sounding both amused and concerned.

"Oh." She opened her eyes reluctantly, then stilled as a shadow moved into the periphery of her vision. It wasn't a very large shadow, really, a darker blotch in the darkness that surrounded them, but it was moving. Dropping, actually, straight for Stephen's unsuspecting head. A spider! Lowering itself on its silken thread! Knowing she was overreacting, but helpless to do otherwise, she jerked in his arms and opened her mouth to warn him, but suddenly the arachnid dropped the last of the way at lightning speed. Prudence instinctively lifted the fan that had been dangling from her wrist all evening and brought it down atop the spider . . . and on top of Stephen's head.

"What the—" Releasing her at once, Lord Stockton covered the crown of his head and stepped back.

"A spider," Prudence blurted, trailing after him as he moved warily away. "Really, my lord. It dropped out of the marble tree and landed on your head. I was just—" She gestured with her fan, her expression brightening as she spotted the dark blob that had been the spider on the light-colored fan Ellie had given her .

"See! I got it." She thrust the fan out toward him and Stephen stumbled and fell onto a couch to avoid it. "Really, there was a spider on your head."

"*Pru?*"

Prudence let the fan drop and swung around at that concerned call. Ellie was walking along the balcony, rubbing her arms and peering uncertainly out into the darkness of the snow-covered gardens.

"Prudence, are you there? Father said he saw you come out here."

"Damn," she said softly and turned back to Stephen. Seeing the way the man was eyeing her as he got back to his feet, she threw her hands up in disgust. The fan, again dangling from her wrist, swung out, neatly clipping him between the legs. Prudence gasped in horror and started toward him as he bent over with a gasp. "Are you—"

"I am fine!" He held up a hand in self-defense, shuffling back away from her. "Just go. Go."

"But—"

"Pru!"

Shaking her head in frustration, she turned and hurried outside to find Ellie.

"You'd better get a look at this, milord."

Stephen glanced up from the books he was balancing to find Plunkett in the open door of his office. The doorman's face looked even more bulldoggish than usual, wrinkled up in concern as it was. "What is it?"

"There's a bunch of women out front."

Frowning at the vague announcement, Stephen stood and followed the man through the kitchens and out into the gaming room. His expression tightened at the sight of the few patrons seated about the room. Business had dwindled more and more with each of Prudence Prescott's antics. There had been a slight dip in the number of clients the night after the riot she'd caused, and the numbers had cut in half after her poisoning. Now there were no more than a handful of men in the place. The damned woman had cost him quite a bit of money. If she were here right now, he would probably wring her lovely neck. Or kiss her senseless. Strangely, he rather thought he might enjoy the second option more. As infuriating as her antics had been—and painful, he added as an afterthought—he spent more time imagining licentious pursuits with her than punishments. And the little episode in Kindersley's office, before he had taken the fan to the groin, had managed only to inflame his imaginings. The young woman truly intrigued him, despite her tendency to cause havoc wherever she went.

Stephen pushed his thoughts aside when Plunkett stopped in front of him. Glancing up, he saw that they had reached the front entrance. His doorman swung the door open and stepped outside, holding it for him to follow. Stephen did and gawked at the scene before him.

"What the hell?" he asked, gaping at a horde of picketing women.

"Hmmm," Plunkett rumbled. "They've been here for the last hour, and it's affecting business. A lot of the women out there are wives or daughters of regulars. It's scaring the men off. Carriages pull up, then pull away just as quickly when the women move toward them."

Stephen didn't really need an explanation. As he watched,

a carriage with the Justerly crest on it drew to a halt before the building. He saw the duke peer out the window at the picketing women; then the protesters started toward the carriage shouting, "Save your soul! No more gambling!" Justerly pulled abruptly back and let the carriage curtains drop closed; then Stephen heard his shout to his driver to get them out of there. The coach lurched away and the women cheered at their success in saving one more soul.

"Damn!" Leaving Plunkett at the door, Stephen stormed out into the mob.

"You truly *are* out to ruin me, aren't you?"

Prudence turned slowly at those words, not at all surprised by Stephen's appearance. She had actually expected him earlier, and thought it very forbearing of him to wait so long to kick up a fuss. "Good evening, my lord. How are you this evening?"

"How am I?" He glared. "I am suffering a financial setback in the person of one Lady Prudence Prescott. No one dares come near this place. I have a total of ten guests in the club right now—all of them patrons who were inside before you and your league of sour-faced dowagers arrived. And they are all terrified to leave lest one of their wives or mothers is out here picketing."

"Is my father one of the men inside?" Prudence asked with a frown.

"Nay."

She smiled in relief at his snapped response. "Then I suppose I can say that your plan is working. Thank you."

"*My* plan?"

Prudence nodded with a smile. "The other night at Ellie's ball you said that if I had such strong feelings about gambling, I should picket and get the gambling establishments closed down."

"I meant that you should picket the House of Commons and get the laws changed and—" He regained control of himself with some effort, then said very calmly, "All you have accomplished, my lady, is another step toward ruining *my* business. Which will not aid *your* cause. Your father is gambling tonight, I guarantee it. Just not in Ballard's."

Prudence looked startled at that suggestion. "Faugh! Of course he isn't. He had to give up his membership to the clubs. He favors your establishment."

"You do not have to belong to the private clubs to get in; you merely need a friend to take you with him as a guest. Your father spends the first part of most nights at White's. He—"

"You are lying. I followed him here that first night, and both times I have been inside Ballard's since, he was—"

"Both times you were inside Ballard's it was late evening," he pointed out firmly.

Prudence frowned. What Stephen was saying was true enough. She had gone late deliberately. When she had first gone disguised as a man it had taken her a good portion of the night to tuck and pin the back of her father's breeches. Even with Ellie's help it had been quite late when she had finally set out. Then, the night she had gone disguised as a serving wench, she had gone late to avoid the kitchen staff, thinking it might be less risky. If what he said was true, and her father did not only gamble here, then she was wasting her time. Wasn't she?

"Ah, well, that is of no consequence. The important thing

here is that my father, like the rest of your patrons, will not show up here tonight. My picketing is still a success."

Stephen glared at her in frustration, then snatched her hand and began dragging her along the sidewalk toward his carriage.

"What are you doing? Unhand me, my lord." She started to bring her sign down on his head, but he caught it with his free hand and tugged it from her, tossing it aside with disgust.

"Must you always carry something to brain men?"

"I do not carry things about with the intention of braining men," Prudence answered with affront.

"Oh? What about that umbrella you broke over Plunkett's head?"

"It was raining earlier in the evening. I brought the umbrella in case it started up again."

"Uh-huh." He sounded doubtful. "And the cane you clobbered Mershone with when you were disguised as a man?"

"Mershone?" Prudence echoed with confusion, then asked, "Was he that hawk-faced fellow?"

"Aye."

"What an awful man. He was mistreating one of your servants and deserved the koshing he got. But I only had that cane as part of my disguise; I thought it was most effective."

"Most effective," she heard him mutter. Prudence made a face at the back of his head.

"You batted me over the head with your fan at the Kindersleys' ball."

"I told you I was sorry about that. There was a rather large spider on your head and—"

"You were just about to beat on me with that sign you're carrying!"

Having no defense for that accusation, Prudence merely

sighed and settled on the cushioned seat, then stiffened when she realized that while distracting her with his accusations, he had managed to get her into his carriage. She lunged for the door.

"Oh, no, you don't!" Stephen grasped her about the waist and tugged her onto his lap, holding her there firmly with one arm as he banged on the carriage wall with the other. The carriage was off at once and Prudence grabbed frantically at his arm to maintain her balance.

"You can release me now," she said once the carriage had settled into a steady trot.

"But I rather like holding you."

Prudence felt her insides melt at that husky announcement and allowed herself the luxury of briefly enjoying his embrace. When she felt his breath on her neck, little tingles of anticipation raced through her; then she let out a breathy sigh and turned in to the caress as his lips claimed the sensitive skin there. However, when his hands closed over her breasts through her gown and the warmth inside her started turning to red-hot heat, she forced herself to struggle out of his arms to the safety of the opposite seat.

Stephen let her go. He was smiling at her when she finally glanced across at him.

"I thought you liked my kisses?"

Prudence flushed. "Aye. Well, it is not proper to—"

"And you are so proper," he gently teased.

Prudence glanced away, trying not to squirm with embarrassment, and shrugged. "I may not always be proper, my lord, but I do have some sense. And once I was away from your . . . influence, I realized that I really did not wish to become involved with someone who is helping my father, and countless others, destroy their families by gambling. Especially a man who should know better. Your own father should have made you sympathetic to this plight!"

Stephen was silent for a moment, the smile gone from his face. She expected him to be angry and strike out at her verbally about her own shortcomings, but was surprised by his quiet reply. "I can understand that sentiment, my lady. I did not feel much differently about the gaming hells my father attended or their owners. I have realized since that the owners are not the ones to blame. Which I am about to prove to you."

Prudence turned her head and peered silently out the window.

"If he were not gambling at Ballard's, it would be somewhere else," Stephen said quietly. "I run an honest establishment and limit how much men are allowed to lose. Should they start to dig too deep, I cut them off and send them home."

Prudence turned back to face him. "Is that supposed to make it all right that you help ruin them—the fact that if it was not you taking their money, it would be someone else?"

Irritation flashed across his face. "That is not what I meant."

"What did you mean then?"

He opened his mouth to answer, then paused to glance out the window as the carriage slowed. "We are here. Come. You will see what I am trying to say."

Opening the carriage door, he stepped down and turned to help her out. Prudence ignored the hand he proffered and glanced at the building they had stopped before. As she stepped down from the carriage, she saw that he had brought her to White's.

"After our discussion at the Kindersleys' ball, I looked into your father's gambling." Stephen urged her up to the window to the side of the door. There was a table there with men seated around it. Prudence knew it was considered the best seat in the house, where one could be seen on display. Her father was not one of the men at the table, she saw with relief.

"As I told you, I do not allow my patrons to play too deep. For him to have lost the large amounts of money you are suggesting, I knew he must be gambling elsewhere. I looked into the matter. He usually comes here first. Then he goes to one or two of the other private clubs, depending on his mood. Then he goes to Ballard's, where he plays cards until well after midnight. At that point, he heads to some of the lesser establishments. He does not appear to gamble large amounts at any of his stops, but when added together, perhaps . . ." He shrugged, then suddenly pointed past the table in the front window toward one further in. "There he is."

Prudence stared at the man he was pointing to. It *was* her father. And he was playing cards. She felt her heart shrivel in her chest. Tonight had been a waste of time. Perhaps all of it had been. And perhaps she'd known all along and blindly done what seemed would help—no matter how ludicrous.

She remained silent and docile as he turned her away from the window and led her back to his carriage, getting inside automatically when the driver opened the door. She remained silent as Stephen gave his driver her address and instructions to take them there. Some part of her thought she should return to the picketing. She had organized it, after all, but now there seemed little use, and she did not have the heart for it. They had all been so excited and buoyed by the fact that they were driving Ballard's customers away that she didn't want to be the one to tell them it was for naught. No doubt *all* their husbands and fathers were merely gambling elsewhere.

"You should give it up, Prudence. Your father simply does

not wish to listen. Nothing you say will sway him. It is some sort of illness. Believe me, I know."

"Aye, I know you do," she said quietly. "Which is precisely why it is so hard for me to comprehend how you can now do to others what was done to your family."

"I am not doing anything. I run an honest establishment. I do not cheat—"

"You say that it is some sort of illness. A compulsion. Are you not then taking advantage of this illness?" When he stared at her blankly, she turned her head away with a sigh. "I am not foolish enough to think that I can make him change his ways. Our talk at Ellie's ball convinced me that I could not do that. Tonight's efforts were an attempt to at least slow his losses down. Perhaps I would have been able to keep my family intact just a little bit longer. I thought—*hoped*—to keep us out of the poorhouse until at least the new year. I see now that even that is not possible."

Stephen pulled back sharply at her words, concern on his face. "Surely it is not so bad?"

Pru's answer was a painful silence, and Stephen frowned, taking in her broken expression.

"Prudence, please," he began, reaching out to caress her cheek, but the carriage stopped. They had reached her home. Pulling free of his touch as the driver opened the door, Prudence stepped out of the carriage and walked through the gate to her home.

*

Chapter Five

*

𝒮tephen leaned back in his chair, the accounts open before him all but forgotten. His mind was not on what he should be doing, but instead taken up with thoughts of Prudence. He could not seem to get his last vision of her out of his mind. Her shoulders slumped, she had looked so defeated as she had walked away. That vision haunted him. *She* haunted him. Stephen hadn't known her long, but she had certainly made an impact on his life in a hurry. She had also livened it up. With her around, almost every day had been an adventure. It had gotten to the point where he had wondered what would come next. The answer now was, Nothing. She hadn't tried anything for a week, not since he had taken her to White's.

Pushing impatiently to his feet, he wandered through the kitchens of his establishment and into the gaming room. Servants were rushing about, cleaning up from last night's business and preparing for tonight's. It had picked up again now that Ballard's was no longer plagued with Pru's own particular brand of havoc.

He would trade it all to enjoy that havoc and her presence again.

Shaking his head at that thought, he walked to the front door and opened it. Plunkett turned questioningly as Stephen glanced around the street's inhabitants. No one would be coming for hours, but Plunkett started work each day as soon as Stephen unlocked the doors. He was there to prevent anyone from sneaking in to steal things while the servants were busy.

"Any trouble?" he asked almost hopefully.

"Nay, my lord. Quiet as the dead."

"Hmm." Stephen couldn't deny his disappointment. He missed her. He missed her presence, her smell, her smile, her apologetic looks as she created chaos and left destruction in her wake.

"Maybe ye should call on her, milord."

Startled by the unsolicited advice, Stephen glanced to his doorman and found the beefy man looking flustered by his own temerity in making the suggestion. But, as uncomfortable as he appeared, it didn't stop him from offering more.

"I only say that because I've noticed how you've been hankering after her, sort of low since she ain't come back. *Everyone*'s noticed." Seeing Stephen's alarm, he added, "Not that anyone would be blaming ye. She's one of them wormy sorts."

"Wormy sorts?" Stephen echoed with amazement.

"Aye. One of them ones who worms under the skin by your heart and sticks there. Kind of charming and naughty and good all at the same time so's you don't know whether to spank her or kiss her."

Stephen considered the analogy solemnly, then nodded. It was somewhat scandalous for this doorman to speak so of a woman of Prudence's rank, but the man had the right of it. "Aye. She is definitely one of the wormy ones." Stepping out onto the stoop, he let the door close behind him. "Perhaps I *will* go call on the Prescotts."

"Are you not going to skate?"

Prudence smiled at Ellie's rosy-cheeked face and shook her head. "You know I cannot."

"Aye, but you have your skates on. I thought mayhap you were going to give it a go. You will improve with practice, Pru."

"That is what you said when we were ten. You do recall, do you not, the time I fell and nearly bit my tongue off?"

"Ah, yes." The other girl grimaced. "Well, why do you have your skates on then?"

"In case Charlotte falls down and hurts herself or needs me. I wanted to be prepared."

"Oh. How sensible."

"There is no need to sound so surprised that I am being sensible, Ellie. I am not a complete nodcock, you know."

"Nay, of course you aren't. I did not mean to make it sound as if you— Uh-oh."

"Uh-oh what?" Prudence asked with a frown.

"Well, fancy meeting you ladies here."

Pru stiffened at that cheerful voice, then turned to glance over her shoulder at Stephen as he joined them at the edge of the ice rink. She hadn't seen him since he had taken her to White's. And had missed him horribly, she admitted to herself, then berated herself for being an idiot. She shouldn't miss him. He was helping to ruin her family, whether deliberately or not. She should loathe the man. But he was so damned handsome, and he had such a nice smile and sweet eyes and— *Damn!*

Without really considering what she was doing, Prudence propelled herself out onto the ice.

Stephen gaped after Prudence in amazement. He had arrived at the Prescott home only to learn that Pru had taken her younger sister skating. Not one to give up easily, he had left the Prescotts', headed straight to the shops to purchase himself a pair of skates, then had come to find her. And find her he had, though he had to wonder at the state of his mind, for it was obvious the woman he was pursuing was quite mad.

"What the devil is she doing?" he asked, watching her perform some sort of dance on the ice. At least he thought it was a dance, though it was one he had never seen before. It consisted of repetitive jerking, then skidding motions of her feet and a wild swinging and flapping of her arms. She careened across the ice.

"Hmmm," Eleanore Kindersley murmured consideringly beside him. "I believe she is attempting to skate, my lord."

"She is?" He let his gaze drift over the other people gliding around the rink. "No one else appears to be skating like that."

"Well, I did say *attempting* to skate."

Stephen raised his eyebrows at Pru's friend, but she didn't notice. She was wincing at something out on the ice. Following her gaze, Stephen winced as well. Prudence had taken a tumble and was now trying to pick herself up. She managed to get halfway back up before her feet slid out from beneath her and she ended back on her behind.

"She doesn't appear to be very good at it."

"Nay," Ellie agreed quietly. "But then she doesn't care to skate. In fact, she did not originally intend to skate today. She only wore her skates in case Charlotte needed her."

"I see," Stephen said softly, watching Prudence gain her feet only to do something like a pirouette and again land on her bottom. Shaking his head, he turned abruptly and moved to the nearest log. Settling on it, he began to undo his boots.

"What are you doing?"

Stephen glanced up at Eleanore Kindersley, then went back to what he was doing. "Putting on my skates."

"Ah. You have never tied skate laces before, have you?"

"Nay." He glanced up with surprise. "How did you know?"

"You are doing it wrong," she explained. Kneeling before him, she took the strings. "Here, let me assist you." Swatting his hands out of the way, she made quick work of the task.

"I hesitate to ask this, my lord," she said, stepping back as he got to his feet. "But have you ever been skating before?"

He paused, looking uncertain, then nodded. "Yes. I am sure I did as a child. At least, I recall drinking hot cider in the cold."

"Oh, dear. Well, perhaps you should remain here. I am sure Prudence—" She turned and fixed on something on the ice. Following her gaze again, Stephen saw that a rather dashing-looking fellow had stopped to help Pru.

"There. You see. There is no need for you to—"

Cursing under his breath, Stephen did not stick around to hear more. He sailed out onto the rink in a manner rather similar to the way Prudence had done moments before, and no doubt looking just as mad as he wheeled his arms and pedaled his feet. Not that he cared. He was more concerned with staying upright on the ridiculously slippery surface and rescuing Prudence from the randy bastard presently using the excuse of helping her as a chance to maul her.

The man was holding her far too close to his chest, in Stephen's opinion. And Prudence, grateful for his assistance, was probably wholly unaware of his no doubt salacious intent.

"Lecher," Stephen muttered under his breath as Prudence started to slip again and the man hugged her closer until they were chest-to-chest. When he got there, he would—

His thoughts ended abruptly as a young boy swished past, bumping him. Stephen promptly lost his precarious balance and landed flat on his back. Grimacing at the pain in his tail-bone, he sat up, then glanced irritably around at a raucous laugh. The young beast who had knocked him off his feet was now skating in circles about him, laughing uproariously. The little demon only reached the top of Stephen's head where he sat on the ice, but he skated like the wind.

Deciding that if the little guttersnipe could skate like that, he himself could, Stephen ignored the brat and started to his feet. He was halfway back up when his feet slid out from beneath him again. The second time he ended doing half a split. Deciding that he needed something to keep his first skate steady while he regained his feet, Stephen hesitated, slid his glove off and set it on the ice before his right skate, then tried again.

Much to his satisfaction, that worked nicely. The glove held the skate in place, allowing him to regain his feet. But then he teetered there, peering down at the glove still lying on the ice. He knew without a doubt that if he tried to retrieve it, he would end up back on his butt. After all the trouble he had gone to getting here, he wasn't risking falling again for one stupid glove.

He would just leave it, he decided as he glanced over to

snarl at the way the libertine was holding Prudence. It was indecent. If anyone was going to hold her that way, it was him and him alone!

Stepping over his glove, he launched himself forward. Careening across the ice at a rather satisfying, if terrifying speed, he reached Prudence and her would-be rescuer in a trice. Unfortunately, once he was sailing along, he had no idea how to slow or stop himself. He was going to crash into the pair. Just moments before impact, he managed to adjust the angle of his skates, thereby sending himself hurtling into only the fellow.

"Stephen!"

It did his heart good to hear that concerned cry from Prudence as he crashed down on top of her would-be rescuer. He gave her a reassuring smile over his shoulder, then glanced back at the fellow who had thoughtfully, if unintentionally, cushioned his fall.

"So sorry about that," he apologized, crawling off and bracing his skate against the man's leg to get back to his feet. "I meant to come to Pru's aid; however I am just getting used to skates again. Need a little practice, I guess. Are you all right?"

Taking the man's groan for a yes, Stephen nodded with satisfaction. Turning, he took Pru's hands.

"Wait. I do not think he is—"

"He is fine. You heard him. Come along. We had best get off the ice before one or both of us suffers an injury. Thanks again, young man," he called, then urged her away, both of them teetering and slipping across the ice.

"Where is your other glove?"

"Hmm? What?" He glanced down at the cold bare hand she was clutching and grimaced. "Oh, yes. Well, I appear to have lost—" He paused as Prudence suddenly tumbled to her knees.

Stephen stared down at her with a dismay that turned to chagrin as he saw the glove she was picking up, the one that had caught her skate and tripped her.

"You found it." Taking the ice-covered glove from her, he shoved it into his pocket, then took her elbow to help her to her feet. He managed to get her up without falling himself, then urged her to the edge of the rink, noting with some pride that he was actually almost skating.

"What are you doing here?" Prudence said in a hiss, pulling free of his hold the moment they stepped off the ice and onto the more stable snowy ground. "I believe I made it plain that I am uncomfortable seeing you when you are aiding in ruining—"

"I know," Stephen interrupted as he followed her to the log he had sat on earlier to don his skates. "You were right."

"About what, my lord?"

"About . . . I did not really realize that . . . When I started Ballard's, I was desperate to regain some of the money my father had lost. He left my mother and I in a bad way and we needed income to survive. I found I was good at gambling. Ironic, since my father was not. After making a small amount, seeing how much certain clubs could take in, starting Ballard's seemed the swiftest way to return my family's estate to what it was. But after that, I was tainted. It seemed only fitting that the club should remain open. I did not consider that I was taking advantage of others just like my father had been taken advantage of. But you are right. I am making money off of the frailties of others."

She considered that silently, then asked, "What shall you do now that you realize that?"

Stephen scowled and wished he could see her face. She was bent forward, undoing her skates, and he couldn't see her expression. He hadn't really planned what he wanted to say to her. He was stumbling around blind. "Well, I suppose I could ban your father from the club."

"Why bother? As you proved, he will just gamble elsewhere."

Stephen frowned, his gaze moving absently over the skaters before he glanced back and complained, "I do not know what else I can possibly do."

"Nay. Of course you do not." She sounded bitter, and Stephen felt at a loss until she straightened and added, "This is not about my father, Stephen. At least not just my father. This is about you—how you make your way in the world."

There was a regret in her eyes that made his heart shrivel. "I—"

"Pru! Guess what?"

Stephen watched helplessly as she turned away toward a young girl who had rushed over to address her. She was a younger version of Prudence, with the same chestnut hair and gamine features. Stephen had the brief thought that Prudence's daughter would probably look very much the same.

"Good. You have already removed your skates," Prudence said, getting to her feet. "'Tis time to return home. Where is Eleanore?"

"Oh, but Pru!" the girl protested.

"Where is Eleanore?" she repeated firmly.

"She said to tell you she had gone home."

"Gone home?" Prudence echoed with disbelief.

"Aye. She said that no doubt Lord Stockton would take us home, and she was growing cold."

"Growing cold, my eye," Stephen heard her mutter irritably as he got to his feet.

"I would be pleased to see you home," he said. He saw the inner struggle take place on her face, but then her gaze landed on her sister and resignation set in. Even as she agreed, he got the distinct impression that she would have walked rather than accept his offer—and would have, were it not for her sister's presence. Ironically, that made young Charlotte one of Stephen's favorite people, and he teased and chatted with her easily, listening with a smile to her chatter all the way to the Prescotts'.

When the carriage stopped in front of their home, the little whirlwind was out the door at once. But when Prudence made to follow, Stephen caught her arm and drew her back, pulling her into his arms for a kiss before she could protest. It was a desperate kiss, a last-ditch effort to bring her back to him, and at first, as she kissed him back he felt hope that it might succeed. But then he felt her become still and withdraw, and her expression when he reluctantly released her killed his brief hope. He saw on her face that he was one of the bad guys. Just as he had seen the owners of the gaming hells his father had frequented, so she saw him—as a vulture.

She exited the coach without a word.

Stephen's mood was grim when he returned to his club. He found dissatisfaction plucking at him as he peered around the gaming room. It was late enough that the place was filling up, and everywhere he looked were the desperate gazes of men risking more than they should, the slumped shoulders of losers. At times like this, it all seemed terribly tawdry and unpalatable, and he seriously considered alternative professions. It was also at times like this that he saw his father everywhere. Right that moment, he was even seeing his father in the face of Lord Prescott, and the man's very presence seemed to mock him.

Prudence rolled onto her back and sighed miserably. Sleep seemed to be beyond her. Her mind was too full to allow it.

She kept thinking of Stephen, seeing his handsome face, remembering his kisses, his touch, his scent, his smile. He had such gentle eyes. She wished—

She threw the bedcovers aside impatiently and sat up to swing her feet off of the bed. There was no use in wishing for things she couldn't have. It was doubtful that Stephen's interest in her went beyond the carnal, and even should he wish more, she could not, in good conscience, have any sort of marriage with a man who made his living off of the weaknesses of people like her father.

Standing, she found her robe and pulled it on, then made her way cautiously through the dark to the door. It was Christmas Eve. She had gone to bed early. The whole household had, except for her father. He was no doubt out losing the last of their possessions. The creditors had stopped allowing Bentley, their butler, to brush them off. The day before, they had started to take things away in lieu of payment. Which was why Prudence had taken Charlotte skating—to keep her from having to witness those nasty encounters.

She had intended to take her little sister somewhere else today, perhaps to visit Ellie, but other than two large bill collectors who had visited rather early, no one had come around. The day had turned out well, and she and her mother had decided to take advantage of their home while they still had it, stringing popcorn to finish decorating the tree. Prudence supposed even creditors had hearts if they were waiting until after Christmas to empty the Prescott home.

She had made her way along the dark hall and down the stairs before spotting the light shining from beneath the kitchen door. Suspecting it was her mother, and knowing she would need cheering, Prudence forced a smile to her face and pushed into the room. Inside she froze. It wasn't her mother; instead, her father sat at the table, looking dazed.

"Father, whatever are you doing home?" she asked with surprise. "Why are you not out . . ."

"I have been banned from everywhere, that is why. Where has all the liquor in this house gone?"

"You *drank* it," she answered distractedly. "Did you say you were banned from *everywhere*?"

He nodded morosely. "Someone went around and paid all my debts, every last one. But in exchange, the owners were to bar me from entry." He shook his head miserably. "I am not even allowed in to drink! Who the hell would do a thing like that?"

"Papa, you are sober."

He glanced up with a startled expression. "Aye. Why does that surprised you?"

"I have not seen you sober in a long time," she said gently. Surprised realization crossed his face; then his gaze moved to the door as his wife entered.

"What is this about?" she asked upon seeing her husband. Her face showed the same surprise at his presence that Prudence had felt.

"Papa has been banned from the clubs. Someone has paid his debts, but he is no longer allowed in them—even to drink." Prudence spoke quietly, then rushed to comfort her mother as she burst into sudden tears. "This is good news, Mam. Everything will be well now."

"I know!" The woman wailed. "It is just that I have been so frightened. When those creditors came and took . . . I feared we would be in the poorhouse by year's end, and—oh, Prudence, we are saved!" She threw her arms around her daughter and held her tightly, sobbing into her shoulder, and Prudence peered over the other woman at her father, unable to keep the accusation out of her eyes. It was not softened by the stunned and slightly horrified look on his face.

He looked away from her angry eyes for a moment, then stood and moved forward to pat awkwardly at his wife's shoulder. "Ah, now, Meg. Don't carry on so," he said uncomfortably. "Things had not got that bad."

"Not got that bad?!" Lady Prescott shrieked, turning on him in the first show of temper Prudence had ever seen from her. "The creditors were here yesterday and this morning. They took my mother's diamond necklace and—"

"What?" Lord Prescott interrupted, looking thunderous. "Why did no one tell me?"

"Because you were never here to tell!" she roared. "You have been avoiding us for weeks now. Dragging yourself back in the middle of the night, passing out in the guest chambers, sneaking out the moment the way was clear . . ."

He flushed guiltily at the accusations, then wearily sank back into his seat.

"I have been an ass, haven't I? I've made you both so miserable." Grasping his wife's hand, he pressed it to his forehead and closed his eyes. "I do not know how it started. John died and I just didn't want to think about it. At first the drink worked for that, but then it wasn't enough. I started gambling. Before I knew it, I had gotten so far in debt that I could not stop. I kept hoping that the next hand would be enough to get me out, but instead I just kept getting in deeper and deeper and . . ." He shook his head, then opened his eyes and peered up at his wife. "I am sorry."

A sob breaking from her lips, Lady Prescott bent to hug her husband tightly around the neck. "I know it was hard losing Johnny like that. I still ache over it as well. But dear God, Edward, this last while I felt sure we had lost you, too."

"Nay." He patted her back soothingly. "Well, mayhap for a while. But I am back now." He blinked, as if looking at the world through new eyes. Sober eyes.

"Thank you, God," Lady Prescott whispered, then added with a smile, "Just in time for Christmas."

"Christmas?" Lord Prescott looked stunned, then vexed. "Damn me, I forgot all about Christmas. I have no gifts for you."

"It does not matter." Prudence's mother gave a watery laugh, joy spreading on her face. "I got all I wanted for Christmas."

Her husband's confusion was plain to see. "What was that?"

"I prayed that you would stop drinking and gambling, that we wouldn't spend Christmas in debtor's prison. And I have that now."

"Damn." He sighed miserably. "I *have* been an ass. I am sorry, love. I will try to be a better husband. I will try very hard."

"That's all a woman could ask," Lady Prescott said quietly, and helped him to his feet.

Prudence watched them head up the stairs, a soft smile on her face. She knew it wouldn't be easy; there were still hard times ahead. There were days her father would be miserable and unhappy for want of the liquor, but there was finally hope . . . and her mother looked so happy. Almost as happy as Prudence felt.

A thought coming to her, she headed for her own room, but not to go to bed. She needed to get dressed. She had someone to thank for this miracle. Someone unexpected.

Chapter Six

"My lord?"

Stephen glanced up from the fire he had been morosely contemplating, and lifted an eyebrow at the sight of his butler.

"You have a guest, my lord," the man announced.

Stephen started to say that he had no wish for company, to send whoever it was away, when he spotted Pru's gamine face peeking around his butler's ample girth. He lurched out of his seat.

"Prudence! What are you doing here?" he cried in astonishment, waving the butler away as he hurried forward to greet her.

"I had to talk to you."

"But you could be ruined if anyone—"

"No one saw me," she assured him quickly. "And I will stay only a moment."

His expression easing somewhat, Stephen nodded and led the way toward the two chairs in front of the fire, gesturing for her to take one. He waited politely while she seated herself, then moved to lean against the fireplace.

"*You* did it, didn't you?" she asked the moment he was settled.

Stephen shrugged, not bothering to ask what she spoke of. He knew she meant her father and his gambling debts.

"Why?"

Uncomfortable under her shining gaze, he turned away, bracing his hand on the mantel and peering down into the flames. "You were right when you accused me of refilling my coffers at the expense of others. For some it is just gaming. Good fun. But for others—like your father—they are suffering an illness. And, as you pointed out, I was taking advantage of that. Once I admitted that to myself, I found I could no longer pretend I wasn't harming anyone."

"So you paid off my father's debts?"

He shrugged as if it were of no real consequence; then a smile tugged at his lips as he admitted, "I managed to save his reputation, I think. I gave a rather clever explanation as to why I was paying all your father's debts." Before she could question him on that, he added, "I also told them that he was not to be allowed inside the gaming halls anymore."

"And they agreed to this?"

His expression turned wry at her obvious surprise. "I do have some influence around town. Most everyone owes me money." He scuffed at the corner of the rug before the fire with his boot, then added, "And then I sold Ballard's."

Prudence leaned forward in her seat. "You what?"

"Well, it shan't be Ballard's much longer. The new owner is renaming it." Sticking his hands in the pockets of his coat, he shrugged again. "I am looking into other ventures. I already have several I may invest in." He turned back to the fire. "Would I be right in supposing that your father is now grumpy as hell, but at home and sober?"

"Aye." When she fell silent, he glanced over his shoulder to see her biting her lip uncertainly, her gaze sliding around the warm and cozy room they were in. Then she heaved a little sigh, straightened her shoulders in a habit he was coming to recognize, and faced him to ask. "Did you do this because you felt guilty?"

Stephen considered her question solemnly as he turned his back to the fireplace. "That may have influenced me; however, I have considered getting out of the business for a while. As for paying your father's debts, that I did for you. I could hardly let the woman I love end up in debtor's prison for Christmas."

"Love?" She looked as if she were holding her breath.

"Aye."

"Oh, Stephen!" Launching herself out of her chair, she threw herself at him. He staggered back against the fireplace as she pressed tiny little kisses all over his face.

"Thank you, thank you, thank you!" she cried between kisses to his nose, his cheeks, his eyes, his chin, and finally his lips. There he brought the spate of little butterfly kisses to an end. Catching the back of her head, he held her still when she would have continued on with her exuberant rampage, and he moved his mouth on hers. Prudence didn't seem to mind. She gave no resistance. In fact, Stephen felt her smile against his mouth before she opened to him, inviting a deeper kiss. He immediately took advantage of the invitation, devouring her with a passion that had him hardening to shameful proportions. His body was reacting like an untried lad's, and he was heeding it's plaintive urgings. Within moments he had Prudence on her back on the fur rug in front of the fire, his hands busy everywhere. One was pushing the skirt of her gown up, the other tugging the top of it down. His lips were leaping from hers to the curve of one breast, then back, eager to taste everything as she writhed, arched, moaned, and sighed beneath him.

"This is not good," he muttered, kissing his way over the curve of her breast. Prudence sighed dreamily and arched against him as he took one erect nipple into his mouth.

"It feels very good to me," she purred.

Stephen smiled against her flesh. She felt it, apparently, and slid her hand into his dark hair. "You are smiling," she said.

"I have been doing that a lot since I met you," he admitted, his smile widening.

"It is the same for me," Prudence confessed on a half giggle, half sigh. He laved her nipple. "I must thank you."

Stephen raised his head to peer at her questioningly. "For making you smile?"

"Aye. For that, and for—"

"This?" he asked, catching the tip of her breast between his teeth and licking in. Releasing it, he added, "Or this?" The hand that had been resting on her thigh rose up to cup the center of her.

"Oh." Prudence pressed into his touch and shook her head a touch frantically on the fur. "If this is being ruined, I think I like it."

Stephen stilled at those words, concern for her gripping him, but she opened her eyes and smiled at him gently.

"Pray, do not stop. I do not wish you to stop." She hesitated, then added, "But I do want to thank you for giving my mother everything she wanted for Christmas."

"Ah." Aroused and pleased by the good he'd done, Stephen rubbed a thumb over the damp nipple he had been suckling, enjoying the way she arched and purred in response. "And what do *you* want for Christmas?"

"Me?" She seemed surprised.

"Aye. You," he said. Then he stilled as he realized that it was Christmas Eve. He could not buy her a gift until the shops reopened. Vexed that he hadn't thought of a gift before this, he warned, "I shan't be able to procure it until after the shops reopen, but—"

"What I want cannot be purchased."

Stephen drew back at that soft assurance. "What?"

"I would like more of *this*," she said huskily. Laughing, she drew his head toward her own.

Stephen allowed her to pull him forward until his mouth was a bare inch away, then paused and murmured, "I am not sure."

"What?"

He couldn't tell if she was more affronted or shocked by his refusal to take what she offered, and he nearly smiled at her reaction, but managed to keep a solemn demeanor. "Well," he amended. "Perhaps I could be persuaded . . . if you were to agree to give me what I want for Christmas in return."

Prudence suddenly looked wary. "What do *you* want for Christmas?"

"All I want in the world for Christmas is for you to make an honest man of me. Marry me, Prudence."

Pru caught her breath at Stephen's proposal, nearly squeezing him silly. She wanted to shriek, "Yes," but she hesitated and pushed at his chest until he eased the embrace. Solemnly she said, "You do not have to marry me. We can stop this right now. No one would ever know. I have escaped notice for far worse. You do not have to feel honor-bound to marry me."

"On the other hand," he said slowly, "I could enjoy you now, tonight, on this Christmas Eve, and every other night so long as we both shall live. I could share your life, have children with you who will look as sweet and be just as cussedly stubborn as you. And I can have you and your harebrained schemes to make the rest of my life an adventure." He smiled crookedly. "It is not a hard choice."

"Truly?"

"Truly," he assured her. "Besides, that clever reason I gave for why I was paying your father's debts . . ."

Confusion covered her expression at the seeming change of subject. "Yes?"

"I said it was because we were marrying and he had to save up for a huge wedding."

"Stephen!" she cried, slapping at his chest.

He grinned unrepentantly and pulled her closer in his arms. "I do love you, Pru, and I want to share my life with you. What of you?"

"Me?" She smiled crookedly at the uncertainty on his face as he asked the question, then made a serious face and tapped her chin thoughtfully. "Hmmm, let me see. Marry my own personal hero? The man who saved my family?"

"No," Stephen said at once, "I do not wish you to marry me for what I did. I do not wish you to marry me out of simple gratitude."

"Ah." Prudence nodded her head with understanding. "Then how about because you make me burn? Raise my passions? Test my mind? Make me smile. Or because my heart sings when you are near? Because when you are away I think of you and wonder what you are doing, and when you are near I wonder what you are thinking and wish you would touch me? Would that be reason enough? Or perhaps because I love you?"

She gasped when he hugged her tightly, then rolled on the floor with her until she lay atop him. Pulling her head down, he kissed her until they were both aching with want; then he leaned his forehead against hers and held her close. Doing so, he whispered, "I do love you. You make me very happy, Pru."

"Ahhhh," Prudence sighed in a quavery voice. "I have changed my mind."

"About what?" he asked, brushing the hair back behind her ears, a loving smile on his face for her and only her.

"All I want for Christmas is for you to say that again," she murmured, a smile trembling on her lips.

Stephen's lips widened. "I believe that can be arranged. In fact, lucky girl that you are, I think I can give you both things."

And he did.

LYNSAY SANDS
The Reluctant Reformer

Everyone knows of Lady X. The masked courtesan is reputedly a noblewoman fallen on hard times. What Lord James does not know is that she is Lady Margaret Wentworth—the feisty sister of his best friend, who has forced James into an oath of protection. But when James tracks the girl to a house of ill repute, the only explanation is that Maggie is London's most enigmatic wanton.

Snatching her away will be a ticklish business, and after that James will have to ignore her violent protests that she was never the infamous X. He will have to reform the hoyden, while keeping his hands off the luscious goods that the rest of the ton has reputedly sampled. And, with Maggie, hardest of all will be keeping himself from falling in love.

___4974-0 $5.99 US/$7.99 CAN